# His
# M...

*From the ~~office~~ to the bedroom…*

## Praise for three bestselling authors – Helen Bianchin, Cathy Williams and Sandra Marton

### About Helen Bianchin:

'Helen Bianchin gives readers a wonderful read with sensual characters, an engrossing premise and a superb conflict.'
—*Romantic Times*

### About Cathy Williams:

'The passion and emotions jump off the page and the characters are energetic and vivid, yet deep and emotional.'
—*Romantic Times*

### About THE BEDROOM BUSINESS:

'Sandra Marton's *The Bedroom Business* spices up the winter months with passionate scenes, zesty characters, an intense conflict and a fabulous love story.'
—*Romantic Times*

# His Boardroom Mistress

## THE HUSBAND
## ASSIGNMENT
*by*
*Helen Bianchin*

## THE BABY VERDICT
*by*
*Cathy Williams*

## THE BEDROOM BUSINESS
*by*
*Sandra Marton*

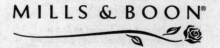

MILLS & BOON®

*MILLS & BOON and MILLS & BOON with the Rose Device are registered trademarks of the publisher.*
*Harlequin Mills & Boon Limited,*
*Eton House, 18-24 Paradise Road, Richmond, Surrey, TW9 1SR*

HIS BOARDROOM MISTRESS
© by Harlequin Enterprises II B.V., 2005

*The Husband Assignment, The Baby Verdict* and
*The Bedroom Business* were first published in Great Britain by
Harlequin Mills & Boon Limited in separate, single volumes.

*The Husband Assignment* © Helen Bianchin 2000
*The Baby Verdict* © Cathy Williams 1999
*The Bedroom Business* © Sandra Myles 2000

ISBN 0 263 84472 2

05-0205

*Printed and bound in Spain
by Litografia Rosés S.A., Barcelona*

**Helen Bianchin** was born in New Zealand and travelled to Australia before marrying her Italian-born husband. After three years they moved, returned to New Zealand with their daughter, had two sons then resettled in Australia. Encouraged by friends to recount anecdotes of her years as a tobacco sharefarmer's wife living in an Italian community, Helen began setting words on paper and her first novel was published in 1975. An animal lover, she says her terrier and Persian cat regard her study as as much theirs as hers.

**Look out for the next sizzling read
by Helen Bianchin:
THE DISOBEDIENT BRIDE
Coming in April 2005, in Modern Romance™!**

# THE HUSBAND ASSIGNMENT
*by*
## Helen Bianchin

# CHAPTER ONE

RAOUL LANIER inclined his head in silent acknowledgment as the attractive airline hostess extended a customary farewell to passengers leaving the aircraft.

Her mouth curved a little wider, and the expression in her eyes offered numerous sensual delights should he choose to extend an invitation to share a drink during her stopover.

The attention she'd bestowed on him during the long international flight had included a friendly warmth that went beyond the courteous solicitousness proffered to his fellow travelers.

It could have proved an interesting diversion, if fleeting sexual encounters formed part of his personal agenda, Raoul mused as he cleared the aircraft and entered the concourse.

As the eldest son and part heir to a billion-dollar fortune, a sense of caution coupled with cynicism had formed at an early age.

Good European genes had blessed him with enviable height, superb bone structure and ruggedly attractive facial features that inevitably drew a second glance. Physical fitness and fine clothes completed a combination that proved magnetic to women of all ages.

A quality that was both an advantage and a curse, he acknowledged with rueful humor as he rode the escalator down to ground level and crossed to the appropriate luggage carousel.

Raoul checked his watch. He had two hours in which to clear customs, take a cab to the hotel at Double Bay, shower and change, before he was scheduled to appear at a business meeting.

Primarily his Australian visit was intended to target the possibility of setting up a Sydney base for the multinational Lanier conglomerate. Wheels had already been set in motion, and if all the details met with his satisfaction, he was prepared to clinch the deal.

Not easily, for he was a skilled tactician whose strategy was recognized and lauded by his peers and associates.

He spotted his luggage, hefted it from the carousel and then strode out of the terminal to summon a taxi.

Brilliant summer sunshine had him reaching for protective sunglasses as he provided the driver with the name of his hotel, then he sank back against the seat in contemplative silence.

The meeting this afternoon held importance. He planned to present a noncommittal persona, and absent himself from the scene for several days, reachable only by cell phone during a sojourn on Queensland's Gold Coast.

Checking up on family. His mouth thinned slightly as his expression assumed reflective thought.

He held filial affection for both his brothers. The

youngest, Sebastian, had recently married and was at present taking an extended holiday in Europe with his new wife.

However, it was Michel who was providing concern, with his marriage of six months in apparent crisis. Seven weeks ago Michel's wife had left New York and flown to Australia to take part in a movie being filmed at the Gold Coast Warner Brothers' studios.

Michel had concluded important European meetings, then followed Sandrine with a view to negotiating a reconciliation. The fact the movie had developed financial problems merely added a bargaining dimension Raoul suspected Michel intended to use to his advantage.

Each of the Lanier brothers possessed a considerable personal fortune, and sinking a few million dollars into a floundering movie wouldn't put a dent in Michel's assets.

A sudden screech of brakes, a muffled curse from the taxi driver, followed by an offered apology captured his attention, and he caught the buildup of traffic, the terrace houses, as the driver swung into the outer lane.

Raoul caught a glimpse of tall buildings stretched skyward in the distance, and estimated it would take ten minutes, fifteen at most, to reach the Ritz-Carlton hotel in Double Bay.

He was no stranger to this large southern hemispheric city, and he held a certain affection for its scenic beauty and stunning architecture, albeit that it was very young in terms of his native France.

*Home* was a luxury two-story apartment in Auteuil filled with antique furniture, marble-tiled floors, oriental rugs, objets d'art.

He had been born and raised in Paris, graduated from one of its finest universities, then was absorbed into the Lanier corporation as a junior executive.

Raoul gave a grim smile in memory of those early days beneath his father's eaglelike tutelage. Henri Lanier had been a hard taskmaster. Ruthless, Raoul conceded, but fair.

Today, Henri presided as the figurehead of a multinational conglomerate, with Raoul and Michel holding equal power. Sebastian, on the other hand, had chosen law, graduated, practiced, then he penned and sold his first novel, and the rest as they say was history.

The taxi slid to a halt outside the entrance to a gracious well-established hotel a short distance from the waterfront.

Raoul handed the driver a folded note, then stepped from the vehicle while the concierge collected his bags from the boot.

Checking in was a simple procedure, and in his room he took bottled water from the bar-fridge and drank it, ordered room service to deliver lunch at midday, then he unpacked a few essentials, showered, shaved, donned a complimentary robe and replaced the receiver on the last of a few calls less than a minute before a steward presented lunch.

Afterward he dressed, checked his briefcase and took the lift to the main lobby. His meeting was scheduled for two. It was now three minutes past the hour. Essential minutes that gave him an edge, unless the man he was due to liaise with was also well-versed in tactical game-playing.

Eagerness inevitably bred punctuality, Raoul acknowledged, especially when the possibility of a large investment was at stake.

The meeting could easily have stretched to an hour. Raoul cut that time in half with clear instruction and assertive demand, leaving no shred of doubt as to who held command.

Afterward he returned to his room, snagged bottled water from the bar-fridge, then he opened his laptop and spent time keying in data and directing it via e-mail to Paris. He made two calls, the second of which was to Michel, alerting him to his arrival the following day.

Raoul flexed his limbs, then stretched his lengthy frame. He needed exercise. The gym? First, he'd exchange the business suit for sweats and sneakers, and take a walk in the fresh air. His plans for the evening encompassed nothing more than ordering in a light evening meal, followed by an hour or two on the laptop, then he intended to fall into bed and catch up on sleep.

The intercom buzzed, and Stephanie reached out to activate it.

'Michel Lanier is here.'

She winced at the receptionist's attempt at a French pronunciation, and stifled a faint smile at the girl's obvious effort to impress. Michel Lanier was, she had to concede, an impressive man. If a woman was susceptible to a tall, dark-haired, attractive male.

'Give me a minute, then show him in.'

It was an integral part of Stephanie's job as a marketing manager to initiate discussions and venture opinions. She liked what she did for a living, it paid well and the rewards were many.

There was satisfaction in utilizing her expertise in film, together with an instinctive grasp of what attracted and titillated public interest, thus improving cinema attendance, and profitability for the film studios, the investors.

This particular movie had gone over budget, over time, financial avenues had been exhausted and a week ago it had been destined not to be completed.

The crux had been Sandrine Lanier, part-time model and actress, who had a minor role in the film, and her husband's willingness to inject a considerable amount of money to salvage it.

Stephanie shuffled the papers she'd been perusing into a folder at the sound of a double knock on her door, and hit the Save button on her computer.

'Michel and Raoul Lanier.'

She successfully hid her surprise as she registered both names, and she stood and summoned a friendly smile as Michel Lanier entered the room.

'Please take a seat,' she instructed, indicating a pair of comfortable leather chairs.

'My brother requested he sit in at this meeting,' Michel Lanier revealed smoothly. 'You have no objection?'

What could she say? 'No, of course not.'

Michel made the introduction. 'Stephanie Sommers. Raoul Lanier.'

In his late thirties, she surmised, and the elder, if only by a few years.

Raoul Lanier stood an inch, maybe closer to two, taller than his brother. His broad frame held a familial similarity, as did his facial features. Except his hair was darker, almost black, and his jaw had the dark shadow of a man who was forced to shave night and morning.

Wide-set gray eyes, dark as slate, were far too knowledgeable for a woman's peace of mind. As to his mouth...its curve held a sensuality that hinted at great passion. Equally she imagined those lines could thin, perhaps become almost cruel if he was so inclined.

His presence in her office hinted *business,* which raised doubt in her mind that Michel Lanier held the sole stake in a financial package aimed at rescuing the film in which his wife played a minor part.

'Stephanie.' He extended his hand in formal greeting, and she took it, choosing to ignore the faint tinge of mockery evident.

His handshake was firm, his touch warm, and she told herself the sensual awareness pulsing through her veins was merely a figment of her imagination.

'Mr. Lanier,' she acknowledged coolly.

One eyebrow rose, and his mouth curved slightly. 'Raoul.' He lifted a hand and indicated Michel with an expressive gesture. 'Otherwise an adherence to formality will prove confusing.'

His accent was slight, but evident nonetheless, and the depth and intonation of his voice curled around her nerve endings and tugged a little, setting her internal protective mechanism on edge.

Charm, he had it. There was also knowledge apparent in those dark eyes, a knowledge that was wholly sensual, sexual, coupled with contemplative interest.

He would be lethal with women, she deduced wryly. Given his looks, his physique, his wealth, he wouldn't even have to try.

With deliberate movements, she crossed around her desk and sank into the leather chair. It was a position of power, and she used it mercilessly.

'I have the figures you requested.' She looked at Michel, and chose to ignore Raoul entirely. 'Together with a rundown of proposals we intend to use in promoting the film.' She picked up a manila envelope and slid papers into it. 'I'm sure you'll find it satisfactory. Of course, we can't begin with promotion until the film is completed. The marketing people will have a private viewing, then discuss which aspects should be highlighted to attract the attention of the viewing public.'

She kept her attention on Michel. 'I believe the producer anticipates another week should wrap up filming, with perhaps a further few days scheduled for reshooting. It would be of added interest to include you in the publicity campaign...both as an investor, and Sandrine's husband.' Her smile was purely professional. 'I trust you'll be agreeable?'

When he didn't respond, she explained, 'It's all part of the bid to protect your investment.' Did she sound cynical? She hadn't meant to, but it had been a long day. 'Do you have any questions?'

'You have another appointment?' Raoul queried silkily.

'Yes, I do.' Stephanie glanced at her watch, and stood. 'I'm sorry I can't spare you more time.' She met Michel's enigmatic gaze, then picked up the manila envelope and held it out to him. 'When you've examined these, please feel free to call me with any queries.'

'I'd like the opportunity to continue this discussion,' Raoul indicated. 'Shall we say dinner, tonight? Michel and Sandrine will join us. I'm staying at the Sheraton Mirage. Six-thirty in the main lobby?'

It annoyed her unreasonably that he took her acceptance for granted. 'I'm sorry, I won't be able to make it.'

'A date you can't break in the interest of business?'

Important business. Or was Raoul Lanier merely employing undue influence in his own interest?

'With my daughter, Mr. Lanier, whom I'm due to collect from the day care center in half an hour.' Her personal file was easily accessible to anyone with the right connections. Eliciting such details would be a breeze for someone of Michel or Raoul Lanier's standing.

His eyes narrowed fractionally. 'It isn't possible for you to hire a baby-sitter?'

She wanted to hit him for attempting to infringe on her personal life. 'Difficult, at such short notice,' she responded stiffly.

'Make the call, Stephanie.'

She disliked being controlled, and she resented this man's aura of power.

There was the temptation to tell him to go to hell, and she barely managed to bite her tongue. Michel Lanier was a wealthy man in his own right, although she couldn't be certain part of his investment wasn't being funded by the Lanier conglomerate. In which case, Raoul Lanier had a legitimate claim.

She could insist on another evening. In fact, she was sorely tempted to do just that. Except it seemed foolish to be irksome just for the sake of it.

Her expression was cool and composed as she inclined her head. 'If you'll excuse me?' She walked to the door and opened it, waiting as both men filed past her and exited the room.

One pair of dark gray eyes held a glimmer of amusement, and her own sharpened, then deepened with silent anger.

He was enjoying this, and didn't appear to give a second's consideration to what it would cost her in time and effort.

She closed the door behind them, then she crossed to her desk and pressed the required digits to connect with the teenage student she relied on to baby-sit. A few minutes later she replaced the receiver, gave a heavy sigh, then walked out to reception.

Michel Lanier was using his cell phone, and she was acutely conscious of Raoul's studied appraisal as she crossed to his side.

'Six-thirty, the Sheraton Mirage foyer,' she confirmed, adding with a certain cynicism, 'I shall look forward to it.'

He withdrew a slim billfold. 'My card, with my cell phone number.'

She wanted to ignore the courtesy, and add with cutting sarcasm that Hell could freeze over before she'd willingly choose to contact him.

Stephanie caught the quick gleam of amusement apparent, and deliberately arched an eyebrow in silent query, held it, then she accepted the card from his outstretched hand, careful to ensure their fingers didn't touch.

Was that an imperceptible quirk of mockery at the edge of his lips? She told herself she didn't give a damn.

Without a further word she turned and retraced her steps.

It was almost five, which allowed her one hour and ten minutes to collect Emma from the day care center, drive to Mermaid Beach, feed and bathe her daughter, then shower, dress, brief the baby-sitter and leave.

Do-able, provided there were no hiccups or delays.

An added bonus was that Sarah, her baby-sitter had offered to arrive early and take up any slack.

Something for which Stephanie was immensely grateful as she stepped into a slim-fitting black dress and slid the zip home. A few strokes of the brush to her strawberry-blond hair restored order to the stylish bob, and she examined her makeup, added a touch of blusher to her cheeks, spritzed her favorite Hermés perfume to several pulse points, then she slid her feet into stiletto-heeled black pumps, caught up a black shoulder bag and stepped quickly into the lounge.

'Bye, darling.' She leaned down and gave Emma a hug. 'Be a good girl for Sarah.' She turned toward the baby-sitter. 'Any problems, ring me on my cell phone. I won't be late. *Thanks,*' she added with heartfelt sincerity.

'Anytime. Enjoy yourself.'

That was debatable, Stephanie perceived as she crossed the path and slid in behind the wheel of her car.

*Business,* she reminded herself as she reversed out from the driveway, and eased the sedan down the quiet suburban street. Tonight is strictly business.

Why, then, did she have the feeling that she'd been very cleverly manipulated?

The distance between Mermaid Beach and the Sheraton Mirage hotel at Main Beach represented a fifteen-minute drive…slightly less, if she was fortunate enough to strike a green light at every traffic controlled intersection.

It was a beautiful summer evening, the sun reflected the day's heat, and Stephanie reached forward to adjust the air conditioning.

High-rise buildings stood like tall sentinels, vying with luxury hotels lining the long gently curved stretch of oceanfront.

The Gold Coast had been her home for almost four years. Years in which she'd mentally fought to put a broken relationship behind her and deal with the bitterness of knowing the man in her life had expected...no, begged, her to terminate an accidental pregnancy on the grounds a baby would represent too much responsibility and wreck his plans. With icy calm she'd handed back his engagement ring and walked out of his life.

It hadn't been easy. Yet Emma made it all worthwhile. She was a dear child, Stephanie's image with soft blond curls with the merest tinge of reddish gold.

A horn-blast shattered Stephanie's introspection, and a slight frown creased her forehead as the car developed a faint bump. Seconds later she didn't know whether to curse or cry as she pulled into the side of the road and brought the vehicle to a halt.

Just what she needed. A puncture, when she hadn't allowed herself a minute to spare. Dammit. She reached forward and popped the boot, then she slid out of her seat and prepared to change the tire. Left front, she determined as she removed the jack and set it in position.

Stiletto heels and a figure-hugging dress didn't make for ideal maneuvering. Nor did she relish wrestling with unfamiliar tools as she attempted to loosen stubborn wheel nuts.

This was one occasion when she was more than willing to put feminine self-sufficiency to one side and welcome male assistance.

Except no car stopped, and she battled with the task, completed the wheel change, replaced tools and then cleaned up as best she could with a packet of moist wipes and a box of tissues.

A quick glance at her watch confirmed she was already ten minutes late, and she reached for her cell phone, extracted Raoul Lanier's business card and keyed in the appropriate digits.

He answered on the second ring, and she identified herself, offered an explanation, an apology, and ended the call before he had the opportunity to say a further word.

Five minutes later Stephanie slid the car to a halt in the Sheraton Mirage hotel underground car park and took the lift to the main lobby.

She saw Raoul at once, his height and breadth of shoulder emphasized by superb tailoring, his dark hair well-groomed.

As she drew close he turned toward her, and he stood watching her approach with an unwavering scrutiny that made her want to check if there was a smudge on her nose or cheek, and wonder whether her hasty cleaning-up had removed every speck of grease and dust.

Stephanie mentally squared her shoulders as she summoned forth a warm smile. She was practiced in the social graces, and adept at handling any situation. It was very rare for her to allow anything or anyone to ruffle her composure.

All she had to do, she assured herself silently, was get through the next hour or two with her dignity intact.

'Sandrine. Michel,' she greeted with ease as she joined them. 'Raoul,' she acknowledged civilly. 'I'm sorry about the delay.'

*Take control*, a tiny voice prompted. 'Shall we go in?'

She didn't miss the faint narrowing of his dark eyes, nor did she mistake the deceptive indolence apparent, and she ignored the slight shiver that feathered its way down her spine.

Raoul Lanier was just a man whose wealth and power were enviable assets in the business arena. She had no interest in him on a personal level, she assured herself.

Why, then, did she feel on edge and about as confident as a seven-year-old child, instead of the twenty-seven-year-old woman she was?

# CHAPTER TWO

THE maître 'd led them to a table with a splendid view out over the pool and ocean. He seated them with reserved politeness, then summoned the drinks waiter.

Stephanie perused the wine list with practiced ease. Her knowledge of Australian wines was comprehensive, and she conferred over a choice of red or white, sparkling or still.

'What would you suggest?' Raoul drawled, mildly amused by her determination to play hostess.

'The hotel carries a selection by a multigold medal vintner. I can recommend their Chardonnay or the Pinot Noir.'

Raoul ordered a bottle of each, and when the wine steward uncorked and presented the wine, Stephanie declined, opting for mineral water.

'The need for a clear head?'

'Of course,' she returned coolly. 'The evening's purpose is focused on discussions about marketing strategies for the movie.' She turned her attention to Michel. 'I trust you've had an opportunity to examine the paperwork?'

'Perhaps we could leave any business discussion until after we've ordered our starter and main?' Raoul suggested imperturbably.

Stephanie directed him a studied glance, and met his level gaze. 'If you'd prefer, Mr. Lanier.'

'Raoul,' he insisted silkily.

'Raoul,' she conceded, imitating his slightly accented intonation. If he wanted to play a game of verbal thrust and parry, she'd prove she could be his equal.

Her resolve deepened the color of her eyes and lent a slight tilt to her chin.

It amused and intrigued him. Most…no, *all,* he mentally amended, women of his acquaintance tended to assume a mantle of coquetry, some subtle, others distinctly blatant, in his presence. Cynicism acquired at a young age had taught him that wealth and social status provided the attraction. Experience hadn't changed his opinion.

A waiter approached their table, conferred over the choice of starters, and at a request from Michel, provided a knowledgeable dissertation regarding the merits of each main dish on the menu before taking their order.

Stephanie lifted her glass and sipped the contents. Despite the apparent social implications, this evening was *business,* and she intended to relay the pertinent aspects of marketing strategy, outline the precise course it would take for this particular film, then she would leave.

If Raoul, Michel and Sandrine chose to linger or move on to the bar, that was their choice.

She replaced her glass onto the table and directed her attention toward Michel. 'I've already outlined the major facets of film marketing strategy in an appendix among the paperwork handed to you this afternoon,' she began formally. She was aware of Raoul's studied gaze, and chose to ignore it.

'Briefly to recap, when the completed film is delivered to us from the studio, it receives a private viewing by several people, about thirty in all. Various meetings are held to discuss the target market, what age group the film will most appeal to, which segments should be selected for the trailer.' It was an involved process, and one in which she excelled. 'We need to determine which shots will appear in press releases to television and the media, overseas and locally.'

Raoul noted the way her skin took on a glow beneath the muted lighting, the small gestures she used to emphasis a point. The liking for her job seemed genuine, and her enthusiasm didn't appear to be contrived. Unless he was mistaken, this was no hard sell by a corporate executive intent on personal success at any price.

'In order to heighten public awareness of the film, we'll organize a fashion shoot with one or more of the prestige fashion magazines, and arrange coverage in at least two of the major national weekly magazines. As well as local and interstate newspapers.'

The waiter approached the table and set down their selected starters, and almost on cue the wine steward appeared to top up their drinks.

'It would be advantageous to utilize Sandrine's modeling connections to the fullest extent,'

Stephanie continued as she reached for her cutlery. 'We'll also arrange for you to be present at a few social events and organize media coverage. Press interviews will be set up with the main actors and a few of the cast, the release of which appear simultaneously to draw public attention to the film.'

'Impressive,' Michel drawled, incurring a sharp glance from his wife.

'Laudable,' Raoul inclined in agreement. 'Perhaps you'd care to elaborate—your degree of dedication to this particular project?'

'Total,' she responded, then qualified evenly, 'With one exception. In terms of personal family crisis, my daughter Emma takes precedence.'

'Not optimum,' Raoul discounted, employing an edge of ruthlessness.

A deliberate strategy to place her behind the eight ball? 'You have no obligations whatsoever, Mr. Lanier?' she posed smoothly. 'No wife or mistress who has license to your time?' Her gaze lanced his, level, unwavering, undeterred by the warning glint apparent. 'Or does *business* consume your life to the exclusion of all else?'

It was possible to hear a pin drop within the immediate vicinity of their table. No one, she imagined, had dared to confront Raoul Lanier in such a manner.

'A subtle query on your part?' Raoul posed with hateful amusement. 'As to whether I have a wife?'

'Your marital status is of no interest to me whatsoever,' she responded evenly. It was the truth. 'And you didn't answer the question.'

Would she be so brave if they were alone? Perhaps, he accorded silently, sufficiently intrigued to discover if the bravado was merely a facade.

'I allow myself leisure time.'

His drawled response set her teeth on edge, and she summoned a sweet smile. 'Sensible of you.'

She had no answer for the sensual tension electrifying the air between them. Or for the insane desire to challenge him to a verbal fencing match. It was almost as if some invisible imp was prompting her into battle, and putting words in her mouth she would normally never utter.

'I hope you weren't too inconvenienced in locating a baby-sitter at such short notice?' Sandrine queried in what Stephanie perceived as a skilled attempt to switch the subject of conversation.

'Fortunately not.'

Sandrine offered a wry smile. 'The Lanier brothers tend to snap their fingers and expect immediate action.'

'So I gather,' Stephanie responded dryly.

'Can I persuade you to try some wine, Stephanie?' Michel intervened smoothly. 'Half a glass won't affect your ability to drive.'

'Thank you, no.'

The waiter unobtrusively removed their plates, inquired if the starter was to their satisfaction, then retreated.

Raoul leaned back in his chair and subjected Stephanie to an analytical appraisal. The subdued lighting emphasized delicate bone structure, lent a soft glow to her skin and accentuated the blue depth of her eyes.

She possessed a lush mouth, full and softly curved, and he watched it draw in slightly, caught the faint tightening of muscles at the edge of her jaw as she became aware of his deliberate assessment.

For one infinitesimal second her eyes blazed fire, and he noted the imperceptible movement as she attempted to minimize a convulsive swallow.

Not so controlled, he decided with satisfaction, aware that it would provide an interesting challenge to explore the exigent chemistry between them.

How would that mouth feel beneath the pressure of his own? There was a part of him that wanted to ruffle her composure, test the level of her restraint, and handle the aftermath.

Stephanie barely restrained the impulse to *hit* him. He was deliberately needling her, like a supine panther who'd sighted a prey within reach and was toying with the decision to pounce, or play. Either way, the result would be the same.

Raoul Lanier was in for a surprise if he thought he could try those tactics with her, she decided in silent anger.

She held his gaze deliberately, and saw one eyebrow lift in a slow arch, almost as if he had read her mind. Mental telepathy? Somehow she doubted he possessed that ability. More likely it stemmed from an innate and accurate knowledge of women.

The appearance of the waiter with their main course temporarily diverted her attention. She looked at the plate placed before her, and felt her appetite diminish to zero.

'The meal isn't to your liking?'

Stephanie heard Raoul's deep drawl, sensed the double entendre, and for a brief moment she entertained tossing the contents of her glass in his face.

*Smile,* a tiny voice urged. This isn't the first occasion you've had to deal with male arrogance, and it sure won't be the last. Business was the purpose for this meeting, albeit that it was being conducted in luxurious surroundings with the accompaniment of fine food and wine.

'Do you have any queries?' she asked of Michel, and incurred his thoughtful gaze.

'You appear to have covered everything for the moment.'

'Perhaps Stephanie would care to give us her personal opinion on this film,' Raoul drawled as he toyed with his wineglass.

'My expertise is with marketing strategy, Mr. Lanier,' she said with grave politeness, whereas underneath that superficial veneer she was seething.

His gaze seemed to lance through every protective barrier she erected, and she hated him for it.

'Surely you have an opinion?' he queried mildly.

'Nothing is a guaranteed success,' she voiced steadily. 'And there are varied degrees of success. I understand both director and producer have a certain reputation in their field, the cast comprises relatively high profile actors, the theme will attract public interest.' Her gaze was unwavering as she held his. 'I can only assure you marketing will do a commend-able job with promotion.'

She glimpsed his cynical smile, saw the hardness in those powerful features and refused to allow either to unsettle her equilibrium.

'A standard response,' Raoul acknowledged silk-ily. 'That conveys precisely nothing.'

She'd had enough. 'You're talking to the wrong person, Mr. Lanier. But then, you know that, don't you? This so-called business dinner is merely a social occasion initiated by you for your own amusement.' She removed her napkin and placed it beside her plate, then she stood to her feet and collected her evening purse. Ignoring Raoul, she focused her at-tention on Michel. 'Enjoy your meal.'

Without a further word she turned from the table and made her way to the main desk. Requesting the bill, she produced her corporate card, instructed the maximum estimated amount for the total be written in, then she signed the credit slip and pocketed her copy.

Stephanie moved into the foyer and crossed to the lift, jabbing the Call button with more force than nec-essary.

Damn Raoul Lanier. He'd succeeded in getting be-neath her skin, and she hated him for it. Hated herself for allowing him to affect her in a way that tore at the foundations of unbiased *professional* good man-ners.

For heaven's sake, where was the lift? Another five seconds, and she'd take the stairs. Almost on command, the doors slid open, four people emerged and Stephanie stepped into the cubicle, then turned toward the control panel.

Only to freeze at the sight of Raoul Lanier on the verge of entering the lift.

'What do you think you're doing?' she managed to ask in a furious undertone.

'Accompanying you down to your car.' He reached forward and depressed the button designating the car park.

An action which galvanized Stephanie into jabbing the button that held the doors open. 'Something that's totally unnecessary. Get out.'

He didn't answer. Instead he leaned forward, captured both her hands and held them firmly while he depressed the appropriate button.

Stephanie wrenched against his grasp in an attempt to get free, without success, and she watched with mounting anger as the doors slid closed and the lift began to descend.

'Let go of me.' Her voice was as cool as an arctic floe.

'When the lift reaches the car park,' Raoul drawled imperturbably.

'You are the most arrogant, insolent, insufferable man I've ever had the misfortune to meet.'

'Really? I'm flattered. I expected at least ten damning descriptions.'

'Give me a few seconds,' she threatened darkly.

She was supremely conscious of him, his physical height and breadth, the aura of power he exuded, and this close his choice of cologne teased her senses, notwithstanding the essence of the man and the electric tension evident between them.

The heightened sensuality was almost a tangible entity, powerful, primeval, riveting. It made her afraid. Not only of him, but herself and the long dormant emotions she'd deliberately tamped down for four years.

The lift came to a smooth halt, and she wrenched her hands free, then exited the cubicle the instant the doors slid open.

'Where is your car?'

She began walking toward the glass doors that led to the car park. 'There's no need to play the gentleman. The area is well-lit.'

She may as well have not spoken, and she drew in a deep breath, releasing it slowly as she deliberately ignored him and increased her pace.

It took only minutes to reach her car, and she extracted her keys, unlocked the door, then stilled as a hand prevented her from sliding in behind the wheel.

'Whatever you're thinking of doing,' she said tightly, searing him with a look that would have felled a lesser man. 'Don't.'

'I was going to offer an apology.'

'For initiating an unnecessary social occasion in the guise of *business*, then conducting a deliberate game of cat and mouse with me?' Her tone was deceptively soft, but her eyes resembled crystalline sapphire. 'An apology is merely words, Mr. Lanier, and I find your manner unacceptable.' She looked pointedly at his hand. 'You have three seconds to walk away. Otherwise I'll alert security.'

'And request you rejoin me at dinner,' he continued as if she hadn't spoken.

'I'm no longer hungry, I don't like you, and—' she paused fractionally, and aimed for the kill '—the last thing I want to do is spend another minute in your company. Is that clear?'

Raoul inclined his head in mocking acceptance. 'Perfectly.' He attended to the clasp and held open the door. *'Au revoir.'*

Stephanie slid in behind the wheel, inserted the key into the ignition and fired the engine. 'Goodbye.'

The instant he closed the door she reversed out of the parking bay, then without sparing him a glance she drove toward the exit.

Minutes later she joined the flow of traffic traveling toward the center of town, and it wasn't until she'd cleared the three major intersections that she allowed herself to reflect on the scene in the hotel car park.

She'd managed to have the last word, but somehow she had the feeling Raoul Lanier had deliberately contrived his apparent defeat. And that annoyed the heck out of her!

'You're home early,' Sarah said with surprise when Stephanie entered the house just before nine.

'Everything all right?' Stephanie asked as she placed her bag down onto the table, and began removing her earrings.

'Fine. Emma is never any trouble. She had a glass

of milk at seven-thirty, and went to bed without a murmur.'

She looked at the textbooks laid out on the table, the empty coffee mug. 'Another coffee? I'm making myself some.'

Sarah stood, closed and stacked her books, then slid them into a soft briefcase. 'Thanks, but I'll take a rain check.'

'I appreciate your coming over at such short notice.'

'It's a pleasure,' the baby-sitter declared warmly. 'You have a lovely quiet house, perfect study conditions.' She grinned, then rolled her eyes expressively. 'Two teenage brothers tend to make a lot of noise.'

Stephanie extracted some bills from her purse and pressed them into the girl's hand. 'Thanks, Sarah. Good luck with the exams.'

She saw her out the door, then she locked up and went to check on Emma.

The child was sleeping, her expression peaceful as she clutched a favorite rag doll to her chest. Stephanie leaned down and adjusted the covers, then lightly pushed back a stray lock of hair that had fallen forward onto one soft cheek.

The tug of unconditional love consumed her. Nothing, *nothing* was as wonderful as the gift of a child. Emma's happiness and well-being was worth any sacrifice. A stressful job, the need to present cutting-edge marketing strategy, estimating consumer appeal and ensuring each project was a winner.

The necessity, she added wryly, to occasionally entertain outside conventional business hours. She was familiar with an entire range of personality traits. In her line of business, she came into contact with them all.

Yet no man had managed to get beneath her skin the way Raoul Lanier did. She dealt with men who'd made flirting an art form. Men who imagined wealth condoned dubious behavior and an appalling lack of manners. Then there were those who had so many tickets on themselves they no longer knew who they were.

She'd handled each and every one of them with tact and diplomacy. Even charm. None of which qualities were evident in the presence of a certain Frenchman.

*He* unsettled her. Far too much for her own liking. She didn't want to *feel* insecure and vulnerable. She'd tread that path once before. She had no intention of retracing her steps.

Stephanie entered the main bedroom, carefully removed her dress and slipped off her shoes, then she cleansed her face free of makeup, stripped off her underwear and donned a long cotton T-shirt before returning to collect her mug of coffee and sink into a deep-cushioned chair in front of the television.

At ten she turned out the lights and went to bed, only to lay awake staring into the darkness as she fought to dismiss Raoul Lanier's disturbing image.

*     *     *

The in-house phone buzzed, and Stephanie automatically reached for it, depressed the button and endeavored to tame the frustrated edge to her voice. 'Yes. What is it, Isabel?'

It wasn't shaping up to be a good day. That little Irish gremlin, Murphy, had danced a jig on her turf from the moment she woke. Water from the shower ran cold from the hot tap, necessitating a call to a plumber. Emma wanted porridge instead of cereal, then requested egg with toast cut into soldiers, only to take two mouthfuls and refuse to eat anymore. Depositing her daughter at day care resulted in an unprecedented tantrum, and she tore a nail wrestling the punctured tire from her boot at the tire mart en route to work.

'I have a delivery for you out front.'

'Whatever it is, take care of it.'

'Flowers with a card addressed to you?'

Flowers? No one sent her flowers, except on special occasions. And today wasn't one of them. 'Okay, I'm on my way to reception.'

Roses. Tight buds in cream, peach and pale apricot. Two, no three dozen. Long-stemmed, encased in cellophane, with a subtle delicate perfume.

'Stephanie Sommers? Please sign the delivery slip for this envelope.'

Who would send her such an expensive gift? Even as the query formed in her mind, her mouth tightened at the possible answer.

He wouldn't...would he?

'They're beautiful,' Isabel breathed with envy as

Stephanie detached an accompanying envelope and plucked out the card.

*"A small token to atone for last night. R."*

Each word seemed to leap out in stark reminder, and she wanted to shove Raoul Lanier's *token* into the nearest wastepaper bin. *Atone? Twenty* dozen roses wouldn't atone for the studied arrogance of the man.

'Shall I fetch a vase?'

Stephanie drew a shallow breath, then released it. 'Yes.' She handed the large cellophane sheaf to her secretary. 'Place these on the front desk.'

'You don't want them in your office?'

'They'll make me sneeze.' A slight fabrication, but she didn't want to be constantly reminded of the man who'd gifted them. 'Take messages on any of my calls for the rest of the afternoon, unless they're urgent, or from Emma's day care center.'

She stepped back into her office, closed the door, then crossed to her desk, picked up the letter opener and slit the envelope.

Quite what she expected to find, she wasn't sure. Certainly it had to be relatively important to warrant special delivery.

Stephanie extracted the slim piece of paper, saw that it was a check, made out to her and signed by Raoul Lanier for an amount that covered the cost of dinner the previous evening. To endorse it, just in case she might be in doubt, there was a hotel business card attached with his name written on the reverse side.

*How dare he?* The dinner was a legitimate business expense. Raoul Lanier had chosen to make it personal.

Well, she knew just what to do with his check. Her fingers moved automatically, and seconds later the torn pieces fluttered into the wastepaper bin.

Stephanie sank into her chair and turned on the screen on her computer. *Work.* She had plenty of it. All she had to do was immerse herself in the electronic checking of pertinent details to dispense the omnipotent Frenchman from her mind.

Except it didn't quite work out that way. His image intruded, disrupting her focus, minimizing her concentration.

It was something of an endurance feat that she completed the day's schedule without mishap, and she closed down the computer as Isabel entered with a sheaf of messages. Three of which she returned, two were put to one side for the morning, and one she discarded.

Raoul Lanier could whistle *Dixie,* she decided vengefully as she slid papers into her briefcase and caught up her bag.

Her gaze skimmed the office in a cursory check before leaving for the evening. She caught sight of the special delivery envelope that had contained Raoul Lanier's check, and she reached for it, flipped it idly between her fingers, then on impulse she bent down and caught up the torn check she'd consigned to the wastepaper bin.

Stephanie took an envelope from her stationery

drawer, placed the torn check into it, dampened the seal, then wrote Raoul Lanier in bold black ink, followed by the name of his hotel.

The Sheraton wasn't that far out of her way, and a wry smile teased her lips as she anticipated his expression when he opened the envelope.

Tit for tat wasn't an enviable modus operandi, but she was darned if she'd allow him to have the upper hand.

It was a simple matter to drive up to the main hotel entrance and hand the addressed envelope to the concierge. Difficult to hide a vaguely exultant smile as she eased the car onto the main road.

Traffic was heavy, consequently it took at least three light changes to pass through each main intersection as she headed for the day care center.

Emma looked slightly flushed, and her eyes held a brightness that foreshadowed an increased temperature. 'I'll see how she fares through the night,' Stephanie declared quietly to the attendant nursing sister. 'I may keep her home tomorrow.'

'Give me a call in the morning.'

An hour later she'd bathed and changed Emma, encouraged her to eat a little dinner, only to have her throw up soon after. Something that occurred with regularity throughout the night.

By morning they were both tired and wan, and at eight Stephanie made a series of calls that gained a doctor's appointment, the office to relay she'd be working from home and to divert any phone calls to her message bank and finally, the day care center.

'Sick,' Emma said in a forlorn voice, and Stephanie leaned down to brush her lips across her daughter's forehead.

'I know, sweetheart. We'll go see the doctor soon, and get some medicine to make you better.'

Washing. Loads of it. She took the second completed load out and pushed it into the drier, then systematically filled the washing machine and set it going again.

A gastro virus, the doctor pronounced, and prescribed treatment and care. Stephanie called into the pharmacy, collected a few essentials from the nearby supermarket, then she drove home and settled Emma comfortably on the sofa with one of her favorite videos slotted into the VCR.

A sophisticated laptop linked her to the office, and she noted the calls logged in on her message bank, then settled down to work.

Emma slept for an hour, had some chicken broth, a dry piece of toast, then snuggled down in the makeshift bed Stephanie set up on the couch.

By evening Emma was much improved, and she slept through the night without mishap. Even so, Stephanie decided to keep her home another day as a precaution.

*Work* was a little more difficult with a reasonably energetic child underfoot, and when she'd settled Emma into bed for her afternoon nap she crossed to the phone and made a series of necessary calls.

One revealed the information she sought, in that Michel Lanier was investing personal, not Lanier corporate funds. Therefore it was solely Michel to whom she owed professional allegiance.

Stephanie opened her laptop, and began sourcing the necessary data she needed to complete a report. Although film was her area of expertise, she worked on other marketing projects and liaised with several of her associates.

It was almost three when the doorbell rang, and she quickly crossed to open the door before whoever was on the other side could ring the bell again.

Security was an important feature for a single woman living alone with a young child, and aluminum grills covered every window and both doors.

Possibly it was a neighbor, or a hawker canvassing door-to-door.

Stephanie unlocked the paneled wooden door and was temporarily unable to contain her surprise at the sight of Raoul Lanier's tall frame beyond the aperture.

He looked vital, dynamic, his broad-boned features portraying a handsome ruggedness that was primitive, compelling. Almost barbaric.

Words formed to demand how he'd discovered where she lived. Then they died before they found voice. All Raoul Lanier had to do was lift the telephone and make a few inquiries to elicit the pertinent information.

# CHAPTER THREE

'WHAT are you doing here?'

Raoul arched an eyebrow. 'Do you usually greet everyone this way?'

'No,' she managed to say coolly.

'And keep them standing on the doorstep?'

He bothered her more than she was prepared to admit. On a professional level, she had no recourse but to suffer his presence. However, this was *her* time, her *home*, which made it very personal.

She was safe. The outer wrought-iron security door was locked. He couldn't enter unless she chose to release the catch.

'I conduct business in my office, Mr. Lanier. I suggest you contact my secretary and make an appointment.'

'In case it slipped your mind, you refused to take my call.'

'I had to do some urgent work on the computer,' she explained, determined not to sound defensive. 'My secretary took messages.'

'I gave her one. You didn't return it.'

She regarded him carefully. 'There was no need, given Michel is investing personal, not Lanier company funds, into the film.'

'As a matter of interest, did the roses make it into your office?'

Stephanie's eyes flared, then assumed cool control. 'I had Isabel put them in reception.'

'And tore up my check.'

'It was a business dinner,' she reminded firmly.

'Business was on the agenda,' Raoul granted in measured tones.

'It was the sole reason I accepted your invitation.'

There was cynical amusement lurking in the depths of his eyes. 'You have since made that remarkably clear.'

'I'm not into playing word-games, nor do I indulge in male ego-stroking.'

He laughed. A deep throaty sound that held a degree of spontaneous humor, and something else she didn't care to define.

'Invite me in, Stephanie.'

'No. Emma is due to wake from her nap anytime soon.'

'Have dinner with me tonight.'

'I don't date, Mr. Lanier,' she added icily.

'Raoul,' he insisted evenly. 'The sharing of a meal doesn't necessarily constitute a date.'

He really was too much! 'What part of *no* don't you understand?' she demanded, and saw his eyes narrow slightly.

'Are you so afraid of me?'

*Fear* had many aspects, and while her personal safety wasn't in question, her emotional sanity was something else entirely. She'd turned the lock on her emotional heart and thrown away the key. This man saw too much, sensed too much, and was therefore dangerous.

'You're wasting your time,' she said quietly.

One eyebrow arched. 'You think so?'

'We have nothing to discuss.'

'Yes,' Raoul argued silkily. 'We do.'

His gaze seemed to sear right through to her soul, and it took enormous willpower to keep her eyes level, *emotionless*.

'In your dreams,' Stephanie reiterated with pseudo sweetness.

His expression didn't change, although his voice was a soft drawl that conveyed innate knowledge. *'Oui.'*

She drew a deep breath, and released it slowly. 'If you don't leave immediately, I'll make a call and have you charged with harassment.'

Stephanie closed the door, and leaned against it for several long minutes, then she drew in a deep breath and moved toward the kitchen. Crossing to the refrigerator she took a can of cola, popped the tab, then she extracted a glass and filled it with the sparkling dark liquid.

Her skin felt heated, and her pulse beat fast at the edge of her throat. Damn him. Who did he think he was?

A hollow laugh escaped into the silence of the room. Raoul Lanier knew exactly who he was. What's more, she had the instinctive feeling he would stop at nothing to get what he wanted.

The question was, *what* did Raoul Lanier want with her?

Sex. Why else did men pursue women, if not to indulge in intimacy?

Hadn't she discovered that to her cost? Ben had said the sweet words and pushed all the right buttons. Until she fell pregnant. Then he became someone she didn't know at all, and she'd walked away, vowing never to trust a man again, ever.

There were men she dealt with in the course of her business life, and despite numerous invitations she'd held steadfast to her rule not to date.

However none had affected her as Raoul Lanier did. Instant awareness. Sexual chemistry at its zenith, she added with silent cynicism.

Electric, primeval, *shocking,* she acknowledged, remembering vividly the moment their gazes met when he'd walked into her office.

Within seconds, it had seemed as if her life came to a standstill and there was only *him.* Invading her senses, warming her blood, staking a claim. As if he possessed a blueprint to her future. It had unnerved her then. It disturbed and unnerved her now.

Her fingers clenched until the knuckles shone white, and she crossed to the sink and discarded the glass.

Do something. Anything. The ironing, she decided. Heaven knew she had enough of it. By then Emma would be awake, and she'd entertain her until it was time to cook dinner.

Two hours later Stephanie settled Emma in front

of the television and slid an educational video into the VCR.

'I'll start dinner, sweetheart.' The house favored open-plan living, and the lounge adjoined the dining room, both of which were visible from the kitchen.

There was chicken and vegetable broth left from yesterday, and she peeled potatoes, carrots and added broccoli to go with the steamed chicken. Better to stick to something fairly bland for the next day or two.

She had just added water to the saucepan when she heard the singsong peal of the doorbell. She reached for the kitchen towel, dried her hands and crossed into the lounge.

'Doorbell,' Emma announced solemnly as Stephanie moved into the hallway.

The only person who popped in without forewarning was her neighbor, and she opened the door with a ready smile, only to have it fade as she recognized the man on the landing.

'What are you doing here?'

'I believe we've already done that,' Raoul said with musing mockery. He held out two brown paper sacks. 'I brought dinner.'

'Why?' she demanded baldly.

'Why not?' he posed lightly.

'Mommy?'

Stephanie closed her eyes, then opened them again, spearing him with a look that spoke volumes before turning toward her daughter. 'It's okay, darling,' she said gently. 'Go back into the lounge. I'll be there in a minute.'

'Hello, Emma.'

His voice was calm, soothing…friendly, *warm*, damn him!

'Hello.' Emma was openly curious, and not at all intimidated. 'Who are you?'

Raoul sank down onto his haunches in one fluid movement. 'A friend of your mother's.'

'What's your name?'

'Raoul.'

'Are you having dinner with us?' the little girl queried solemnly.

'Would you like me to?'

Oh my, he was good! Stephanie shot him a glance that would have felled a lesser man.

'Yes.'

*Unfair,* she wanted to scream.

'Mommy?'

'I'm sure Raoul—' she hesitated fractionally over his name '—has plans for the evening.'

'Do you?' Emma asked, her eyes wide with curiosity.

'No plans,' Raoul assured.

Dammit, he was enjoying this!

'You can watch my video,' Emma invited, offering a generous smile.

'I'd like that.'

Stephanie met his eyes, glimpsed the silent query lurking there and wanted nothing more than to close the door in his face. 'I don't think it would be a good idea.'

'I promise to be on my best behavior,' Raoul declared solemnly.

Don't you get it? she wanted to demand in anger. You're *not* welcome. And never will be, a silent voice echoed.

He inclined his head, aware that she was teetering on the edge, and anything he said at this point could work to his disadvantage.

'Please, Mommy.'

Blind trust. To a child, everything was simple. If only it was as simple for an adult!

Stephanie inserted the key and unlocked the security door. 'Come in.' Her voice was polite, but lacked any pretense of enthusiasm or graciousness.

'You're big,' Emma declared as he entered the lobby, and he smiled.

'Maybe it's because you're small.'

'I'm three,' the little girl pronounced proudly.

Raoul indicated the paper sacks. 'If you lead the way, I'll deposit these in the kitchen.'

It was a comfortable one-level house, relatively modern with average-size rooms. Raoul's presence seemed to diminish them, and she was supremely conscious of him as he followed her down the hallway.

It was almost as if all her fine body hairs stood on end in involuntary protection. Which was crazy, she silently chastised. Already she was fast becoming a mass of nerves, and he hadn't even touched her.

*What would you do if he did?* Don't think about it. It's not going to happen.

She crossed around behind the kitchen counter in an unconscious attempt to put some space between them.

There was already two saucepans simmering on the stove, and she indicated them as he placed the sacks down. 'I usually feed Emma about this time.'

'Then perhaps we can eat together.'

Stephanie opened one sack, and removed plastic containers that revealed tandoori chicken, steamed rice and a selection of vegetables. The second sack contained a crusty baguette, a selection of cheeses and a bottle of wine.

It offered a tasty feast, and surpassed the broth, boiled chicken and plain vegetables she'd intended to share with Emma.

'I'll fetch an extra plate and cutlery.'

'Tell me where they are, and I'll attend to it while you set out the food.'

'You can sit next to me,' Emma said in a bright voice.

Oh Emma, *don't.* This is a one-off, not the beginning of a friendship.

'It will be a pleasure.'

'I'm a big girl now. I can eat all by myself.'

It was meaningless chatter, and Stephanie didn't know whether to smile or sigh as her daughter regaled their reluctantly invited guest with the names of her friends at the day care center, her swimming lessons, a recent birthday party, videos she liked to watch and the much anticipated event…a trip to the theme park Movieworld on Saturday.

'Mommy's got tickets,' Emma assured as she finished the last of her vegetables. 'You can come, too.'

Oh, no, he can't. 'Mr. Lanier is a very busy man, darling. Besides, you may not be well enough to go,' Stephanie qualified quickly. 'We'll have to wait and see.'

She didn't want to spend time with him, even in the company of her daughter. And he knew. She could sense the faint amusement evident as she stood to her feet and began collecting plates and cutlery together.

'You can watch my video with me while Mommy does the dishes.' Emma began to hop down from the chair, then she paused. 'Please leave the table, Mommy?'

Stephanie felt her heart tug at Emma's earnest attempt to remember her manners. 'Yes,' she said gently, watching as her daughter unhesitatingly accepted Raoul Lanier's hand.

How could Emma be so friendly with someone she'd only just met? A man, when Emma came into contact with so few men. *Especially a man of Raoul Lanier's caliber.* Someone Stephanie had disliked on sight.

*Dislike* wasn't an adequate description, she decided cynically as she crossed to the sink and began rinsing plates.

His mere presence attacked the protective wall she'd built around herself. She liked to think she had total control, and responsibility for her life and everything in it rested solely with *her*. She didn't need a man invading her space, her time, her emotions.

Unless, of course, a woman was sufficiently fortunate to find the right man. Someone who would recognize and respect a woman's needs, who would give as well as take.

*Get a grip,* a skeptical voice derided silently. You're content with the status quo, remember? You have a home, a good job and a child who is the light of your life. What more do you want?

*Nothing,* she assured herself, and knew she lied.

The rinsed plates and cutlery were consigned to the dishwasher, and she dealt with the saucepans with more diligence than was necessary.

Stephanie reentered the lounge and almost halted midstep at the sight of Emma seated beside the man she wished was anywhere else but *here*.

They looked *comfortable* with each other, and she wasn't sure she liked it. Be honest, and admit you hate it, an inner voice taunted.

What's more, Emma was giving Raoul a running commentary on the video as it played, drawing his attention to the various figures in and out of costume.

A glance at the screen was sufficient for Stephanie to determine the video had only a few minutes left to run, and as the credits rolled Stephanie reached for her daughter's hand as she deactivated the VCR. 'Time for your bath, sweetheart.'

For a moment it seemed Emma might object, then she slid off the cushioned seat and stood.

'I'll come back and say good-night,' she assured Raoul with childish earnestness as he unwound his length in one fluid movement.

'Mr. Lanier has to leave,' Stephanie said firmly, willing him to do just that. Her voice gentled, 'You'd better say good-night now.'

Emma looked at him with unblinking solemnity for all of twenty seconds. 'Good night.'

Stephanie began to lead her daughter from the room, only to have Emma pause and ask wistfully,

'Will you come and see us again?'

Raoul looked from the child to the mother, and back again. His smile was gentle. 'I'd like that.'

Emma grinned unabashedly, and broke into a skipping gait as she followed Stephanie from the room.

Oh hell, Stephanie cursed silently as she ran water into the bath and began undressing her daughter. How did you tell a three-year-old not to like someone? Explain that adult judgment was based on more than superficial appearance? And the reason for her mother's dislike was seeded in distrust and fear?

It was far beyond the comprehension of a child, and because of that it would be unfair to issue a reprimand.

Raoul focused his attention on the number of picture frames lining a mahogany dropped table, and moved close to examine them.

Emma as a baby; sitting clutching a teddy bear that was almost of a similar size to the child; standing; perched on Santa Claus's knee in a store studio shot; seated on a tricycle.

There was a photo of an older couple whom he deduced were Stephanie's parents, but nothing of the man who was Emma's father.

He lifted a hand and threaded fingers through his hair. If he had any sense he'd let himself out of the house and drive back to his hotel where at least three hours' work awaited him on the laptop. He had international telephone calls to make, data to check. He'd be lucky if he got to bed before midnight.

Not that it mattered much, he reflected wryly. The past few nights hadn't been given to peaceful sleep. His mind had centered too often on a strawberry-blond blue-eyed young marketing executive who held no qualms in challenging him to a verbal sparring match at the slightest provocation.

His gaze strayed to the television, caught the moving images in color and endeavored to focus his attention on a geographical program featuring a safari park in Africa.

The sound of a childish voice had him turning toward the door, and seconds later Emma skipped into the room ahead of Stephanie.

'I'm going to bed now.'

She was her mother in miniature. The hair was a few shades lighter, but the eyes were bright blue, and the features held the promise of fine bone structure.

'Good night, Emma.'

'I'll see you out before I put Emma down,' Stephanie ventured coolly.

'If you trust me in your kitchen, I'll make coffee

while you put Emma to bed. There's something I want to discuss with you.'

She didn't believe him. He could see the faint wariness, the doubt. And the need not to make an undue fuss in front of her daughter.

'I'll be back in ten minutes,' she accorded with resignation. 'Coffee and sugar are in the pantry. Milk in the refrigerator. I take mine white with one sugar.'

She reentered the lounge to find two cups filled with steaming coffee set on the occasional table, and the aroma of freshly ground coffee beans teased her nostrils.

'You've made a conquest,' Stephanie indicated as she picked up a cup.

Raoul inclined his head. 'With Emma,' he acknowledged in an accented drawl. 'But not her mother.'

'Nor are you likely to,' she assured coolly. There was a part of her that silently screamed for him to leave, *now*. She didn't want him in her house, her lounge, and she especially didn't want him creating havoc with her emotional sanity.

He didn't shift position, yet there was a stillness evident in his stance, an intense watchful quality that sent prickles of alarm scudding down the length of her spine. 'No?'

One single word that held a wealth of meaning she didn't want to explore. 'Why don't you cut to the chase?' A bald suggestion that evoked a cynical smile.

'Your unbiased opinion on the projected success of the movie Michel is investing in.'

'I wouldn't hazard a guess,' Stephanie offered evenly. 'There are too many dependent factors.' Her gaze speared his. 'Now, if you don't mind, I must ask you to leave. I have a report I need to work on.'

A lazy smile curved his mouth. 'A businesslike indication the evening is at an end?'

'Yes.' She wrestled with her conscience, and added, 'It was thoughtful of you to bring dinner. Thank you.'

'How polite.'

She detected mockery in his tone, and ignored it as she led the way toward the front door. There was a heightened awareness that played havoc with her nerve endings. Dammit, she could almost *feel* his presence as he walked in her wake, and she hated her reaction as much as she hated *him*.

Stephanie slipped the latch, opened the door and stood to one side to allow him clear passage. 'Good night, Mr. Lanier.'

'Raoul,' he insisted quietly. 'There is just one more thing.'

'What?' she managed to ask with remarkable steadiness.

'This.'

His hands captured her face and his head lowered down to hers before she could utter any protest, and then it was too late, for his mouth had taken possession of her own in a kiss that was so incredibly evocative it stirred her emotions and sent them rocketing out of control.

Dear heaven. It was all she could do not to lean in against him as he deepened the kiss to something so intensely sensual her whole body quivered in re- action.

This is *insane,* a tiny voice cautioned. What in hell are you *doing?*

With determined resolve she reached up and wrenched free of his hands, his tantalizing mouth, at the same time taking an unsteady step backward in an attempt to put some space between them.

Her breathing came in ragged gasps, and she could only stand looking at him with a combination of dis- may and shock.

She wanted to scream *how dare you?* Twin flags of color tinged her cheeks, and her eyes darkened to the deepest sapphire. 'Get out.'

The words emerged in a damning whisper, and he pressed a finger to her mouth, tracing its slightly swollen curves with a gentleness that almost undid her.

'*Au revoir, cherie.*'

He stepped past her, and she closed the door, at- tached the safety chain, then she turned and leaned her back against the solid wood.

She closed her eyes against his image, then opened them again. As much as she blamed *him,* she also apportioned herself some of the blame. For not only responding, but *enjoying* the feel of that skillful mouth as it possessed her own.

Stephanie pushed herself away from the door and collected the empty coffee cups from the lounge and carried them into the kitchen.

Menial chores completed, she entered the small room she'd set up as a home office, activated her laptop and spent three hours on the report.

It was late when she went to bed, and after two hours spent tossing and turning, she switched on the bed lamp and read for an hour before falling into a deep sleep filled with a vivid dream about a nightmarish character who bore a striking resemblance to Raoul Lanier.

# CHAPTER FOUR

THE weekends were strictly devoted to mother-and-daughter time. Saturday morning Stephanie put Emma in the car and drove to a park with a play area, grassy banks bordering a meandering ornamental lake where children could feed the ducks.

For more than an hour Emma ran and played with some of the other children, scrambled over the jungle gym and had several turns on the swing.

Then it was time to drive to the local shopping center, collect the week's groceries before returning home for lunch. While Emma had her afternoon nap, Stephanie caught up with the housework, after which Emma engaged in swimming lessons held at the local pool.

Stephanie inevitably planned something special for dinner, and when the dishes had been cleared away and Emma was bathed and in bed, she'd curl up in a chair and slot a rented video into the VCR.

The pattern rarely changed, and she told herself she was content. Or she had been, until five days ago when a tall ruggedly attractive man with a fascinating French accent invaded her life.

Last night his touch had awakened feelings and emotions she didn't want to think about. Yet conversely, they infiltrated her mind and upset her equilibrium.

Stephanie let her thoughts wander from the actors on screen depicting unrequited love between two people from opposite ends of the social structure.

Another week, she determined, then the film would wrap. That was when her job would step into a higher gear as she organized television interviews, photo and fashion shoots, and the pièce de résistance, the gala dinner and dance.

Her involvement with Michel and Sandrine would be at a premium. Her contact with Raoul would hopefully be minimal.

Then Michel, Sandrine and Raoul would fly out from the Gold Coast to New York, Paris…and her life would revert to normal.

Sunday brought the coveted visit to Movieworld, and Stephanie took pleasure in seeing all the sights, experiencing the acted thrills and spills through the eyes of her daughter. Emma could barely keep awake toward the end, and after such an exciting day she willingly had her bath, ate an early dinner, then climbed into bed.

Monday brought a return to their weekday routine, and Stephanie focused on her schedule as she checked and wrote up her diary.

A cocktail party on Tuesday evening, followed by the gala dinner Saturday night meant she needed to enlist Sarah's baby-sitting services, and she made the call.

The day fled swiftly, the afternoon proving fraught

as last-minute checks revealed a few glitches she needed to chase up and eliminate. Her car, which she'd dropped in for its customary service, needed a replacement part that hadn't arrived by courier in time for the mechanic to finish the job. A temporary loaned vehicle sufficed, and when she arrived home it was to discover a stray dog...a very large dog, she surmised, had somehow gained entrance through the day and had dug up nearly all of her garden plants. He'd also scared their cat half to death judging by his perch high up a tree.

Adding insult to injury, the dog had had a ball trying to drag washing from the clothesline.

It should have been Friday the thirteenth, Stephanie muttered beneath her breath as she set about rescuing the cat, gathering up broken plants, then she retrieved the washing and sorted clothes into Mend, Discard, Wash.

Surprisingly she slept well and woke to a beautifully sunny day with the promise of soaring temperatures and high humidity.

Stephanie favored slim-fitting stylish business suits for office wear, and she owned several that she mixed and matched with a variety of silk blouses. She coveted a sophisticated look, actively promoting an image of skilled efficiency, knowledge, nous.

This morning she selected a tailored skirt and jacket in deep sapphire blue. No blouse, black stiletto heels, her only jewelry a watch and slender neck chain.

The day progressed without a hitch, and she arrived home with forty minutes in which to bathe and feed Emma, shower, dress, then leave at six to attend an invitation-only cocktail party held in a very prestigious penthouse apartment at Main Beach.

Speed and organization were of the essence, and not for the first time she wished she had an eight-hour-a-day job that began when she walked through the office door in the morning and ended when she left late afternoon. And after-hours social obligations didn't form part of her salary package.

If that were the case, she wouldn't be able to afford this pleasantly furnished brick and tile house with its swimming pool, situated a short walk from the beach and a major shopping center. Nor would she own a relatively late-model car, or possess such a fashionable wardrobe of clothes.

For some reason she viewed the evening's cocktail party with unaccustomed reluctance. She need only stay a short while, she reminded herself as she put the finishing touches to her makeup, then she added earrings, a matching pendant, and slipped her feet into black stiletto-heeled pumps.

Basic black in a classic design, Stephanie accorded as she checked her appearance in the long cheval mirror. Short sleeves, scooped neckline, smooth-fitting, with black lace overlaying the skirt and finishing in a scalloped hemline a modest few inches above the knee.

She flicked a glance at her wristwatch, caught up her evening purse and walked out into the lounge where Sarah was entertaining Emma with a new picture storybook.

The little girl had already been bathed and fed, and Stephanie crouched low to bestow a hug. 'Be a good girl for Sarah. Love you.'

'Yes. Love you, too,' Emma responded, tightening her arms around her mother's neck for a long minute.

Special, Stephanie accorded silently. The love of a child was unconditional, and therefore something to treasure.

'Okay,' she issued as she kissed her daughter's cheek and broke contact. 'Time to go.'

She could handle the daily routine of leaving Emma in care, for there was no other option. However, leaving her at night proved a wrench every time, no matter how she rationalized that she only socialized when the job demanded it.

Tonight's soiree was being held in a penthouse apartment situated opposite the Sheraton Mirage to celebrate soaring sales of an imported line of luxury lingerie. Successful advertising, publicity, promotion and marketing had attracted the eye of the Gold Coast's glitterati, resulting in a runaway success. The firm's European director had opted to fly in from Milan to inspect the firm's first Australian boutique and, rumor had it, to inspect his recently acquired apartment in the luxurious Palazzo Versace.

Stephanie reached Main Beach at six-thirty, parked in the underground car park beneath the complex, then rode the lift to the main foyer. Directions to the designated penthouse were easy to follow, and minutes later she'd cleared security and was led by a hostess into a large formal entertaining area filled with mingling guests.

A waiter appeared almost instantly and proffered a tray containing a selection of hors d'oeuvres. They were bite-size, and Stephanie took one, then at the waiter's encouragement, she selected another. There was champagne, which she declined in favor of flavored mineral water.

'Isn't this something else?'

She turned at the sound of a familiar voice, and offered the advertising executive a warm smile. 'Something,' she agreed, following his gaze as it encompassed the luxurious furnishings, magnificent tiling, the expensive paintings adorning the wall, each of which appeared to be genuine originals.

The million-dollar view out over the Broadwater, the many high-rise apartment buildings to the hills in the distance was picture-perfect by daylight. In another hour, when darkness fell, it would provide a fairyland of light against the backdrop of an indigo sky.

'It would appear lingerie does very well.'

'It's high-quality luxury, exceptional workmanship,' Stephanie stated, and incurred a slightly cynical smile.

'And ruinously expensive.'

'It has the name,' she said simply.

'Which we help promote.'

She inclined her head. 'Successfully.' Her gaze skimmed the room, touching on the occasional familiar face. A waiter proffered a tray of savories, and she accepted one, aware of hunger pangs and the knowledge she wouldn't eat dinner.

'If you'll excuse me,' she indicated minutes later. 'There's someone I want to talk to.'

During the next hour she mixed and mingled with fellow guests, some of whom she knew, others who clearly represented the cream of Gold Coast society.

Their host was a charming Italian whose attractive good looks caused more than one female heart to flutter in anticipation of gaining his attention.

Stephanie found it mildly amusing to observe the subtle, and not so subtle, attempts to flirt and charm him into more than a fleeting conversation. Some of it was merely harmless game-playing, which he dealt with the ease of long practice.

Anytime soon an announcement would be made, the host would deliver a gratifying speech, there would be the obligatory champagne toast, coffee would be offered, then she could leave and drive home.

Her gaze shifted, made restless by some indefinable shift in the room's occupants. Her skin's surface contracted in an involuntary shiver, almost a gesture of self-defense, and a slight frown creased her forehead. What on earth...

Then she glimpsed a tall broad-shouldered frame, and the breath caught in her throat at the sight of a familiar dark well-groomed head.

It couldn't be...could it? Her attention was riveted

as she watched the man turn toward her, and had her worst fears confirmed.

Raoul Lanier.

His features were unmistakable. The sculpted bone structure, broad cheekbones, the slant of his jaw, the wide set of those dark gray eyes. And the mouth.

Her eyes honed on that sensuously curved mouth, and remembered how it felt to have it close over her own. A slight tremor shook her slender frame, and she controlled it, barely.

With a sense of mesmerized fascination she watched as he paused to utter a few words to the person he was speaking to, then he turned and began making his way toward her.

For one wild moment she considered leaving. And she almost did, except instinct warned he would probably follow.

As he drew close she ignored her body's reaction and consciously took a slow steadying breath, aware the room and its occupants faded into obscurity.

There was only him, and an acute awareness she was loath to acknowledge.

'Stephanie.'

'Don't tell me,' she began in a voice edged with cynicism. 'Our host is a friend of yours.'

Raoul's eyes assumed a musing gleam. 'We attended the same university.'

'Sheer coincidence, of course,' she continued wryly. 'That you both happen to be in Australia at the same time. Staying not only in the same state, but the same city.'

He inclined his head, and moved in close to make room for a guest intent on beckoning the waiter.

Their bodies almost touched, and she instinctively moved back a pace.

Had he known she'd be here? 'I wouldn't have thought feminine lingerie would interest you.' She'd meant it to be a cutting remark, but as soon as the words were out of her mouth she realized their implication.

'It depends on the woman,' he intoned with dry amusement. 'And whether I'm sufficiently fascinated to want to remove it.'

The very thought of those clever hands easing a bra strap off a smooth shoulder, fingers skillfully manipulating a clasp, then lingering at the curve of a feminine waist before sliding lacy briefs down over slender hips...

*Stop it.* Wayward thoughts and a vivid imagination could only spell trouble.

'If you'll excuse me,' Stephanie said firmly, intending to remove herself as far away as possible from this disturbing man.

'No.'

She looked at him in silent askance, unaware that her eyes deepened in color and assumed a warning sparkle. 'What do you mean—*no?*'

His fingers closed over her elbow. 'Let me introduce you to Bruno.'

She shot him a fulminating glare. 'Get your hand off me.'

'*Merde,*' he swore softly. 'You try my patience.'

'Should I offer to mediate?' an amused male voice intruded.

Stephanie turned and came face to face with her host. A man whose eyes held wisdom and astute knowledge.

'Are you not going to introduce me to this young lady?'

'Bruno Farelli,' Raoul indicated smoothly. 'Stephanie Sommers.'

Bruno took her hand in his and lifted it to his lips. 'Stephanie,' he acknowledged. 'A pleasure.' His dark eyes gleamed with latent humor as he indicated Raoul. 'You do not like this man?'

'He irritates the hell out of me.'

Bruno's amusement was barely restrained. 'Interesting. Women usually fall at his feet.'

'How—' she paused deliberately, then continued with pseudo sweetness '—foolish of them.'

'Raoul must bring you to dinner,' Bruno drawled. 'My wife will enjoy your company.'

'I don't think—'

'Adriana was unable to join me tonight. My daughter did not travel well on the long flight.'

'I'm sorry,' Stephanie said with genuine sympathy.

He regarded her for several long seconds. 'Yes, I do believe you are,' he accorded quietly, pausing as his personal assistant drew close and murmured a brief message. Bruno nodded, then cast Stephanie and Raoul an apologetic glance. 'We will talk later. Now I must say a few words to my guests.'

The words were practiced, but sincere, and the

small surprise was a sneak preview of next season's new lingerie designs, which three models displayed to perfection. Expertly choreographed, the brief parade provided a tantalizing glimpse of what would appear in the boutique a few months from now.

It was a masterly stroke, and a successful one, judging by the buzz of voiced approval. Many of the women would purchase to titillate their husbands, whilst some of the men would designate a gift to a mistress, Stephanie deduced with a degree of cynicism.

'Can I get you another drink?'

Her glass was almost empty, and she surveyed it speculatively, not wanting to offer any encouragement for Raoul to remain at her side. 'I think I'll wait for coffee.'

'Which probably won't be served for another half hour,' Raoul drawled, and she offered him a witching smile that didn't reach her eyes.

'Then you mustn't let me keep you.'

Amusement tinged his expression. 'A politely veiled directive?'

'However did you guess?'

He was silent for several seconds, then he ventured with dangerous softness, 'Did Emma's father hurt you so badly?'

She met his gaze with fearless disregard, aware he saw more than she wanted anyone to see. It unsettled her, and attacked the carefully constructed wall she'd erected guarding her emotions.

A mix of emotions warred with each other as she

sought to control them. 'It's none of your business,' she managed to say with equal quietness.

There was a ruthlessness evident in those compelling features she found disconcerting.

'Does it not occur to you that I might choose to make it my business?'

'And if I choose not to let you?'

He was silent for several long seconds. 'Do you think you can stop me?'

She deliberately raked him from head to toe, and back again. 'You'd be a fool to even try.'

'I've been accorded many things,' Raoul said with indolent amusement. 'A fool isn't one of them.'

She'd had enough. Enough of this indomitable man, the party, and she wanted nothing more than to leave. Except her boss would undoubtedly frown on her early departure.

'Excuse me,' she voiced coolly. 'There are a few business associates I really should speak to.'

He let her go, watching as she eased her way across the room, pausing to chat momentarily before moving on. She possessed a natural grace, a fluidity of movement that reminded him of a dancer on stage.

'Lovely evening,' a pleasant feminine voice intruded, and he shifted his attention to the strikingly beautiful young blonde at his side, who, he acknowledged cynically, was aware of every feminine ploy and not averse to using each and every one of them.

Her conversation was scintillating with just the right degree of sexual promise in the full mouth, the touch of her hand on his arm.

Yet she didn't interest him, and all too frequently he found his attention straying to an attractive blue-eyed strawberry blonde who was as intent on fighting the sexual tension between them as he was in pursuing it.

Stephanie sipped the contents of her glass and fought the temptation to check her watch.

'All alone?'

Her heart sank a little as she summoned a polite smile.

'Samuel,' she acknowledged. As an advertising executive, Samuel Stone was almost without equal. As a man, he possessed one fatal flaw: he believed he was God's gift to women.

'You *have* moved in exalted circles tonight. The elder Lanier brother, and none other than Bruno Farelli himself paying you attention.' He moved close and ran an idle finger down the length of her arm. 'Nice going, darling. I wonder who you'll choose.'

'Neither.'

'Thus leaving the coast clear for me?'

Stephanie swept him a cool glance. 'When are you going to stop playing this wearisome game?'

His smile held a slightly cruel twist. 'You're the one I haven't caught, Stephanie.'

'You never will,' she stated dryly.

'Never is a long time, darling, and I'm remarkably persistent.'

'Two years, and you still haven't got the message.' She shot him an exasperated look. 'How many times do I need to spell it out?'

'You do disinterest well.'

This was becoming tiresome. 'It's for real, Samuel.'

'Why don't I believe you?'

'Because you have a serious ego problem.' She caught sight of two waiters setting up urns, cups and saucers. Thank heavens!

'Come out with me afterward. We'll go on to a nightclub, dance a little, get comfortable…'

'No.' She turned away from him only to have his hand take possession of hers. 'Don't do this, Samuel,' she warned in a deadly quiet voice.

'I believe the lady said no,' a faintly accented voice stated with dangerous silkiness.

Oh Lord, this was just what she needed. Two men at daggers drawn in a bid for her attention. She should have been flattered. Instead she felt vaguely sickened.

'I was hoping to change her mind,' Samuel indicated, releasing her hand.

Raoul's gaze was intent. 'I would say your luck just ran out.'

Samuel inclined his head in an elaborate bow. 'See you around, Stephanie.'

Not if I see you first, she vowed silently.

'You work with him?' Raoul queried when Samuel was out of earshot.

'Liaise,' Stephanie enlightened. 'Advertising and marketing go hand-in-hand.' She drew a deep breath and released it slowly. 'If you'll excuse me, I'll go get some coffee.'

'I'll join you.'

She gave him a sharp look, opened her mouth to decline his company, then closed it again.

'Emma has fully recovered?'

'Yes.' She was conscious of being unobtrusively led toward the table where coffee and tea were being dispensed. 'Yes, she has.'

'Two coffees. One black, the other white with one sugar,' Raoul instructed, then with a cup held in each hand he indicated the wide expanse of floor-to-ceiling glass. 'Let's go take a look at the view.'

Darkness had descended, and the many high-rise buildings appeared as brightly lit towers set against an inky sky. There were boats anchored in the vast marina, and the water resembled dark satin ribboned by the reflection of an ascending moon.

Stephanie stood in silence and sipped her coffee, increasingly aware of Raoul's close proximity as she focused on the immediately adjoining restaurant complex. Patrons enjoying their meal were partly visible, and there were couples, families, strolling along the boardwalk, pausing from time to time to admire some of the large cabin cruisers moored side by side.

It was a peaceful sight, with the sound of music providing a background to the chatter and laughter.

A powerful engine sprang to life from the marina, and minutes later a fully lit cruiser eased out from its berth and headed toward the main channel.

'This reminds me a little of the south of France,' Raoul revealed, indicating the marina. 'Have you traveled at all?'

'North America.' It seemed ages ago, a part of her past she no longer chose to dwell on.

'A holiday?'

'Yes.' A conducted tour in the company of the man she was to marry. Post Ben, pre-Emma.

'You visited New York?'

'I loved the beat of the city, the pulse of life. Seen as a tourist,' she ventured quietly. 'I imagine everyday reality causes it to lose some of the glamour.'

She finished the last of her coffee. 'I really must leave. Sarah has exams tomorrow, and I promised not to be late.'

'I'll walk you to your car.'

'There's no need. I parked in the Mirage shopping complex, and the area is well-lit.'

'Come, we'll find Bruno and you can tell him you've enjoyed a pleasant evening.'

'I can do that quite well on my own.'

He took her cup and placed it down onto a nearby side table along with his own.

'You don't listen, do you?' Stephanie vented with angry resignation as he accompanied her across the room.

Bruno was engaged in conversation with two men, and he looked up as Raoul drew close.

'You are leaving? So soon?'

'It's been a lovely evening,' Stephanie complimented with a warm smile. 'Thank you.'

'I will be in touch with Raoul about dinner. Toward the end of the week?'

'I don't think—'

'We'll confirm with you,' Raoul indicated smoothly.

Stephanie waited until they gained the main foyer before trusting herself to speak. 'Just what did you think you were doing back there?'

'Specifically?'

'Accepting a dinner invitation on my behalf!'

'My exact words conveyed we'd confirm.'

She shot him a baleful glare as they passed through the front entrance. *'We?'* Her voice rose a fraction. *'You* can make whatever plans you like!'

'I intend to. Be aware they'll also include you.'

'The hell they will!' They gained the pavement, and she turned to face him, anger emanating from every pore. 'I don't need a bodyguard, and I especially don't need you to assume a role in my life.' She undid the clasp of her evening purse and extracted her car keys. 'Good night!'

She'd parked the car at street level, and there was only a short distance to walk. She gained less than half a dozen paces when Raoul fell into step at her side.

'You are, without doubt, the most infuriating man I've ever had the misfortune to meet!' she vented furiously as she reached her car.

'In that case, I have nothing to lose.' In a swift synchronized movement he brought her close, slid one hand to cup her head as he captured her lips with his own.

For several long seconds she fought against succumbing to the melting sensation threatening to destroy all rational thought. Her hands lifted to pummel his shoulders, only to fall onto each forearm as she opened her mouth to him.

Oh God, she begged in silent plea as his tongue took an evocative exploratory sweep. Don't do this to me. Why, *why* were her emotions at such variance with the dictates of her brain? All it took was his touch, and she fell to pieces.

Raoul sensed the moment she gave in, and he deepened the kiss, taking her to new heights in emotional intensity.

Her response drove him to cup her bottom and lift her close against him. He wanted more, much more, and the temptation to invite her to his hotel suite was imperative. Except such an action would destroy any advantage he might already have gained.

Instead he eased the pressure, lightening the kiss until his lips brushed gently back and forth over her own, and he slid his hands to cradle her face as he slowly lifted his head.

Her eyes were wide, dilated, and filled with shimmering moisture. The sight of those unspilled tears caused his gut to tighten, and undid him more than any words she might have uttered.

He brushed his thumb over the lower curve of her lip, and felt its faint tremor. He wanted to draw her back into his arms, and simply hold her. Rarely had he glimpsed such naked vulnerability in a woman's eyes, and there was a part of him that seethed in silent anger against the man who had put it there.

He saw the effort it cost her to regain control, to gather her defenses together and step back from him.

His hands slid down her arms and settled on her wrists. 'Stephanie—'

'I have to go. Please.'

The last word held a slightly desperate edge, and he released her, took the keys from her nerveless fingers, unlocked the car door and saw her seated behind the wheel.

Stephanie fired the engine, then barely resisted the temptation to reverse at speed, then send the car tearing out onto the road.

It was only supreme control that stopped her, and she didn't cast Raoul so much as a glance as she eased into the flow of traffic.

She wasn't conscious of having held her breath until she released it in a long pent-up groan. *Why* had she allowed herself to fall into that kiss?

A choked laugh caught in her throat. Raoul Lanier hadn't really given her an option! Except she hadn't fought him, and she should have. For her own emotional sanity, not to mention her peace of mind.

She drove automatically, conscious of the traffic, the intersections, the computerized lights as she traversed the main highway toward Mermaid Beach.

Yet she retained a vivid image of how Raoul's mouth had possessed her own, the slide of his hands, and her body's damnable reaction.

She had sworn after Ben that she'd never allow another man to get close to her again. She'd trusted one, and had that trust broken. Just as she had loved, and discovered her interpretation of *love* and Ben's didn't match.

There was Emma, dear sweet innocent Emma. It was enough. She didn't want or need a man to complicate her life. And she especially didn't need Raoul Lanier, who, in a week or two, would board a plane and jet off to the other side of the world to take up where he left off with his life.

He probably had a mistress.

Now why did that cause her stomach to perform a painful somersault? She didn't *like* the man, she definitely disliked the way he affected her, and she had no intention of allowing a personal relationship to develop between them.

Stephanie reached the fringes of suburban Mermaid Beach, and minutes later she turned into her driveway, activated a modem and garaged the car.

Indoors, Sarah relayed all was well and gathered up her books, then Stephanie kept watch until the girl reached her home safely before locking up.

Emma slept peacefully, and Stephanie tucked in the blanket, moved the teddy bear, then quietly retreated to her own room.

# CHAPTER FIVE

IT HADN'T been the best of mornings, Stephanie reflected as she checked her computer's electronic mail. No doubt compounded by the fact she hadn't slept well and was nursing a headache.

One message was headlined as Urgent, and she uttered a soft curse as she clicked it open. The date for the movie's photographic shoot needed to be rescheduled. Could she contact the Sheraton management, organize a suitable time to check the proposed layout, liaise with the photographer and confirm this afternoon?

She reached for her phone, only to have it beep, and she automatically lifted the receiver. 'Yes?'

'I have Raoul Lanier on hold,' Isabel intoned.

Stephanie's stomach immediately curled into a tight ball. 'Have him call back.'

'Okay. Any message?'

Not one you could repeat, she ruminated darkly. 'No,' she managed to say evenly. 'Can you get me Alex Stanford on the line? Try his cell phone.' The photographer was one of the best, and with luck he'd be able to spare half an hour to go over the proposed shots.

Thirty minutes later she'd tied it all together, and

ignoring her scheduled lunch break she slid into her car and drove to Main Beach and the Sheraton Hotel.

Alex was waiting in the lobby when she arrived, and together they descended the central staircase, walked out to the pool area, tossed around indoor and outdoor locations, the portrayed mood she wanted to convey, and fixed on a few possible time frames for the following week, subject to confirmation.

Stephanie extracted her diary, wrote in the dates and times, noted contact names at the film studio, advertising, wardrobe.

'Okay, that's it,' she assured, replacing the diary into her satchel. 'I'll ring when I've pinned it down. Thanks,' she added with a genuine smile as they reentered the lobby. 'I appreciate your help.' Her cell phone rang, and she wriggled her fingers at Alex as he departed for the lift, then she took the call.

Five minutes later she pushed the cell phone into her bag and made for the central stairs leading up to reception. Her stomach grumbled, reminding her she'd had to forego lunch, and she contemplated whether to cross the footbridge to the shopping complex for a coffee and sandwich, or whether she'd simply stop somewhere and pick up something to eat on the way back to the office.

She reached the top of the stairs and made her way through the foyer. Coffee and a sandwich in a café overlooking the Broadwater won out.

'Stephanie.'

It was an instantly recognizable male voice, the

drawling faintly accented tone causing all her fine body hairs to stand up in protective self-defense as she turned to face the man who had indirectly caused her a sleepless night.

Raoul Lanier. Looking every inch the powerful executive, attired in a dark business suit, crisp white shirt and dark silk tie. Expensive tailoring emphasized his breadth of shoulder, accentuated his height and added to an overall aura of sophistication.

She looked…fragile, Raoul decided as he subjected her to a studied appraisal. Her eyes were the deepest blue, and there were faint shadows apparent that indicated she hadn't enjoyed a peaceful night's sleep…any more than he had. Something that pleased him.

Stephanie saw that he wasn't alone. Bruno Farelli, an attractive blonde, and a young child were with him.

Her cool gaze was controlled, her slight smile a mere facsimile. 'Raoul, Bruno,' she acknowledged.

'A pleasure to see you again,' Bruno enthused, and indicated the woman at his side. 'Allow me to introduce my wife, Adriana, and our daughter, Lucia.'

The little girl stole her heart, she resembled a miniature angel, beautifully dressed with gorgeous blond curly hair and a winsome smile.

'Adriana.' Stephanie's features softened as she greeted the child. 'Hello, Lucia.'

'Bruno mentioned you,' Adriana offered warmly. 'We have just emerged from a long lunch.'

Stephanie responded an appropriate platitude. 'I hope you enjoy your stay here.'

'You must join us for dinner,' Adriana pressed with a smile. 'I believe you have a little girl of Lucia's age. It would be delightful for them to meet. Are you free tomorrow evening?'

Oh hell. How did she handle that? With grace, she decided reluctantly. Bruno Farelli was a very influential man, and the agency she worked for was handling his account. To refuse would not only be impolite, but a bad move, professionally. She could only hope Raoul Lanier wasn't included in the invitation.

'Thank you, I'd like that.'

'Shall we say six, at our apartment?'

Her cell phone rang, and she reached for it, ascertained the combination of digits displayed in the window, and offered an apologetic smile. 'I'm sorry, I'll have to take this. If you'll excuse me?' She focused her attention on Adriana. 'Six, tomorrow evening. I'll look forward to it.' She inclined her head briefly, then she turned and activated the call as she made her way toward the main entrance.

Definitely a latte and sandwich, she decided minutes later, and she ordered, then ate beneath a shade umbrella, opting to check Bruno's lingerie boutique window display whilst in the shopping complex.

It was almost three when she entered the office, and what remained of the afternoon was caught up with numerous phone calls together with the completion of a lengthy report.

Consequently it was well after five when she collected Emma from the day care center, and the headache that had bothered her most of the day developed sufficiently to warrant medication.

At eight, with Emma safely asleep, she took a leisurely shower, luxuriating in the relaxing jet of warm water as it soothed the kinks from her neck. Rose-scented soap left her skin silky smooth and exuding a delicate fragrance. Toweled dry she added matching dusting powder and pulled on a freshly laundered T-shirt.

Not exactly an ultrafeminine image, she mentally derided as she caught a glance of her mirrored reflection. Not that it mattered one little bit, for there was no man in her life to tease and tantalize with silk and lace.

Nor did she want one, she silently assured as she applied a thin film of night cream to her face, smoothed the excess onto her hands, then switched off the light and crept into bed.

So why did she lay awake haunted by one man's profile? And have her thoughts stray as she imagined how his skin would feel beneath her touch? Would his muscles flex as he sought control? And at what point would he lose it?

He had the look, the touch, she acknowledged, that promised unbridled primitive passion. The skill and intimate knowledge to drive a woman wild.

Thinking just *how* wild was an infinitely dangerous exercise, for it brought a vivid reminder of her relationship with Ben...a man who had taken his pleasure without consideration for her own. And she, through reticence and naiveté, had enjoyed the closeness and warmth, while longing for more.

Blind trust and immature love, she acknowledged with innate honesty. Had she been older, wiser, in the ways of men, she'd have seen the weakness, the selfishness for what it was. Instead she had made excuses for him and blamed herself for his shortcomings.

*Fool.* How long before she would have seen him for what he was? Her pregnancy had been an act of God...and a gastro bug, which destroyed the contraceptive pill's effectiveness at the most crucial part of her cycle.

Emma, dear sweet Emma. Ben's reaction had been so abhorrent, from that moment Emma had become *hers,* solely hers.

With a determination Stephanie barely recognized in herself, she'd left Sydney, family and friends, and relocated to the Gold Coast, carving a niche for herself at what she did best...marketing. She'd worked up until two weeks before Emma's birth, taken a month's maternity leave, then returned to the workforce.

Her mother visited twice a year, and took Emma back to Sydney for a few weeks, and Stephanie returned there for her annual holidays.

For almost four years she'd been happy and content with her life. Until now, when Raoul Lanier had appeared on the scene, disrupting her carefully chosen lifestyle, attacking her libido, and causing her to long for something that could only bring grief.

The only way out was not to see him again. A silent bubble of laughter rose and died in her throat. How did she do that, when he had involved himself in one of her work assignments? Everywhere she went, he seemed to be *there*. Legitimately, she had to concede.

She closed her eyes then opened them again to stare into the room's darkness.

A week or two, then he'd be gone. Surely she could survive that length of time?

The shrill peal of the phone jerked her instantly into a sitting position, and she reached for the bedside lamp with one hand and the extension receiver with the other.

Her voice was breathless, startled, apprehensive, and she inwardly cursed herself as she checked the time.

'Did I wake you?' Raoul's voice was deep, and vaguely husky.

She wasn't conscious of holding her breath, until it released in a rush. 'No.' She clutched the receiver, and mentally counted to three. 'No, you didn't. What do you want?'

'You neglected to return my call.'

'I wasn't aware it was necessary,' she said coolly. 'Besides, I understand my secretary asked you to call back.'

'I didn't have the opportunity until now.'

'It couldn't wait until tomorrow?'

'Michel requests you fax him an update on estimated marketing and advertising expenses. He wants to check them against the preliminary figures. Have you a pen and paper handy? I'll give you his e-mail address.'

'Just a minute.' She opened the pedestal drawer and extracted a pad and pen. 'Okay, what is it?' She wrote it down, then repeated it. 'I'll get on to it first thing in the morning.'

'There is just one more thing,' he drawled.

'And that is?'

'I'll collect you and Emma at five forty-five tomorrow evening.'

She closed her eyes and opened them again. Why, for one minute, had she thought he might not be included in Bruno's invitation? 'No. I'll drive to the hotel.'

'*Sacré bleu,* why must you be so independent?'

'You're already staying at the Sheraton,' she stated with cool logic. 'Why collect me?'

'You would prefer to drive home at night to an empty house with a young child in your care?'

This was too much. *He* was too much! 'I would *prefer* it if you weren't there at all tomorrow night,' she flung angrily.

'My presence unsettles you?' Raoul pursued with mocking amusement.

'You flatter yourself,' she said icily. 'If there's nothing else you need to discuss, I'd like to go back to bed. And in future,' she added for good measure, 'please keep business calls to business hours.'

He laughed, a deep-throated chuckle that incensed her to such a degree she hung up on him.

Insufferable man. She thumped her pillow, snapped off the light, then pulled up the covers and settled down to sleep.

Except sleep was never more distant, and she cursed him to hell and back as the dark hours crept slowly to midnight and beyond.

The insistent peal of the alarm clock brought her sharply awake, and she depressed the button before slipping wearily from the bed.

Feed and dress Emma, feed the cat, take out the trash, make coffee, eat, pack Emma's lunch and fill drink bottles ready for day care...

Stephanie went through the motions automatically, completed essential household chores, then she dressed for work, delivered Emma to the day care center and drove in to the office.

It proved to be a day where anything that could go wrong, did. She needed every organizational skill she possessed to arrange the smooth transition from delivery of stock to television promotion. A company drivers' strike provided a delay while she arranged alternate mode of transport. Wardrobe didn't supply the right size or the right color for the model promoting the product. Phone calls weren't returned, and she had to chase up advertising.

When she left the office at five all she wanted to do was collect Emma, go home, relax and unwind.

Instead she needed to bathe and dress her daughter, grab a quick shower, throw on some clothes, apply makeup...all in the space of twenty-five minutes.

There was a part of her that wanted to ring and cancel, except that would amount to a cop-out, and she was damned if she'd allow Raoul Lanier the satisfaction. She'd attend, and enjoy herself. For Emma's sake, and that of her hosts. The indomitable Frenchman could, she decided, go *jump* for all she cared.

It was nothing short of a miracle that she was ready on time. Elegant evening trousers with matching camisole in a deep ultraviolet highlighted her cream textured skin and emphasized her eyes. Emma wore a pale blue print dress with white shoes and socks. Her very best outfit, Stephanie mused, taking pleasure in her daughter's delightful anticipation of the evening ahead.

From a personal aspect, she hadn't had the opportunity to give it more than a passing thought. Now that they were on the verge of leaving, the prospect of spending yet another few hours in Raoul Lanier's company bothered her more than she wanted to admit.

'Okay, sweetheart,' she said gently as she collected her keys and evening purse. 'Let's go.'

They made it to the front door, only to have the bell peal as Stephanie reached to open it, and her heart raced into overdrive at the sight of Raoul Lanier standing on the porch.

'You shouldn't have come,' she said at once, doing her best to remain polite in Emma's presence.

He spared her a long hard glance. 'I said I would collect you.'

He was angry, she could tell from the set of his jaw, the slight thickening of his accent. It was becoming a battle of wills—*hers, his*—and for some reason, despite her determination, she felt she was treading shaky ground.

Raoul turned to greet Emma, who, an innocent traitor, appeared delighted not only to see him, but excited at the prospect of being driven in a different car.

A large late-model sedan, Stephanie saw at once. 'I'll need to get Emma's booster seat,' she indicated, and crossed to the garage. 'She's under the legal age to be able to travel without it.' One of the reasons I would have preferred to use my own car, she added silently, then caught Raoul's perceptive look, and knew he wasn't fooled in the slightest.

Three more minutes, and their cars would have passed in the street. He wanted to shake her. Independence in a woman was a fine thing, but this particular young woman was intent on carrying it too far.

Raoul drove with care, traversing the northbound highway with the ease of a man well used to handling both left- and right-hand drive.

Emma's excited childish chatter precluded the need to search for conversation, and Stephanie experienced a mixture of apprehension and trepidation as Raoul swept the car into the underground parking lot beneath the Palazzo Versace.

Save your nerves for a few hours' time when you leave, she admonished silently. Although with luck, Raoul would indulge in a few glasses of wine during dinner, and she could insist on taking a taxi home.

Two hours, three at the most, then she could leave, social obligation complete, and thereafter contact with Bruno Farelli would be restricted to office hours and confined to business matters.

Some hope, she realized with a sinking heart, as the evening progressed. *Luck* wasn't on her side, in any respect.

Emma and Lucia, with the natural instinct of children, bonded immediately. To the extent it seemed as if they'd known each other from the cradle.

Adriana's warmth and sparkling humor made it impossible to retain a polite distance. Both she and Bruno were friendly convivial hosts who went to great pains to ensure Stephanie felt at ease.

They would have succeeded handsomely if it hadn't been for Raoul's presence. For it was *he* who set her nerves on edge. He who caused her heart to beat faster as she forced herself to sample the various courses, sip a little wine, and converse with apparent ease.

Did any one of them realize just how tense she was beneath the relaxed facade? Could anyone detect the way her pulse thudded at the base of her throat? Or how her body tingled with electrifying awareness because of the man seated at her side?

The food was superb, she was certain of it, except her taste buds appeared to have gone on strike.

This was madness. A divine insanity that had no base in her reality.

How long before she could escape? There was dessert still to come, followed by coffee. Another hour?

'Which theme park would you recommend for Lucia's benefit?' Adriana queried. 'We are only on the Coast for such a short time.'

'Dreamworld is wonderful,' Stephanie answered automatically. 'And Seaworld. Each have various rides and attractions. I've taken Emma to both, and while she enjoyed Seaworld, Dreamworld was her favorite.'

'Bruno has Saturday free. We'd love you and Emma to join us. The girls get on well together, and it would be so nice for Lucia to have Emma's company.'

'Dreamworld,' Emma parroted with excitement. 'Please, Mommy.'

'*Si,*' Lucia echoed. 'Dreamworld.'

'English, Lucia,' Adriana admonished gently.

'Perhaps Stephanie already has plans for the weekend,' Raoul indicated, offering her a silent challenge to refuse.

'Saturday is fine,' Stephanie answered evenly in a determined effort to prove she wouldn't rise to his bait. 'Thank you. We'd be delighted to join you.'

Adriana looked pleased as she stood and gathered up the dinner plates. 'I'll get dessert. I hope you like tiramisu?'

'Love it,' Stephanie assured. 'Can I help with anything?'

'You're very kind, but everything is organized.'

Coffee followed the superb dessert, and it was almost nine when Stephanie indicated she must leave.

'It's been a lovely evening,' she said warmly, extending her thanks. 'I'll look forward to Saturday.' She meant it, for Adriana was delightful, and Emma would love sharing the adventures of Dreamworld with Lucia.

'Let me have your telephone number.' Adriana beckoned for her to cross to an escritoire, where she extracted pen and paper. 'I'll ring and arrange a time to meet.'

Stephanie withdrew her cell phone. 'I'll call a taxi.'

Adriana gave her a thoughtful glance, and opted to remain quiet.

A few minutes, the dispatcher relayed, as a taxi had just dropped someone off at the Sheraton.

Collecting Emma, bidding her hosts good-night, was achieved in minimum time.

'Cancel the taxi,' Raoul instructed with deadly quiet as they made their way toward the lift.

'No.'

His expression hardened, and his eyes resembled dark gray slate. 'Cancel, Stephanie,' he voiced quietly. 'Or I will.'

She shot him a cool glare, which changed to scandalized surprise as he calmly took the cell phone from her hand, pressed Redial, and canceled the taxi.

She badly wanted to tell him to go take a flying

leap, except such behavior would only startle Emma. It would have to wait, she decided vengefully, until they were alone.

Stephanie was supremely conscious of him as they rode the lift down to the car park, and it took every reserve of strength not to wrench Emma from his arms.

Who did he think he was, invading her life, taking charge, issuing orders? It was a wonder steam wasn't escaping from her ears as she banked down her anger.

Fortunately Emma's excitement resulted in practically nonstop chatter during the fifteen-minute drive to Mermaid Beach, which meant Stephanie was able to respond to her daughter and totally ignore the man behind the wheel of the car.

The instant Raoul pulled into her driveway she undid her seat belt, and no sooner had he brought the car to a halt that she slid from the passenger seat in a bid to extricate Emma as quickly as possible.

'There's no need for you to get out,' Stephanie said tightly as he copied her actions. 'I can manage.'

'I am sure you can,' he evinced silkily as he crossed to her side. 'Let me take Emma.'

She didn't want him in the house. 'No. I'm fine. Say good-night, darling,' she bade Emma seconds later, only to give a startled gasp as Raoul removed the keys from her fingers and pushed one into the lock of the front door.

Naturally he got it right the first time, and she

clenched her teeth in exasperation as he followed her indoors.

Stephanie threw him a look that should have felled him. 'I'd like you to leave. Now.'

'Put Emma to bed, Stephanie,' Raoul drawled in a deceptively silky voice. He smiled at the little girl nestled in her mother's arms. 'Good night, poppet. Sweet dreams.'

'Kiss good night,' Emma said with unblinking solemnity, and held out her arms.

Raoul leaned forward and brushed a soft childish cheek with his lips, then watched as Stephanie turned away and moved down the hallway.

Did he have any idea what that gesture did to her? Almost before her eyes man and child were forming an affection that had no place to go. It wasn't fair to Emma, she decided as she undressed her daughter and went through the routine of getting her ready for bed.

It took a while for her to settle, given the excitement of the evening and the prospect of a visit to Dreamworld. But halfway through the usual nighttime story the long silky lashes began to droop as she drifted to sleep.

Stephanie waited a few minutes, then she adjusted the covers, turned down the light and gently closed the door as she left.

Raoul was in the lounge, one hand thrust into a trouser pocket, and he raked her slender form with compelling intensity as she crossed to stand behind a single chair.

'Don't presume to judge me by Emma's father.'

Her eyes flashed blue fire and her chin tilted as she threw him a venomous glare. 'You know nothing of Emma's father.'

'I know he holds no importance in your life.' He indicated the picture frames holding pride of place on the dropped table. 'There is no evidence of his existence.'

Anger flooded through her like an unstoppable tide, and the desire to shock caused a flow of words she had no intention of uttering.

'Ben is dead.'

If that stark announcement surprised him, he gave no evidence of it, and that infuriated her further.

'You want to know details?' she vented. 'We were childhood sweethearts who grew up together, fell in love and got engaged. Then I fell pregnant. A classic mistake caused by a low dosage pill and a gastric attack.' Her expression sobered, became shuttered as some of the pain returned.

'The man I thought I knew as well as I knew myself suggested I *take care of it* on the grounds a child would complicate our lives.' Her face paled at the memory of those ghastly arguments. 'I refused.' She felt her features tighten as scenes flashed through her mind. The anger, the stinging retribution. 'He opted out and took a flight to Canada, only to die a few months later in a skiing accident.'

She drew a deep calming breath, then released it, hating herself for the tirade, and hating him even more for goading her into it.

'You intend excluding all men from your life, because one man ran away from responsibility?'

She'd dealt with this four years ago. Dealt with the pain of rejection, the degree of guilt for Ben's death. She didn't want to revive the past, for she'd learned the hard way that it had no part in her future.

'I want you to leave.'

'Not yet.'

'Who do you think you are?' On impulse she picked up a nearby ornament and hurled it at him only to see him field and catch it.

The action horrified her, and she stared at him in stunned disbelief for several long seconds.

'Dammit! What do you want from me?' The query came out as a strangled whisper.

'The opportunity to prove I'm not Ben.' His voice was dangerously quiet, and she was unable to look away.

'To what end?' she demanded, sorely tried. 'You're on the Coast how long? A week, two at the most.' Her gaze pierced his. 'Then what? You move on, New York, Paris...wherever. I can qualify a pleasant sojourn, but what about Emma? How does she deal with someone who affords her affection, then leaves?'

'I want to be with you.'

His meaning was unmistakable. 'Are you suggesting we scratch an *itch?*'

Her scandalized expression amused him. 'When I take you to bed,' he vowed silkily, 'it won't be merely to *scratch an itch.*'

'No,' she denied heatedly. 'Because you won't get anywhere near my bed!'

Raoul regarded her silently for a few seconds. 'You are so sure about that?'

She wasn't sure about anything where he was concerned. Already he'd managed to get beneath her skin, and that in itself was dangerous.

'Go find some other woman to fill your needs. I'm not into experimentation.'

'Neither am I,' Raoul assured pitilessly. 'And if I merely wanted a woman to *fill my needs,* why would I choose to continually do battle with *you?*'

'Because I make a change, and therefore present a challenge?'

'Is that what you think?'

'Damn you,' Stephanie snarled, almost at the end of her tether. 'What else is there for me to think?'

'You could try to trust me.'

'I trusted a man once,' she flung heatedly. 'Someone I'd known all my life. Why should I trust *you,* someone I've known for only a week!'

'Because I give my word that you can.'

'Words are easy,' she said bitterly.

She wasn't aware of him moving, yet he was close, much too close, and there was nothing she could do to escape his descending head as he claimed her mouth in a kiss that took her by complete surprise.

She expected force...a fierce unprincipled onslaught that was nothing less than an invasion.

Instead his touch was tactile, an evocative exploration that was incredibly gentle. Bewitching, enticing, it mesmerized her with a magic all its own, hinting at hunger and passion withheld.

Heat coursed through her veins, arousing acute sensuality, and her body swayed into his, craving closer contact as her arms slid up his shoulders and clung.

Raoul deepened the kiss, slowly and with infinite care, eliciting a response that drove him to the brink.

This wasn't the time, or the place, and he gradually withdrew, lightly brushing her lips with his own until they sought and rested against her temple.

How long they stood like that she wasn't sure. Long seconds, maybe minutes. Then he shifted a hand and cupped her chin, forcing her to meet his gaze.

'You want to deny *this*?' He cradled her face, and felt a tremor race through her body. 'Reject what we might have together?' He smoothed a thumb over her lips. 'I want you. For all the right reasons. I need you to want to take the first step.'

He lowered his head and kissed her, lightly teasing her tongue with his own, then he withdrew.

'I'm going to walk out the door. You have the number of my cell phone. If you don't ring me before I reach the hotel, I won't attempt to see you again.' He ran his thumb lightly over her lower lip, then pressed the pad against the slightly swollen center. 'Okay?'

'I don't want this,' she said in a desperate whisper.

'Wrong,' he denied gently. 'You don't want to be hurt.'

'That, too,' she admitted wretchedly, and he smiled.

'One day at a time, *cherie,* hmm?'

She wasn't capable of uttering a word.

He placed his hands over her own and gently disentangled them from his shoulders.

Her eyes clung to his, wide, dilated, unblinking as he stepped back a pace. She saw his lips curve into a faint smile that held quizzical warmth, and something else.

Then he turned and left the room. She heard the faint *snick* as the front door closed and the lock engaged, and seconds later his car engine purred into life, only to fade with distance.

Stephanie didn't move, she simply stared into space as she tried to collect her thoughts.

If she rang him, her life would never be the same. Yet if she didn't...would she live to regret not having taken that chance?

*Life* was all about chance. You could choose whether to welcome it with both hands. Or you could choose extreme caution, question every possibility, and never realize a dream.

What did she have to lose?

A hollow laugh rose and formed a lump in her throat. Oh *hell.* She was damned if she did, and damned if she didn't.

Impulse stirred her to action, and she extracted Raoul's business card, then made the call.

He picked up on the third ring. 'What took you so long?'

'A fight with my subconscious,' she answered honestly.

'*Merci.*'

His voice sounded deep and impossibly husky, and did strange things to her equilibrium.

'Good night.' She cut the connection, then stood in reflective silence.

What had she done? She was mad, *insane*. To contemplate aligning herself with someone of Raoul Lanier's caliber was akin to riding a tiger. But what a ride, a tiny imp taunted mercilessly.

Too restless to sleep, she retrieved fresh linen and made up the bed in the spare room ready for her mother. She also dusted, and put out fresh towels.

Then she made a cup of tea and flicked through the channels on cable television in the hope of finding something engrossing to watch, only to switch it off and pick up a book.

# CHAPTER SIX

A *DELIVERY* of roses, a dozen beautiful pale pink buds sheathed in cellophane arrived in reception midafternoon, and Stephanie ignored her secretary's curiosity as she extracted the card.

*Dinner tonight. Seven. Raoul.*

'Shall I fetch a vase?'

She looked up at the sound of Isabel's voice. 'Thanks.'

'Your three-thirty appointment is waiting in reception. Shall I show her in?'

'Give me a few minutes, I need to make a call first.'

Seconds later she punched in a series of digits, and tried to calm her shredding nerves as she waited for Raoul to pick up.

A kiss didn't mean anything, despite the fact it was very skillfully executed and pushed all the right buttons, she conceded rationally, only to stifle a groan. Who did she think she was kidding?

'Lanier.'

His voice was deep, businesslike, and she forced herself to respond in kind. 'Stephanie.' She turned away from the desk and looked at the scene beyond the plate-glass window. 'Thank you for the roses.'

She felt like a gauche teenager, which was ridiculous!

'My pleasure.'

The husky faintly accented voice seeped into her body and curled around her nerve endings. She lifted a shaky hand and pushed back a stray tendril of hair.

It was crazy to feel so distracted, and her fingers tightened on the receiver as she sought composure. 'I can't make it tonight. My mother is arriving from Sydney on the evening flight.'

'You need to collect her from the airport.' He sounded vaguely amused, almost as if he *knew* the struggle she was having in order to remain calm.

'Yes. I'm sorry.'

'I'll look forward to meeting her—'

'Raoul—'

'When I collect you and Emma tomorrow,' he continued. 'Adriana mentioned meeting in the hotel foyer at nine-thirty.'

'It will be easier if I drive to the hotel.'

'We've been down this path before,' Raoul drawled. 'Nine-fifteen, Stephanie.'

'I don't like domineering men,' she retorted, and heard his soft husky laughter. Her voice assumed a definitive coolness. 'I have a client waiting.'

'Tomorrow, Stephanie,' he reminded a bare second before she disconnected the call.

'Nanna's coming, Nanna's coming. Big airplane,' Emma chanted on the way home, during her bath, over dinner and all the way down to Coolangatta airport.

'*Nanna.*' Stephanie had to physically restrain her from running to the entry doors the instant Emma caught sight of her grandmother walking the concourse.

'Celeste.' Stephanie greeted her mother with an affectionate hug, and took her carry-on bag so Celeste could gather Emma into her arms.

There wasn't a chance to get a word in edgeways as Emma excitedly regaled every detail about day care, her friends, the beach, the pool. Nonstop childish chatter ruled as Stephanie collected Celeste's bag from the luggage carousel.

'How are you, darling?' Celeste inquired of her daughter when there was a temporary lull.

'Fine,' Stephanie answered warmly. 'The job is going well.' She shot Celeste a quick smile. 'As you can see, Emma is great.'

'Dreamworld,' Emma chorused from the rear seat. 'Tomorrow me and Mommy and Lucia, and Raoul—' she struggled getting the name out '—are going to Dreamworld. Can Nanna come, too?'

'We'll talk about it later, sweetheart,' Celeste conceded.

It took a while for Emma to settle after they arrived home, and it was almost nine when Stephanie entered the lounge.

'I made some tea, darling.' Celeste indicated the sofa. 'Now come and sit down.'

'How is Dad?'

Celeste smiled warmly. 'Philip is fine. Still working too hard, but he enjoys the legal process, and criminal law is his life.'

It was lovely to catch up on all the news. Family comprised several cousins, aunts and uncles, her grandparents, and it was almost eleven when Celeste caught sight of the time.

'I think we should go to bed. We have plenty of time over the weekend to chat.'

'Would you like to come to Dreamworld with us tomorrow?' Stephanie asked as she straightened cushions and switched off the lamp.

'You're going with friends, aren't you, darling? I might just relax at home, and prepare a roast for dinner.'

Ever the mother, Stephanie conceded affectionately. Roast dinners, baking tins filled, extra for the freezer. She placed an arm around Celeste's waist as they traversed the short hallway. 'I've already washed curtains and bedspreads,' she warned with a smile. 'So don't even *think* about any spring-cleaning, okay?'

'I like to do things for you. I don't get the chance very often.'

Stephanie switched on the light in the spare bedroom. 'Sleep well, Celeste. I'll see you in the morning.'

A bright sunny day, with the promise of high temperatures, Stephanie saw as she opened shutters and let the light in.

It was early, only seven, but Emma had already stirred, and she popped an educational video into the VCR. 'Sit quietly,' she said. 'I'll get you some juice, then we'll have breakfast.'

Celeste joined them, and at eight-thirty Stephanie dressed Emma, packed a holdall with sunscreen cream, snacks, juice, bottled water, the utilitarian first-aid necessities and the seemingly hundred and one things needed when taking a child out for the day.

Then she quickly changed into stonewashed jeans and a blue singlet top, added a blouse, then tended to her makeup.

Emma had positioned herself on a chair beside the window overlooking the front driveway, and Stephanie heard her excited voice calling, 'Raoul's here. Raoul's here, Mommy.'

'There's no such thing as a quiet arrival,' Stephanie said wryly as Celeste rose to her feet.

'Oh my,' Celeste murmured as Raoul entered the hallway.

Attired in casual dress jeans, a navy polo shirt and trainers—sunglasses pushed high—he resembled something out of the pages of a men's fashion magazine.

Stephanie performed introductions. 'My mother, Celeste Sommers. Raoul Lanier.'

'A pleasure,' Raoul inclined, and Stephanie could almost sense his effect on her mother.

'Raoul, Raoul.' Emma launched herself at him, and he caught and lifted her high against his chest.

'*Bon jour,* Emma,' he greeted solemnly.

'Dreamworld. Got a cap.' She put a hand over the cap pulled down over her hair. 'Can we go?' She turned to her grandmother. 'Bye, Nanna.'

'Have a nice day,' Celeste said warmly.

Raoul took Emma to the car while Stephanie set the booster seat, and within minutes Raoul reversed down the driveway and headed toward the highway.

They entered the theme park shortly after ten, and both Emma and Lucia chattered with delight as the adults indulged them in a variety of rides and other features suitable for the very young.

Stephanie was supremely conscious of Raoul at her side, the light momentary brush of his hand at her waist, her shoulder. His smile did strange things to her composure, and her whole body seemed like a finely tuned instrument awaiting his touch.

It was madness, a madness she couldn't afford. For four years she'd marshaled her emotions and vowed never to allow another man to get beneath her skin. Now, no matter how hard she tried to avoid it, Raoul had skillfully managed to penetrate her defenses.

Could he sense her ambivalence? Probably, she perceived wryly. He seemed to have developed the uncanny knack of reading her mind, anticipating her thoughts.

Together with Bruno, Adriana and Lucia, they watched the tigers, rode the paddle steamer and witnessed the little girls' awe at the enacted mock train robbery.

There were several stops for liquid refreshment as

the day wore on, and after an alfresco lunch both little girls began to tire.

'I'll take her,' Raoul indicated when Stephanie lifted Emma into her arms, and as she was about to protest Emma leaned toward him with arms outstretched.

What could she say? To refuse would seem churlish. Besides, Emma was only copying Lucia, who was happily settled in the curve of her father's arm.

It didn't take long for two little heads to droop against two male shoulders, and Stephanie tried to ignore the sight of her daughter nestled comfortably in Raoul's arms. It looked natural, much too natural, and there was a part of her that wanted to tear Emma away.

Don't get too close. It's unfair, she longed to hurl at him. But with Bruno and Adriana within hearing distance, there wasn't much she could do except appear relaxed and at ease with the situation as they wandered in and out of several tourist and souvenir shops.

Lucia stirred a short while later, and almost on cue Emma lifted her head, focused on her surroundings and pointed to where several cartoon costumed characters were mingling among the crowd.

'Kenny Koala,' Emma chanted with renewed energy, and there were photographs taken with each costumed character, then after time-out for refreshments, they slowly made their way toward the main gate.

'It's been a lovely day.' Adriana leaned forward

and caught hold of Stephanie's hand. 'Thank you for bringing Emma. Lucia has had a wonderful time.'

'We've hired a cruiser and crew to tour the waterways tomorrow,' Bruno relayed as they reached their respective cars. 'We would like to have you join us.'

Raoul inclined his head. 'Stephanie?'

She'd been on edge all day in his company. The thought of spending yet another day with him sent her stomach fluttering with nervous tension. 'It's very kind of you, but my mother is visiting from Sydney.'

'Bring her, too,' Adriana encouraged warmly. 'Please, it will be fun to spend another day together, our last on the Gold Coast, for we leave on Monday.'

Stephanie didn't have the heart to refuse. After all, she wouldn't be alone with Raoul. 'I'll check with Celeste and see if she has anything planned, then call you.'

There was a general exodus of people and cars from the theme park, consequently it took a while to gain clear passage onto the highway. Although once there, Raoul was able to pick up speed, and it was after five when he pulled into her driveway.

Extracting Emma, the booster seat, took essential minutes, and Stephanie could hardly refuse Raoul's help. It followed that he came into the house, and Celeste seemed bent on offering him a drink, inquiring about the day, which together with Emma's excited verbal contributions took some time.

He could, she decided with unwarranted cynicism,

have politely declined the drink and retreated within minutes. So why hadn't he?

Worse, he looked very much at ease and far too relaxed for her peace of mind as he conversed with Celeste. Cruising the waterways and an invitation to join them the next day was presented with superb verbal strategy, achieving his objective with a skill she could only admire.

'I'll be delighted.' Celeste beamed warmly. 'Perhaps you'd like to join us for dinner?'

*No,* Stephanie silently cried, don't do this. But it was too late.

'Raoul may have plans,' she interjected quickly, willing him to refuse.

'No plans,' he returned easily, meeting her gaze as he offered a faint musing smile. 'Thank you. Celeste.'

Fine, let Celeste entertain him. *She* had things to do. Bathing Emma was one of them, not to mention unpacking the holdall of drink bottles, fruit and a number of other comestibles essential to a day out with a young child.

'If you'll excuse me?' She extended her hand to Emma. 'Bathtime, sweetheart.'

Emma's cheerful questions and observations provided a welcome distraction, and afterward Stephanie took time to freshen up. Although she refused to change on the grounds that it would seem as if she'd done so strictly for Raoul's benefit.

'Raoul insisted on buying wine to go with dinner,' Celeste indicated as Stephanie entered the kitchen.

'He should be back soon.' She expertly turned the roast vegetables and slid the pan back into the oven. 'He seems nice, darling.'

*Nice?* He was many things, but nice? Determined, overwhelming. *Lethal.*

'No comment?' Celeste teased, and caught her daughter's wry glance.

At that moment Raoul returned, and Stephanie busied herself setting the table, then helped Celeste dish the meal.

Her mother was an excellent cook, and Stephanie fought hard to do justice to the food on her plate.

'Do you have family, Raoul?'

Here we go, Stephanie inwardly groaned. The maternal need for background details. She studiously avoided looking at him as she helped Emma with her vegetables.

'Two brothers, Michel and Sebastian. Michel is currently in Australia with his wife. Sebastian and Anneke recently married and are at present touring Europe.'

'Your parents live in France?'

'My mother died a few years ago, but my father resides in the family home and continues to take an active interest in business.'

'Do you live in a big house?' asked Emma, her expression solemn as she waited for his answer.

'Some of the time.'

'Do you have a dog?'

He gave Emma a warm smile. 'Yes, two of them. And two cats, some hens and ducks, geese and a parrot who tells everyone who comes near him to have a happy day.'

Emma's eyes became very round. 'A parrot talks?'

Raoul's eyes gleamed with latent humor. 'Yes,' he enlightened gently. 'He really does.'

'Is it very far away?'

'Raoul lives in Paris, darling. Many thousands of miles on the other side of the world,' Stephanie elaborated.

'Can we come visit?' Emma ventured, innocent of distance.

'I would like that.'

'Shall I serve dessert?' Stephanie queried as she rose to her feet and began stacking cutlery and plates.

A delicious lemon pie was an excellent complement, and she waived Celeste's offer to take care of the dishes.

'You cooked, I'll do the dishes,' she said firmly.

'I agree,' Raoul added as he stood and pushed in his chair. 'You go and sit down. I'll help Stephanie.'

He probably hadn't cleaned a dish in his life. 'Thanks,' she said sweetly. 'You rinse, I'll stack the dishwasher, then you can attack the pots and pans.'

He shot her a dark gleaming glance, almost as if he divined her thoughts, and set about proving her wrong with quick deft thorough movements she found hard to keep pace with. He scoured pots and pans with considerable skill, and when they were all done he wiped down the sink bench, then leaned one hip against the bench and watched her finish up.

'Why don't you go put Emma to bed, while I make coffee?'

It was worth it just to watch those beautiful dark blue eyes dilate and pink color her cheeks. As long as she was angry he didn't have anything to lose, he determined as he caught hold of her chin and possessed her mouth in a brief hungry kiss.

'How dare you?' she whispered furiously, and heard his quietly drawled response,

'Easily.'

She walked from the kitchen without offering a further word, and when she returned he was seated comfortably opposite Celeste, conversing as if he'd known her mother for years.

It was an acquired trait, an entrepreneurial strategy someone kindly disposed would term *charm*. Was it genuine? Celeste seemed to think so, and her mother was no fool when it came to judging character.

'If you'll excuse me, I must leave,' Raoul intimated and rose to his feet. He took hold of her mother's hand and lifted it to his lips. '*Merci*, Celeste, for the meal and your company.'

'I'll see you to the door.' A few minutes and he'd be gone, then she could relax.

He was close, much too close as she preceded him down the hallway, and before she had a chance to open the door he cradled her face and took possession of her mouth in a kiss that tugged at the very depths of her heart.

When he lifted his head she could only look at

him, her breathing as unsteady as her rapidly beating pulse.

'*Bonne nuit, mon ange,*' he bade gently. 'Until tomorrow.' He pressed the pad of his thumb to her lower lip. 'I'll be here at nine.' His mouth curved with sensuous warmth. 'Sleep well.'

He opened the door and moved lightly down the steps to his car, and Stephanie watched as he slid behind the wheel, then reversed down the driveway.

She closed the door, secured the locks, then reentered the lounge.

Celeste wisely didn't comment on the faint color tinging her daughter's cheeks. Instead she mentioned a new social club she'd joined in Sydney, discussed two recent movies and refrained from mentioning Raoul's name. At ten, she stifled a faint yawn, then indicated the need for an early night.

Stephanie followed her down the hallway, closing lights as she went, and in her own room she stripped off her clothes, then indulged in a leisurely shower before slipping into bed to lay staring at the darkened ceiling.

She must have slept, because when she woke sunlight was streaming through chinks in the wooden shutters at her window.

A tap at her door brought her sitting up in bed, and Celeste entered with a cup of coffee in her hand.

'Morning, darling. I thought I should wake you. It's after eight.'

Oh hell. 'Raoul will be here at nine.' She threw

aside the bedcovers and reached for her robe. 'Where's Emma?'

'Watching one of her videos. She's had breakfast, and I've packed the holdall with most of the things I think she'll need.'

Stephanie took a sip of the strong, sweet coffee and felt its reviving effect. 'Thanks, Celeste. I'll grab something to eat, then change.'

Stephanie chose fatigue-style beige shorts, a pale blue singlet top and slid her feet into trainers. Makeup was a thorough application of sunscreen cream, a light dusting of powder, and lipstick.

Raoul arrived at nine, looking ruggedly attractive attired in casual navy shorts and a white short-sleeved polo shirt. He was fit and tanned, with the muscular build of a man who enjoyed exercise and physical fitness.

It was easy to imagine him playing tennis, racquetball, or training in martial arts. He had the look, the physique, and displayed an aura of control.

It was a beautiful day, the sun warm, with just the slightest breeze stirring the palm fronds and tree leaves.

'Going on a boat,' Emma relayed during the drive to Marina Mirage.

A very large luxury boat, Stephanie saw as Bruno led them through the security gate and indicated the berth where the cruiser lay moored.

For the wealthy tourist, private charter was ideal. Captain and crew, plus catering staff ensured a very

pleasant excursion without any of the attending has-
sle.

Celeste took delight in Lucia, and the little girl
reciprocated twofold.

'You remind her of her beloved Nonna,' Adriana
confided as they settled in the spacious midsection
fitted and furnished as a luxurious lounge.

It was evident Raoul and Bruno shared the ca-
maraderie of long friendship, and Stephanie felt her
pulse race each time she met his gaze.

He stirred her emotions in a way no man had ever
done before. And he knew. It was there in the faint
gleam in his eyes, the sensual pull of his mouth as
it curved to form a smile.

Throughout the day he made little attempt to touch
her, and then it was merely a light brush of his hand
on her arm. Emma was generous in her affection,
trusting with the unaffected instinct of a child. As far
as her daughter was concerned, he was Santa Claus
and the Easter Bunny rolled into one.

*And you,* a persistent little gremlin taunted. What
is he to you?

Someone, she conceded cynically, whom she need
regard with caution. There was the fear of being hurt,
of being let down. And having to pick up the pieces.
She'd done it once, and she didn't want to do it
again.

*Don't think about it,* she chastised silently. Enjoy
the day for what it is—the company of charming
people—and just *be.*

The captain cruised the coastal waterways, the

main Nerang river and the larger inland canals. So many beautiful homes lined the water frontage, many with large cabin cruisers moored at individual jetties. Landscaped gardens, huge stands of palm trees and swimming pools.

The captain gave a commentary on various landmarks, and relayed anecdotes about several different men who had made and lost fortunes during the spasmodic ''boom and bust'' cycles over the years.

After lunch the cruiser headed through the main channel to Sanctuary Cove, then retraced its path via Couran Cove, Stradbroke Island, passed Seaworld theme park, and slid into its berth at Marina Mirage shortly after six.

It had been an incredible day, and Stephanie said so, thanking Bruno and Adriana as they disembarked.

'Please, join us in our apartment for an hour or two.' Adriana issued the invitation with warm enthusiasm. 'I can make a salad, the men will cook steaks on the open grill.'

'But you're leaving tomorrow, you must need to pack—'

'Only a few things,' Adriana assured. 'It is easier to have a wardrobe in each of our apartments. Please, it would give us pleasure for you to visit for a while.'

'The girls are tired,' Stephanie indicated. 'It's been a long day for them.'

'I don't think an hour will make much difference,' Celeste offered as they cleared the security gate and entered the shopping complex.

Two against one, Stephanie reflected wryly. Make

that three, she mentally adjusted as she caught her daughter's expression. Held in the curve of Raoul's arm the little girl looked enchanting, her gold-blond hair so fair against the darker features of the man who carried her.

Seared steaks, fresh salads, eaten with a crusty baguette cut in thick slices, and washed down with a light wine, then followed by coffee made for a appetizing repast, and a fitting relaxed end to the day.

It was almost eight when Raoul drew the car to a halt outside the house, and he released a sleeping Emma from her booster seat, then carried her indoors.

'Third door on the left,' Stephanie instructed, leading the way down the hall. 'I'll change and put her to bed.'

Five minutes later she entered the lounge. 'Can I get you some tea, coffee? A cold drink?'

'Not for me, darling,' Celeste declined, and Raoul shook his head.

'Thanks, but no. I must get back to the hotel. I have some work to do before I catch the early morning flight down to Sydney.'

He was leaving? For how long? And why did she suddenly feel *empty?*

'I'll be back Wednesday evening, Thursday if I encounter any delay.'

He turned to Celeste and bade her good-night, and Stephanie saw him to the door.

'Thanks for a lovely day.'

His smile caused her toes to curl. 'I will phone from Sydney.'

She met his mouth without conscious thought, angling her head to fit his, in a kiss that was dazzling in its intensity, and all too brief.

## CHAPTER SEVEN

STEPHANIE deliberately sought a hectic work schedule to ensure there was little time to focus much thought on Raoul. For eight hours each day she was mostly successful. Nights were the worst, for no matter how hard she tried, his image came far too readily to mind.

He even managed to invade her dreams, and more than once she woke in a state of restless anticipation only to discover the image in her mind was precisely that…an image.

He rang twice, relatively brief calls which were confined to inquiries about her day, and Stephanie was able to elicit only that he was deeply involved in delicate negotiations that could delay his return.

Flowers were delivered to her office on Tuesday, with the words ''Missing you, R'' on the card. Stephanie kept them at work where the air conditioning helped keep them fresh.

Deciding what to wear to the gala dinner on Saturday evening caused a thorough appraisal of her wardrobe, and she withdrew three suitable gowns, then discarded each one of them.

What she needed, she determined, was something really spectacular…not flamboyant, but quietly and expensively spectacular.

She found it at an exclusive boutique. A figure-hugging design in black with thin jeweled straps, and the saleslady's approval merely added to her own. The price tag was astronomical, but worth every cent, she assured as she arranged for the hemline to be altered.

So far, the marketing strategy for the film was on schedule, and she made a note to ring Alex Stanford. She really wanted a preview of the shots he'd taken.

Wednesday evening Stephanie arranged for Sarah to baby-sit while she and Celeste went to a movie, a charming tale with an all-star cast featuring English women living in Italy during World War II. Afterward they stopped for coffee in one of several boutique cafés lining a trendy street current in vogue at Broadbeach.

'I'm so pleased to see you enjoying a social life, darling,' Celeste said gently as they waited for their order.

'You mean Raoul,' Stephanie responded without preamble.

'Yes.'

She shook her head in silent negation, assuring, 'It isn't going to happen.'

'I think you should leave your options open.'

A teasing smile curved her lips. 'Celeste, are you suggesting I sleep with him?'

'I'm your mother, darling. Mothers don't encourage their daughters to—'

'Indulge in wild sex,' Stephanie completed, offering Celeste a wicked grin.

'You deserve to be with someone,' Celeste ventured quietly.

A waitress delivered their coffee, and Celeste discussed the movie they'd just seen, the quality of the acting...a subject that lasted for the time it took to savor the superb lattes, before driving the short distance home.

The next day Raoul rang to say he'd be back on the evening flight, and the anticipated pleasure of seeing him again was overwhelming. She'd tried to tell herself she hadn't missed him, but knew she lied.

Friday morning there was another delivery of flowers. Flower, she corrected, unsure how to view the single red rose in its cellophane cylinder. The accompanying card held no message, just the initial *R*.

Lunch was a sandwich eaten at her desk and washed down with bottled water as she ran a check on the photo stills that had arrived by courier from Alex Stanford. He'd noted his selection, and she agreed with him. The shots were good, very good.

The lead actress, Cait Lynden, looked great alongside the two professional models. The lead actor, Gregor Anders, had perfected the right angles to portray himself to the best possible advantage.

Michel Lanier should be well pleased. Especially, with the photo stills of Sandrine. There was something about her, some indefinable quality that commanded a second glance. Add unaffected appeal, exquisite bone structure, and you had a visual winner, Stephanie qualified.

The glossy fashion magazine was due to hit the newsstands next week, the interviews and photo segments would appear in two of the weekly women's magazines the same week. A comprehensive one-on-one interview with Cait Lynden and Gregor Anders was scheduled for the magazine section of the Sunday newspaper in three major states, and television interviews were due to air in two weeks' time.

Then there were the social pages. Cocktail party, the gala charity dinner, to which some of Brisbane and the Gold Coast's social elite were invited, together with photographers and journalists to note and record the event.

It was all part of a well-presented media package aimed to attract public interest, a teaser to encourage paying cinema customers, Stephanie accorded wryly.

It would be nice, she reflected ruminatively, if the movie broke even. Although Michel Lanier could well afford to take the loss.

Filming had finished, and next week the marketing team would attend a private screening and decide which segments should appear as trailers. Meetings, conferences, release dates. It was a comprehensive and exacting project.

Stephanie reached for the phone and made a series of calls, logged data into her computer and ran another check on the table seating for the charity gala dinner to be held in the Grand Ballroom at the Sheraton.

She needed to collect her new gown for the event,

and a call to the boutique ascertained the alterations were complete.

It was almost five-thirty when she parked the car at the Marina Mirage shopping complex. Ten minutes later she emerged from the boutique, an emblazoned carry-bag in hand.

With luck, if the traffic wasn't too heavy, she'd be able to collect Emma from the day care center and be home just after six. Celeste was preparing Emma's favorite meal, and they planned a quiet evening together.

Stephanie stepped onto the escalator and idly scanned the ground floor with its marbled tiles, an attractive water fountain and tables set out for casual alfresco dining.

She glimpsed a familiar male head, and recognized Raoul...in the company of a tall stunningly beautiful woman with dark hair pulled back into a sleek knot, classic features, exquisite makeup and a figure to die for.

Worse, one hand was curled round Raoul's forearm. They looked...*cozy,* Stephanie decided.

Did hearts stop? She was willing to swear hers did. And there was a sudden searing pain in the region of her stomach.

At that precise moment he lifted his head and saw her. For a shocking few seconds his expression assumed a still quality, and he removed the woman's hand from his arm, murmured a few words at her protest and moved toward the base of the escalator.

There was no way Stephanie could avoid him, and

although it took considerable effort she summoned a polite smile as she stepped off.

'Raoul,' she acknowledged with cool formality.

'*Mon ami,* are you not going to introduce us?'

French, Stephanie deduced, huskily feminine and infinitely feline.

'Of course,' Raoul inclined with unruffled ease. 'Ghislaine Chabert. Stephanie Sommers.'

Ghislaine stroked a hand down Raoul's forearm, gifted him a witching smile, then transferred her attention to Stephanie. Her eyes hardened and became cold. 'You are one of Raoul's business acquaintances?'

Oh my. A tigress. With sheathed claws and a mean disposition. 'Michel's,' Stephanie corrected succinctly.

'Stephanie is in marketing.'

Perfectly shaped eyebrows lifted fractionally. 'Ah,' Ghislaine inclined with condescension. 'Sandrine's little movie.'

This could only get worse, and she didn't intend hanging around to discover how much worse. 'If you'll excuse me?' She cast Raoul a measured glance, and inclined her head toward Ghislaine. 'I'm already late to collect my daughter.'

'I'll walk you to your car.'

'Please don't bother.' She stepped to one side and began walking to the set of central escalators that would take her down to the car park.

He said something to Ghislaine in French, brusque

words that were totally incomprehensible, then caught up with Stephanie in a few long strides.

She should have known he'd follow her. Without breaking step she continued toward the escalator, all too aware he was right behind her.

He snagged her arm as she stepped off the escalator and turned her to face him.

'Whatever you're bent on surmising—*don't*,' Raoul warned silkily.

'You haven't a clue what I'm thinking,' Stephanie declared distantly.

'Yes,' he reiterated. 'I do.'

'You read minds?' she flung icily, and glimpsed the cynicism in his smile.

'Yours is remarkably transparent.'

'There is no point to this conversation.'

'*Sacré bleu,*' he swore softly. 'You try the patience of a saint. Ghislaine,' he informed hardily, 'is the daughter of an old family friend, who arrived unannounced, and not by my invitation,' Raoul continued hardily, wanting to kiss her senseless until the doubt, the insecurity, disappeared.

'You don't need to explain,' she declared coolly.

Oh, yes, he did. With concise honesty, right now. 'Ghislaine has booked herself into the same hotel. She's not *with* me,' he said with deliberate emphasis. 'She never has been.'

She directed him a level look. 'Why are you telling me this?'

He wanted to smote his fist against something

hard. 'Because Ghislaine is a femme fatale who finds it amusing to play games.'

Stephanie took in a breath and released it as an exasperated sigh. 'I'd love to stop and chat, but I have to pick up Emma.'

'And you don't believe a word I've said.'

She retained his gaze fearlessly. 'You're free to do whatever you like with whomever you please.' She looked pointedly at his hand on her arm.

'You're making obstacles where there are none.'

'No,' she refuted as he released her. 'I'm making it easy.'

Dignity won out every time, she assured silently as she crossed through two rows to where she'd parked her car. Except dignity didn't do a thing for the way her nerves were shredding into numerous strands. Nor did it help ease the painful ache in her stomach.

She unlocked the door and slid in behind the wheel, then she fired the engine and sent the car up to ground level.

Perhaps it was as well she'd planned a quiet evening at home with Celeste and Emma. She needed time to think.

When Raoul rang at eight, she had Celeste tell him she was putting Emma to bed. She didn't return his call.

Her mother wisely maintained a silent counsel, for which Stephanie was grateful. Maternal advice, no matter how well-meaning, wasn't high on her list tonight.

Together they viewed a video, followed by a program on cable, before reaching a mutual agreement to retire.

There were too many images invading her mind to promote sleep, and Stephanie didn't even try. Instead she plumped an extra pillow against the bed head and picked up a book.

Two hours later she snapped off the bed lamp and stared into the darkness.

Tomorrow was going to be a long day, followed by an even longer night. There were press interviews and photographers scheduled to cover the film cast at Movieworld. She needed to take Celeste and Emma to the airport for the midday flight to Sydney. Then there was the gala dinner.

Would Ghislaine inveigle an invitation? It wouldn't be difficult to acquire one. The Grand Ballroom was large, the staff adept at setting up an extra table or two at the last moment, providing seating wasn't already at maximum. All Ghislaine needed to do was have a discreet word in the right ear and pay for the privilege.

Stephanie stifled a muffled curse and thumped her pillow.

The image of Ghislaine *clinging* to Raoul's arm was vivid in her mind. And how had the Frenchwoman known where Raoul was staying?

She vowed it didn't matter. But it did. It mattered a lot. Despite her efforts to prevent it, he'd managed to scale every protective wall she'd erected, and was close to invading her heart.

Raoul's warning returned to haunt her. Ghislaine liked to play games, huh? Well, let the games begin!

It was a wrench depositing Celeste and Emma at the airport, and Stephanie experienced a mixture of acute loss and emotional deprivation as she hugged Emma close in a final farewell as they passed through security. Watching the jet taxi down the runway, then ascend, was never a good idea. Maybe, when Emma grew older, she'd be able to discard the practice. But now, the little girl was so young, so vulnerable…yet so excited and happy to embark on an adventure.

Emma would have a wonderful time, Stephanie assured herself as she slid into the car and drove toward the car park exit.

It was *she* who needed to adjust to an empty house, the lack of childish chatter and laughter. The umbilical cord connecting mother to child, although cut at birth, was never really severed, she mused as she gained the northbound highway.

Stephanie stopped off at home, heated a slice of Celeste's quiche and ate it, checked her answering machine, then she collected a container of commercially bottled water from the refrigerator and returned to her car.

Dedication to the job was a fine thing, and she could easily have delegated an appearance at the Movieworld shoot. Except she considered it important to be present for any on-the-spot decisions. It was precisely that dedication to detail that had seen her rise through the marketing ranks.

Away from the comfort of air conditioning the heat was intense. As the afternoon wore on, dispositions became frayed, artistic temperament increased and the suggestion they move to another location brought voiced dissent from a few.

'It'll add another dimension,' Alex Stanford assured as he packed his camera and hefted the bag over one shoulder.

'Okay,' Stephanie indicated, trusting his judgment. 'See you there.'

She'd almost reached the car when her cell phone rang.

'Not returning my calls is becoming a habit of yours,' Raoul's voice drawled close to her ear.

Her pulse rate picked up and quickened to a faster beat. 'It's been quite a day.'

'I'll pick you up at seven.'

'Please don't,' she responded quickly, aware of the need to be at the hotel early.

'Stephanie.' His voice acquired a warning edge she chose to ignore.

'Once we're seated, I'm off the hook,' she relayed succinctly. 'Prior to that, I'll be working the job. You'll be superfluous.'

'What time do you have to be there?' His slightly accented voice sent a shiver feathering down her spine.

The sound of a car horn distorted audible clarity, and she put a hand over one ear. 'I have to go,' she indicated.

'Six-fifteen?'

She would have argued, endorsing her decision to meet him at the hotel, except she didn't have the time to conduct a verbal sparring match. 'Fine.'

The afternoon was fraught, and by five even the television camera crew were relieved to dismantle equipment and head for their vehicle.

Consequently it was five-thirty by the time Stephanie reached Mermaid Beach, and home. Forty-five minutes in which to shower, wash and dry her hair, apply makeup and dress didn't present an enviable time frame.

With speed and efficiency she managed it…just. The doorbell pealed as she was in the process of attaching ear studs, and she quickly slid her feet into stiletto-heeled pumps, spritzed perfume to a few pulse points, then she caught up her evening purse and headed for the front door.

The breath caught in her throat at the sight of him. It wasn't the dark evening suit, nor the snowy white pin-tucked shirt, but the man himself and the significant aura of power he exuded. There was a sense of strength, an innate quality that had little to do with his muscular frame or chiseled facial features.

'We really should leave,' Stephanie said coolly.

The gown did wonderful things for her, it was precisely the reason she'd seriously challenged the limit on her credit card. Her job called for what she termed "a working wardrobe," yet the motivation for the purchase of this particular acquisition had been personal rather than professional.

'Beautiful,' Raoul accorded gently, and glimpsed pleasure appeared briefly before she masked it.

'Thank you,' she returned solemnly. He made her nervous, and she hoped it didn't show.

No other man had the power to arouse such a complexity of emotions. Why *this* man? she asked silently as they traveled the northbound highway toward Main Beach.

It was a question that increasingly haunted her with each passing day. *What are you going to do about it?* an elusive imp persisted. *Have an affair?* One week of heaven, followed by a lifetime of attempting to deal with it?

A silent bubble of hysterical laughter died in her throat. Never had she been so prey to such a range of ambivalent feelings, swinging like a pendulum from *go for it and to hell with the consequences* to *don't do this to yourself.*

'You're very quiet,' Raoul observed, shooting her a discerning glance as they neared their destination.

'Just a hectic day,' Stephanie revealed evenly. She was still angry with him, but mostly she was angry with Ghislaine.

'Fragile egos, interrupted schedules that went way over time?'

And that only accounted for the *day.* She offered him a rueful smile. 'How did you guess?'

Six-thirty For Seven on the invitations meant there were guests already mingling in the lounge area outside the hotel ballroom.

The prestigious yearly event in aid of charity ensured attendance by the social glitterati, and the very reason why Stephanie had seized the marketing opportunity to have key members of the cast attend. The publicity potential was too good to miss.

Four leading European fashion houses with boutiques in the upmarket Mirage shopping complex had compiled a fashion parade with models displaying the new season's releases.

However, it was the fragile egos that had her running a personal check of the table seatings. The charity organizers had arranged their own tables, but the few set aside for important guests and dignitaries required personal attention.

Stephanie located the tables up front, ran a check on place names, made one change, then returned to the lounge, caught sight of Alex Stanford and crossed to confer with him about the shots she wanted.

'Where are our exalted stars?' Alex queried. 'Bent on making an entrance?'

'Michel and Sandrine have just arrived,' she indicated. 'There they are talking to Michel's brother.' And Ghislaine.

Now why didn't that surprise her?

At that moment the main doors opened and the guests began entering the ballroom. Women wearing designer gowns and sufficient jewelry to warrant security measures, while the men observed the formal evening wear, black tie dress code.

Michel and Sandrine drew near, closely followed by Raoul and Ghislaine.

'You are joining us?'

Stephanie met Raoul's enigmatic gaze and held it. 'Soon. I need to have a word with the photographer.'

Ghislaine slipped an arm through Raoul's and cast Stephanie a brilliant smile. *Mine,* the gesture stated.

The Frenchwoman looked stunning, her gown a strapless, backless masterpiece that shrieked European couturier. A single strand diamond necklace looked expensive, and was matched with a bracelet and ear studs.

Stephanie greeted Michel and Sandrine, acknowledged Ghislaine, then she excused herself and went in search of Alex Stanford.

Five minutes later she entered the ballroom and began weaving her way toward their designated table. There was still no sign of Cait Lynden or Gregor Anders, she saw at a glance. However, Tony the film's director was seated at an adjacent table with the producer, two of the Warner Brothers Movieworld executives and their wives. And Ghislaine.

Whose influence had Ghislaine used to secure a seat at one of the main tables? Raoul? Possibly Michel? Stephanie assured herself she didn't want to know.

She slid into her seat just as the lights flickered indicating the opening speech was about to begin, and suddenly there was Cait Lynden and Gregor Anders, their progress to the head of the room spotlighted and captured by a clutch of professional photographers.

It was almost amusing, Stephanie alluded wryly,

if only one could manage to see the humour in the situation. Michel was under siege from the expressive attention of the lead actress, who, it appeared, was intent on displaying subtle designs on Sandrine's husband.

Whereas on the adjacent table, Ghislaine was doing her very best to garner Raoul's attention.

The charity chairwoman gave an introductory speech, followed by a word from the mayor, then the waiters emerged bearing trays containing the starters.

The food was attractively presented, but Stephanie merely forked a few morsels, and barely did justice to the main course.

'Some more water?'

Stephanie cast Raoul a polite glance. 'Thank you.'

His eyes darkened fractionally, and he restrained the desire to rattle her composure.

The announcement the fashion parade was about to begin precluded the need for silence, and Stephanie was grateful as the room lighting dimmed and spotlights highlighted the catwalk.

Beautiful clothes in several categories, although emphasis was placed on after-five and evening wear, specifically aimed, Stephanie conceded, for the society women in attendance. Expertly choreographed and commentated, the parade provided forty minutes of glitz and glamour.

There was a time lag before the serving of dessert and coffee. It was then the photographers sought to capture their shots, and she employed diplomacy when Cait Lynden instructed a photo be taken with

Michel, who had given prior instructions that any photo taken of him must also include his wife.

'Both Lanier brothers?' Alex Stanford suggested, motioning for Raoul to join Michel and Sandrine.

'Why not include the marketing manager?' Raoul countered smoothly as he stood to his feet. He held out a hand. 'Stephanie?'

'Alex has been instructed to involve me in a group shot with Tony, the producer and the Warner Brothers Movieworld executives.'

Raoul was too skilled in psychological manipulation to condone defeat. 'I imagine Alex is not limited to the number of film rolls he is able to use?'

Alex, sensing a display of wills and mildly amused by its possibilities, merely endorsed Raoul's suggestion by motioning her into position. 'Let's do it, Stephanie.'

To refuse would seem churlish, and she slid to her feet and stood where Alex positioned her, between Sandrine and Raoul with Michel at his wife's side.

Raoul slipped an arm along the back of her waist, and she stood completely still as all her senses kicked into vibrant life.

She was suddenly conscious of every breath she took, and consciously regulated each and every one of them in a bid to reduce the rapid beating of her heart. She could feel the thud of it reflected in the pulse at the base of her throat, her wrists, and the warmth it generated deep inside.

Even her skin seemed acutely sensitized, and she

was willing to swear heat whispered through every vein in her body.

Stephanie almost jumped as his fingers caressed the base of her spine, then moved to the back of her waist in a slow, soothing pattern. Was he aware of the effect he had on her? She hoped not.

'One more,' Alex called, and the flashbulb caused a second's blindness.

'Not so difficult, *oui?*' Raoul murmured musingly as they moved back to their table.

'Do you always get your own way?'

'Yes.'

Guests were moving between tables, socializing briefly with friends and acquaintances before the evening wound down to a conclusion.

Stephanie placed a hand over her glass as he lifted a bottle of wine. 'No, thanks.'

Raoul's smile held sensual warmth. 'The need for a clear head?'

'I rarely drink,' she said quietly, frozen into immobility as he lifted a hand to her cheek and trailed his fingers down to the edge of her mouth. Her eyes widened, their depths darkening as the pupils dilated, and she barely controlled an involuntary shiver as he traced the sensitive chord of her neck and rested briefly in the hollow there.

'Stephanie, I need you to be part of the executive group shot,' Alex Stanford intruded, and the mesmeric spell was broken.

Thankfully, she assured silently as she followed the photographer. It wasn't easy to slip away, for the film director and producer were in a gregarious mood, so too were the Warner Brothers' executives, and almost fifteen minutes passed before she was able to leave.

Sandrine was not in evidence, nor were the two dignitaries who comprised part of the table seating. Raoul and Michel were engrossed in conversation, and seated in an empty chair...*her* chair...was Ghislaine.

It would have been polite for the Frenchwoman to move, but Ghislaine obviously had no intention of observing conventional good manners.

Stephanie collected her glass, and crossed to another table where two of her associates were seated. If Ghislaine wanted to command Raoul's attention, she could have the figurative floor all to herself.

It didn't help that Samuel Stone occupied a chair next to the one empty seat at the table. Nor that he'd generously imbibed of the wine, and had moved on to spirits. Maybe if she ignored him, he wouldn't even notice her presence.

Fat chance, Stephanie accorded within seconds. She'd merely exchanged one awkward situation at one table for a worse situation of a different kind at another table.

'Darling Stephanie.' Samuel leaned close, much too close, and lifted his glass. 'I salute you.'

'Thank you.' She wasn't quite sure what he was saluting her for, but it seemed prudent to agree with him.

'You're good,' he continued. 'Very, very good,

darling.' He curved an arm over her shoulders. 'Why don't you come work for me?'

Wouldn't that be a move in the wrong direction, she derided silently.

Instinct caused her to glance toward Raoul. He looked completely at ease, his posture relaxed, his features portraying studied interest. Yet almost as if he could sense her attention his gaze shifted, and his gaze locked with hers.

She saw him say something to Michel and Sandrine, then he rose to his feet and moved toward her.

# CHAPTER EIGHT

STEPHANIE indicated her intention to leave. 'If you'll excuse me?'

If Raoul thought she'd calmly return to their designated table and watch Ghislaine continue her *clinging vine* performance, he was sadly mistaken!

She'd only taken two steps when he drew level.

His eyes were dark. Too dark, she discerned.

'We've been invited, together with Michel and Sandrine, to party on at the hotel's nightclub. I understand the cast, studio marketing and advertising executives intend to transfer there.'

She looked at him carefully. 'And Ghislaine?'

Something moved in those dark depths, and a muscle tensed at the edge of his jaw. 'She's free to do as she pleases.'

'As I am,' Stephanie responded quietly. 'Now, if you'll excuse me, I need to freshen up.'

'Damn.' The curse fell from his lips with restrained anger. 'Why would I choose to spend time with her, when I prefer to be with you?'

'She's French, gorgeous, eminently suitable and she adores you,' she responded flippantly.

'And if I do not adore her?'

The mere thought of him adoring another woman made her feel slightly ill. Yet some irrepressible imp goaded her to offer, 'Consider the amalgamation of two family fortunes.'

'Go freshen up, Stephanie,' he drawled. 'Before I say something regrettable.'

Without a further word she turned and made her way toward one of the exit doors.

'Mind if I join you?'

Stephanie caught the faintly wry tone, glimpsed an edge of exasperation evident and offered Sandrine a wicked smile.

'On an escape mission?'

'You've got it in one.'

A queue in the powder room meant they were in for a short wait.

'Now that filming is over, I imagine you'll be returning to New York,' she began in an attempt at conversation.

'We're flying down to Sydney tomorrow for a few days before heading home on Tuesday...sans Cait Lynden,' she concluded quizzically.

A faint chuckle emerged from Stephanie's throat. 'Like that, huh?'

'Oh, yes.'

Even an unsuspecting bystander couldn't have misinterpreted the lead actress's marked play for Michel's attention. Although having witnessed the occasional exchanged look between Michel and his wife, she doubted Sandrine had anything to worry about.

'For what it's worth, Ghislaine has been on the scene for several years,' Sandrine offered gently.

'The Lanier men don't waste time going after what they want. If Raoul wanted Ghislaine, he would have had a ring on her finger by now.'

'It really doesn't interest me.'

'Doesn't it?'

Was Sandrine especially intuitive? Or was she merely attempting to elicit an indication of Stephanie's feelings?

Somehow the latter didn't ring true. She was spared a response as a stall became empty and the actress moved forward to occupy it.

Minutes later they took time for makeup repairs, then together they emerged to find Raoul and Michel examining the picturesque waterfall adjoining the lounge area. Cait, Gregor and Ghislaine stood close by.

'Into battle,' Sandrine murmured, and Stephanie successfully hid a faint smile. *Battle* could very well be the operative word if Cait Lynden continued to monopolize Michel's attention.

The hotel nightclub was situated on the next floor, and the exclusive club was alive with people. Funky music emitted from strategically placed speakers, and subdued lighting added to the overall ambience.

Stephanie hadn't frequented a nightclub since she broke up with Ben, and she was quite content to observe rather than participate.

Cait and Ghislaine made a good pair, she determined as she observed each young woman's attempt to encourage Raoul and Michel onto the dance floor.

'Do you want to escape the performance?'

There were any number of females present who would have drooled at the chance to dance with Gregor Anders. Stephanie wasn't one of them.

'Your bête noire has just entered the milieu,' Gregor intoned cynically. 'Do you really want to have to fend him off?'

A surreptitious glance confirmed Samuel Stone's presence, and if she had to choose between the two, Gregor got her vote.

'This really isn't my scene,' she assured as he drew her onto the crowded floor.

'So…treat you gently?'

Her faint laugh was genuine. 'No fancy flamboyant moves,' she warned.

'We could try for up close and personal.'

'Considering the beat of the music, that might not be wise.'

'Where's your sense of adventure?' He pulled her close, and expertly led her through a set of basic steps. 'Well, well,' he murmured close to her ear. 'An update in the manhunting stakes sees Cait cast aside by Michel, who has very wisely made it clear he prefers his wife. And there,' he revealed with theatrical timing. 'We have Raoul giving Ghislaine the flick.' He executed a sweeping turn. 'Now we see the elder Lanier brother beating a path toward us. *You*, my dear, appear to be his target.'

'You're mistaken.'

'Want me to play the shining knight?'

'And have those good looks marred?' she countered, and saw him wince.

'I agree. He's a formidable quarry, in more ways than one. Prepare yourself for takeover.'

Stephanie sensed Raoul's presence a few seconds before he drew level, and her whole circulatory system immediately went into overdrive.

She was willing to swear the blood traveled faster through her veins, and her pulse seemed to jump to an accelerated beat. Even her skin's surface prickled with awareness.

'Do you mind, Gregor?' The voice was a deep drawl that held an edge of steel.

Gregor didn't mind at all. He didn't even feign reluctance. So much for the shining knight offer!

'Be my guest.' The words scarcely left his lips than he faded away between the milling patrons.

The music changed from fast and funky to a soulful ballad, and Raoul drew her close against him.

She should object, and pull back a little, but although the mind dictated, her body chose not to obey. She fit perfectly, and there was a part of her that wanted to lean in and just drift.

For a few minutes she did just that, succumbing to an insidious sensuality that intensified with every passing second. Treacherous, primal, *raw*.

The music changed, and she told herself she was glad. Sexual passion in any form wasn't on her agenda. Especially with a man who lived on the other side of the world, and to whom she was merely a passing fancy. Someone to be his social partner and occupy his bed for a limited time.

Even the thought of engaging in sex with him

turned her bones to liquid. Instinct warned that this man would not take his pleasure without thought for hers, and just thinking how he could pleasure her was sufficient to set her pulse racing into overdrive.

Dangerous. Infinitely dangerous, she perceived, unwilling to admit even to herself that with each passing day her resistance was gradually ebbing away.

Was he aware of it? Probably, she conceded, for he was far too attuned to her psyche. Having someone anticipate her thoughts, her actions, made her feel uncomfortable. And guarded.

'We're leaving,' Michel indicated, then he turned toward his brother. 'I'll ring you early Monday morning.'

Raoul inclined his head, and Sandrine leaned forward to touch her cheek to Stephanie's, murmuring 'good luck' as she did so, then drawing away she offered Stephanie a warm smile. 'I hope we get to meet again.'

Words, sincerely meant, but expressing a desire for something that would probably not eventuate. Nevertheless, Stephanie returned the words in kind.

'Stephanie!'

Oh Lord, Samuel Stone, more than a little the worse for wear and on a mission, from his determined expression.

'Dance with me.'

'We were about to leave,' Raoul drawled. 'Perhaps another time?'

Not if she could avoid it. 'Sorry, Samuel.'

'C'mon, Stephanie.' He reached out and caught her arm in a viselike grip. 'Let's give it a whirl.'

'I think not, my friend.' Raoul's voice was deceptively quiet, like steel encased in silk.

Samuel's expression assumed alcohol-induced belligerence. 'Staked a claim, have you?'

Raoul didn't move an inch, but the air suddenly seemed charged with threatening promise. 'Yes,' he acceded with hard inflexibility.

For a heart-stopping few seconds Stephanie froze, unaware of the room, the people, the noise. There was only Raoul, and the indomitable power he portrayed.

Then Samuel released her arm and spread his hands in a conciliatory gesture. 'Your round, ice princess,' he conceded with deliberate mockery, and melted through the crowd.

'Trouble, darling?' Ghislaine arched delicately.

Lose one, gain one, Stephanie accorded silently. 'Nothing to be concerned about,' she said with an edge of mockery.

'Raoul is very good at defending a woman's honor.' Ghislaine cast him a sultry look. 'Aren't you, *mon ami?*'

'Good night,' Stephanie issued when Raoul didn't answer.

'Oh really, darling?' The pout had been practiced to perfection. 'You're leaving so soon? It's early.'

'For you, possibly,' Stephanie remarked steadily. 'But my day began at dawn this morning.'

'Why interrupt Raoul's enjoyment? I am sure you can take a taxi home.'

'No,' he said with chilling softness. 'That isn't an option.'

'Aren't you taking chivalry a little too far?' Ghislaine queried with a hint of disdain.

Raoul placed an arm along the back of Stephanie's waist. '*Bon nuit,* Ghislaine.'

His tone held indolence and the smoothness of silk.

'I'm impressed,' Stephanie declared as he propelled her toward the entrance. 'Do you do this often?'

'Do what, precisely?'

They exited the nightclub and made their way to the lift that would take them down to the car park.

'Defend one woman and destroy another, both at the same time.'

'You have a way with words,' he alluded cynically, and she cast him a dazzling smile.

'It's one of my talents,' she assured.

'I have to fly down to Sydney tomorrow,' Raoul informed as they rode the lift. 'I had a call this afternoon to say the deal has been finalized and the contract will be ready for my signature on Monday.'

Her heart plummeted. Finalizing the deal meant there was no reason for him to stay.

'Will you take a direct flight from Sydney to Paris?'

He cast her a sharp glance, saw the carefully composed features, and noted the visible pulse beat at the base of her throat. Not so composed, he conceded with satisfaction.

'I intend returning to the coast Monday evening.'

She wasn't aware she'd been holding her breath, and she released it slowly, evenly. 'I see.'

They reached the car, and Raoul freed the lock. 'Do you?'

Now, there was a question. How did she answer it without incriminating herself? Best not to even try, she bade silently as she slid into the passenger seat.

He fired the engine and eased the car toward the main exit, then gained the divided road that led to the main southbound highway.

'No answer?'

'There isn't one,' she said simply.

Brightly colored neon detailed shops and cafés as they passed through the heart of Surfers Paradise.

Motels lined both sides of the highway. It was a vibrant colorful city, geared for the tourist dollar, and offered a multitude of entertainment services.

The flow of traffic at this hour of the night was smooth, and it seemed only minutes before they drove through Broadbeach and entered the fringes of Mermaid Beach.

Raoul brought the car to a smooth halt in her driveway, and cut the lights and the engine.

She released her seat belt, then undid the door clasp and slid out, aware he was duplicating her actions.

'There's no need for you to come in.'

He crossed around and held his hand out for her keys. 'Yes, there is.'

At that precise moment she was prepared to agree with Ghislaine. There was a limit to chivalry.

'I'll be fine,' she assured as he unlocked the door and switched on the lights.

'Are you afraid of me, *cherie?*'

Confrontation was admirable, but right now she wasn't sure she cared for it. 'No,' she answered honestly.

It was herself she was afraid of. Afraid that if he kissed her, she might not be able to control her emotions. And if she relinquished that control, she knew precisely where it would lead.

To experience his lovemaking would be…incredible, she qualified. To take him to her bed, and wake to his touch… Dare she?

She looked at him, saw the strength evident, the heat carefully banked, and felt her body leap with answering warmth.

Stephanie made her way through to the lounge, aware he followed close behind. Her composure was rapidly falling into shreds, and she mentally chastised herself. Nerves were hell and damnation. Raoul was just a man, like any other.

A lot you know, she silently derided. It's four years since I was intimate with a man, and I feel gauche, awkward…dammit, *scared* in a way that has nothing to do with *fear*.

This could, he cautioned, disintegrate in a second. She was a complex mix that comprised integrity and honesty, with a well of passion a man could drown in if he wasn't careful. Yet there was also deep-seated pain and distrust.

'Go make some coffee,' he said quietly.

So he wasn't about to seduce her…at least, not right now. She should have felt relieved, but instead there was a sense of delaying the inevitable, and that in itself only worsened the state of her nerves.

Stephanie entered the kitchen, filled the carafe with water and set it into the coffeemaker, measured out and added ground coffee beans.

'I imagine Celeste has rung to confirm their safe arrival?'

He'd moved so quietly she hadn't heard a sound, and she spared him a quick glance as she extracted two cups and saucers from a cupboard.

'Yes. Everything's fine.' A few steps to the refrigerator to retrieve milk. 'Would you like something to eat?'

When she closed the refrigerator door he was there, and she felt her eyes widen as he took the milk container from her hand and set it on the bench.

'You. Just you.'

He didn't give her time to protest as he drew her close, and his mouth fastened on hers in a slow evocative tasting that became a feast of the senses.

Impossibly sensual, it dispensed all rational thought as she angled her head and indulged in an emotional ride that swept her high to a place where there was only the man, the moment…and desire.

Dear heaven, it was all she could do not to slip

her hands beneath his jacket and tear the garment free. Loosen the buttons on his shirt in her need to touch his skin. To feel the warmth, the pulsing life of muscle and sinew, to savor the taste of him. And have him taste her.

The kiss deepened into possession as his hand slid to her derriere and pulled her close against him. His arousal was a potent force, electrifying and primal as she instinctively reached for him.

She felt a tremor race through his body, and for an instant she gloried in the power, the supreme, albeit brief moment of having him at her mercy.

Then the control was all his as he took his mouth from her own and began trailing a tantalizing path down the edge of her neck, drifting to tease the hollows at the base of her throat, before slipping low to the soft swell of her breast.

A beaded shoestring strap slid off one shoulder, and a faint groan escaped from her lips as he bared one breast, then shaped it, stroking the creamy contour until she thought she'd go mad.

His lips sought the sensitive peak and tantalized it with his tongue, grazing it with his teeth as he held her on the knife edge between pleasure and pain.

When he took the distended peak into his mouth and suckled she arched up against him as sensation arrowed through her body.

It was almost more than she could bear, and she made no protest as Raoul slid an arm beneath her knees and lifted her high into his arms.

His mouth returned to claim hers, and she wound

her arms around his neck as she kissed him back, exulting in the sensation he was able to evoke.

It was relatively easy to discover which bedroom was hers. Feminine in soft peach and pale mint green, an antique bed, and numerous lacy pillows stacked against the headboard.

He shrugged off his jacket, discarded the bow tie and paused to brush light fingers down her cheek as she sought to free the buttons on his shirt.

In tandem they slid off shoes, then Raoul sought the zip fastening at the back of her gown and slid it free.

She was beautiful, slender curves, delicate bone structure and pale skin. Lacy bikini briefs were the only item of clothing protecting her from total nudity, and he shrugged off his shirt and dispensed with his trousers in two fluid movements.

Stephanie could only admire his physique. The well-honed muscular chest and shoulders, the taut waist and flat stomach.

The state of his arousal gave her a bad moment, and her insides involuntarily clenched at the thought of accommodating him.

He curled a hand round her nape and shaped her head as he took possession of her mouth, kissing her with such eroticism she almost cried at the sweet sorcery of his touch.

One tug was all it took to pull the covers from the bed, then he tumbled her down onto the sheeted mattress and knelt over her.

His eyes were dark and slumberous, and his

strength was a palpable entity as he buried his mouth against her neck.

Stephanie lifted her arms and linked them at his nape, only to have him gently disengage them and carefully place them above her head.

She felt a tremor race through her body as he traced a path to her breast, explored at leisure, then trailed down to the soft indentation at her waist.

A faint gasp escaped her lips as he moved lower, and she whimpered out loud at the path traced by the tip of his tongue.

Raoul took intimacy to a new level, evoking a response from her that was wild and wanton. Libidinous, she added, as sensation spiraled through her body, taking her higher than she'd ever been before.

Dear heaven. If this is what he could do with his mouth, how on earth would she survive when he took possession? Go up in flames? Self-destruct?

*Both,* Stephanie acknowledged a long time later as she lay cradled against him on the edge of sleep.

Every nerve ending had flared into impassioned life as he'd begun a slow invasion, stirring her emotions to fever pitch with long hungry kisses that dispensed with any inhibitions. She'd met and matched his rhythm in a wild pagan dance that surpassed her wildest imagination.

She'd thought he might vacate her bed, shower, then dress and leave.

Instead he curved her close in against him and

stroked her hair, pausing every now and then to brush light fingers across her cheek.

Her body ached, and she was willing to swear she could still *feel* him deep inside.

She wasn't conscious of drifting off to sleep, except she must have, for she came slowly awake at the soft tracing movement at her waist. Fingers slid over one hip and brushed against her thigh, and she shifted restlessly as he began an evocative pattern.

Stephanie leaned forward and nipped the skin close to one male nipple, and had the satisfaction of hearing his intake of breath.

'So you want to play, hmm?'

In one fluid movement he pulled her on top of him, and she arched back in a supple feline movement.

'You woke me,' she protested teasingly, loving the feel of his hands as they shaped her body, her breasts, and took a tantalizing path down to where she straddled him.

'Now I have your full attention?'

Oh, yes, he had that. She wriggled a little, and took pleasure in his husky groan, the heat of his arousal pressing against her.

With provocative intent, she moved a little, causing a sexual friction that was just as electrifying for him as it was for her.

In one swift movement he curved a hand around her nape and pulled her head down to his, taking possession of her mouth in a manner that left her weak-willed and malleable.

When he released her she rose with graceful fluidity, then carefully positioned herself and took him deep inside.

She had control, and she used it mercilessly as she rode him hard and fast, then eased to a slow erotic pace that had him growling low in his throat as he rolled her onto her back.

At some stage they both slept, and woke late to the sun streaming in through the curtains.

Together they rose from the bed and showered together…a long shower as Raoul pulled her high against him and she curved her legs over his hips in one final passionate coupling, then they dressed and breakfasted on strong coffee, eggs and toast.

It was after ten when Raoul caught her close and bestowed a lingering kiss. 'I have to leave,' he said gently. 'I'll call you from Sydney.' His smile held a warmth that made her stomach curl. 'Take care, *cherie*.'

Without a further word he slid in behind the wheel of the car, fired the engine, then reversed out onto the road.

Stephanie stood watching until the car was no longer in sight.

# CHAPTER NINE

THE day stretched ahead, presenting a number of possibilities. However, the first priority was to put a call through to Celeste.

Stephanie crossed to the phone and punched in the required digits, then listened to Emma relay an excited account of the flight, the drive with her beloved 'Poppa,' playing with Jake the dog and a visit to the beach as soon as she woke from her afternoon nap.

'Sounds like fun,' Stephanie said lightly when Celeste came back on the line.

'It is,' her mother assured. 'And you, Stephanie? Did everything turn out well last night?'

Now there was a question she couldn't answer with total honesty! Revealing to your mother that you'd just experienced the best sex in your life, not once but several times in the past eight hours wasn't exactly a confidence she felt inclined to share.

'Really well,' she responded easily. 'We achieved the necessary publicity, there were no mishaps. It was very successful.'

'And Raoul?'

Oh my. 'He seemed to enjoy himself.' A masterpiece in understatement! 'He left this morning for Sydney. Business,' she elaborated.

'But he'll be back?'

'Yes.'

'Good.'

*Don't,* Stephanie urged silently. It can't go anywhere, because there's nowhere for it to go.

'I'll ring tomorrow evening,' she indicated, then added gently, 'Thanks, Mom. I know Emma will have a wonderful time.'

Housework beckoned, the washing and some ironing, and when it was all done she went down to the local supermarket and bought milk, bread and a few essentials.

Afterward she curled up in a comfortable chair and indulged in the luxury of reading several chapters of a seven-hundred-page historical saga. The rich texture of the writing kept her enthralled until the natural light began to fade, and she was about to switch on the lamp when the shrill insistent peal of the telephone had her reaching for the receiver.

The male voice was deep, husky and the slight accent identified it as belonging undeniably to Raoul. Just the sound of it sent primitive awareness radiating through her body.

'How are you?'

'Fine.'

His throaty chuckle did crazy things to her equilibrium. 'That's it? Fine?'

'What would you have me say?' she countered unsteadily, and wondered if he was aware just how he affected her.

'It can wait, *cherie.*'

There was a part of her that ached to see him again, yet there was also caution and a certain degree of despair. If only she had a casual attitude to sex without needing any meaningful emotional attachment, she could view the interlude for what it was...a brief affair with no strings.

'Michel and Sandrine are joining me for dinner tonight.'

Stephanie curled her fingers over the receiver. 'Enjoy,' she bade lightly. 'What time is your meeting tomorrow?'

'Early afternoon. I'll call you.'

'Okay.'

'*Bonne nuit, cherie,*' Raoul drawled. 'Sleep well.'

She didn't, of course. There were too many thoughts chasing through her brain for an easy rest, and she woke next morning with the distinct need for a few hours more sleep.

However, the day awaited, and her work schedule was bound to be hectic.

A shower, followed by cereal and fruit, then she changed into a pencil-slim black skirt, added a peach-colored camisole and pinstriped black jacket, tended to her makeup and caught up her keys before heading for the car.

Only to discover she had a flat tire. The curse she stifled was pithy, and adequately described her frustration. Changing tires was becoming a habit, she muttered beneath her breath as she shrugged off her jacket and tossed it onto the passenger seat.

She crossed to the rear of the car, popped the boot, removed the spare tire, the jack and set to work.

After it was done, she retrieved her keys and went back into the house to wash up.

An essential call into the local tire mart to drop off the damaged tire for repair took up valuable time, added to which traffic was heavy, taking at least three changes of lights to get through each intersection, and consequently she was late entering the office.

Coffee, hot, strong and sweet helped, and she went through her diary, made a number of notations, then logged on to her computer.

The interoffice phone rang and she reached for it.

'I have a Miss Chabert on the line,' Isabel revealed. 'She insists on speaking to you personally.'

Ghislaine? What on earth could she possibly want? 'Put her through.'

'Ghislaine,' Stephanie greeted with polite civility.

'Stephanie. We should do lunch.'

Oh, no, we shouldn't! 'I'm really busy right now,' she responded calmly.

'Meet me at the Terraces. One o'clock.'

The imperious demand grated, and she drew in a deep breath, then released it slowly. 'I can't—'

'Be there.'

This was a joke, a very bad joke. It was almost laughable, except instinct warned there was no humor in the situation at all. 'I can't think of a thing we have in common.'

'Raoul.'

'There's nothing to discuss,' she said quietly, and replaced the receiver. Jealousy, she perceived, was an ugly state of mind.

Lunch was a salad sandwich she sent out for, and ate at her desk. Washed down by bottled water, it sufficed as sustenance as she made necessary calls, checked paperwork and determined the film's scheduled release date. It was important to prompt public interest by running the trailers on television and follow-up media coverage in the trade magazines. She made a note to check with advertising.

At three she broke for coffee, qualifying she needed the caffeine to get her through the afternoon. The way things were going, she'd need to take work home.

It was after four when reception alerted a Ghislaine Chabert was at the desk. Stephanie muffled an unladylike curse. She didn't have time for this. Whatever bee Ghislaine had in her bonnet, this was neither the place nor the time to deal with it.

'You told her I'm busy?'

'Miss Chabert insists on seeing you.'

She quickly checked her diary, then made a split-second decision. 'All right. Show her in.' She stood and smoothed a hand over her hair. 'Ring me when my four-thirty appointment arrives.'

Lipstick was an essential repair, and she'd just recapped the tube when her secretary gave her door a peremptory tap prior to swinging it wide.

The Frenchwoman swept in on a cloud of perfume, expensive couture clothing, her face an exquisitely made-up mask.

Calm, composed, in control, Stephanie reminded herself of the affirmation as she indicated a chair.

'Ghislaine. Do sit down.' She crossed behind her desk and remained standing. With a cool, calculated action she cast her watch a deliberate glance. 'I can spare you five minutes.'

'I'd prefer to stand.'

They faced each other across the desk like two opposing enemies. Stephanie watchful and distinctly wary, while Ghislaine played the haute dame to the hilt.

'Leave Raoul alone. He is *mine*.'

Straight to the point, with as much subtlety as a sledgehammer. Stephanie deliberately arched one eyebrow. 'Really? The purpose of your visit is to warn me off?'

Ghislaine raked Stephanie's slender form with scorn. 'Why else do you think I am here?'

'Are you done?' she posed quietly, already regretting her decision to have Ghislaine enter her office.

'No, I am not nearly done,' the Frenchwoman responded bluntly. 'Raoul didn't come back to the hotel last night. Was he with you?'

'I don't think that qualifies an answer,' she said carefully, and saw Ghislaine's expression harden.

'You are just a diversion, someone new, different,' the other woman said scathingly. '*Temporary*.'

Stephanie felt the anger flare, and sought measured control. A catfight here, now, didn't form part of her agenda! 'I think you'd better leave.'

'Stay away from him.'

'What if he chooses not to stay away from me?'

'Our respective families want us to marry. I intend to see that it happens.'

She caught the vindictiveness, the irrational sense of purpose in those hard dark eyes, and experienced a chill of apprehension. 'Then I must wish you *good luck*,' she said evenly. 'And ask you to leave.'

Almost on cue the phone buzzed, and she picked up the receiver, listened, then replaced it onto the handset.

'My client is waiting.' She crossed to the door, and opened it. 'Goodbye, Ghislaine.'

'Don't underestimate me' was issued as a silky warning as the Frenchwoman exited the office.

Stephanie took a deep breath, very much in need of a minute or two to dispel her anger, then regain a measure of composure.

Ghislaine was a witch, possibly a dangerous witch with a problem. Sandrine's words came to mind, but it offered little reassurance.

Meantime, she had a job to do, and keeping a valued client waiting overlong in reception didn't form part of her plan.

It was after six when she arrived home, the owner of two new tires, for when she'd called in to collect the repaired spare, the young man shook his head.

'Couldn't fix it, ma'am. It'd been cut.' At her faintly puzzled expression, he elaborated, 'Slashed. With a knife, I'd say.'

How? More importantly, *who?* 'I guess I need a new tire.'

'Two, in the front, make 'em even.'

She didn't even blink. 'Can you do it now?'

'We're due to close soon.'

'Please. I really need my car.'

'Okay, for you I'll make an exception. Take a seat.'

Ten minutes later she wrote a check, then slid into the car and drove home.

Indoors, she changed into shorts and a singlet top, then crossed into the kitchen. She'd prepare a tossed salad and have it with some cold chicken, then follow it with fresh fruit.

After she'd shower, pull on a robe, and put in a few hours at the laptop. But first she'd call Celeste and catch up on Emma's day... A ferry ride and a visit to Taronga Park Zoo, she learned, and tomorrow they were going to ride on the monorail.

'You're spoiling her,' Stephanie protested, and heard her mother's chuckle.

'No, we're having fun.'

It was reassuring not to be missed, but she experienced a very real feeling of loss at not hearing her daughter's voice, the hugs, the kisses.

*Work,* she determined, as she set the laptop onto the dining-room table more than an hour later, would occupy her mind.

It did, and she became immersed in entering data, saving it on disk ready to print out at the office in the morning.

The doorbell ringing startled her, and she checked her watch, wondering who on earth would call in at nine in the evening without using the telephone to check it was okay.

The security door was locked, she had a safety chain on the door, as well as a peephole. There was no sense pretending she wasn't home, for the lights indicated otherwise.

The doorbell rang again, jerking her into motion, and she moved quickly to the front of the house.

One look was sufficient to determine it was Raoul who stood on her doorstep, and with nerveless fingers she dealt with the chain, the lock and undid the security door.

'Hi.' As a greeting it was inane, and Stephanie felt the warmth creep into her cheeks as he let his gaze roam over the short silk robe, her bare legs, before returning to settle on her expressive features.

'Were you in bed?'

He sounded indolently amused, and she ran a check on the tie of her robe, then pulled the edges more tightly together.

'No,' she said quickly. 'I was working.'

He was something else, his height and breadth of shoulder impressive. His exclusive brand of cologne teased her senses, and her eyes were mesmerized by the sensual curve of his mouth. He'd removed his jacket and held it hooked over one shoulder.

'Aren't you going to ask me in?' he queried gently, and she stood aside at once.

'Of course.'

Raoul stepped down the hallway and she followed him. 'Would you like some coffee?'

He came to a halt in the lounge and turned to face her. 'Not unless you're making some for yourself. Otherwise a cold drink will do fine.'

She went to the refrigerator and fetched a can of cola, pulled the tab, then extracted a glass and handed both to him.

'Did you eat on the plane?' Of course he'd eaten on the plane, she derided silently. It was after nine, for heaven's sake!

He poured the dark sparkling liquid, then took a long swallow. 'Yes.'

'How was your meeting?' She was aware of the need to make polite conversation, and equally aware he found it amusing.

'Successful.' He placed the empty can down onto the bench, and subjected her to a slow, warm appraisal.

'The contract is signed, the deal completed.'

'Then there's nothing to keep you here.'

The glass followed the empty can, and he leaned one hip against the edge of the bench. 'Yes,' he denied indolently. 'There is.'

Something twisted inside her stomach.

His gaze didn't waver, and she felt as if she was teetering close to a precipice.

'*You,*' Raoul stated solemnly.

That was certainly direct. But in what context? Given Ghislaine's venomous revelation, there was only one possibility.

'As a temporary diversion?' she posed, and saw his gaze narrow fractionally.

'A diversion from what?'

'Ghislaine, and your forthcoming marriage.'

He didn't move, but it seemed his long muscular frame uncoiled and became a formidable force.

Stephanie caught a glimpse of the persona he undoubtedly presented in the business arena. There was a dangerous stillness apparent, a waiting, watchful quality that revealed nothing and gave no hint of his reaction.

'Ghislaine possesses a fanciful imagination,' he drawled. 'Fostered by overindulgent parents in a desire to link Chabert to Lanier.' Facial muscles shifted and reassembled over chiseled bone structure. 'A business merger is out of the question, and there are no marriage plans.'

'Ghislaine appears to think differently.'

'And you believed her?' His voice was quiet, deadly.

Her eyes sparked blue fire, and the anger she'd managed to hold at bay for the past few hours rose to the surface. 'She was very convincing.'

'Yes,' he acknowledged cynically. 'I imagine she was.'

'There's no purpose to this,' Stephanie refuted, sorely tried.

'I disagree.'

Her chin tilted. '*Why?* The result remains the same.'

'You're so sure about that?'

I'm not sure about anything, damn you! But even with the most generous heart, I can't see it happening any other way. A proposal and happy-ever-after belong in fairy stories.

'Raoul,' Stephanie commanded unsteadily. 'Go home. Please.' She wanted him out of here, now, before she did something totally stupid. As it was, her eyes ached with repressed emotion. 'I really do have a few hours work ahead of me.'

He looked at her, saw the tiredness, the emotional strain evident, and subdued the anger he wanted to direct against Ghislaine for having caused Stephanie grief.

Without a word he caught hold of her shoulders and pulled her into his arms, curving a hand beneath her nape as he slid the other down to splay over the slight curve of her bottom.

She twisted against him in an attempt to break free, then fought against dissolving into him as his lips sought the vulnerable hollow at the edge of her neck.

'Don't.' The word emerged as a despairing groan. She didn't want this. She couldn't afford the sweet slide into emotional ecstasy, and she doubted her ability to survive the exquisite passion without fragmenting into a hundred shimmering pieces.

How long they stood together she had no idea. There was the sensation of it being right, as if some ephemeral force was at work. And dear heaven, it was so *good* to lean against him, accept his strength, his assurance.

Like this, she didn't care how long it lasted. It was enough he was here, and they had the night. So what if there were too few nights left? The truth was she didn't want to deny herself the ultimate pleasure of shared intimacy with him. Was that so bad?

Slowly, gently, he disentangled her arms and stood back a pace. Then he caught her chin between thumb and forefinger, lifted it, and tried not to drown in those dark sapphire depths.

'Go do whatever it is you have to do to finish on the computer,' Raoul bade easily. 'I'll get the coffee.'

Stephanie opened her mouth to protest, only to close it again. Her lashes swept wide as he tucked a stray lock of hair behind her ear, then he trailed his fingers down the curve of her cheek and let them rest against the edge of her mouth. He leaned down and dropped a soft kiss on the tip of her nose, then he pushed her gently in the direction of the table, and the computer.

It took her almost two hours, and there was a sense of satisfaction in pressing the Save key and transferring the data onto disk.

She'd been conscious of Raoul sprawled comfortably at ease on the large sofa in the adjoining open plan lounge. He had the television on low, and he looked totally relaxed. Every now and then she'd been conscious of him sparing her a watchful glance, and experienced the answering tremor as her body leaped in response.

With automatic movements she closed down the program, then disconnected the power inlet.

She didn't hear Raoul move, and a slight gasp escaped her lips as she felt his hands close over her shoulders.

His fingers began a deep soothing massage of her shoulders and neck muscles, gradually easing out the kinks until she sighed and let her head roll forward in a gesture of total acceptance.

It felt so good, so very good, it was all she could do not to express her pleasure in a purr of gratitude. When he began on her scalp she closed her eyes and surrendered to the magic.

There was little sense of the passage of time, and she made a token protest as his hands slid to her shoulders, then caught hold of her waist.

In one fluid movement he lifted her into his arms and carried her down the hall to the bedroom.

'Raoul—'

'Don't think,' he said huskily as he swept aside the covers and tumbled down onto the bed with her. His lips caressed the edge of her mouth. 'Just feel.'

He discarded his clothes with ease, shrugging out of his shirt, discarding trousers, shoes and socks, briefs, then he gathered her close and began a long, slow loving that had her begging for release.

It was flagrant, evocative, as his mouth took a tortuously slow path over every inch of her body. Caressing, tasting, in a supplication that drove her wild. The blood sang in her veins as sensation spiraled to impossible heights, and he caught her as she fell, only to wreak havoc as he sent her soaring again and again.

Skillful fingers knew where to touch, to stroke, as

he paid sensual homage to every pleasure spot, each heightened nerve ending. Just as she thought she'd experienced it all, he followed the same path in a tasting feast that made her cry out in all-consuming ecstasy.

Her whole body was one pulsating ache, and her response was unrestrained as she captured his head and dragged his mouth to her own.

He took her then, melding his body to hers in one powerful thrust, stayed there, then began a tantalizing withdrawal, before plunging deeper in a slow primal rhythm that built in pace until there was only the raw passion of two lovers in perfect accord.

Afterward they slept, held close in each other's arms in a tangle of sheets as the moon disappeared and the night became shrouded in darkness.

At some stage Stephanie stirred, felt the soothing slide of fingers down her back, and settled comfortably against warm skin and muscle, subsiding easily into relaxed somnolence.

The shrill sound of the alarm was an impossible intrusion, and Stephanie automatically reached out to close it, only to come in contact with a hard, muscular forearm intent on the same task.

'Six-thirty,' a slightly accented male voice drawled with a degree of amusement. 'Time to rise and shine.'

'Shower's mine,' she voiced drowsily, then yelped in shocked surprise as his hand slid down to create renewed havoc, bringing her to orgasm with such tactile skill it stole her breath. 'I think I should get up.'

Raoul's mouth nuzzled the soft hollow at the base of her neck. 'Only think?'

'Affirmative action is essential,' she said weakly, and slid out from beneath his grasp. 'Otherwise I'll be late.'

He rolled onto his back and linked his arms behind his head. Then he smiled, and Stephanie felt the powerful tug of desire.

She couldn't imagine anything she'd rather do than sink down onto the bed and give in to the hunger, the sheer sensual pleasure of his touch. To gift him a similar pleasure.

What would it be like to wake every morning like this after a night of exquisite lovemaking, only to do it all over again?

Sex. She closed her eyes, then opened them again. Very good sex. It wasn't—*couldn't*—be anything more. Could it?

Oh God. What she felt wasn't love. *Was it?* Realization washed through her body, quickly followed by apprehension. *No,* she screamed a silent denial. This wasn't happening.

Raoul observed the play of emotions chase across her expressive features, saw the shocked surprise evident in her eyes before her lashes swept down in a protective veil, and caught the faint tremor as she lifted a shaky hand to tuck back her hair.

His gaze narrowed fractionally as she caught up her robe and made for the en suite.

Minutes later she stepped into the shower stall, turned on the water and picked up the bottle of shampoo. Only to have it taken out of her hand within seconds of wetting her hair.

'You can't—'

'Yes, I can,' Raoul drawled as he poured thick liquid into one cupped palm, then he massaged it over her scalp.

When he was done, he picked up the soap and began smoothing it over her body. It became a teasing, evocative action that brought a groan to her lips.

At this rate, she'd need to forego breakfast. But oh dear Lord, it would be worth it just to savor his touch, to gift him a similar supplication.

'Raoul.' His name silvered from her lips, and anything else she might have said remained locked in her throat as his mouth closed over hers in a kiss that became a possession all of its own.

Nothing else mattered as he slid her arms up to link at his neck, and when he lifted her close she simply held on, exulting in the shape and feel of him, his strength, his earthy taste and raw sexuality.

She could almost believe he was bent on assaulting her senses…in an attempt to achieve what? she wondered idly as she snagged a towel and removed some of the excess moisture from her hair.

Soft color stained her cheeks at the thought of her craven response, and how easily he was able to achieve it. In his arms she became a wanton, eager to sample every sexual delight he cared to introduce.

Toweled dry, she went through the personal routine, collected fresh underwear, then hurriedly selected an elegant trouser suit, applied makeup, brushed her hair and slid her feet into high-heeled pumps.

Stephanie didn't even bother running a check on the time. It hardly mattered what the clock said, when it was obvious she was going to be late.

She caught up her bag, crossed to the laptop and retrieved the disk, then moved toward the front door.

He was right behind her, his holdall in one hand, his personal laptop in the other. He'd shaved, and in place of the suit he wore tailored trousers and a dark polo shirt.

Stephanie crossed to the garage, used the remote to open the automatic doors, then swore beneath her breath when she saw her car had a flat tire. Something she wouldn't have noticed had she not crossed around to the front passenger side to shift a garden rake, which seemed to have slid forward and lay resting against the bodywork of her car.

'Problems?'

Stephanie gestured toward the front wheel. 'This is the second time I've had a flat tire in two days,' she vented angrily. 'If this one is slashed, too, I'm going to report it to the police.'

'Slashed?' Raoul queried with deceptive quiet, and she inclined her head.

'That's what the guy at the tire mart said. He fitted two new tires for me last night.' She pushed a hand through her hair, and stifled an inward sigh. 'I'll get the spare.'

'Leave it,' he instructed. 'I'll drive you.'

'Dammit, I *need* my car.'

'And collect you from work. Give me the remote module, a spare key to the car and I'll take care of it.'

She opened her mouth to argue, then simply closed it again as he brushed the knuckles of one hand lightly along her jaw.

'No contest, *ma cher.*'

It was easier to do as he said, and as he negotiated traffic she retrieved her cell phone and called reception, alerting her imminent arrival.

Stephanie reached for the door clasp the moment Raoul swept to a halt outside the entrance to her office building, and she uttered a hurried 'thanks' as she slid from the car.

# CHAPTER TEN

As MORNINGS went, Stephanie's was a doozy, and losing an hour merely made a bad situation worse. Everything that could go wrong, did. Worse, her secretary had called in sick, and her temporary replacement didn't have a clue.

Coffee, hot sweet and strong helped some, and she prioritized paperwork, telephone calls, and didn't stop until one, when she deemed it sensible to take a lunch break. Otherwise she'd never make it through the afternoon.

There was a café close by, one of a few which catered for staff working in the many tall office blocks in this part of Southport, and Stephanie covered the short distance, choosing a table outdoors.

Numerous spreading tree branches provided shade, and there were bright striped awnings and umbrellas to protect patrons from the heat of the summer's sun.

The food was superb, the service swift, and within a very short space of time she was presented with a chicken and salad focaccia sandwich and a cappuccino.

It was a beautiful day, and from where she sat she could see the park, the sparkling waters of the main channel, and beyond it the architectural white sails of the Marina Mirage shopping complex soared against the background of blue sky. Next to it stood the condominium complex of the beautifully designed Palazzo Versace.

A view, she conceded with warmth, to die for. The café was well patronized, but not sufficiently so to warrant anyone requesting to share her table, and she took time to enjoy the food, the ambience. Entitled, she assured, by virtue of working late at home last night.

Thinking about what had happened *after* she'd closed down the computer last night set every nerve-end tingling alive. Dangerous, she mused, definitely dangerous to focus overlong on the passion Raoul had aroused...and her answering hunger.

Tonight's cocktail party for the marketing executives was a ''must attend'' function. Although she need only stay an hour, two at the most, and she'd be able to leave.

Stephanie finished her sandwich, drained the last of her cappuccino, then paid her bill at the counter and walked out into the sunshine.

She hadn't covered more than a few steps when a feminine slightly accented voice said her name.

No, please tell me it isn't Ghislaine, she prayed silently, only to turn and discover her prayers unanswered. What on earth was the Frenchwoman doing in this part of town?

'I took the wrong exit from the shopping center,' Ghislaine offered in explanation. 'I was looking for a taxi rank.'

'Way wrong,' Stephanie agreed. 'You can either

retrace your steps to the center and get directions for the right exit, or,' she suggested, wondering why she should be so helpful, 'I can ring the taxi company and have them send a car here.'

'Oh, *here* would be wonderful.'

It took only minutes to organize, and she replaced the cell phone into her bag. 'You'll have to excuse me. I need to get back to the office.'

'Before you go,' Ghislaine began with pseudo sweetness. 'I want to thank you.'

'For what?'

'Discrediting me with Raoul.'

Stephanie's stomach executed a painful somersault at the thought Ghislaine had probably deliberately set up watch on the off chance she'd frequent her usual lunch venue today.

'You managed to do that all by yourself,' Stephanie responded carefully.

'Raoul rang me this morning, suggesting we meet for coffee at the Terraces.' Her eyes glittered with ill-concealed anger. 'I looked forward to a tête-è-tête. Surely my visit to your office was private?'

Stephanie could almost visualize Ghislaine sharpening her metaphorical claws.

'Or do you always run to your men and tell tales?'

*Grr.* She was inclined to unsheathe her own! However a scene on a public street simply wasn't on her agenda. Silence, in some instances, was more effective than mere words.

'Who are you? A nonentity with no noble breeding, no social standing, *nothing!*' Ghislaine stated with scathing insolence.

'Whereas you are eminently qualified in each criterion?'

'*Yes,* damn you!'

Stephanie felt her blood heat. 'Sadly, blue blood and lineage don't necessarily guarantee desire.'

'*Bitch.*' She took a step forward and swung the palm of her hand, narrowly missing her target as Stephanie twisted her head to one side.

'Perhaps I should remind you that verbal defamation can warrant legal prosecution, and physical abuse will land you in court.'

'Raoul belongs to *me.*'

There was no way she was going to stand here and take any more of Ghislaine's verbal vitriol. Without a word she stepped forward and began walking.

'Don't you *dare* turn your back on me. I haven't finished with you!'

She didn't pause, or even bother to look back. A mistake, she learned seconds later, as something heavy careened into her back and almost sent her sprawling to the pavement.

A shoulder bag, she saw as she straightened, and swung with Ghislaine's weight behind it. 'That amounted to deliberate assault.'

Ghislaine's attractive features were brittle with fury. 'Where are your witnesses?' She gave an expressive shrug. 'As far as I'm concerned, you tripped. Pity you didn't fall.'

This had gone quite far enough! 'You want to go

the distance, Ghislaine? Raoul won't be impressed to learn you paid someone to slash my tires. Not once, but twice.' Her eyebrows rose. 'You didn't think I'd find out?'

'I don't know what you're talking about.'

Stephanie drew breath, and aimed for the kill. 'No? What did you think your scare tactics would do, Ghislaine? Send me running in the opposite direction?' She shook her head. 'I don't frighten that easily.'

'He just wants you for sex!'

'If that's true,' she opined carefully. 'Why me, when you're so willing to service him?'

Ghislaine looked as if she was going to throw the mother of all hissy fits, for her face paled, then tinged pink. Her eyes assumed a glassy look, her mouth thinned, and if it was possible for steam to emit from a human's ears...

'If you weren't on the scene—'

'It would be some other woman,' Stephanie offered. 'Accept it for the truth, and move on.'

'As you will?'

A horn blast close by alerted the taxi's arrival, and Ghislaine stepped across the grass verge and slid into the rear seat. Seconds later the taxi accelerated down the road.

Within minutes Stephanie walked through the entrance foyer and took the lift to her floor. Outwardly she appeared composed. No small achievement, when inside she was a mess of conflicting emotions, uppermost of which was the need to hit out in restrained anger at Ghislaine's obsessive behavior.

'You have two urgent calls to return, three faxes are on your desk and your three o'clock appointment has rescheduled thirty minutes early.'

It was back to work with a vengeance, and she continued at a punishing pace until five. The worst of it had been dealt with, and what hadn't could wait until tomorrow, she decided wearily as she shut down the computer, collected her bag and exited the office.

Raoul was waiting for her in the downstairs foyer, and her heart skipped a beat at the sight of him. His dark suit was perfectly tailored, his grooming exemplary. He really was something else, she conceded as she drew close. She'd miss him like hell when he left.

'Hi.'

Her greeting was bright, too bright, Raoul decided as he took in her pale features, the air of fragility apparent.

'Tough day?' he queried lightly, and saw her faint grimace.

'An understatement.'

With a swiftness that surprised her he captured her mouth with his own and kissed her. Thoroughly.

She could only gaze at him in startled surprise when he lifted his head, and he smiled, watching her eyes darken and dilate. 'You looked as if you needed it.'

She did, but not for the reason he imagined.

Traffic was heavy, and it took twenty minutes to reach Mermaid Beach.

'I'll go shower and change,' Stephanie intimated as they entered the house. 'Help yourself to a drink.'

He let her go, and crossed into the kitchen, selected something nonalcoholic from the refrigerator, then entered the lounge.

The bank of framed photographs caught his attention, and he picked up one of Stephanie holding Emma as a young baby.

He traced her outline with his finger, his lips curving slightly at her celluloid smile, the brave tilt of her head. Strong, courageous, she possessed integrity, passion, and a sense of self he found admirable.

Emma's father had been a fool, he accorded silently. In more ways than one.

Raoul replaced the frame and crossed to the window, then stood looking out over the grass to the neat bordered garden running the length of the fence separating the house next door. Flowers bloomed in carefully tended clumps, and there were shrubs, a few palm trees indicative of the tropical Queensland climate.

Stephanie found him there as she entered the lounge, and he turned, taking in her slender frame, the light red-gold hair styled in a neat bob, the delicate facial bone structure.

'Stunning,' he complimented, noting the way the electric-blue silk emphasized her cream-textured skin and highlighted her eyes.

'Shall we leave?'

Raoul caught up his keys and followed her out to the car. 'You'll need to give me directions.'

'It's not far.'

The private home was owned by a wealthy client who was known for his generosity and his penchant for entertaining. Located in a one-way street running parallel to the foreshore, the extensive three-level mansion was one of many very exclusive homes overlooking the ocean.

There were perhaps thirty invited guests sipping champagne and indulging in bite-size canapés.

'The purpose of this soiree is business?' Raoul inclined as more guests drifted into the large lounge.

'Definitely. Charles is one of the firm's most influential clients.' Stephanie wrinkled her nose at him. 'Who likes to lead into the festive season with the first of the pre-Christmas cocktail parties.' A faintly wicked smile tugged the edge of her lips. 'Yes, I know. It's only the first week in November.'

During the ensuing hour they mixed and mingled, together and separately as Raoul was drawn into conversation while a guest snagged Stephanie's attention.

She was good at her job, he perceived. Her interest was genuine, and she had a head for dates and figures that earned her respect from her peers.

His gaze lingered as she laughed spontaneously at someone's joke, then moved easily into conversation.

At that precise moment she lifted her head and looked at him, aware instinctively that he'd been watching her, and she smiled, offering him a slightly raised eyebrow in silent query.

Was it possible for two people to communicate without words? Did he sense that she wanted him so badly she could almost feel his touch?

Stephanie felt the heat rise deep inside, sensed the prickle of awareness scud across the surface of her skin, as she endeavored to contain her wayward thoughts.

With a sense of fascination she watched as he murmured a few words to the man he was with, then he made his way toward her.

'Having fun?' she lightly teased as he drew close, and almost melted beneath the warmth of his smile.

'By any definition,' Raoul drawled, and lifting a hand he trailed the pads of his fingers across her cheek.

Her eyes flared, and she was willing to swear her lower lip shook a little in involuntary reaction. She felt her body sway fractionally toward his, almost as if it had a mind of its own.

'Hungry?' He let his hand trace the length of her arm to her wrist and threaded his fingers through hers. 'For food?' she countered with a wicked smile, and felt the faint pressure as his fingers curled around her own.

'That, too.'

'I know of an intimate restaurant not far from here that serves the most divine Italian food.' She waited a beat. 'We could take some home and have a feast.'

'You don't want candlelight, Chianti and Andrea Bocelli singing sweet ballads on the CD player?'

She felt a bubble of laughter rise in her throat. 'Well,' she conceded, offering him a deliciously seductive smile. 'If you insist on an authentic ambience.'

They left a short while later, and it took only minutes to reach the small restaurant situated in a long block of shops fronting the southbound highway.

Owned and operated by an extended Italian family, they were greeted at the door by a courtly uncle, served wine by the eldest son, a daughter served the food, while both parents and the uncle's wife reigned in the kitchen.

The aroma of fresh herbs and spices mingled with wine and a host of tantalizing sauces, and there was music…

'Pavarotti,' Raoul drawled as Stephanie opted for a table, 'Making me wait, hmm?' he murmured with a teasing smile as he followed her to a spare table on the far side of the room.

'It's called anticipation.'

'I'll get my revenge later.'

Her eyes gleamed with wicked humor as they each took a seat. 'I'm trembling.'

'As well you should.'

Raoul ordered a mild red Lambrusco, and they settled on a starter each and followed it with another, rather than a main, choosing a clear soup, followed by spinach and feta ravioli served with mushrooms.

*'Perfecto,'* Raoul declared when they finished the dish and ordered coffee.

It was after eleven when Raoul paid the bill and they left. The night was warm, and the sky held a myriad of stars, heralding another fine day tomorrow.

How many more days did she have left? Two, three? Don't think about it, a small voice cautioned. They had the night, and it was enough. It *had* to be enough.

Yet how could it be, she agonized hours later as she lay spent beside him. A long, slow loving so incredibly tender she'd almost wept as he brought her to orgasm, then just as she thought it was over he took her soaring to impossible heights and beyond.

Afterward she had pleasured him, embracing every muscle, annointing every inch of skin in a flagrant trail that left him groaning with a need so intense it was almost beyond control.

What followed was nothing less than a pagan coupling, primitive and unrestrained as they were driven by an intoxicating frenzy that was wild, erotic and totally shameless.

Slowly, with infinite care, Stephanie slid out from beneath the covers, caught up her robe and moved silently down to the lounge.

Moonlight slipped through the partly open shutters, and she adjusted them slightly to ensure a clear view of the yard. Everything was still, and the moon cast long shadows from the few trees and shrubs.

In the distance a dog barked, then quietened, and

she stood gazing out into the opalescent night, silent and lost in introspective thought.

It was there Raoul found her, after stirring and finding an empty space beside him, and he'd moved quickly, silently, through the house until he reached the lounge and saw her slender form outlined beside the window.

Something tugged at his heart. She stood so still, so obviously lost in thought. How long had she been there?

Her arms were crossed at her midriff, and she looked so alone, almost forlorn.

'Unable to sleep, *cherie?*' he queried quietly as he moved to stand behind her. He slid his hands around her waist and drew her back to rest against him.

Stephanie felt his lips caress the delicate pulse beat at the edge of her neck, and let herself sink into him.

'It's a beautiful night,' she said huskily, and felt a sensation arrow through her body as he nuzzled an earlobe.

'*Oui.*' His fingers splayed down over her stomach and slid between the opening of her robe. 'I have to fly back to Paris at the end of the week.'

Her heart lurched, then stopped beating for a few seconds. Pain seeped through every pore in her body, and she could almost swear she forgot to breathe.

The moment she'd been dreading had finally arrived. Why, in her wildest dreams, had she hoped that it wouldn't?

What could she say? *Don't go?*

'I want you with me.'

Paris? *Paris.* It wasn't possible. How could she even consider it? What about Emma? Celeste was wonderful, but she couldn't expect her mother... Besides, there was her job. 'We live different lives on opposite sides of the world.' She was breaking up inside. 'But we don't—'

'Have a future?' His hands slid to her shoulders and he turned her around to face him. 'Yes, we do.'

Pride was responsible for the way her chin lifted, and her gaze was steady. 'As sometime lovers who spend a week or two together whenever the timing is right?'

'No. I have something different in mind.'

'I'm not *mistress* material,' she assured sadly.

His teeth showed white as his mouth curved to form a musing smile. 'I'm relieved to hear it.'

'I have a child, a career,' she stated.

'This career, *here,* is too important for you to give up?' Raoul queried.

'I have responsibilities, financial commitments.'

'If the financial commitments were removed?'

'What are you suggesting?'

'Marry me.'

Shock deprived her of the ability to speak, and when she found her voice, the words emerged as little more than a whisper. 'What did you say?'

'Marry me,' Raoul repeated gently.

'You're not serious?'

'I can assure you I have never been more serious in my life.'

'But—'

'If a career is so important to you, I can arrange a position in marketing, or any field you choose.'

She didn't doubt it. 'Raoul—'

'I have an apartment in Auteuil, and a home in the Chinon wine region of the Loire Valley. Emma will delight in spending weekends and holidays there.'

'You're going too fast,' she protested.

'No,' he denied quietly. 'I want you with me, as my wife, wherever I happen to be in the world. Emma is a part of you that is everything to me. Perhaps in a few years there will be a sister or brother for her to love and care for. But for now, we share whatever the future holds...together.'

Stephanie felt the prick of tears, and fought hard to control them.

'I have important meetings in Paris next week. Four days, *mon amour,* then I'll be back and we will arrange our wedding. Your parents will return to Paris with us for Christmas.'

*Christmas* was only weeks away. 'It's too soon...we can't—'

'We can. Easily.' Money, sufficient amounts of it, had a power of its own.

'You love me.'

It was a statement, not a query. She could only wonder at her own transparency, and how long he'd known.

He cradled her face in his hands, glimpsed the fleeting emotions, and appraised each and every one of them. 'I took one look at you that first day on the film set,' he revealed softly. 'And knew my life would never be the same again.'

Any minute soon she'd wake and discover this was nothing more than wishful thinking on the part of her subconscious mind.

'Be with me, stay with me. Eternity. *Je t'aime, mon coeur.*'

Her bones turned to liquid, and she wound her arms around his neck and pulled his mouth down to hers, initiating a kiss that reached to the very depths of her soul.

'I fought against becoming emotionally involved with you every step of the way,' Stephanie revealed in a voice just above a whisper. 'I tried so hard to convince myself you were a complication I couldn't afford. But everywhere I turned, there you were. I couldn't seem to escape you.'

His lips were creating an evocative path at her temple, and she could almost feel his smile.

'You noticed.'

'You didn't play fair. You charmed my daughter, not to mention my mother.'

'They were my strongest allies.'

'It was almost as if you had a hidden agenda.'

'Assignment,' Raoul corrected, and nuzzled her soft curve at the edge of her neck. 'Father to Emma. And husband…*yours.*'

It took her a moment to catch her breath, then a slow sweet smile curved her lips. 'Reverse the order,' she teased unmercifully. 'And I might think about it.'

'Might you, indeed?' Raoul growled huskily. He swept an arm beneath her knees and lifted her against his chest.

A bubble of laughter escaped her lips. 'What is this, persuasion?'

'Sweet torture,' Raoul assured huskily. 'Until you say *yes*.'

It didn't take long. Not very long at all.

## CHAPTER ELEVEN

THEY were married by a Celebrant in a civil ceremony held in a restored nondenominational church set in beautiful gardens by the river. Stephanie's father gave her away, Celeste was matron of honor, and Emma the flower girl.

The bride wore a short cream dress overlayed with scalloped lace, while the groom was resplendent in a perfectly tailored black suit.

Afterward they ate fine food and drank Cristal champagne.

Two days later Raoul, Stephanie and Emma, together with Celeste and Philip flew to Paris where they held another ceremony, a reaffirmation of their vows, for the benefit of Raoul's family.

Sandrine and Michel attended, as did Anneke and Sebastian. Henri stood proudly as head of the family, and Madeleine, the elderly matriarch, gave her blessing and thanked Stephanie for introducing a great-grandchild into the family. Premature, perhaps, for the legal adoption that would change Emma's surname from Sommers to Lanier would not be official for a while.

Two Lanier wives hid a secretive smile, and remained silent. It was too soon to share the news that next Christmas, God willing, there would be two babes for Madeleine to fuss over.

Raoul noted Stephanie's faintly wistful expression and linked her fingers with his own.

'Happy?'

She turned her head toward him, and her radiant smile took his breath away.

'Yes,' she said simply, amazed that he needed to ask, when every night she responded to his lovemaking with such a wealth of unbridled passion. 'How would you feel about—'

'*Oui.*'

'I didn't finish.'

He lifted her hand to his lips and brushed a lingering openmouthed kiss to the pulsing veins at her wrist. '*Mon coeur,* you don't need to.'

Her eyes sparkled with wicked humor. 'You read minds?'

'Yours, *mon amour,* is particularly transparent.'

'That's something I'm going to have to work on,' she said with mocking amusement, and heard his soft husky laughter.

'You are the other half of me, part of my soul. I look at you, and know your mind, your heart, as well as I know my own.'

'*Tu es ma vie. Je t'adore.*'

His mouth brushed her temple. '*Merci, mon ange,*' he said gently, and felt her fingers tighten around his own.

Life, he acknowledged, didn't get any better than this.

**Cathy Williams** is originally from Trinidad but has lived in England for a number of years. She currently has a house in Warwickshire which she shares with her husband Richard, her three daughters Charlotte, Olivia and Emma and their pet cat, Salem. She adores writing romantic fiction and would love one of her girls to become a writer although at the moment she is happy enough if they do their homework and agree not to bicker with one another.

**Look out for Cathy Williams's next sexy story:
IN THE BANKER'S BED
On sale April 2005, in Modern Romance™!**

# THE BABY VERDICT
## by
## Cathy Williams

# CHAPTER ONE

'THE big boss wants to see you.'

Jessica looked at the petite, blonde secretary she shared with her boss, Robert Grange, and grinned.

'Has anyone told you that you're wasted as a secretary, Millie? You have a special talent for making the most innocuous statements sound dramatic. Really, you need to be in a TV soap.' She rested her briefcase on the ground next to her and began riffling through the post, sifting out bits, leaving some for her secretary to open. 'That tax information I need still hasn't come through,' she said distractedly, ripping open an envelope and glancing through the contents. 'Why can't people get their act together? I asked for that information two days ago.'

'Jess,' her secretary said, 'you're not hearing me. You've been summoned! You need to get your skates on and not stand there flicking through the mail!'

Jessica looked up from what she was doing and frowned. 'I'm due to see Robert in fifteen minutes' time,' she said. 'What's the problem?'

'The problem is,' Millie told her in a long-suffering voice, 'you're thinking of the wrong big boss. Bruno Carr is in your office waiting for you.'

'Bruno Carr?' She glanced along the corridor. 'What does Bruno Carr want with *me?*' She had been working at BC Holdings for nine months, and during that time she had not once laid eyes on the legendary Bruno Carr. BC Holdings was just one of a multitude of companies he owned. His headquarters were in the City somewhere, and

5

he rarely deigned to visit some of his smaller companies. Once a month, Robert would journey to the City with a case bulging with documents, proof that profits were where they should be, finances were running smoothly and employees were doing what they should be doing.

'I have no idea,' Millie said now, throwing a cursory glance at her perfectly shaped nails, today painted jade-green to match the colours of her suit, 'but he doesn't look like the kind of man who appreciates being kept waiting.'

Well, what kind of man *does* he look like? Jessica wanted to ask. She felt a thread of nervous tension snake through her body and she did a quick mental calculation of what she might possibly have done to warrant Bruno Carr descending on her.

'You should have *asked* him what he wanted,' she hissed, her brown eyes flicking between the corridor and her secretary. 'That's what secretaries are *for*.' She was very rarely thrown off balance by anything, but the sudden unexpectedness of this was enough to disconcert her.

'People don't ask Bruno Carr questions like that!' Millie exclaimed in a horrified voice. 'He comes in, says what he wants, and you just nod a lot and do it.'

'Well, he sounds a particularly pleasant kind of individual.'

A great, big, overweight, pompous man who went around stamping on the little people and issuing orders by royal decree. This was all she needed on a freezing January Monday morning.

'Where's Robert?' she asked, postponing the inevitable for as long as she could. Her lawyer's instinct told her to get as much information about what was going on as she possibly could, even if Millie was being particularly unforthcoming.

'Meeting. He was told to go ahead without you.'

'I see.'

'Guess that means that the great Bruno Carr wants to see you all on your lonesome,' she whispered confidentially. 'Sounds ominous, if you ask me.'

'I don't recall asking you,' Jessica said automatically.

'Well, I'd better go along in.' Whatever it was she had done, it had clearly been a grave crime against Bruno Carr's enterprises, for which she was to be punished by immediate dismissal. Perhaps she had inadvertently taken home one of the company's red marker pens with her, and he had somehow discovered it. From the sound of it, he was just the sort of man who would see that as reason for instant sacking. And why else would he have sought her out, making sure that he gave no warning in advance, if not to confront her with some misdemeanour?

She retrieved her briefcase from the ground and mentally braced herself for the worst.

'Could you bring us in some coffee in about ten minutes' time, Mills?' she asked, running her hands along her neatly pinned back blonde hair, just to make sure that there were no loose strands waiting to ambush her composure.

'You mean if Mr Carr allows it...'

'You're being ridiculous now.'

She pulled herself erect and headed down the corridor, pausing briefly outside her door and wondering whether she should knock or not. There was no remote reason why she should knock to enter her own office, but, then again, barging in might be another nail in her coffin.

It was frustrating. She could admit, without any false modesty, that although she had been at the company for under a year she was doing a brilliant job. She had a sharp, alert mind and a willingness to work any number of hours to get a job done. What could he possibly have found to criticise in her performance?

She found herself knocking angrily on the door, then she pushed it open and walked in.

He was sitting in *her* chair, which was turned away from the door so that only the top of his head was visible, because he was talking on *her* phone, his voice low and staccato. She stood for a few seconds, glaring at the back of the leather swivel chair, knowing how those bears had felt when Goldilocks had swanned in in their absence and usurped their property.

'Excuse me. Mr Carr?' she said, folding her arms and injecting as much crispness into her tone as was possible, just in case some of her annoyance oozed out.

He turned around very slowly and she stared at him, mouth open, as he slowly finished his telephone conversation and leant forward to replace the phone. Then he sat back, folded his arms, and looked at her without saying anything.

She had been expecting thinning grey hair. She had been expecting middle-aged spread caused by too many rich lunches and not enough exercise. She had been expecting bushy eyebrows, wobbling jowls and a tightly pursed mouth.

Why had the wretched Millicent given her no warning of what the man looked like?

True, there was arrogance stamped on those hard features, but any arrogance was well contained in a face that was the most powerfully sensual she had ever seen in her life before.

His hair was almost black, his eyes shrewd, cool, and wintry blue and the lines of his face were perfectly chiselled, yet somehow escaping from the category of routinely handsome.

Handsome, Jessica thought, was a combination of features that blended well together. Perhaps it was his expression and a certain mantle of accepted self-assurance, or maybe it was the overall impression of brains and power, but there was some intangible element to the man sitting in front of her that catapulted him into a category all of his own.

'What are you doing in my chair?' she asked stupidly, forcing down the immediate physical impact he had made on her and trying to retrieve some of her composure back from where it had been flung to the four winds.

'*Your* chair?' His voice was low, velvety and coldly ironic.

She instantly felt her hackles rise. It was easy to work out what his type was: the wealthy, clever, powerful, good-looking bachelor who assumed that the world lay somewhere in the region of his feet.

'Sorry. I meant *your* chair in my office.' She smiled sweetly and continued to look at him with a steady, unfaltering gaze.

Her momentary lapse at being confronted with such intense masculinity had now been put away in a box at the back of her mind, and her self-control was once again reasserting itself.

It never let her down. It had been her companion for such a long time, seemingly all twenty-eight years of her life, that she could avail herself of it effortlessly.

He didn't bother to answer that. Instead, he nodded briefly in the direction of the chair facing him, and told her to sit down.

'I've been waiting to see you for the past...' he flicked back the cuff of his shirt and consulted the gold watch '...twenty-five minutes. Do you normally get into work this late?'

Jessica sat down, crossed her legs and swallowed down the lump of anger in her throat.

'My hours are nine to five—' she began.

'Clock watching isn't a trait I encourage in my employees.'

'But I left work at a little after ten last night. If I got in at a little after nine, then I do apologise. I'm normally up and running here by eight-thirty in the morning.' She bared her teeth in a semblance of politeness and linked her fingers together on one knee.

'Robert sings your praises...' he looked at the piece of paper lying in front of him, which she recognised, upside down, as her CV '...Jessica. I take it, by the way, that you know who I am?'

'Bruno Carr,' she said, tempted to add *Leader of the Universe*.

'You're younger than I imagined from what Robert has told me,' he said flatly. He looked at her speculatively through narrowed eyes, as if weighing her up, and she wondered what her age had to do with the price of sliced bread. Instead, she thought, of making disparaging comments on her age, why didn't he just cut to the nub of the matter and tell her why he was here? In her office, sitting in her chair, having used her telephone.

'Would you mind very much if I had a cup of coffee? Before I launch into defending my age?' That one she couldn't resist, and he raised his eyebrows, unamused.

'Millie,' he buzzed, 'two coffees, please.' He leaned back into the chair, which dwarfed her even though she was tall, but appeared made for him. Even though he was camouflaged by his suit, she could see that he had a muscular, athletic physique and was tall. He would be, she reckoned, one of those rarities: a man she would have to look up to, even when she was in heels.

In record time there was a knock at the door and Millie fluttered in with a tray, on which were two cups, with saucers, instead of the usual mugs, a plate of biscuits and cream and sugar.

'Will there be anything else?' she asked, smiling coyly and hovering.

Oh, please, Jessica thought wryly. Was this the same delicate, porcelain girl who could make mincemeat of men? Bruno's presence had obviously reduced her to the archetypal eyelash-batting, empty-headed bimbo she most certainly was not. No wonder the man wore that aura of invincibility about him, if women dropped like ninepins every time he was around.

'For the moment.' He looked appreciatively at a blushing Millie and gave a smile of such profound sensual charm that Jessica's breath caught in her throat for the merest fleeting of seconds. Then she steadied herself and reached forward for the cup on the tray.

Yes, men like Bruno Carr were a dangerous species. The sort who should carry health warnings stamped on their foreheads so that women knew to steer clear of them.

Jessica's mouth tightened as her mind flicked through the pages of her past, like a calendar blown back by a strong wind.

She remembered her father, tall, elegant, charming, always talking to her mother's friends, making them feel special. It was only later, as she had grown up, that she had realised that his activities had extended well beyond merely talking and that his charm, never applied to his wife, had been only skin-deep.

'Now,' he said, once Millie had disappeared out of the door, 'you're doubtless wondering why I'm here.'

'It's crossed my mind.' After all, she thought acidly, it's hardly been your policy in the past to fraternise. At least not with the members of *this* particular offshoot company, however hugely profitable it was.

'Has Robert said anything to you about his health?' Bruno asked, leaning forward with his elbows on the desk.

'About his *health*?' Jessica looked at him, confused. 'No. Why? Is there something wrong?' She knew that over the past three months he had been leaving work earlier than usual, but he had told her that a man of his age needed to wind down eventually, and she had believed him.

'Have you noticed *nothing* about his hours recently?' There was cool sarcasm in his voice and she stiffened.

'He hasn't been working very much overtime…'

'And he's been delegating quite a substantial amount of his workload onto you. Am I right?'

'A bit,' she admitted, wondering why she had never questioned that.

'And yet you didn't put two and two together? Hardly a very positive trait in a lawyer. Shouldn't lawyers be adept at ferrying out information and making assumptions?'

'I apologise if I didn't see anything sinister in his behaviour,' she said with equal coldness in her voice. 'Believe it or not, cross-examining my boss wasn't part of my job specification.' She could feel her anger going up a notch and was alarmed more by the fact that he had managed to arouse such a reaction in her than by what he had said.

Outbursts of emotions were not something that she was accustomed to dealing with. From a young age, as she had stood on the sidelines and watched the antics of her father and the misery of her long-suffering mother, she had learned to control her emotions, to keep them under lock and key.

'Are you telling me that he's ill?' she asked tightly, worry in her voice.

'Stomach ulcer. He's on medication for it and has been for a while, but he's now been told that he needs to have a sabbatical. At least six months away from the stress of a work environment.'

'How dreadful. I wish he'd said something to me. I would have relieved him of far more of his workload.' She thought of her boss—tall, grey-haired, kindly, always encouraging her and never backward in his praise when she'd done a good job at something—and felt a stab of guilt.

Bruno was right. *Why* hadn't she put two and two together and worked out that he was not well?

'It's unfortunate,' Bruno said, watching her face and reading her reaction, 'but it's not terminal.'

'I'm afraid I don't know a great deal about stomach ulcers…'

'I gathered that from the expression on your face.' He raked his fingers through his hair, and she watched, half mesmerised by this simple gesture.

'I've told him,' Bruno said, 'that the sooner he leaves the better. There's no point jeopardising his health for the sake of a job. Which,' he continued slowly, 'brings me to you, and the reason I'm here.'

'Right. Of course.' She was still dazedly thinking of all the signs she had missed over the past few months.

'You're Robert's second in command. I gather that you're good at your job.'

What did he expect her to say to that? 'I do my best.'

'I've read your CV. For someone who's so young, you appear to have excelled in your previous job, and in your law exams.'

*Appear to have excelled?* What was he trying to tell her? That he doubted what was in front of him?

'Why didn't you go down the line of barrister?' he asked, not looking at her, still flicking through the sheets of paper in front of him.

'I thought about it,' Jessica said, still smarting from his

tone of voice. 'In the end, I decided that working within a company would give me more of a sense of stability and fulfilment. Of course, I still have friends in the field of criminal law and I try and go to as many court cases as I can.'

'As a hobby?' He glanced up at her, his eyes unreadable, and she wondered whether there was an element of sarcasm there.

'It's as useful a *hobby* as any I can think of,' she said a little sharply.

'Useful...if a little solitary.'

'Which is no bad thing, as far as I am concerned.'

He looked at her fully then, not saying anything for such a long time that she began to feel uncomfortable. Then he pushed himself away from the desk and stood up, his hands in his pockets, and began pacing the room, finally ending up by the window, where he remained standing, resting back against the ledge.

He was even taller than she had originally thought, and his body had a toned leanness to it that reminded her of something dangerous and unpredictable. Some kind of predatory jungle animal. Or perhaps, she thought, aware that she shouldn't stare and therefore carefully averting her eyes to a point slightly to the side of him, that was simply the overall impression he emanated.

'You'll have to cover for Robert during his absence,' he said, looking at her, his blue eyes calculating. 'Naturally, you'll be financially compensated.'

'That won't be a problem.' She could hardly carry on talking to the upper-left angle of the window, so she looked him fully in the face, and felt that disturbing awareness again.

Whatever was wrong with her? She didn't even care for the man! He was about as jovial as a barracuda. Not the sort of man she went for at all. Her boyfriends, short-lived though they tended to be, were all fashioned in the same mould: easygoing, considerate, occasionally a little dull. But men she could handle.

She had seen firsthand how debilitating it could be to live a life over which you exercised no control. She had watched her mother wither over the years as she had endured her husband's brutal infidelities, tied to the house because she had been told repeatedly that she was incapable of doing anything on her own.

Jessica had fashioned her escape from that stifling atmosphere with the precision of a military campaign. While her teenaged friends had spent their days swooning over boys and experimenting with make-up, she had buried her head in her books, working with the single-minded passion of someone who needed to furiously dig a tunnel before they could see the outside world.

She had no intention of ever handing over control of her life to someone else. She had studied hard, worked hard and every step of her career had been built on determination and lessons learnt in the past.

'I already work very closely with Robert, anyway,' she said, snapping back to the present and focusing on the man standing in front of her. 'I know most of his client base. The rest I can familiarise myself with easily enough.' A temporary promotion. She breathed a little sigh of relief. And to think that she had hovered uncertainly by that office door, convinced that she was about to be handed her walking cards.

'Will that be all?' she asked, standing up. She smiled and extended her hand.

'No.'

'I beg your pardon?'

'No, that will not be all, so you might as well sit back down.'

A man accustomed to giving orders. A man who by-passed the polite preliminaries of conversation that most people took for granted.

She withdrew her hand, feeling a bit idiotic, and sat back down.

'You don't think that I travelled out here merely to inform you that you've got a promotion, do you?' His voice was cool and amused, and it was an effort for her to continue looking at him without dislike.

'I know,' she said, 'that was silly of me, wasn't it?'

He frowned, and she struggled to contain a sudden urge to grin.

'Do I hear a little edge of sarcasm there?' he asked mildly.

'Of course not!' Her brown eyes were innocently shocked at such a suggestion. 'I wouldn't dare!'

'You haven't asked when Robert is due to leave.' He returned to the chair behind the desk, sat back down and then pushed it away so that he could cross his legs, ankle on knee.

'I assumed...' What had she assumed? 'I guessed that it would be in a couple of months' time...?'

'At the end of the week.'

'The end of the week!' Jessica looked at him, startled. 'The end of *this* week? But how? Why hasn't he said anything to me? Surely he'll need longer than four days to tie up loose ends...'

'Are you beginning to regret your optimism in filling in for him?'

'I'm just expressing surprise at the suddenness of it all,' she told him coldly. 'I'm also a little bit taken aback that he didn't see fit to inform me before this.'

'You have me to thank for that,' he said bluntly. 'This development happened overnight, literally, and I told him that it would be better for me to talk to you. In fact, it was essential that I did.' He paused, as though contemplating what to say next. 'His mother lives in America and two days ago she suffered a stroke. I told him that it made sense for him to combine his leave with a visit out there to see her. He'll speak to you about this when he gets in this afternoon, then he'll call a staff meeting some time tomorrow.'

'I see.'

'The reason I made a point of coming out here to tell you all this yourself—'

'When you almost certainly would have had better things to do,' Jessica muttered to herself.

'Sorry? I missed that.' He leaned forward slightly, and she flashed him a brilliant smile.

'Nothing important. Just thinking aloud.'

'This sudden development comes at a rather inconvenient time.'

'Inconvenient for whom?' she asked.

'I'll ignore that question,' Bruno told her, narrowing his eyes. 'It borders on impertinence.'

Which it did. She felt colour steal into her cheeks. Had she forgotten that this man was her boss? Had she forgotten that she should toe the line and not risk her career for the sake of emotion?

'I'm sorry,' she said honestly. 'I suppose I'm just shocked and worried about Robert. It's been sprung on me out of the blue.'

What a limp lettuce of an excuse, she thought. She could feel his shrewd eyes on her, assessing, and she waited for him to inform her that sarcasm was not something he would tolerate. Sarcasm, she suspected, was not something he had probably ever had to deal with.

He chose to disregard what she had said, though.

'Two days ago,' he said instead, 'I received this.' He withdrew a letter from his jacket pocket and shoved it across the desk to her, then he sat back and watched while she opened it and read the contents several times over.

Bruno Carr was being sued. Personally. A component for a car, manufactured by one of his plants, had resulted in a near-fatal car crash.

'This,' he explained softly, 'is why I thought it important to come and see you myself.'

Jessica looked up briefly before re-reading the official letter. 'To see if you considered me capable of dealing with this…'

'That's right. And you're not what I expected.'

'Is that why you expressed concern about my age, Mr Carr?' She carefully placed the sheet of paper on the desk in front of her and sat back, with her fingers linked on her lap.

A legal issue was something she could deal with. The personal confrontation with Bruno Carr had brought out feelings in her she hadn't even known existed, at least not for a very long time. But this. She took her time considering him.

'You think that because I'm relatively young I'm incapable of doing a good job.'

'You lack experience,' he said flatly. 'You are also a woman.'

'Perhaps I could address those concerns of yours one at a time?' When she smiled, her jaw ached because of the effort, and her fingers were itching to hurl something very heavy at him. Precisely what century was this man living in?

'Firstly, age has nothing to do with competence. I can't deny that I haven't got three decades' worth of experience behind me, but then I can assure you that I am more than capable of dealing with this lawsuit.' The only way to deal with Bruno Carr, she decided, was not to be cowed by him. He would smell out any hint of uncertainty from her with the unerring precision of a shark smelling blood, and he would promptly take his lawsuit somewhere else. Careerwise, it would be death for her.

'Of course, I shall need immediate and unrestricted access to any information, technical or otherwise, that I consider necessary...'

He nodded fractionally, and continued to look at her, waiting for her to say her piece, upon which he would deliver his verdict.

'Fine. Now, secondly, yes, I am a woman.' Camouflaged as it was by her genderless working garb. In a man's world, frilly dresses were off limits—not that she had ever been one for frilly dresses anyway. A suit told the world precisely what she wanted it to know, which was that she was to be taken seriously. Even outside the working environment, she steered clear of frocks and short skirts, preferring jeans and clothes that were tailored and smart rather than provocative. It was only when she stripped at night that she saw the reflection of her own body in the mirror—tall, slender, but with full breasts and long legs. A good figure, she knew. It was as well to conceal it.

'However,' she continued, 'women comprise a high percentage of the working arena these days, in case you hadn't noticed. I'm sure if you cast your eyes around you'll discover that there are quite a few spread throughout your various companies.'

'Ah, but none of them is poised to defend my name in a lawsuit, are they?' he pointed out smoothly.

'And why do you think that a man might be more competent at the job than a woman?' she asked, changing tactic. She fixed him a cool, implacable stare, one of her specialities when it came to withering any member of the opposite sex who might be overstepping her boundaries. He stared back at her, unperturbed.

'Because women are prone to outbursts of hysteria when the going gets too tough, and I, frankly, don't think that that will do at all in this instance.'

Oh, good grief, Jessica thought to herself. *Was she really hearing this?*

'Outbursts of hysteria?' she asked politely, with her head tilted to one side. 'When the going gets tough?' She laughed dryly. 'Possibly with the women you tend to associate with, but I can assure you that there's a whole army of them out there who don't react in any such way when faced with a challenge.' She paused, and added for good measure, 'And by challenge I don't mean colour co-ordinating our clothes or debating what shade of nail polish we should wear on our next date.'

He looked away and she caught something that looked remarkably like a stifled smile, although she couldn't be sure, because when he once again looked at her his face was serious.

'Robert has every confidence in your ability,' he told her. 'And that's counted heavily in your favour. If it were up to me, I would say that a young, inexperienced woman would not come high on the list of people I would choose to handle this.'

I'm going to have to work fairly closely with this man if I get this job, Jessica thought grimly. I'm going to have to quell the urge to strangle him.

'Well,' she informed him with a cool little smile and a slight shrug, 'there's nothing more I can say to convince you that I'd do a good job. If you don't feel one hundred per cent confident of my abilities, then, of course, you must look elsewhere.'

The interview, as far as she was concerned, was finished, but she was deeply reluctant to stand up, just in case he ordered her to sit back down again.

He saved her the decision by standing up himself and moving around the desk towards her.

For a second she felt a recurrence of that vague, unspecified alarm that had wrong-footed her previously, then it subsided and she rose to her feet. In her heels, she reached just to the level of his mouth, and she averted her eyes hurriedly because, almost unconsciously, her mind registered that it was a disconcertingly sensual mouth.

'I'm prepared to give you the benefit of the doubt, Miss Stearn,' he said, reaching out to shake her hand.

'And I'm flattered,' she replied, withdrawing her hand almost immediately, 'especially since I realise that it goes against your better judgement. I'll do a good job.'

'Oh, I hope so,' he drawled, looking down at her, 'for both our sakes.'

'Quite.' She abandoned all attempts at smiling. Why bother? If he could be brutally frank with her, then she would be as brutally frank back, within reasonable limits.

'And I feel I should warn you that I'm intolerant of incompetence, especially when my reputation is at stake.'

'Thanks for the warning. I'll bear it in mind.'

She watched as he walked towards the door, then as he was about to open it he turned and looked at her over his shoulder.

'You're quite the hard nut, aren't you?' he said in a speculative voice.

Was he surprised? She supposed so. Quite unexpectedly, she had a vision of the sort of women he appreciated, and she could guarantee that not a single hard nut would be among them.

'I'm not about to agree or disagree with that, Mr Carr. You're entitled to your own opinion.'

He nodded, half smiled, and then closed the door behind him, and it was only then, as her body sagged, that she realised quite how much strain she had been under.

The news about Robert had come as a shock. He had seemed fit enough. Hadn't he? She frowned and tried to remember whether there had been any give-away signs of ill health. Then, uneasily, it crossed her mind that perhaps there had been and she had just failed to recognise them because she'd been so wrapped up in her work. Her concentration on her job was single-minded and complete, which, she acknowledged, was great when it came to climbing ladders and winning promotions, but there was a great big world out there and…was it passing her by?

No. Surely not. She had a successful, rewarding career. How could anything be passing her by? Every goal she had striven for had been achieved. She should feel nothing but satisfaction.

Of course, her love life was not exactly thrilling. In fact, it was positively non-existent at the moment. Her relationship with Greg had ended six months ago, which had been roughly its duration. She uncomfortably remembered his criticism of her—that she had been obsessed with her career.

*You're quite the hard nut, aren't you?*

There's nothing wrong with wanting to be independent, she told herself fiercely. If her mother had been financially independent, she would have had the courage to leave the man who had made her life hell.

There's nothing wrong with me, she thought, and, if it's the last thing I do, I'll prove that I can take this case and win it.

# CHAPTER TWO

JESSICA looked at her watch, stretched, and debated whether she should telephone Bruno Carr or not. It was eight o'clock, she was still at work, and she needed information. If she was to win this case, she thought with a sense of self-righteous indignation, then he would have to be more available to answer questions. For the past week he had been abroad on business, and, however much information she could gather from various members of various departments, sooner or later he would have to avail himself.

She eyed the phone warily, as though fearing that it might metamorphose into something unpleasant at any moment, then, making her mind up, she dialled his direct work extension and was on the verge of hanging up when she heard his voice down the other end.

Irrationally, she felt a flutter of nerves.

'Mr Carr? This is Jessica Stearn here. I've been trying to reach you for the past week, but I gather you've been away on business.'

'New York.'

'Well, I'm glad you're back because there are one or two questions I need to ask you.' She shuffled some bits of paper in front of her, then began to doodle on her notepad.

'Fire away.'

'I think it might be better if this is done face to face. It's important that you familiarise yourself with every aspect of the case so that every question that's thrown at you on the stand can be dealt with.'

23

'It wasn't my intention to go into the witness box unprepared,' he said dryly.

'Perhaps we could meet some time tomorrow?' she asked, glancing at her diary.

'Why not now?'

'Now?'

'I take it you're still at work.'

'Yes, I am, but—'

'No time like the present. Now, do you know the address of my office here?' He rattled it off, and she hurriedly scribbled it alongside her complicated doodle. 'Get a cab. You'll get here quicker.'

'Yes, but—'

She heard the flat hum of the dialling tone and stared at the receiver in her hand with an expression of stunned amazement. He'd hung up on her! He'd decided that now was as good a time to answer questions as any, and hadn't even had the common politeness to ask her what her plans for the evening might be!

Was he so used to getting his own way that he simply took it for granted that the rest of the human race would fall in with whatever he wanted?

She stood up, slipped on her jacket and coat, grabbed her handbag from the low, square table in the corner of her office and hurried out of the building.

The more she thought about his attitude, the more exasperated she became. She could very nearly convince herself that she had really had exciting plans for the evening, when in fact her plans had included no more than a quick, pre-prepared meal in front of the television, a few law articles she wanted to have a look at, and then bed.

Hardly heady stuff, she knew, but she had been working since eight-thirty in the morning, and a low-key evening was just what she felt she needed.

It didn't help that she had to trudge two blocks and wait fifteen minutes before she managed to hail a taxi. Thursday nights were always busy. Late-night shopping and the remnants of the January sales were enough to encourage even the laziest into the streets. She watched as taxi after taxi trundled past and was in a thoroughly foul temper by the time a vacant one pulled over to the side for her.

I need a long soak in a bath, she fumed silently to herself, staring out of the window at the bright lights and the people, hurrying along to minimise the length of time they spent in the cold. Her suit felt starched and uncomfortable, her make-up had almost vanished completely and she wanted to kick off her shoes and let her feet breathe.

His office block in the City was quite different from where she worked. Large, with a lot of opaque glass everywhere, and, when she entered, a profusion of plants strewn around an enormous reception area, in the centre of which the large, circular desk, manned by an elderly man in uniform, was a bit like an island adrift in the middle of an ocean.

A group of three men in suits was standing to one side, talking in low voices, and they glanced around automatically as she entered the building, but aside from them it was empty.

Because, she thought, everyone else has left to go home and relax, or else get dressed before stepping out to paint the town red.

Jessica couldn't remember the last time she had painted the town red. She had a sneaking suspicion that she had never painted it red—or any other colour, come to think of it.

During her more active moments, when she'd been involved with a man, few and far between though they had been, she had gone to the theatre or had meals out.

Somehow, she didn't think that that fell into the 'Red Paint' category.

'Mr Carr, please,' she said to the man behind the desk, now feeling gloomy in addition to exasperated and inconvenienced.

He lifted the receiver, spoke for a few seconds, and then nodded at her.

'Mr Carr's expecting you,' he said, and she resisted the impulse to tell him that she knew that already, considering she had been summoned half an hour ago. 'Fourth floor, last office on the right. He said it'll be fine for you to make your own way up.'

'Oh, grand!' Jessica said with a large, beaming smile. 'That must mean that he trusts me not to nick anything *en route*.'

She was standing outside his office door at a little after eight-thirty, quietly determined that she would stay no longer than half an hour. Long enough to brief him on the details of the case, find out his thoughts firsthand, and then anything more detailed could be arranged via their secretaries.

That way, she would be back at her apartment in North London by ten at the latest, just in time to catch the news, microwave a meal and read for half an hour. Any law books would have to wait for another day.

The thick, mahogany door was slightly ajar, so she knocked and pushed it open without waiting for a reply. The room, obviously his secretary's, was empty. Jessica glanced around it, unconsciously noting that it was larger than most of the top directors' offices she had been into in her lifetime, if a little lacking in character. A comfortable, functional room that spoke of high-octane efficiency and an ability to get on with the job without distraction.

She strode purposefully towards a further interconnecting

door, knocked and, without thinking, pushed it open. He had been expecting her, hadn't he?

Obviously not, because he was not alone, and his companion was not a fellow senior worker who might have popped in for a five-minute chat. Not unless his fellow senior workers resembled Barbie dolls.

'I—I'm sorry,' Jessica stammered, embarrassed, 'I had no idea that I was interrupting…'

'Come in.'

Bruno looked not in the least disconcerted by her abrupt arrival. His female companion, however, clearly didn't welcome the intrusion. She turned from where she was half sitting on his desk and looked at Jessica with no attempt to disguise her annoyance.

'You could have knocked,' was her opening line. Her voice, high and girlish, matched the rest of her. She was the perfect male fantasy package. Jessica acknowledged that without a trace of envy. Petite, curvy, with full breasts bursting out of a tight-fitting, long-sleeved top, a skirt that was short enough to leave little to the imagination, and high shoes, which had been discarded. The blonde hair hung in curls past her shoulders and her face was angelic, even if the expression on it wasn't.

'I didn't expect…' Jessica began, not quite knowing where to go from there.

'You never said that your so-called meeting was with a woman!' the girl accused Bruno, pouting.

'I think it's time you left, Rachel,' he said, patting her arm to encourage her off the desk.

'But we need to talk! You promised!' She wriggled unhappily off the desk and stepped into her shoes. Her face was a mixture of frustration and pleading.

'Perhaps you could come over to my place when you're

finished here.' She turned to Jessica. 'You won't be long, will you?'

'No, I don't plan—'

'Close the door behind you after you leave, Rachel,' Bruno interrupted, swerving back behind the desk and tapping into his computer.

Oh, charming, Jessica thought. Was this how he treated all his women? She edged into the room, uncomfortably watching as the dismissed blonde stormed out of the office, slamming the door behind her, then she sat down facing him and placed a sheaf of papers on the desk between them.

'I won't keep you,' she said icily. 'I had rather planned one or two things this evening...'

'Oh, really? What?' He looked up from the computer with a mildly curious expression.

This was not what she had expected. Fool that she was, she had anticipated some sort of apology, if only for the sake of politeness.

TV, a microwave dinner and an early night did not seem the appropriate admission. However, she could not bring herself to tell an outright lie. Instead, she said, 'I need to consult a couple of references in some law books at home...'

'Another fascinating hobby of yours, is it?' The blue eyes glinted with sardonic humour. 'I shudder to think what your dull moments are comprised of.'

Oh, what a keen sense of humour, she thought acidly, excuse me if I don't fall off my chair laughing.

How could she have forgotten quite how irritating the man was?

'I've read every detail of the case that's being put forward,' she said, ignoring his remark completely and tapping the sheaf of papers on the desk. 'And I've highlighted the areas we particularly need to concentrate on.'

He obligingly picked up the lot, scanned through them, replaced them on the desk and asked her if she had eaten.

'I beg your pardon?'

'Have you eaten? Had dinner? Consumed food within the last three hours?'

'I know what you mean,' Jessica snapped, 'I just have no idea why you're asking.'

'It's late. I think we might just as well go out for a quick bite. We can go through all this tomorrow when we're feeling more alert.'

'You're kidding, aren't you?' But he didn't seem to be. She watched, bewildered, as he strolled across to the two-seater sofa by the bookshelf, picked up his jacket and slung it on, followed by a camel-coloured trenchcoat.

'There's a good Italian just around the corner. I can always get a table there.' He stopped to look at her. 'Coming?'

'This is ridiculous,' Jessica spluttered, getting to her feet and feeling utterly manipulated as she shoved all the paperwork back into her briefcase. 'With all due respect, this has been a pointless exercise for me.'

'Oh, I don't know,' he mused, eyebrows raised, 'a meal out is surely more fun than looking up a few legal references...'

'I would say that depends entirely on the company involved,' she muttered stiffly.

'If it's any consolation, we'll talk business for the duration of the meal. How about that?' His phoney, soothing tone of voice got on her nerves even more, and she took a few deep breaths and controlled her temper.

'I'm not dressed for a meal out,' she pointed out, because a wayward thought had suddenly crossed her mind: she didn't want to be alone with Bruno Carr unless there was the reassuring presence of files, desks and computers around.

'Oh, I don't know.' He gave her a leisurely look. 'I'm sure Gino has witnessed the sight of a working woman in a suit before. This *is* the twentieth century, after all, as you were so adamant about pointing out the last time we met.'

He opened the door, stood aside, and she brushed past him with a lofty expression. Diplomacy is the better part of valour, she told herself on the way down in the lift. She was doing this because he was her boss and refusing point-blank was hardly a tactful manoeuvre. If any other man had treated her with such high-handed arrogance, she would have dismissed him on the spot.

That was a comforting thought.

They walked quickly and in silence to the restaurant. In this part of London, there were fewer people about. There were no trendy boutiques to attract the shoppers and not enough fashionable clubs to entice the young and the beautiful.

It was also too cold for dawdling. Within ten minutes they were at the restaurant, which was surprisingly full with an after-work crowd, but the proprietor immediately recognised Bruno and showed them to a table in the furthest corner of the place.

It occurred to Jessica that his girlfriend, or lover, or whoever the small, well-endowed blonde was, would not be impressed to find that his important business meeting had translated itself into a meal at the local Italian.

A suspicious thought began playing at the back of her mind, but she lost it as they were handed menus and the dishes of the day were explained with elaborate, Mediterranean flamboyance.

She had meals out with girlfriends on a fairly regular basis, but it had been a while since she had had a meal out with a man, and against all better judgement she found herself sneaking glances at Bruno as he contemplated the menu in front of him and ordered a bottle of white wine.

It was a unique experience to walk into a room and know that female heads were surreptitiously turning in their direction as they watched and assessed from under lowered lashes. She did not have the immediately captivating face of someone who aroused curious second looks. She was not unattractive, but she knew, deep down, that the few attractions she did possess were played down. Her mind and intelligence were what she wanted on display, rather than her physical attributes. It felt peculiar to be speculated upon by perfect strangers, even if it was simply because she was in the company of Bruno Carr.

He looked up suddenly from the menu and she dropped her eyes, ruffled to think that he might have caught her stare and followed the train of her thoughts from it.

'So,' he said lazily, 'shall we launch immediately into a work-related discussion or would you like to have a glass of wine first?'

Why did she get the impression that, although he recognised her intelligence, he was secretly laughing at her?

'I do have it in me to converse about things other than work,' she told him coldly, unsettled by his attitude. She felt as though he was toying with her, in much the same way that a cat toyed with a mouse. 'I just thought that that was my reason for flying over to see you at this time of the night.'

He ignored that part of her little speech. 'Other things than work...well, I guess that means...play?' He had ordered a bottle of white wine, and he looked at her as he tasted a thumbful, nodded, and then waited while two glasses were poured. 'So, aside from law books and court cases, what other forms of play do you indulge in?'

He tilted his head slightly to one side, sipped his wine and contemplated her with a gravity which she knew was fake. He was highly amused by her and she found it exasperating.

'I'm sure you know,' she informed him calmly, taking a mouthful of wine and savouring the taste on her tongue, 'considering you had my CV in front of you in my office and it was all listed there. But, in case you forgot, I enjoy going to the theatre, reading and foreign travel. What about you?' She looked at him without blinking and decided that two could play that game. 'Oops, sorry. I saw firsthand in your office what sort of play you enjoy indulging in.'

*Had she said that?*

*Had she gone completely mad?*

He grinned at her wickedly. 'I do enjoy going to the theatre, reading, and foreign travel as well. But I'll admit there are other, more absorbing types of play I prefer.'

'Right.' She could feel colour stealing into her cheeks, and she hurriedly drank some more wine. 'Now, shall we discuss this case? At least go over a few things? I'm sure you have a hectic schedule tomorrow and the less—'

'Dear me. Surely you can do better than that.' He shot her a surprised look. 'Just when I thought that we were going to have a little chat about these…things other than work you enjoy talking about.'

'Okay. Then let's talk about why you ordered me over to see you only to drag me out here the minute I step foot through the door.'

'Drag you out here? You have a way with words, don't you?'

'I'm sorry,' Jessica said stiffly, 'I didn't mean to appear rude.'

'Oh, feel free to speak your mind. I appreciate honesty in a person.'

'In that case, I might as well tell you that I'm a great believer in discussion. I don't like being commanded to do things. I realise that you're my boss...'

'And have the authority to tell you precisely what I want you to do...?' His voice was soft and when he drank his wine he continued to look at her over the rim of his glass.

'Theoretically.' The conversation seemed to be getting out of hand and she wondered when they had veered away from the conventional boss-employee line of chit-chat. 'You did say that you wanted me to be honest,' she said a little defensively, in anticipation of criticism.

'Oh, I know. And there's no need to look so alarmed. I'm not about to invoke the wrath of Khan on you for your temerity. After all, we *will* be working together to some extent. We might as well make sure that we can co-operate. I'm a great believer in the open forum.'

'Except for tonight.'

'Except for tonight,' he agreed, half smiling.

'Because...?' She looked at him, and tried to let that suggestion of great charm wash over her. 'Because...' Bruno Carr did things for a reason. 'You wanted me at your office...at that precise moment...because...' It suddenly clicked. 'Because you wanted to get rid of your girlfriend and my appearance was the most convenient way of doing that...am I right?'

'You have a suspicious mind,' he answered, leaning back slightly as plates of food were put in front of them, and vegetables were distributed with flourish. 'It must be the lawyer in you.'

'I don't like being used, Mr Carr.'

'Why don't you call me Bruno? I encourage first names among my employees. Good for company morale. Makes people feel more comfortable.'

'But that's an illusion, isn't it?' Jessica said in a steely voice. 'As tonight proved. You wanted me over because it was an expedient way of getting your girlfriend to leave.'

She could see that he was getting uncomfortable with her persistence but the thought of such blatant manipulation of her stuck in her throat.

'Oh, for God's sake, you're like a dog with a bone. If it makes you feel any better to hear me admit it, then, yes, you're right. You telephoned, and the idea occurred to me that an unavoidable business meeting was just what I needed.'

Jessica finished her glass of wine and it was immediately refilled.

'That's despicable.' She thought it, yes, but she was still amazed when it popped out of her mouth, almost as though any connection between thought and action had been severed. She knew that she ought to apologise. Whatever he said about first names and appreciating honesty and trying to make his employees feel comfortable, he still owned the company she worked for.

But she found it difficult not to voice her objections. She had spent too many years witnessing the price of her mother's silence.

'Why didn't you just tell the poor woman that you were tired of her?'

'*The poor woman?*' All trace of charm had disappeared from his face and he glowered at her. 'You have no idea what you're talking about when you refer to Rachel as *the poor woman*, and I have no idea why I'm bothering to elaborate on any of this with you.'

'Guilt?' she suggested. 'Guilt that I saw through your little manoeuvre? A basic sense of decency in realising that I need some kind of explanation? Even if I *am* only an employee? I wouldn't suggest this normally, but you did say that you enjoyed the open forum.'

He shook his head and raked his fingers through his hair, then he shot her a frustrated, perplexed look from under his lashes. 'So, I gather, do you,' he commented, eyebrows raised, and she smiled serenely at him.

'I'm not in the habit of being quite so outspoken—'

'Not in the habit! God, I should think you send men running in the opposite direction as fast as their legs can take them the minute you confront them with your brand of open forum chit-chat!'

Jessica went bright red and stabbed a few of the vegetables on her plate with misdirected aggression.

'This is ridiculous,' she muttered, eating a mouthful of food that now tasted like sawdust. 'All of this is beside the point. Whatever your reasons for getting me to your office, and whether I approve of them or not, the point of my being here is in my briefcase on the ground.'

'Oh, no, you don't,' he told her darkly. 'You generated this topic of conversation, and we'll finish it.'

'Like you said, you don't owe me an explanation...'

'But we'll be working together and I don't intend to spend my time being treated like some kind of inhuman monster.'

'Does it matter, just so long as we get the job done?'

'Yes, I rather think it does.'

Jessica didn't say anything. She concentrated on her food and waited for him to speak.

'And would you like to know why? Because I wouldn't want you to think that I spend my time chasing women. We'll be working together, and I can't have you feeling threatened, now, can I?' Which, she thought, neatly put her in her place.

'I feel so much better for that. Thank you for setting my anxious mind at rest.'

'Where do you get it from?'

'Get what from?'

'That special talent you have for biting sarcasm? I can't see Robert dealing all that well with that viperlike tongue of yours.'

'Robert,' Jessica informed him stoutly, 'is a sweetie.' And I'm not normally prone to biting sarcasm, she thought to herself, but then again the rest of the human race don't provoke me quite like you do.

'Oh, good grief.' He closed his knife and fork and signalled for another bottle of wine.

Had they consumed one already? She had barely noticed what she had been drinking, and, looking down, she realised that she had done justice to her plate of food, also without noticing.

'And just to clear the air,' he informed her, 'I don't walk around treating women like second-rate citizens.'

'I'm sure you don't.'

'That's right, so you can wipe that supercilious expression off your face.'

'Look, there's really no need…'

'Rachel, just for the record, started off as a bit of fun, but I discovered that she wasn't as content as I thought just to have a good time. Pretty soon, she…she…'

'Wanted more?' Jessica said helpfully.

'Oh, you're aware of the phenomenon, are you?'

'Not personally.'

'Well…' he shrugged and adopted a hangdog expression '…what can a man do?'

The blue eyes scoured her face with boyish bewilderment.

'Oh, please!' Jessica told him awkwardly, recognising that this was the essence of true charm. Bruno Carr, arrogant and self-confident that he was, would never veer into the arena of cruelty, because he genuinely liked women.

His natural instincts were to persuade, even when seduction played no part in a hidden agenda. The ability to flirt was as inherent with him as the ability to breathe. He did it without thinking, which was why he was so adept at it.

'Women.' He raised both shoulders expressively. 'Sometimes I don't think I understand them at all.'

'Really. Now I wonder why I find that so hard to believe.'

'Rachel started talking about the importance of families, of having children, the benefits of settling down.'

'Poor, misguided girl,' Jessica said without a trace of sympathy in her voice for him. 'And what a dreadful predicament for you, I'm sure. One minute, you have a willing, vivacious partner, the next minute she's gazing into jeweller shops and dropping hints about permanence.'

'I'm not the marrying sort,' he said. 'Some men are and some men aren't.'

'You mean it's all in the genes?'

'Whereas all women are. Eventually.'

'Ah. I see.' She nodded slowly. In a strange, masochistic way, and even though she still resented his high-handed behaviour and was appalled by his train of thought, she found that she was enjoying this conversation. She must be mad.

'I mean,' he said, 'you come across as being the archetypal career woman, but, if you were to be brutally honest with yourself, wouldn't you agree that when you see the odd pram being pushed you get a certain pang?'

'What kind of pang?'

'A pang of longing. Something to do with a biological clock, I gather.' He poured another glass of wine for them both.

'Well, not that I've ever recognised, but I suppose if your theory's true then I must subconsciously have that pang lurking in there somewhere.' How come the conversation was suddenly featuring her in the starring role? Her mind was feeling a little unreliable from the wine.

'And you don't?'

Jessica shook her head and frowned. 'I thought we were talking about you,' she said, thinking furiously.

'We were, but then somehow we've ended up talking about you. I think it's important to have some insight into the people who work with me.'

'You mean you enjoy prying into their lives?'

He grinned, and then laughed, and she gave him a wry smile in return.

This was beginning to feel just a little too dangerous for her liking, although she had no idea why. They were simply, at least for the moment, getting along. She got along with lots of people. Most of the human race, in fact. So why did *this* make her feel uneasy? When he raised the bottle to her glass, she shook her head and covered it with the palm of her hand.

'I've drunk enough already,' she told him honestly. 'Any more and I'll be fit for nothing in the morning. I don't have much of a head for alcohol.'

'Lack of practice?'

'Something like that.'

'You mean you don't spend the occasional night seeing the dawn rise with a glass of champagne in your hand?'

'Not routinely, no,' she said. Her hand slipped from round the rim of the glass to the stem, and she curled her fingers lightly around it, not meeting his eye.

Did *he* do that sort of thing on a regular basis? The blonde bombshell looked like the sort of woman who appreciated overblown gestures along those lines, and presumably she was merely an indication of the type of female he went out with.

'Actually,' she said, looking at him, 'I thought people only did that sort of thing in third-rate movies.'

His mouth twitched, but at least he didn't burst into laughter. She had a sneaking suspicion that if he had her remark would somehow have backfired in her face, making her appear dull and unadventurous.

'I take it you don't approve...?'

'Does it matter what I think or not? Oh, I forgot, you like to have insight into your employees. Well, as a matter of fact, I neither approve nor disapprove. I just think that it's not my style.'

'And what *is* your style?'

His voice was a low murmur and his eyes on her were suddenly intense. She felt her skin break out in a faint film of perspiration. It was the wine, of course. Between them, they had managed to drink the better part of two bottles, and that simply was not something she was accustomed to doing. One glass, yes. But virtually a bottle? She was surprised that all she saw on his face was a look of curious interest. She should rightfully be seeing three faces, all blurry, and all with different expressions.

'Work!' she told him, plucking the word from out of the blue.

'Work,' he repeated obligingly. 'I take it that my limited time on getting insight has been exhausted?'

Jessica looked at her watch and realised that they had been at the restaurant far longer than she had imagined.

'I must be getting back!' she exclaimed.

'Before the carriage turns into a pumpkin?' he asked with dry amusement.

'I don't have a carriage,' she answered, choosing to ignore any possible innuendo. 'In fact, I shall have to take a taxi back to my place. I only hope I can find one.'

'Why don't you walk back with me to the office, and I can give you a lift home?'

'That won't be necessary.' A lift home? She thought not. Whether it was the drink or not, the night seemed to have taken her onto unfamiliar ground. She had no desire to prolong the experience. Unfamiliar ground was territory she felt should be better left unexplored. She had never been able to control her background. She had watched in helpless silence as her parents had waged their unremitting cold war and as soon as she had been able to she had left, first to university, then to London. She had learned to exercise control over her life and that had always suited her.

Bruno Carr, however, was not a man who slotted easily into any sort of category she could handle.

As she reached for her briefcase and her bag she realised that the conversation between them had had all the elements of a free fall. How had that happened?

She could feel his eyes on her, and she refused to look at him, at least until she had managed to get some of her thoughts in order.

'It'll be a damned sight more convenient if I give you a lift home,' he said.

'No, thank you. Honestly.' Why was she in such a panic at the suggestion? It made sense. 'Perhaps I ought to telephone for a taxi.' She looked around her, searching for inspiration.

'Come on,' he said, signing his credit-card slip, tearing off his copy, and then standing up. 'Before you collapse in distress at the thought of getting into a car with me.'

She heard the amusement in his voice with a sinking heart. What must he think of her? Another hysterical woman, overreacting at something utterly insignificant. Hardly professional behaviour, was it?

She took a few deep breaths to steady herself.

'I must appear quite ridiculous,' she said in a calmer voice, rooting around for something sensible to say, 'but I had no idea that the evening would be this late, and...' Inspiration! 'I completely forgot that my mum was supposed to call tonight...'

'Ah. Important call, was it?'

'My sister-in-law was due to have her baby today...' Or around now, anyway. 'Mum lives in Australia with my brother and his wife,' she explained. True enough. Three weeks after her father had died, her mum, faced with sudden freedom, had taken flight to the most distant shores possible and was having a wonderful time out there. 'She'll be terribly disappointed that I wasn't at home. Anyway, the sooner I get back the better, so if you don't mind I'll just jump in a taxi and tell him to go as quickly as he can...' She knew that she was beginning to ramble, so she stopped talking and smiled brightly at him. What a pathetic excuse.

'Of course. At times like these, every second counts.' He ushered her out of the restaurant, and as luck would have it hailed a cab within seconds.

'There now,' he said, opening the door for her and peering in as she settled in the back. 'Feel better?'

She felt a complete fool, but she smiled and nodded and tried to inject an expression of relief on her face.

'Tomorrow,' he told her. 'My office. Eight-thirty.' He stood back slightly with his hand on the door. 'Make sure you bring your brain with you. You've got important work ahead of you. Can't have your head addled with thoughts of babies.' With which he slammed the door behind him, and Jessica ground her teeth together in sheer frustration and watched as he strode off along the pavement in the direction of his building.

# CHAPTER THREE

'I SHALL have to look at a drawing of the part in question. Is there any chance at all that it could have been made slightly askew? Grooves in the wrong place? Too many grooves? Too few? Anything at all that might have caused that car to malfunction?'

'Don't be ridiculous.'

Jessica sighed and looked across the table to where Bruno was sitting, his chair pushed back, his legs loosely crossed, with a stack of papers on his lap.

The boardroom was enormous, but he had insisted from the start that it was the only place that could guarantee his uninterrupted time. She still felt dwarfed by its vastness, however, and their voices had that hollow quality peculiar to when people spoke in cavernous surroundings.

'You'll be asked that in the witness box,' she said calmly, 'and I don't think that the answer you just gave me is going to do.' They had been working closely together for three weeks and this was not the first time that she had had to remind him that his answers would have to be laboriously intricate, leaving nothing to the imagination. He had a tendency to bypass all those tedious details, which he assumed everyone should know without having to be told.

'Why not?'

Jessica sighed again, this time a little louder. It was late, her eyes were stinging and she was in no mood to launch into a debate on the whys and wherefores of what could and couldn't be said on the stand. He tapped his fountain pen idly on the stack of papers and continued to look at her through narrowed eyes.

She was certain that he knew precisely how to make her feel uncomfortable. He knew that she was fine just so long as they stuck to their brief, but an errant gesture or a look that hovered just a fraction too long was enough to make her feel hot and bothered. She never showed it, but he could sense her change in mood and was not averse to preying on it for a bit of fun.

'You're being difficult,' she said at last. 'It's late. Perhaps we should wrap it up for the day.' She stood up and he followed her with his eyes, leaning back and clasping his hands together at the back of his head.

She had thought, initially, that she would become immune to his overwhelming personality and those dark, striking good looks, but she hadn't. In the middle of a question, or as he swivelled to one side when he spoke on the telephone, or even at the end of a long day, when he stretched so that his taut, muscular body flexed beneath the well-tailored suit, she could feel her eyes travel the length of his body, she could feel her mouth become suddenly dry.

Now, she dealt with her own treacherous and aggravating response to him by doing her utmost to avoid eye contact.

'*Being difficult?* Explain what you mean by *being difficult.*'

Jessica didn't answer. She walked across the room, removed her jacket and coat from the hanger and then walked back to her pile of papers. Without looking at him, she began sifting through them, pausing to read snatches of reports, then she stuffed the lot into her briefcase and snapped it shut.

'I'm tired too,' she said, meeting his stare reluctantly. 'It's been a long week.'

'You're right,' he surprised her by saying. 'Friday is the

worst day to work late. Don't you agree?' He had slung his jacket over the back of the leather chair, and he stuck it on, tugging his tie off and shoving it into his pocket. Then he undid the top button of his shirt.

Jessica followed all of this with a mortifying sense of compulsion, then she blinked and dragged her eyes away.

The end of the case couldn't come a day too soon as far as she was concerned. Working alongside Bruno Carr was stretching her nerves to breaking-point, and she couldn't quite work out why.

'Fridays are meant for relaxing. Winding down before the business of the weekend.'

She shrugged and made no comment.

'I'll see you on Monday,' she said, facing him.

'I'll get the lift down with you.'

They walked together to the lift and as the doors shut he turned to her and said, 'Big plans for tonight?'

'Not big, no. And you?' His eyes were boring into her but she refused to look at him.

'Small plans, then?'

She clicked her tongue with impatience. There had been no more prying into her personal life, not since that unsettling meal out three weeks previously, but for some reason he was in the mood to stir and she was handy.

'I shall put my feet up and relax.'

'Isn't that what you did last Friday?' he mused thoughtfully, and she clenched her fists tightly around the handle of her briefcase.

'Is it?' she asked innocently, refusing to become bait for his sense of humour. 'I forget. I'm surprised you remember, actually.'

'Oh, I remember everything. It's one of my talents.'

'Along with your modesty.'

He laughed under his breath. 'I hope we aren't working

you too hard...' His voice was speculative, paternal and didn't fool her for an instant. 'I wouldn't want to be accused of coming between you and your love life.'

The doors pinged open, and Jessica breathed a sigh of relief. Bruno was tenacious. When he got hold of something, he was like a dog with a bone, which was fine when it came to work, but when he started directing it at her private life she had an instinctive urge to dive and take cover.

'I'll make sure not to accuse you of any such thing, in that case,' she answered politely. They walked out of the building and into dark, driving rain.

'Have a good weekend.' He strolled off in the direction of the company's underground car park, and five minutes later she saw him sweep away, his car sending up a fine spray.

Jessica held her briefcase awkwardly over her head, ventured to the side of the kerb and waited for a vacant cab which, after fifteen minutes, was beginning to resemble a hunt for the proverbial needle in the haystack.

She should have walked to the underground, but her feet ached, and now it seemed pointless.

She was on the point of returning to the office and calling a taxi when a low-slung, sleek car slowed down and finally stopped in front of her. The window purred down and Bruno contemplated her wet, shivering form with a grin.

'Friday nights can be a bit difficult, especially wet Friday nights. Care for a lift?'

There was no possible excuse she could come up with this time. She could hardly tell him that she was having a grand time right where she was, huddled under her briefcase in a futile attempt not to become absolutely soaked to the skin.

He clicked open the passenger door and she hurried

round to the side, cursing fate, the weather and her idiocy in not walking to the underground, whatever the pathetic state of her aching feet.

'Thanks,' she said, slamming the door behind her. 'Filthy night. I'm afraid I'm dripping all over your seat.' She was feeling more bedraggled by the minute.

'I'm sure the car will recover from the shock of it,' he said gravely. 'Where to?'

She gave him her address, and leaned back, closing her eyes.

'What were you doing back at the office anyway?' she asked, easing her feet out of her shoes but not kicking them off completely.

'Oh, just some work I had to collect.'

'But...' She turned to look at his profile. 'Did you get what you returned for?'

'No. I saw your wet, forlorn shape and decided to do my good deed for the week instead.'

'How considerate.' As fast as the windscreen wipers cleared the screen, it became blurred with more running water.

'That's the sort of person that I am.'

He seemed, she thought, in a remarkably good mood considering he had found himself having to drive miles out of his way to deliver her to her house.

'I hope,' she said suddenly, 'I'm not ruining your plans for the evening.'

'Not at all. Don't give that another thought. I'd planned on spending the night in, actually.' He paused. 'Painting my nails and washing my hair.'

In the darkness, Jessica grinned. She had never known a man who could switch from aggressive to funny with such ease. In fact, she had never known a man whose personality was so complex. He could be ruthless, single-minded, persistent, utterly exasperating and madly, unbearably sarcastic. He could also be charming, witty and disconcertingly easygoing. Perhaps he had a split personality.

'Carry on along this road until you come to the next junction, then turn left.'

'How's your sister-in-law's baby?' he asked, after a few minutes' silence.

'My sister-in-law's baby?'

'The one she was due to have on the very day you couldn't possibly accept a lift home with me because you had to get back for a telephone call from your mother.'

'Oh. That sister-in-law. That baby.' That convoluted excuse. 'Both well and doing fine.' She had had the baby three days later, so as far as lies went that one was pretty close to the truth.

'Must be glad to have your mother out there to help,' he said casually, and Jessica didn't reply. She was not a revealing person by nature, and she seldom, if ever, discussed her family with anyone. Her background and all the attendant heartache was something she kept to herself.

'Guess so.'

'How long has your mother been over there? Seems a very far-flung place to go and live.'

'My brother was out there,' she said shortly, staring out of the window. Through the rain and the darkness, the lights looked like watery splashes of colour against a black, velvet background.

'But you were over here,' he pointed out, and she didn't say anything.

'I take it your silence means that I'm treading on delicate ground.'

'You're treading on ground that's none of your business,' she told him bluntly. 'Go straight over the traffic lights and my street's the third turning on the right.'

'How does your father fit into all this?'

Her fists curled into tight balls and she felt a knot of acid bitterness gather in her stomach. She had so successfully managed to slot her father into a disused cupboard in her mind that every time his memory was pulled out and dusted down, for whatever reason, she was overcome with the same, familiar feelings of anger.

'He died seven years ago,' she said tightly.

There must have been some indication of how she felt in her voice, because he glanced swiftly at her before turning back to the road.

'Should I offer you my sympathies?'

'You can offer whatever you care to.' Her father had spent his years ruling his house with a reign of terror, bellowing at her and her brother, lashing out at whoever had happened to be closest if his mood had happened to be off-key. Sympathy was the least appropriate feeling she could be offered, but there was no way that she would tell any of that to the man sitting next to her behind the steering wheel.

'My house is the third on the right. Bit hard to see in this weather, but you can just drop me off here.'

He slowed the car down and as she turned to face him, ready with her neat phrases of thanks and hope-it-wasn't-too-much-of-a-bother, he said, killing the engine and resting his head against the window, 'A cup of coffee would be nice. These are hellish conditions to be driving in.' He rubbed his eyes with his thumbs and she felt a pull of sympathy. He had been under no obligation to pick her up and drop her at her house, and whatever he had said about having no plans for that evening she was pretty certain that he had had. He was not a man to enjoy the comforts of a solitary meal, a cup of cocoa and a late-night movie, on a Friday night.

'Sure.' She got out of the car, only realising how thoroughly she had been drenched when the weight of her coat threatened to drag her to the ground. Her hair was still damp as well. She would look like a scarecrow in the morning.

'And perhaps you could rustle up something for us to eat,' he suggested, following her to the front door, then into the house.

In winter, she always made sure that she left the hall light on, so that when she returned home the place wasn't in complete darkness. And the heating had switched itself on three hours previously, so that it was beautifully warm inside. She felt some of the chill drain out of her bones.

'Rustle you up something to eat?' she asked, removing her coat and jacket and looking at him with incredulity.

'Nothing fancy. Just whatever you were going to do for yourself.' He was looking around without making it glaringly obvious, and he followed her into the small sitting room, with the large bay window overlooking the street. It was her favourite room in the house, the one she spent most of her time in, and had been decorated in warm, rich colours—deep greens and terracottas—and she had replaced the sixties-style electric fire with a real one, seldom used but beautiful to look at.

He strolled around it, dwarfing it in a way no one ever had before, looking at the photos of her mother and her brother with his family in their carefully chosen wood and silver frames. Did he notice that pictures of her father were conspicuously absent?

'I think it might be a good idea if you change,' he said out of the blue, turning to look at her, and she flushed. Yes, that had occurred to her but, no, she had had no intention of doing any such thing. Her working garb, however damp and bedraggled, was, somehow, her protection.

'Do you ever stop giving orders?' she asked politely.

'It's a bad habit of mine. You'll catch your death of cold if you stay like that.'

Jessica glared and watched as he removed his jacket, tossed it on to one of the chairs and sat down, stretching out his long legs in front of him.

'I won't be a minute,' she muttered.

Never mind bad habits, she thought, the man had some insufferable traits. She shut the bedroom door behind her, hesitating briefly, then locking it, though why she had no idea, and she stepped out of her shoes with a sigh of relief. Then she hurriedly flung on a white tee shirt and a pair of jeans, and replaced her shoes with the pair of worn, flat-heeled sandals she wore around the house.

She glanced at her reflection in the mirror and then unpinned her hair, which had optimistically started the day as a perfectly coiled chignon. With speed born of habit, she plaited it, one long, blonde plait. Not exactly a sophisticated hairdo, she thought, but it would have to do.

When she returned, it was to hear rummaging in the kitchen, and she found him there with two wineglasses in his hand.

'I see you had some wine in your fridge.'

'Go right ahead and make yourself at home.'

'Care for a glass?' The bottle was on the kitchen table and, with a huge sigh of resignation, she nodded and he poured them both a glass.

'I really wouldn't want to keep you from whatever you had planned,' she began, folding her arms, uncomfortably aware that despite his casual attitude he had taken in her change of clothes, her alteration from businesswoman to homebody.

'Your hair is much longer than I thought.'

He had noticed *her hair*? What else had he noticed?

'There's not much to eat here. I'm not accustomed to cooking for someone else without preparation.'

'You wouldn't be trying to get rid of me, by any chance?' he asked, sitting on one of the chairs by the table and looking at her. There was amused challenge in his blue eyes and she went pink.

Was he a mind-reader or was she just a lot more obvious than she thought?

And what would he think if she admitted that she felt uncomfortable being in her house with him? She knew what he would think. He would think that he made her nervous, he would think that she felt more than merely the polite indifference of employee towards employer, which she had been at such pains to cultivate over the past few weeks. He would think that she was attracted to him.

She should have laughed at this conclusion, but instead of laughing to herself she felt a sudden surge of alarm.

'Of course I'm not trying to get rid of you!' she denied, her voice high. 'I just can't believe that you haven't got something more interesting to do on a Friday night than sit here and have a dreary meal with one of your employees.' It seemed a good idea to remind him that he was her boss.

'Between Rachels at the moment,' he said, and she could hear laughter in his voice.

So he was temporarily lacking in female companionship. That would account for the fact that some of that unused charm was spilling over onto her. He probably couldn't help himself. Under normal circumstances, she would be the last woman in the world he would look at twice, but they had been working closely together for a few weeks, albeit not always in perfect harmony, and he was without the distraction of a mistress.

'Poor old you,' she gushed with overdone sympathy. 'Your brain must be missing the intellectual stimulation.'

She paused, and then added, grudgingly, 'I apologise, that was uncalled for. She seemed a perfectly nice girl.' When in the company of men, she thought to herself.

'Oh, I think I'm doing all right on that front at the moment.' He tilted his glass towards her with a mocking salute, and she turned around and began foraging through the cupboards in search of something palatable for them to eat.

Her dietary requirements were virtually non-existent. Living on her own, she ate when she felt like it and very rarely cooked for herself. Pre-packaged foods were the norm, or else fresh bread and cheese. Sometimes, when she was particularly tired or particularly lazy, a bowl of cereal filled the gap.

She located a can of tuna and some tinned sweetcorn and then scoured the fridge for whatever else might be lurking there. Three tomatoes, she found, a bag of mushrooms which she had planned on using two days previously and half a tub of cream, which she surreptitiously sniffed just in case.

Clearing out her fridge on a daily basis was always one of her New Year's resolutions, and thus far never one that she had actually got around to putting into practice.

'Would you like a hand?' he asked from behind her and she shook her head.

'No. But I feel I should warn you that cooking was never one of my strong points, so don't expect anything exquisite.' She glanced over her shoulder to see him wearing that amused grin of his, the sort of grin that implied that her discomfort was a never-ending source of enjoyment to him.

'Oh, don't apologise. Lack of culinary skills is a trait I thoroughly approve of in a woman.'

'Strange. I thought that the way to a man's heart was through his stomach.' It was all right having this conversation with him while her back was turned away and while she could busy herself with the frying of mushrooms and tuna and all the ingredients that seemed to be converging into a colourful mishmash of food. Lord only knew what it would taste like. Whenever she cooked for someone else, she always made sure that a recipe book was close to hand. Spontaneous creations were things she tried to avoid at all costs.

'My point exactly.'

Jessica risked a look at him from over her shoulder, to gauge whether he was joking, but his expression was serious.

'Am I supposed to ask you to clarify?'

'I would have thought that I was being fairly obvious.'

'In other words, the way to your heart is firmly blocked off with a "No Trespassing" sign.'

Actually, she didn't need him to spell that out for her. One look at him was enough to tell her that he was a man who preferred the freedom to do precisely what he pleased without the obstruction of a wife. He worked long hours, was away for long stretches of time on business. In between, she assumed, he liked simple, undemanding recreation with someone who didn't tire him by challenging his intellect.

Her voice was light when she spoke. She stirred the contents of the saucepan, hoping that her mysterious, thrown-together concoction would not taste too appalling, and when she gauged that it was nearly cooked she put a pot of water to boil for some pasta. Then she sat down at the kitchen table and took a sip from her glass of wine.

She idly wondered what he would look like in jeans and a tee shirt. He had the sort of physique that was designed to look good in clothes. Wide shoulders, lean hips, long, muscular legs. Her heart began to beat a little faster.

'Was that Rachel's downfall?' she asked curiously. It
occurred to her that this was hardly a typical boss-employee
kind of conversation. She had had many amiable chats with
Robert, her immediate boss, about his family, his grand-
children, his holiday plans. None of them had carried this
intangible air of treading on delicate ground. She could feel
herself stepping too close to quicksand, but when she
looked a bit harder, to see if she could recognise the danger,
there was nothing there.

He had given her a lift home because of the weather.
She had invited him inside through politeness. She was now
cooking him a meal out of guilt at having spoilt his evening. Where was the danger in that?

And if they weren't consumed with work talk, then what
was the problem there? It was hardly as though she feared
that he might suddenly draw a deep breath and lunge for
her.

'I enjoy the family life,' he said with a careless shrug,
'just so long as it belongs to someone else.'

Jessica didn't answer. She tossed some pasta into the
boiling water and then remained where she was with the
glass in her hand, leaning against the kitchen counter.

She could understand what he was saying. The companionship of married life was never something that had beckoned. Her friends had taken to making dark comments
about shelf-life, and intimating that they would arrange a
love life for her if she didn't want to do it herself, and she
always laughed at their underhand persistence. She simply
could not conceive what it would be like to be tied to the
cooker, waiting on a man hand and foot. As her mother
had done for so many years.

'How do you feel about the lawsuit?' she asked, changing the subject abruptly. She didn't like it when her mind
started wandering down the road of men and marriage and

families, even if her response was to deny their importance in her life.

'Isn't that a question I should be asking *you*?' he returned, helping himself to more wine and watching her lazily as she began moving around the kitchen, opening drawers, pulling out crockery and cutlery.

She could feel his blue eyes on her and it made her skin tingle. It was a new experience for her. Normally, she had no difficulty in treating men as her equals but now, for some reason, she was acutely aware of her body, her movements, her hair dangling against her back. Her tee shirt was baggy and unrevealing, but she could feel the weight of her breasts beneath it, she could feel her nipples pushing against the thin, silky bra. A thin film of perspiration broke out over her body and when she began setting the table she found that she was purposefully avoiding his gaze.

'I don't think we have a problem,' she said, draining the pasta and tipping the contents of the frying pan into a casserole dish. 'When do you think I'll be able to have a look at those drawings?' She put the pasta and the tuna on the table and indicated for him to help himself.

'Oh, haven't I mentioned? Ralph Jennings delivered them to me this afternoon. I've got them in my briefcase, as a matter of fact.'

'You have?' She paused and looked at him with surprise. 'You should have mentioned that sooner. We could have gone over them at work.'

'You can have a look after we've eaten.' He began helping himself and she looked at him with sudden dismay.

Inexplicably, she didn't want him hanging around after dinner. She had anticipated feeding him and sending him on his way in the minimum amount of time.

'You haven't got a problem with that, have you?' he

asked, glancing up to catch her eye, and she shook her head hurriedly.

'No. I just feel a little…tired… I'm not sure I'll be able to concentrate fully…'

'It's a drawing,' he pointed out dryly. 'Fairly self-explanatory. It'll take ten minutes for me to run through it with you.'

'Yes. Fine,' she said dubiously, sitting down.

'Good. And don't worry about the concentration aspect. Even at half tilt, your brain is better than a lot of men's I've come across in my business dealings.'

'Thank you very much for the compliment.' She was certain that there had been a time when she would have been thrilled at what he had just said, but now she had a hollow feeling of disappointment. She supposed that it was akin to being described as 'one of the lads'. Was that *ever* a compliment for a woman? Who wanted to be 'one of the lads'?

For the first time ever, she wondered what it would be like to be remarked upon for her looks as opposed to her brains. Her boyfriends had always appreciated her intelligence, had warmed to the fact that she had definite opinions on most things, and she had never found that a matter for complaint.

Now, she thought, What would it be like to be a Rachel? Blonde and fluffy and undemanding, with bedroom eyes and a smile that promised sex?

Ridiculous notion, she told herself shakily.

But now that the thought had taken root, it began eating away inside her, nibbling insidiously at all her firmly held beliefs that intelligence in a woman was what mattered, that men who were attracted to the outside packaging were not the sort of men she could ever be interested in.

She heard his voice wash over her as he discussed intricacies of the lawsuit, and she knew that she was responding with all the correct answers, but it was as if she was suddenly functioning on autopilot, while her brain wandered along its merry way.

She was not an unattractive woman. She knew that. True, she might not be overtly sexy in the way that the Rachels of this world were, but neither was she a picture of plainness. Her problem, she realised, was her inability to play up her good points. Her figure was quite acceptable, but she never wore tight clothes. Her long, well-shaped legs were always hidden under calf-length skirts or trousers. Her hair, thick and long and naturally blonde, was always pinned back severely into her neck. Her approach was essential in her career, but it hardly turned heads, did it?

Just thinking like this flustered her, and she couldn't wait for the meal to finish, hastily rejecting his offer to help with the washing-up, rambling on about doing it herself after he had gone because she found it strangely relaxing. Good heavens. Washing dishes was something she found strangely tedious, but the thought of standing next to him at a kitchen sink and doing a mundane domestic chore was almost beyond her level of tolerance.

'What about the drawings?' he asked, after she had cleared the table and positioned herself by the kitchen door in readiness for his departure. He stood up, stretched slightly, and she dragged her eyes away from him.

'In the sitting room, I guess,' she said brightly, with a sinking heart. She had forgotten the wretched drawings.

They walked through to the sitting room, where the lighting seemed mellow and intimate after the fluorescent glare of the overhead kitchen lights, and she sat down on the edge of the sofa and waited as he pulled some papers out of his briefcase.

Then he sat next to her and spread the drawings out on

the low, square coffee-table in front of them. His weight had depressed the sofa. She could feel her thigh lightly touching his and she did her utmost to ignore the sensation. She peered obligingly at the various angles he was pointing out to her, and she nodded and made all the right noises under her breath, but her eyes were mesmerised by his long fingers, and against her his thigh was scorching through her jeans, making all her nerve-endings come alive.

'These are the originals,' he said, inclining very slightly to look at her, and their eyes tangled, brown with blue. Their faces were so close that she could see the fine lines around his eyes, could appreciate the dark thickness of his eyelashes. Could eyelashes be sultry? There was something sultry about his eyelashes. 'Naturally, I shall get copies for the court appearance next week.'

'Naturally,' Jessica said faintly.

'If you want to hang on to these for the weekend…? Have a look at them?' He was looking at his watch, standing up, and she wondered whether he had had enough of her company now. The novelty of conversing with an intelligent woman was wearing off. It was time for him to be on his way. His mind was already striding ahead, planning the rest of his weekend. Was there a replacement Rachel hovering somewhere in the wings? Probably.

'Yes, that would be helpful.' She levered herself off the couch and plastered a bland but wide smile on her face. 'Now, I think my work with you is pretty much finished,' she said, holding on to the smile with difficulty, but loath to let go of it because she had no idea what it would be replaced by. 'So next week I shall take up permanent residence once again at my own office.' She walked him to the door, arms folded.

'And take over where Robert left off.' He turned to her

with a smile. 'Whatever the outcome, you appear to have done a thorough job on this damned lawsuit.'

'As thorough as any man?'

He raised one eyebrow expressively. 'Is that a hint that you want an apology from me?'

'I wouldn't be so mad,' she said wryly, and in the awkward intervening few seconds, as she wondered what next to say, he solved the dilemma by holding out his hand.

'Good work, Miss Stearn. You have the job.' He grinned as he shook her hand, then he was gone. Out of the door, into his car and away into the night.

On a handshake.

She shut the door reflectively behind her and the last thing to go through her head that night was the foggy image of his mouth on hers, his hands exploring her body, his body against her. No handshake. Just something else.

# CHAPTER FOUR

IT WAS in the newspapers. Bruno Carr, after all, was news. He might not be a movie star, Jessica reflected, or a TV personality, but he had the looks, the money and the charisma to grab headlines. The newspapers carried the same image—Bruno emerging from court with his name fully cleared.

Red-nosed, dosed up with paracetamol, and in bed, Jessica read the full commentary in the business section of the newspaper and then re-read it four times.

We did it! she thought. She might have been an important part in piecing together all the evidence, but it had taken a great deal of persistent hard slog, and she had no doubt that her four staff who had worked overtime and weekends to make sure that the case was wrapped up in the minimum amount of time were feeling as euphoric as she was. If a little less under the weather.

It was just a shame that she couldn't have been at the court to witness the victory herself.

She blew her nose into some tissues and flung them into the waste-paper basket which she had strategically placed next to the bed, and which was becoming progressively fuller.

Bruno Carr had swept into her life like a tornado, and now that her part had been played he would vanish without leaving a trace. She lay back on the pillows, closed her eyes and succumbed to feelings of maudlin self-pity.

It was this wretched bug, of course. That was why she felt so low. She had spent the weekend feeling vaguely washed out, and that had progressed onto the familiar aching bones, fever, runny nose and desire to keep the curtains tightly drawn. She hadn't had flu in years. Normally, she was as healthy as a horse.

'Your immune system's up the spout,' her friend Amy had informed her, when she had telephoned earlier in the week to cancel their dinner arrangement. 'You need to take a break.'

So here I am now, she thought glumly, taking a much-deserved break. Who in their right mind would choose to go for a week's vacation to somewhere hot, exotic and sunny when they could lie in bed, sneezing and running a fever instead? That was what standing in the driving, cold rain waiting for a non-existent taxi did for a girl.

She punched the pillows, buried her head in them with a stifled groan, and was debating whether she should bother to leave the bed at all for the rest of the day when the doorbell went.

Through the pillows, it was a muffled noise, and Jessica muttered a venomous, 'Go away' to whoever had the nerve to call when she was indisposed.

The rings became less polite and more insistent, and she eventually dragged herself out of bed, slung on her dressing gown and padded across to the front door.

When she yanked it open and saw Bruno standing outside, his hand poised to press the bell again, she scowled ferociously, aware of the less-than-stunning picture she presented with her runny, red nose and her hair flopping every which way as though it hadn't seen a comb in years.

'How are you feeling?' he asked, and her scowl deepened. It was eleven-thirty in the morning, she was still in her pyjamas and dressing gown, the kitchen was proudly sporting dishes that had not been washed for two days. It seemed a particularly stupid question. 'Everyone's very concerned about you. They seem to have been under the illusion that you have an in-built immunity to ill health.' He grinned slightly. 'Naturally I rushed over because if that's the case you're about to go down in medical history. There could be a fortune in it for you.'

'I feel the way I look,' she told him, pulling her robe tighter around her and reaching behind with one hand to try and get her hair into some sort of order. 'Congratulations, by the way. I read several versions of it in the newspapers.' She gave him a wry look. 'Not that it would take a genius to work out what the outcome had been. You'll have to be careful not to blind people with your high spirits.'

'Mind if I come in? It's freezing out here. Won't do your cold any good at all if you have to stand by an open door having a conversation with me.'

Come in? A social call? He stared at her, refusing to be willed away, until she eventually stood aside to let him in, then she shoved the door shut behind her.

'I'm not good with people when I'm ill,' she told his back as he headed in the direction of the sitting room, for all the world as though he belonged there. 'I'm snappy, short-tempered and I'd really rather just be left alone to get on with my recuperation.' She stood with her hands on her hips and watched as he removed his jacket, dropped it inelegantly on the coffee-table, and then settled into a chair.

'Yes, quite a victory.' He didn't pause to let her answer. 'As you couldn't make it to the court, I thought I'd drop by to congratulate you personally on the result.'

'I didn't do it on my own,' Jessica informed him, thawing slightly but still not enough to view his presence in the house with warmth. 'We all worked very hard to make sure that it got resolved as quickly as possible.'

'And I have congratulated them all myself.'

'Right. That's very good of you.' She paused and sneezed, fishing a tissue out of the pocket of her dressing gown.

'Have you been to a doctor?'

He wasn't going to oblige by vanishing through the front door. Jessica reluctantly sat down on the sofa and tucked her feet underneath her.

She would never have admitted it in a million years, but the thought of being seen by him in all her snuffling lack of glory was enough to make her cringe with self-consciousness. She had always maintained that the body was infinitely less important than the mind, but right now she would have given her right arm to at least have had the foresight to have changed into normal clothes earlier on. Instead of blearily thinking that it involved just too much effort.

'Doctors can't do anything for viruses,' she said. 'You just have to wait for them to take their course.'

'You look a wreck.'

'Oh, thank you very much,' Jessica replied, knowing that it was perfectly true, but nonetheless not caring for his observation. 'It did occur to me when I got up this morning that I should camouflage my red nose under six layers of cleverly applied make-up, but my eyes were watering too much for me to see what I was doing, and I gave up halfway through. 'Course, if I'd known that I was going to be bombarded with visitors, I might have persisted in my efforts.'

'Tut-tut. You certainly weren't kidding when you said that all good humour flew through the window the minute you got ill.'

'Did I say that?'

'Along those lines. Now, why don't you stay where you are and I'll go and fetch you a cup of tea?'

'That's very kind, but, really, there's no need. I appreciate your gesture in coming over here...' ha, ha '...but I'd really rather be on my own. And I'm sure you can think of better ways of celebrating your victory than sharing a room with me and thousands of contagious little germs....' She yawned, only remembered to put her hand over her mouth halfway through, and squashed herself into a more comfortable position on the sofa.

'Nonsense! You should have someone around here, though, to help out if you're ill. Is there no one who could come round and look after you?'

'I don't need looking after!' Jessica said, more sharply than she had intended. 'I'm perfectly capable of looking after myself.'

'I take it that means no.' He stood up, waving her back down when she attempted to follow suit, and she heard him as he headed to the kitchen, then the muffled noises of him making them a cup of tea.

Why had she become so defensive just then? He had asked a perfectly reasonable question and she had jumped down his throat, and the worst of it was she knew why. She had no one. Oh, she had a handful of friends. They went out and had a good time every so often, but there was no one who could come around and look after her if she ever needed looking after.

She was twenty-eight years old, successful in her career, owned her own house and could afford to go on holiday whenever she cared to, but what did all that count for when at the end of the day she had no one to share any of it with?

She couldn't remember thinking this way before. She had measured her worth as she'd climbed the steady ladder of success. She had watched as her friends had married, settled down, in a couple of cases had their first children, and she had never felt the stirrings of envy. She had been vaguely curious as to how their lifestyles would change, but she had held on to her own steady fortunes in the never-ending stormy waters of chance with a feeling of relief.

'Not everyone needs a caretaker,' she announced as Bruno walked back in with a mug of tea in his hand, and he looked at her questioningly.

'You've lost me.'

Jessica took a sip of hot tea, made a face, and then looked at him as he settled on the sofa, which meant that she now wouldn't be able to stretch out her legs if she wanted to.

'I can look after myself,' she told him. 'I don't want you to feel sorry for me.'

'I don't recall mentioning that I did.'

'You don't have to mention it. You can imply it without saying so in so many words.'

'Okay. If it makes you feel happier, I won't feel sorry for you.'

There he goes again, she thought with exasperation, patronising. He *did* feel sorry for her, and it had nothing to do with her temporary ill health. He felt sorry for her because he compared her to the women he knew, women who went out every night and owned a wardrobe full of designer outfits, women whose lives were never free of men, who skirted from one relationship to another without pause in between. She could feel it in the way he looked at her sometimes.

'Good,' she said, disgruntled.

'How are you eating?'

'With my teeth, like everyone else.' His concern, for some reason, was catapulting her into another bout of self-pity. When was the last time anyone had brought her a cup of tea? she thought, on the verge of tears at this point.

'I see your cold hasn't done away with that viper tongue of yours.' His mouth twitched, and she steadfastly refused to look at him. She cradled the mug in her hands, feeling the warm, rough texture under her fingers. It was vaguely soothing.

'Have you eaten?' he asked bluntly.

'Why? Are you about to offer your talents as in-house chef?' The man was simply trying to be pleasant, but for some reason she found it hard to stomach. She wished he had stuck to the brief he had initially presented to her—of a man who was ruthless, self-assured, autocratic and took pains to hide none of those qualities. She couldn't cope with his wit, his sense of humour and, worst, his attempts to be considerate.

'Look,' he said, standing up, 'I'm beginning to wish that I hadn't bothered to drop by. If you'd rather lie and wallow in your misery, then far be it from me to disturb you.' He reached down for his jacket, and Jessica took a deep breath.

'I…' she struggled, looking at her fingers. 'I…I'm…'

'I haven't got all day. Spit it out.'

Wasn't that more like it? He damned well knew what she wanted to say, but he was going to make sure that he didn't let her off the hook.

'I'm sorry if I appeared rude.'

'You didn't *appear* rude. You *were* rude.'

Jessica blushed. 'Okay. I apologise.' This seemed insufficient. He still had his jacket in his hand, and she now realised that she desperately did not want him to leave. She didn't want her final impression on him to be of an ill-mannered, surly, belligerent woman who had neither the good grace nor common courtesy to express her thanks to someone who had paid her a visit out of kindness. Much as she loathed the thought of being seen as a charity case, which was what his kindness implied.

'I'm so accustomed to my independence that I don't deal very well when my body lets me down. I have a pile of work waiting for me at the office, and I simply cannot afford to take time off to be ill.'

'The place won't self-destruct because you're out of it for a few days.' He sighed, and she eyed him surreptitiously as he dumped the jacket back on the coffee-table and looked at her. 'So have you eaten? A simple yes or no answer will do.'

'Not much,' Jessica admitted reluctantly.

'I'll make you something.'

Before she could object, he sauntered off and she lay back and closed her eyes. She wouldn't swap her lifestyle for any of her married friends' lifestyles, of course she wouldn't, but for a minute she conceded that there might be one or two advantages to the married life. One of them had to be a husband who fetched cups of tea when necessary. None of her previous boyfriends had ever come near to fitting any such role, and Bruno Carr, despite the fact that he could bring a grin to her lips at the least expected moments, was definitely not the sort of man who could ever be a contender, but... She imagined someone thoughtful, caring, kind, good background and a dab hand at cooking. Might not be too bad after all.

She was nodding off when Bruno said from over her, 'Wake up, Sleeping Beauty. Feeding time.'

Jessica rubbed her eyes and sat up, swinging her legs over the side of the sofa to accommodate the tray he was carrying.

'Nothing very fancy, I'm afraid.'

He set the tray on her lap, and her mouth watered at the sight of two slices of toast smothered in creamy scrambled egg. Much better than anything she could have produced herself, but then scrambled eggs had always been a problem for her.

'Thank you very much,' she said, tucking into the food, and only realising the depth of her hunger when she bit into the toast and egg. She had eaten nothing for the past day and a half. 'Tastes delicious.'

'Things have a tendency to, when someone else does the cooking.' He perched on the coffee-table and regarded her.

'You do this often, do you?' she asked absent-mindedly, concentrating on feeding her hunger as rapidly as she could without appearing utterly inelegant in the process.

'I think this is a first for me,' he told her dryly, and she shot him a quick, surprised look.

'Clever of you to avoid going out with women who catch the occasional cold,' she said mildly. 'Or do you just avoid them when they're careless enough to get ill?'

'Care to fill me in on precisely what you're saying?'

'I'm not saying anything.' She ducked her head and concentrated on eating.

'Oh, yes, you are. I've noticed something about you. You're good at initiating criticism, in that cowardly, backhanded fashion of yours, but you don't like it if it's pursued, do you? You're not up to defending anything you say.'

'It wasn't meant to be a criticism,' Jessica mumbled, mortified at what he had said, which was perfectly true. 'It was just an observation.'

'I don't make it a habit of cooking for women, any more than I make it a habit of having women cook for me.'

'Should I consider myself flattered, in that case?' She asked the question without thinking about it, but when she looked at him his eyes were cool and speculative.

'You can consider it anything you want to. As far as I'm concerned, it just means that you're not my woman.'

He let the words sink in, in all their brutal simplicity. She was his employee, and that was the full extent of it. Beyond that, she meant nothing at all to him, and so whether she made him a meal, or he cooked her some eggs, was irrelevant. Theirs was not a relationship and so was not threatening.

'But that's not why I came here. I came here to congratulate you on the court case, and found you ill and clearly incapable of looking after yourself...'

'I am perfectly capable of looking after myself!' Jessica retorted indignantly.

'So you've told me. Is that why you looked as though you hadn't eaten for a week?'

'I didn't get around to it...' she returned, feeling more and more like a charity case, and hating it.

'So I made you something to eat.' He shrugged and stood up.

Does he think that I'm trying to attach significance to that? she wondered, with a growing sense of shame. Did he think that she was after him, looking for ways of misinterpreting simple actions into something meaningful?

Yes. Of course he thought that. She could feel herself getting hot and flustered and horribly embarrassed.

He was the archetypal eligible bachelor. She suspected that he would have spent his entire adult life being pursued by women. It would hardly surprise him if he thought that she had joined the queue. She cringed inwardly. Good Lord, he was warning her off him!

'Yes, I know. I know, I know, I know. I'm being a bore. It's this inactivity. I hate it. I need to be *doing*.' She transferred tray from lap to table.

'Makes you feel like a worthwhile member of society, does it?'

Jessica closed her eyes and rested her head against the

back of the sofa. 'Something like that. Either that or I'm an undiagnosed hyperactive and in desperate need of medication.'

'You should try slowing down now and again.'

She half opened her eyes and looked at him. 'Do you?'

'No, but I'm a man.' He waited for her expression to change and then burst out laughing. 'Works a treat every time! Now you have a steaming cold to contend with and high blood pressure from trying to stifle your little flare of self-righteous anger at my remark, but at least the wallowing inclination's disappeared for the moment. Now, doctor's orders: I shouldn't bother coming into work for the rest of the week.' He eyed her up and down in the manner of a scientist sizing up a particularly stubborn strain of bacteria.

'I'll see how it goes,' Jessica said vaguely, not caring for his jovial brand of high humour. Of all the things he made her feel, feminine was not in the list and she wondered whether it was his deliberate ploy to remind her that any concern for her was purely altruistic.

She remembered Rachel, with the flaxen hair and baby-doll look; Rachel who had made the mistake of becoming a little too clingy and therefore had had to be dispensed with. Did he imagine that she might have seen his small act of kindness as encouragement?

She began standing up and he waved her down.

'Actually, I haven't quite said what I came to say,' he informed her, slinging on his jacket.

'Which is?'

'You and your team have done a fine job, and I want to recognise that.'

'I'm sure it's enough for you to tell them that personally,' Jessica said, omitting to mention that a bonus would probably do the trick even more.

'Which is why,' he carried on, ignoring her input, 'I wanted to ask your advice.'

'*My* advice? Where's my diary? I should make a note of this red-letter day.'

'I'll put that remark down to ill health.' He gave her another wolfish grin. 'You know your team far better than I do.'

'True.' She nodded sagely, then, unable to resist the temptation, added, 'They really don't see much of you, considering you *are* their boss.'

He frowned, and she smiled placidly at him.

'I thought a weekend away might be a nice idea...'

'A weekend away? Where?' She hoped he wouldn't suggest a health farm. She couldn't think of a single member of her staff who would appreciate a weekend at a health farm. They were all far too young to see the advantages of a place that offered only nutritional food on their menu and a complete absence of alcohol.

'Somewhere hot, I think, don't you?'

They both automatically looked in the direction of the bay window, through which leaden skies promised the worst of English weather.

'I'm sure they would be thrilled,' Jessica said, with genuine sincerity. 'This weather's awful, isn't it?'

'Grim.'

'When did you have in mind?'

'This weekend, actually. If the office could do without manning for a couple of days.'

'*This weekend?*' The man obviously had no touch with reality if he thought that tickets to anywhere in the Med could be bought at such short notice. 'And of course the office would be manned. Why shouldn't it be?'

'By whom?'

'Well, me for a start, and then there are the secretaries

and all the other people who have had nothing to do with the lawsuit…'

'Fourteen in all, including yourself.'

'You want to take the entire office on a weekend to somewhere hot?' She gave an incredulous laugh.

'What are your objections?'

'Oh, none at all!' Jessica informed him airily. 'Of course, the airlines might have a few. I doubt any of them could fly thirteen people over to sunny Spain at a moment's notice!'

'Whoever mentioned sunny Spain? Which, incidentally, wouldn't be all that sunny at this time of the year. And what do airlines have to do with anything?'

'Well, how else would you suggest they travel?' she asked, with a hint of saccharine sarcasm in her voice. 'Swim?'

'I own a small private jet.'

'You…own…a…private…jet… Of course, don't we all? What household is complete without one?'

'I also own an island in the Caribbean,' he drawled.

*'You own an island in the Caribbean?'* She stared at him, open-mouthed.

'Of course. Don't we all? What household is complete without one?'

Jessica went pink. Why was it that her mouth seemed to develop a will of its own the minute this man was around?

'So you're planning on whisking my entire office off to your private island, in your private jet, for a long weekend.'

'That's about the size of it. Do you think that they would appreciate the gesture?'

'Appreciate might be understating their reaction.' She thought that they might just keel over from shock, and one or two of the older ones, Mary and Elizabeth, in their fifties, might well have to be resuscitated.

'And what about you?'

'What about me?'

'You're included in the list of invitees. I take it you'll be over your cold by Friday?'

She didn't want to go. Private jets to private islands with Bruno Carr lurking in the background somewhere were not her idea of a relaxing time.

'I'm not sure that it'll be possible for me to come as well.'

'Why not?'

'Because...I've already missed enough work, what with having to do so much on this court case. I need to get back to the office and catch up with what's been going on.'

'It can wait a few more days.'

She fidgeted in silence for a while, unable to pinpoint why she felt so apprehensive at a free weekend break in the sun.

'When was the last time you had a holiday?' he asked lazily, and she frowned and thought about the question.

'Some time ago,' she finally admitted. 'My lifestyle doesn't seem to accommodate holidays.'

'Your lifestyle doesn't seem to accommodate holidays?' She heard the irony in his voice and flinched.

'I'm a very busy woman,' she told him stiffly. 'I haven't got the time to go gallivanting around the world at a moment's notice.' What she found she meant was that the years seemed to have rushed by. She had been so wrapped up in her exams, then in her jobs, proving her worth, working all out so that she could stake her claim for financial independence, that she had barely noticed the passing of time. It had been five years since she'd had anything resembling a real holiday. Yes, she had had the occasional long weekend, and a few days off around Christmas, but a fortnight relaxing somewhere, far away from the madding crowd, was a luxury she had almost forgotten existed.

'Of course, it's a very generous offer...'

'Isn't it?' he said coolly. 'But not one you feel you can accept...'

'If I hadn't had these past couple of days off work, ill...'

'In that case, I'm sure you won't mind breaking the news to the rest of your staff that you rejected my offer on their behalf. I'm sure they'll understand.'

He turned around and was heading towards the door, and she scrambled after him.

'What do you mean? Are you telling me that if I don't come, then the bonus break's off for everyone else?'

He stopped abruptly and swung round to face her, so that she very nearly catapulted into his chest.

'Got it in one.'

'That's not fair!'

'Why not? I won't be there for the first day or so, if at all. I need the security of knowing that there'll be someone loosely in charge.'

'They're all adults!'

'Your choice.' He shrugged and looked at her, and eventually she sighed.

'Okay. I'll go. I should be fine by then.' Besides, if Bruno Carr wasn't going to be there, then she would be able to relax, and she needed a rest. Her body was telling her so.

'My secretary will contact you with all the details by Thursday afternoon.'

He rested his hand on the door handle, and then said, in passing, 'It's gratifying to know that you *are* capable of thinking of someone other than yourself.'

'And what is *that* supposed to mean?' she demanded as he opened the door and began heading towards his car.

He didn't bother to turn around. He just called out, in the voice of someone utterly indifferent to what she might or might not think of his remark, 'Why don't you take to your bed and think about it?'

Then he was gone, leaving her speechless with indignation. Yet again.

# CHAPTER FIVE

BRUNO CARR was beginning to occupy quite a bit of space in Jessica's head. But he wouldn't be around and the change in weather would do her good.

She kept those two things uppermost in her mind as she boarded the private jet on the Friday.

It was cold and blustery, and, not quite knowing what the temperatures would be when they landed, she had bundled herself up in jeans, a tee shirt, long-sleeved shirt and thick jumper.

Not everyone in the team of eleven was quite so restrained. Ronnie, the youngest of the secretaries, had braved the British elements in a short, flimsy skirt, which blew around her as she climbed the metal staircase, causing great jollity amongst the six young men behind her, and at the top of the stairs she posed, giggling, in an imitation of Marilyn Monroe until Jessica called dryly for her to get in before she caught her death of cold.

'I'm so excited,' she confided to Jessica as they buckled in. 'I've never been abroad before.'

'Never?' Jessica asked incredulously. True, Ronnie was only eighteen, but she was still surprised that there were people left who had not had a holiday abroad at some point in their lives.

'My dad hates flying,' she explained in a high, breathless voice, peering out of the window even though the view was nothing more impressive than the runway, barely visible in the darkness. 'So we always took our holidays in England.'

'What happened to the rest of the skirt, Ron?' one of the

men asked, pausing to grin at the blonde teenager, and she stuck her tongue out. 'Did it go on holiday ahead of you?' General guffaws all round, and Jessica rested her head back and closed her eyes with a smile.

Thank goodness she had made the effort. She would never have been forgiven by her staff if she had squashed the idea flat.

The bonus, when it had been put to them, had been met with uncontainable enthusiasm. Even Mary and Elizabeth, after tut-tutting about short notice and wondering what their respective husbands would do for supper, had greeted the scheme with delight.

They all needed a rest. They had worked hard over the past few weeks, and they deserved a break. And, Jessica thought as the plane slowly began its ascent, as breaks went, they didn't really get more impressive.

Four days of tropical bliss. They wouldn't even need to think about cooking, because housekeepers would be there, taking care of the food, the cleaning and, from the sound of it, pretty much everything else.

She heard the excited chatter around her as the plane cut a path through the sky, and decided that this was going to do her the world of good after all.

Her flu was on the way out, but she still felt lethargic, and work would have been a strain had she gone back. It also occurred to her that it had been a very long time since she had relaxed totally. Over the past couple of years, her breaks had tended to involve decorating the house. Enjoyable enough, because she quite liked the mindless physical exertion of wallpapering and painting walls, but she would hardly describe it as flaking out.

Before that, she dimly recalled a disastrous week in Portugal with her boyfriend at the time. After only nine months of going out, it had been a last-ditch attempt to energise their love life. Instead, he had fallen head over heels in love with a girl on holiday from Manchester, and Jessica had spent the week sunbathing on her own and listening patiently to his attempts at apology.

Holidays had always made her apprehensive. She could remember going on holiday with her parents, fearfully trying to have a good time with her brother in an atmosphere of frozen politeness, waiting for her father to do something to break the temporary cease-fire.

This short break would be different. She was not expected by anyone to have a good time. She could do precisely as she pleased. Lie on the beach with a book, or else doze with her hat over her face, and let time sweep past her, for once. She had brought a couple of novels with her, making sure to leave behind any law books.

The background noise of the engines eventually lulled her into a kind of sleep, and she was roused when they were told to fasten their seat belts in preparation for landing.

Then she sat up, and peered curiously through the small window as a small island took shape. There seemed to be nothing to it. A dot of land in the middle of sea. There were some lights to indicate the landing-strip, but the darkness prevented her from making out any details, and she settled back as the plane bumped along the ground and finally screeched to a stop.

There was a chorus of voices as everyone reached for their bags, and Ronnie said, grinning, 'I can't believe we're here!' Her blue eyes gleamed. 'Can you believe Mr Carr—oops, Bruno—*actually owns an island*?'

'Amazing, isn't it?' Jessica said, half smiling and half yawning, as she stood up. 'The lengths some people will go to to guarantee a bit of privacy for themselves.'

'I don't even have privacy in the bathroom at home,'

Ronnie was saying cheerfully to her as she yanked out her enormous holdall from underneath the seat in front. 'You wouldn't believe how long teenage boys spend preening themselves!'

'I can imagine!' Jessica returned with a laugh. Her father had been a stickler for timekeeping. She and Jeremy had never seen the bathroom as somewhere to indulge. There had been no preening in front of the bathroom mirror, or reading a book in the bath. Life had always been too disciplined for such indulgences. Most of all, mess had been unacceptable. Every morning, before school, her father would push open the bathroom door and check that everything was spick and span, or else there would be hell to pay, and such lessons were to be avoided at all costs.

Outside, there were two Jeeps waiting for them, but the very first thing they all noticed was the incredible heat. Even at this hour of the night the air was warm, with a lazy breeze doing its best to keep the temperature down. Jumpers were pulled off and shoved over handles of holdalls, and Ronnie, with gleeful satisfaction, raised both arms in the air and asked who was laughing at her outfit now. In her frothy short skirt and skimpy top, she was certainly the most sensibly dressed for the weather, albeit a bit on the overdressed side.

They climbed onto the Jeeps, chatting, and as they bumped along the makeshift road, through a forest of tall, swaying palm trees and bush, Jessica could feel the heat turning her jeans into rubber and her tee shirt into cling film. She hadn't travelled with much. One small case with the barest of essentials. A couple of tee shirts, some shorts, some swimsuits and a cardigan, *just in case,* although, feeling the heat, she had no idea what had possessed her to include this last item in the packing.

The house was a matter of a few minutes' drive away,

and it was already so late by the time they arrived that they were shown immediately to their rooms, none of which was shared.

Lord only knew how many rooms the place had. Jessica, her eyes heavy with exhaustion, vaguely noticed lots of wood everywhere: wooden floors, wooden ceilings, and a labyrinthine network of areas, leading to various different parts of the house.

Her room was large and airy with an overhead fan and a soft mosquito net draped over a double-sized bed. There were rugs on the floor and through an opened door she saw an *en suite* bathroom. It was all very luxurious, she thought, dumping her bag on a chair. The thought of having a shower was tempting, but the thought of changing into her pyjamas in under five seconds and flopping on the bed underneath the mosquito net was even more so.

She switched on the fan, felt obliged to peer through one of the large, veranda-style windows, then slipped on her striped pyjamas, and within ten minutes she was asleep.

When she next opened her eyes, it was to find sunlight streaming into the bedroom, and she groggily realised that it was after ten in the morning.

Through sheer habit, she felt her stomach go into knots at the thought of having overslept. It was something she rarely did, if ever. Her father had never allowed it, and her body had adapted to suit from a very early age.

When she pushed open the slatted wooden window, it was to be greeted with the most perfect sight she had ever seen in her life before. The house was on the beach. White sand and turquoise sea were visible through a latticework of palm trees.

She dressed quickly, flinging on a black bikini, then she grabbed her sun cream, a pair of shades, her hat, a book and rushed out of the house.

'About time you got up!' she heard Ronnie's voice from behind her, and she waved and laughed.

'Where's everyone?' she asked.

'Sunbathing, swimming, exploring! I'm back out in a couple of minutes. Can't waste this weather!'

'No. We might not see it again till summer rolls round in England. If it decides to!'

How on earth could a few hours on a plane make such a difference? She couldn't believe that she had devoted so much time to feeling guilty about work, imagining the mounds of it collecting in her in-tray with relentless, sneering persistence, thinking about how much of her weekends would be eaten up in trying to reduce the swelling pile. As she stepped onto the sand and felt it slipping warmly through her bare feet, work seemed like something vaguely unpleasant that was happening millions of light years away.

Mary and Elizabeth, paired off as usual, were further along the beach, two portly figures modestly attired in dark-coloured one-pieces and shaded with broad-brimmed straw hats. Further along, Ronnie's cronies were fooling around in the water.

Jessica waved and then found herself a more secluded part of the beach, under a palm tree, and she lay down on her towel and slowly plastered herself with sun cream.

The sound of the sea was lulling, a lazy, lapping noise as the water washed against the sand, ebbing away, with the steady in and out rhythm of something alive and breathing. She had brought her book with her, but the glare in her eyes was too strong to read comfortably, and after five minutes she gave in to the irresistible impulse to close her eyes and drift off. Sea, sun, sand, a cool breeze, tranquillity, and a deep, velvety voice in her right ear saying, 'You have to be careful, you know. With your complexion, there's a good chance you could end up looking like broiled lobster.'

Jessica's eyes flew open to confront Bruno Carr standing over her, with two cold drinks in his hands. The vision was so unexpected that she blinked a few times, convinced that the heat must have caused some dreadful mirage to appear. On the fifth blink, she realised that this was no mirage.

'What are you doing here?' she said, sitting up, desperately aware of how much of her body was exposed in her black bikini. Every nerve in her body seemed to have gone on red alert, and, although she did her best to keep her eyes plastered to his face, she was all too aware of his muscular body, more tanned than she would have expected, and clothed only in a short-sleeved cotton shirt, unbuttoned, and a pair of trunks.

Thank goodness for her sunglasses! At least they offered her some protection from the shock of seeing him here. And where was her hat? She grabbed it from next to her and stuck it on, so that her face was instantly half covered.

'Care for a drink?' He handed her a glass of something long and cold, and she took it from him quickly with a bright, 'Thanks.'

'What are you doing here?' she repeated, in a more normal voice. 'I thought you said that you weren't going to be coming.'

'Did I?' He looked at her with an expression of amazement. 'You must have misunderstood. I said that I might not be able to come over for the full time, but as you can see...' he sipped his drink, and, disturbingly because it threatened a longer stay than she wanted, sat down on the edge of her towel, so that she had to make a few imperceptible adjustments to further the distance between them '...I managed to make it over.'

'So I see,' Jessica mumbled.

'Call me a fool, but I couldn't resist the temptation of seeing you without your handy working-woman face on. Efficient cool lawyer by day, efficient cool lawyer by night—didn't make sense. So I rearranged my affairs to see if I could catch a rare glimpse of the only occasionally spotted Jessica Stearn—woman.' He chuckled, thoroughly amused at his wit, and she refused to indulge him by responding.

'Sometimes I wonder how you manage to be so successful,' she said tartly, 'when bird-spotting is such a great pastime of yours.'

'I don't think I said that. Quite.' He shot her a dark, outrageously flirtatious look and grinned. 'Only one species in particular.'

Unable to find a suitable response to that, Jessica resorted to a look of complete disdain, which made him grin even more.

'What do you think of it?'

'Fine. It's your house, after all.'

'No,' he said softly into her ear, which made her shift over a bit more in alarm, 'I meant what do you think of the place, not what do you think about my being here.'

'Oh.' She turned to look at him, and before she knew what was happening he reached out and removed her sunglasses in one neat movement.

'Could you please return those?' she asked, opening her hand.

'I dislike talking to people when they're hiding behind dark glasses.'

'I. Am. Not. Hiding. Behind. Anything,' Jessica said stiffly, thoroughly unnerved, which of course had been his intention as she well knew. 'The glare from the sun makes my eyes water.'

'Rubbish.' He stretched out on the towel next to her, and

out of the corner of her eye she could see a few curious looks coming their way. Mary and Elizabeth had both stopped reading their books—what a coincidence—and were staring across in their direction, attempting to look as though they were admiring the general scenery.

'You are going to start rumours,' Jessica told him in a low, furious voice. He had shoved the sunglasses behind him, firmly out of reach.

'What kind of rumours?'

'Rumours…that…that…' She spluttered into silence, and he gave her a slow, lazy smile.

'I'm merely sitting down to have a chat with one of my employees.'

Jessica ground her teeth together in sheer frustration.

'So…what do you think of this little slice of paradise?' He lay down with his hands behind his head, and her eyes reluctantly followed the long, athletic lines of his body.

'It's beautiful. You're very lucky to have this as a bolt-hole. Do you come here often?'

'When I need to unwind.'

'Good. Well.' Making her mind up, she stood up and he promptly yanked her back down in such a smooth, unhurried gesture that she half toppled onto him, but managed to straighten herself with the speed of light.

'Not so fast. I'm enjoying our little conversation.'

'Glad one of us is,' Jessica muttered indignantly.

'And so are you. Why pretend? You might want to scurry away like a terrified rabbit…'

'Me? A terrified rabbit?'

'Oh, yes. Once you're dragged away from your work—'

'I am perfectly controlled, inside and outside the working environment!' she snapped, cursing the heat that had flooded through her.

'You mean, you'd dearly like to be. Your face lets you

down, though,' he murmured thoughtfully. 'It's too expressive.'

'That's never been a problem before I met you!' she blurted out truthfully, horrified into sudden silence by the admission. 'You...you...'

'Yes? I'm all ears.'

'Are absolutely insufferable. And I'm going to swim.'

She stood up and headed down towards the water, burning with embarrassment.

She shouldn't have worn the bikini, though she actually looked better with fewer clothes. She had the sort of long, slender body that was rendered shapeless by too many layers. She should, she thought, finally reaching the water's edge with relief, have stuck to the one hideous one-piece she had brought with her, but then how on earth could she have known that he would turn up like a bad penny?

She would simply remain in the water, splashing about in an aimless fashion, until he vacated her towel. Every so often she glanced in his direction, half expecting him to come in for a dip while she was there, but eventually he eased himself off her towel, gave her a brief wave and strolled down the beach, stopping to talk for quite some time to Mary and Elizabeth, then further along to the remainder of the crowd whose high-spirited activities had become progressively more sluggish in the heat.

Jessica watched from the water, alternately floating on her back, then ducking and swimming under the cool, clear sea, then when the coast was clear she emerged with relief.

Why had he decided to come? Was it because he knew that his presence would throw her into a state of turmoil, and he found the condition highly amusing? He had said as much. He saw her as an object of curiosity and that thought stung. It made her feel like a freak and perhaps to him she was.

When she strolled back into the house an hour later it was to find an impromptu buffet laid out on the extensive back lawns, and Bruno holding court.

Ronnie, clad only in her bikini top, which had clearly been designed as a cleavage enhancer, and a colourful sarong skirt, was flirting in a kittenish manner, which involved lots of giggling, and even Carla, who was engaged and rarely strayed from the topic of her fiancé, was laughing at something Bruno was saying, and looking rather coy.

Jessica, having thrown some baggy shorts and an even baggier tee shirt over her bikini, helped herself to a plate of food and positioned herself on the sidelines, politely listening to Bruno's amusing accounts of trips he had taken abroad and still burning from what he had said to her earlier on.

'Sheep's eyes,' he was saying now, to an audience that appeared to be hanging on to his every word, 'I assure you, are most definitely one of life's more acquired tastes.'

He glanced in her direction, his eyes lingering momentarily on her outfit, which left everything to the imagination, and she feigned an interested look in what he had been saying.

'And have you any unpleasant experiences to recount from trips abroad, Jessica?'

Of course, he *would* involve her in the conversation, wouldn't he? Knowing that that would be the very last thing she wanted.

'Well...there was the time I very nearly had my leg chewed off by a school of barracuda while swimming in the Indian Ocean,' she said to no one in particular. 'Fortunately I was rescued in the nick of time by a passing helicopter, which airlifted me to safety. The perfect rescue if it weren't for the fact that we immediately flew into a freak storm and very nearly crashed. As it was the pilot lost control and fainted and I had to take over.'

'No!' Ronnie cried in amazement, and Jessica grinned at her.

'You're right. No. My trips abroad have all been spectacularly uneventful, I'm afraid.' At which point, with lunch out of the way, the party broke up, going in different directions, mostly indoors to recover from the effects of the morning sun.

Jessica retired to a bench under a tree to finish eating, and gave a little sigh of resignation as Bruno approached her and then proceeded to sit down next to her.

'This will start the rumour mill going,' he said with amusement. 'If this house had net curtains, then I'm sure a few of them would be twitching.'

'Ha, ha, I'm glad you find the thought of that funny.' She stabbed a piece of tomato and stuck it in her mouth.

'Did you have a nice swim this morning?' he asked, and she threw him a sidelong glance.

'Very nice, thank you.'

'I must say, I was impressed by your exciting anecdote about avoiding death by barracuda in the Indian Ocean. Well, until you said that you'd fabricated the whole thing.'

'Which you had known from the start anyway,' she said, sticking her empty plate on the bench next to her and wondering whether it was her imagination or whether he was flirting with her. It was hard to tell with a man like Bruno because he was intrinsically charming. He had the ability to invite the illusion that you were somehow special, simply because when he conversed he had the knack of making you feel as though every pore in his body were focused on whatever you might be saying.

You'd be a fool, of course, to be taken in by any such illusion.

'True,' he said lazily, stretching one arm along the back of the bench, and tilting his face up to the sun, which speckled through the leaves of the tree.

'Because,' Jessica said coolly, 'hard-working career girls like me who have no time for anything exciting in their lives couldn't possibly have exciting adventures, could we?'

Once the words were out of her mouth, she couldn't quite believe that she had said them. What had possessed her? She sounded like a teenager suffering a fit of pique, instead of a mature adult who had her life totally under control.

It was just…that he made her feel, somehow, as though she had missed the boat somewhere along the line. As though there was a huge, exciting life out there, happening to other people, while she remained locked indoors, too scared to venture out. She wasn't sure why she felt that way, but she knew that she never had until he had come along. He was just so *damned charismatic*. She had watched all the faces at lunchtime, focused on him, alight with enthusiasm.

'That remark,' he told her, not bothering to look at her when he spoke, 'has absolutely nothing to do with anything I said, and everything to do with how you feel about yourself.'

'That's utter nonsense and you know it,' Jessica muttered uncomfortably. Rather than risk going down this route of personal confrontation, from which, she knew, she would emerge the loser, she decided to change the topic of conversation altogether. She even managed to inject a note of cheeriness in her voice when she asked him about the island and the house.

'Who maintains it when you're not around?' she asked. Aside from the house, there were extensive grounds, and they were well tended. She suspected that, in the tropics, foliage grew at a rate of knots. He would need a full-time gardener just to stop the place from becoming a jungle.

'I employ three gardeners, who work all year round.' He yawned, which made her feel like yawning as well. It was the heat. 'And when I'm not here, Vicky and Sandy, the housekeepers who are here at the moment, come across twice a week by boat to make sure that everything's ticking over nicely with the house. But it's used frequently. Friends, family, et cetera.'

'This heat is sleep-inducing, isn't it?' she said politely, already making her excuses for leaving, and he turned to look at her, reading her mind.

'I always think there's something particularly time-wasting about sleeping during the day, don't you?'

'No.'

'Why don't we go for a little walk? Something I want to show you.'

'What?' Panic.

'Come on.' He stood up and waited for her to follow suit, which she didn't. 'You make remarks,' he said mildly, 'about being thought of as unexciting, but you refuse to stray from your carefully monitored path, don't you?'

'And what is *that* supposed to mean?' She looked up at him, shading her eyes with her hand.

'I tell you that I want to show you something and your immediate reaction isn't one of curiosity, it's one of wariness. You act as though anything you aren't familiar with is necessarily going to be unpleasant. Isn't that why you didn't want to come over here? Too scared to try anything out of the ordinary?' He began walking away, and Jessica sprang to her feet and stumbled behind him, matching her pace to his, arms folded, with a look of tight-lipped defensiveness on her face.

'I don't think that's fair!' she panted, wiping her forehead with the back of her hand. Over her bikini, which she had kept on, the tee shirt was clinging to her body like a second skin.

'No, but it worked.' He raised his eyebrows tellingly. 'That's the problem about the truth. Gets a person running around after it, hell-bent on proving it's a lie.'

'That's a ridiculous, homespun piece of amateur psychology!'

'Well, you *could* always retire for a siesta,' he said mildly.

'I never said I wanted a siesta!'

They were inside the house now, which was thankfully much cooler, and she glanced briefly around to see whether anyone was lurking nearby, but wherever they were it wasn't in the sprawling bowels of the living area.

'Well…' he stuck his hands into the pockets of his khaki-coloured shorts and appeared to give the matter some thought '…you could always retreat to the very furthest corner of the house with a book.'

'You are…impossible!'

'Because I'm doing you the great disservice of making you think? Truth hurts. Isn't that how the saying goes?'

'Because you think you can swan around making sweeping assumptions about other people! Because you think you have a right to air your views, whether someone wants to hear them or not!' She started to turn away, and he reached out and caught her by her arm, spinning her around to face him.

'Tell me something, has *no one* ever criticised you in your life before?'

Jessica stood absolutely still, red-faced and trembling. 'In abundance,' she heard herself say. 'About the way I looked and the friends I never had because I was never allowed them, and the grades I got which were never quite good enough.'

'Your father?' Bruno asked quietly.

'He was never satisfied. With any of us. I...I...' Jessica bit her lip and told herself that if she cried, if she did the unthinkable and burst into tears, she would take a vow of silence and retreat to the nearest convent.

'Which makes sense.' He took a strand of her hair and pushed it away from her face. 'Look, you go relax. I'll see you later, I'm sure.'

He began walking away, and after a moment's hesitation she ran after him and said, without preamble, 'If the offer still stands, I'll come with you to see...whatever it was you wanted to show me...'

'You sure about that?' he asked, looking at her narrowly, and she nodded.

They walked out together, onto the beach, while her mind furiously went over what he had said to her and what she had said to him. He was right, she thought with a pang of shame: she projected a veneer of hard, single-minded ambition and she had fought hard to get where she was. But her detachment was off-putting, and she knew that her demeanour did not invite criticism. Oh, she was fine if something critical was said about her work, but she did not encourage personal criticism. Bruno Carr was the first man who had ever bluntly spoken his mind, and she had, she thought, confused, dropped all her defences and confided in him.

They turned the corner of the beach and continued walking as the lush vegetation became denser.

'Small question,' Jessica said, determined now to be bright and cheerful and to pretend that their conversation had never taken place. 'Should we have a map?'

He turned and raised both eyebrows expressively and she

felt a shiver of awareness dart down her spine. He was perspiring and there was a certain animal heat about him that made her limbs feel slightly uncontrolled.

'Map? Map?' He gave her a wolfish grin. 'Only wimps need maps! I can orient myself anywhere in the world just by glancing at the sun.'

'Good job it's a very small island,' she returned with a shaky laugh. 'That has the ring of famous last words before two people end up hopelessly lost and going round in circles.' She had an insane desire to wipe a trickle of perspiration from him with one finger, and lick it away.

'Oh, ye of little faith.' He turned away, whistling under his breath, and continued weaving his way through the bush and coconut trees until they finally arrived at another strip of white sand, narrower and more coral-strewn than the area by the house. Moored to a tree was a small boat, with a small engine and a couple of oars inside. Jessica stared at it, uncertain as to what her reaction ought to be. It wasn't what she had been expecting. She had thought he had wanted to point out something of peculiar natural beauty— a rare flower, or tree or shrub. Certainly not a boat.

'*Et voilà!*' he said, turning to her, and she looked at him dubiously.

'It's a boat,' she said finally. 'What's it doing tethered way out here?'

'Sheer cussedness on my part.' He began loosening the rope that secured it to the tree trunk. 'I enjoy the sweaty, physical exertion of getting here. Also stops it being used randomly by visitors when they come.'

'What are you doing?' she asked, stifling another of those little panic attacks that seemed to strike whenever she was faced with the prospect of being alone with him.

'What does it look like?' He glanced briefly at her. 'I'm going to take you to a part of the island that's only accessible by boat.' He pushed it towards the water and she watched his sinewy body with trancelike concentration, then she gathered herself and smiled. No overreacting, she told herself. No ridiculous teenage hysterics—he's being the perfect host and wants to show me as much as he can because he knows that when I get back to England I'll return to my nose to the grindstone.

'Great!'

He looked at her with amusement. 'Hop in.'

'The engine works, doesn't it?' She climbed into the boat which was bobbing in the shallow, seaweedy water and he climbed in after her.

'Let's hope so. Rowing can be tiring work.'

'But doubtless something you see as another challenge.' She was looking around as she spoke, and missed the glint of laughter in his eyes.

'Doubtless.' He pulled twice on the cord to start the engine, and it put-putted into life with the high-pitched whine of a sewing machine. Then he sat back down on the bench facing her and picked up speed as they cleared the shallow water and headed out to sea. He explained the layout of the island, and as he spoke she looked off to the horizon and tried to ignore her heart hammering madly against her rib-cage. Within five minutes he slowed the engine and headed inland towards a cove, very small, with a backdrop of thick trees and bush. The water was clear enough for her to see the grains of sand at the bottom of the sea bed. Swimming-pool water. Idyllic. But deserted.

'Great place to swim,' he announced as he killed the engine and allowed the boat to drift towards shore. 'The water's incredibly warm just here.'

'Brilliant!' Jessica said faintly.

'Isn't it?' He stood up, steadying himself, then stepped out of the boat and pulled it up onto the sand. There was that thread of laughter in his voice that made her think that he could read her mind, see inside her head to every thought. 'I knew you'd agree!'

Tentatively she climbed out, keeping her eyes firmly averted from him.

'And don't look so terrified,' he whispered in her ear, making her jump, 'the sea is clear of man-eating barracuda. Relax. Nothing around here bites…' He gave a low laugh, then moved away from her. 'It's absolutely perfect.'

Yes, she thought. Wasn't it?

# CHAPTER SIX

BRUNO stripped off his shirt, then his shorts, and Jessica was relieved to see that he was wearing a pair of swimming trunks underneath. Dark green, and low slung, so that she could see the arrow of dark hair running from his navel downwards, disappearing beneath the trunks.

How on earth was he so *bronzed*? She wondered whether he had Italian or Spanish blood in him. He certainly bore no passing resemblance to any English man she had ever seen on a beach. She had long come to the conclusion that English men on beaches were not sights for sore eyes. With no clothes to hide them, their whiteness was almost blinding. Even men who looked passable enough in their suits were rendered laughable when caught with nothing on but a pair of trunks on a beach somewhere.

She retreated to the shade of a coconut tree and looked at Bruno out of the corner of her eye. He had strolled towards the water's edge, and was obviously contemplating swimming out.

'Why are you lurking there?' he shouted over to her, and Jessica hurriedly plastered her gaze somewhere else, shading her eyes with her hands. 'You must be baking with all those clothes on!' She saw the flash of white teeth and felt the familiar bristle as she caught the laughter in his voice.

'I'm fine,' she told him. She could feel the sweat trickling under her armpits and at the back of her neck, where some coils of hair were glued to her skin.

'Join me for a swim!' he commanded, walking towards her, and she eyed him warily. There was no one around, and it was very unlikely that anyone would suddenly appear on the scene. For a small island, this was a remarkably remote spot.

'Can't.' She flashed him a smile. He moved, she thought, with the grace of a panther.

'Why not?' He raked his fingers through his hair and half turned away, so that he was looking out to sea, his face in profile.

'Sun's too hot out there. This is the worst time to be in the sun if you're fair, and I forgot to bring my sun cream.' She shrugged her shoulders helplessly. 'So you go ahead and have a swim. I must say, the water looks very inviting.' She sighed wistfully and gazed at the calm, turquoise sea, as clear as a pool. 'Maybe I'll have a dip in a minute.'

'Well, you're probably right,' Bruno told her sympathetically. 'You just stay well wrapped up, and take refuge in some shade.' He folded his arms and flicked his eyes over her. 'You know, I have a tin with some oil clothes on the boat...I could always rig up a hat of sorts for further protection...' So much for that air of sympathy, she thought crossly.

'That won't be necessary.' She headed off for the nearest tree, sat down, and watched as he walked at a leisurely pace towards the sea, then pushed out, moving quickly away from shore, until his form became smaller and smaller.

She felt a sharp pull of anxiety when he disappeared altogether.

Where the hell was he?

She could remember him telling them that there were no currents around the beach because of coral reefs further out, but then, since when was he an expert on the tidal movements of the ocean?

She stood up, squinting against the glare, her body reaching forward as she tried to distinguish any bobbing figure that might be his. When he finally surfaced, waving at her, she clicked her tongue with irritation and promptly sat back down. Then she lay on her back, stretched her legs out in front of her, and closed her eyes.

Her heart was still beating fast at the thought that he might have been swept out to sea, even though she knew that it had been a ridiculous, passing urge to be worried about him.

If there was one person in the world who could take care of himself, it was Bruno Carr. An ocean current would have to be particularly reckless to think that it could carry him away. She doubted that he had ever been carried away by anything or anyone in his life. His life was utterly and completely in control. Events were things, she imagined, which he manipulated for his own ends, just as he no doubt manipulated the people around him.

A slight breeze blew, and without opening her eyes she hoisted her tee shirt over her head, then folded it roughly and shoved it behind her, pillow-style.

She was on the verge of drifting off into a delicious doze when she felt a spattering of water on her, and her eyes flew open.

There he was, standing over her, and with the sun behind him his face was thrown into shadow. She jerked up into a sitting position, ready to throw him the well-rehearsed smile, to find that he wasn't smiling at her. That ironic, amused grin which seemed permanently to play on his lips whenever he was in her company had been replaced by something else.

He was looking at her. *Really looking at her.* She could feel her skin begin to prickle, and she had to clear her throat before she spoke because she knew that, if she didn't, her words would trip over one another in nervousness.

What was he playing at?

'Good swim?' she asked, in a high voice, and he didn't say anything. 'Wish I could have ventured in…' she volunteered in a cheery voice.

'You look very different when you're asleep.'

'What?' Jessica looked at him, shocked by the intimacy of the remark.

'You heard me.' He sat down alongside her, and every nerve in her body went into immediate overdrive. He leaned against the trunk of the coconut tree, with his long legs stretched out in front of him, loosely crossed at the ankles, and proceeded to look at her.

'How long were you…standing there…staring at me?' She tried to inject some righteous anger in her voice, but failed. She was very much aware that if she shifted a few inches to her left, she would touch him. The thought of that sent a wave of faintness through her.

'Not staring…observing.'

'Oh, right. And the difference is enormous.'

She couldn't maintain his stare, so she turned away and looked out across the white sand, across the water to the sharp blue line of the horizon.

She couldn't believe that she was sitting here, her toes sifting through the castor-sugar sand, next to a man who had swept into her life like a tornado, and feeling things that she knew were absolutely out of order. It was almost as though the change in the scenery had cast a spell on her, released some invisible plug on her emotions.

*Why, for God's sake, was her heart doing such feeble things? Beating like a damn drum just because a man had looked at her?*

'When you're asleep—'

'I wasn't *asleep*. I had my eyes closed.'

'When you're asleep,' he drawled, paying no notice to her interruption, 'you look soft and defenceless.'

'Everyone looks defenceless when they're asleep,' Jessica said shortly, uncomfortable with the conversation. Her fingers played restlessly with the edge of her shorts.

'What made you stop trusting the human race?' he asked softly, and without warning he placed one finger under her chin and tilted her face towards his.

Jessica opened her mouth to say something clever, but when she tried to speak she found that her vocal cords had dried up. She thought she could hear her heart, if that was possible. She could almost hear the surge of her blood crashing through her veins.

'Was it just your father or was there a man as well to compound the problem?' he asked.

'No.' She made a small movement to look away, but he stilled her.

'What, then?'

'I…' She couldn't believe that she was having this conversation. Worse. That she felt compelled to confide in him. The heat was magical, turning her brains to mush. 'I'm afraid my childhood…left a lot to be desired.'

'Your father…'

'Was a tyrant.' There was fierceness in her voice, and she frowned at him. 'He ruled the household with a rod of iron. We weren't allowed…to do anything. Running in the house, shouting…' Her memories were so real that she felt as though she had been swept back into time. 'We all crept around like mice, too afraid to even laugh when he was around.' She looked nervously at him, waiting for him to say something dismissive about what she had told him, but his gaze was steady and unfaltering, and utterly serious.

'The worst of it was…my mum…she must have been full of laughter once…but by the time I grew up, all that had been sucked out of her. All the joy...gone.' She met his eyes without flinching. 'He fooled around, you see. Mum was someone who stayed at home, raising the children and looking after the house, and all the other women...' She shook her head, bewildered now, as she had been then, when she had first overheard her parents arguing behind a semi-closed door. 'He saw nothing wrong in what he did, and when Mum eventually tried to leave, she found that she couldn't. Her self-confidence had taken such a battering over the years that she no longer had any faith in herself. So, you see...' she shrugged lightly and blinked '...I learned pretty fast that it was up to me to sort my life out. I couldn't trust anyone else to do it for me. Aren't I a sad creature?' She attempted a laugh, but it was wobbly and unconvincing.

He stroked some hair from her face, and his fingers burnt her flesh.

'Absolutely not.' He gave her a slow smile. 'No more than the rest of us sad creatures that inhabit this good planet of ours.'

'Are you telling me that you had a miserable childhood?'

'Virtually trouble free,' he admitted, and she gave a low, shaky laugh.

'Now, why do you think I would have guessed as much?' she asked lightly.

'No idea. You tell me.'

She hoped he wasn't seriously expecting an answer to that.

'Shouldn't we think about leaving?'

'Why?'

'Why? Because...'

'Ah, those rumours...might start flying around again...'

'No!'

'Well, then...' he shook his head thoughtfully '...I guess the sun is beginning to make you feel a bit dizzy...'

'The sun's fine...' Enough of a cool breeze to dilute the intensity.

He smiled, a slow, lazy smile, and raised one eyebrow expressively. 'Then the only other reason I can think of is that you're afraid to stay here alone with me...are you? I make you nervous, don't I? I can see it in your body movements. The minute I get too close, you shift a bit just in case I touch you. Why do you think that is? Are you scared that I might make a pass at you...?'

Jessica could feel herself holding her breath. She could also feel the slow, burning flush that spread outwards and upwards, engulfing her.

'I'm afraid of no such thing!' she protested, instantly mortified at the thought that he might be laughing at her, feeling sorry for her with her silly sob stories.

'You should be...'

It took a few seconds for the impact of what he had said to sink in, but when it had her mouth flew open and remained parted. A slow, hot excitement uncurled inside her, like a spiral of smoke. The first sign of a conflagration.

He cupped her face with his hand, and then everything seemed to happen in slow motion. His head lowering to hers, his mouth touching hers, then the feel of his tongue as the kiss became deeper and more urgent.

She had never felt this response before, had never felt dizzy with want.

She reached up and clasped her hands behind his head, and returned his kiss with an abandoned passion she never would have thought possible.

Their tongues met and clashed, wet and thrusting, and she moaned as his fingers slid under the strap of her bikini top, tugging it down.

'God knows, I've wanted to do this…' he groaned, his voice husky and thick. She arched back, fiddling with the clasp at the back, until the bikini top was off and her breasts, larger than they appeared under the camouflage of clothes, hung unrestrained.

Her nipples had hardened into aching peaks, and she shuddered uncontrollably when his fingers began rubbing and teasing.

'Big nipples,' he murmured into her ear. 'I like that.' His tongue flicked wetly in her ear, sending electric currents through her, and then he began licking her neck, while he massaged one full breast with his hand.

In the olden days, ladies swooned. Jessica thought that this must have been what it felt like. As though all her bones had turned to liquid.

She cradled his head, squirming and gasping as he trailed his mouth lower, along her collar-bone. The anticipation of that mouth suckling on a nipple was akin to ecstasy. She urged his head down, and groaned softly as wetness enfolded the pink, throbbing peak. He sucked, pulling her breast into his mouth, arousing the nipple with his tongue, and she ran her hands over his hard, muscled torso, loving the feel of his skin beneath her palms.

'Feel good?' he asked, and she opened her eyes and smiled drowsily at him.

It felt so good that she couldn't bear his mouth away from her body, and, sensing her need, he slowly continued to explore her breasts, running his tongue on the underside, nibbling their softness, teasing her nipples until she wanted to scream.

He slid his hand underneath the elasticised waistband of her shorts, and pulled them down. She wriggled, then kicked them off, parting her legs.

Her wetness down there surprised her. How was it that

she had never reached these amazing heights of pleasure before? Was it because, for the first time in her life, she felt as though she had truly relinquished all control?

He placed the flat of his hand between her thighs and gently rubbed. In response, she reached down and found his pulsating manhood, looking at him so that she could enjoy his own surrender of self-control.

'Take your time,' he murmured, his eyes burning, and she sighed.

Time, she knew, was something they had very little of. Before they knew it, it would have crept up on them, and they would have to leave this idyll behind. But for the moment she put all such thoughts to the back of her head as she eased her body down, down so that she could explore him the way he had been exploring her.

Her mouth drifted sensually over the flat planes of his stomach, feeling his muscles tense and harden under her, then she nuzzled his erect member, licking the shaft, then covering it with her mouth, and as she did so she felt him stiffen, and his breathing become more rapid.

With her hands, she stroked and caressed him, wanting to give him as much pleasure as he had given her, wanting to take her time as well so that what was happening between them, remarkable as it was, would stretch out as long as possible.

She realised that she didn't want this to end. She didn't want to roll away from him and face the present once again.

Sex, which had always been something pleasant enough that had tended to happen at the end of an evening out, had been transformed into something wild and hungry and surging with passion and yearning.

She could feel her body reaching out for him and when he moved to urge her onto her back, she eased her bikini bottom off, so that her soft, blonde, damp curls were exposed to the balmy air.

This ultimate intimacy was a first for her. She watched his dark head descend lower, until his mouth nuzzled against those damp curls.

His tongue found her swollen, throbbing bud and flicked against it, and she moaned and moved against him, pushing herself up. One hand was entwined in his hair, the other loosely thrown over her face, as she panted under the waves of exquisite pleasure rushing through her.

She gyrated her hips, and the pressure of his tongue became stronger. His hands were spread underneath her firm buttocks, and he urged her on until the waves of pleasure became an irresistible crashing force.

She felt her body tense and tighten, then shudder uncontrollably.

But still he kept licking, teasing every ounce of energy out of her body, so that the one powerful climax merged into a series of utterly wonderful shivers of intense fulfilment.

When he finally thrust into her, a deep excitement filled her, unlike anything she had ever experienced before. His mouth covered hers in a hungry, urgent kiss, while one hand cupped her breast and massaged it.

Jessica cried out, a deep, hoarse cry that didn't sound as though it could possibly come from her, and as she felt him reach his own soaring heights her body stiffened in wild response.

How long had time stood still?

When she next opened her eyes, it was to find him looking down at her with the same drowsy contentment that she was feeling and she gave him a tremulous smile.

'Perhaps I will risk a swim in this heat after all,' she murmured, tracing his features with one finger, which he grasped and put into his mouth, so that the smile became a giggle of delight.

'Sounds like a good idea.' He eased himself off her, and they faced one another on their sides.

'If I can only find the energy to get up.'

'Feeling a little drained, are you?'

'Just a bit.' She ran her hand lightly along his side, and then along his upper thigh. She felt, amazingly, as though she had been asleep all her adult life, and was now awake for the first time. Her body was still tingling in the aftermath of their lovemaking.

'Well, no time like the present,' he said, without moving, and he lay flat on his back with his hands folded behind his head and stared upwards for a few seconds, before transferring his gaze to her.

She moved to start slipping back on the bikini, and he stopped her.

'But what if someone comes along?' she whispered nervously as they stood up and began strolling down to the water. She glanced back over her shoulder, and he laughed and rumpled her hair, which looked a mess.

'I guess they'd be in for a shock.'

'That's fine for you to say,' Jessica told him sternly, kicking at the water as they stepped in. 'When we get back to England...' it seemed a million miles away, and the thought of it filled her with a sudden, shocking feeling of disappointment, which she immediately stifled '...you'll vanish back into that ivory tower of yours, but I'll be left with the whispering and knowing looks...'

'True,' he agreed readily. 'But what's a little whispering and a few knowing looks to a determined young woman like yourself?' He grinned and began splashing her with water, and she returned the favour with equal enthusiasm until they were both drenched, and all thoughts of being overseen were lost in the sheer physical activity of swimming.

Swimming and touching, soft, wet strokes that made her want to return to the little patch of sand under the tree and make love to him all over again.

Her hair hung down to her waist like a sheath of dark gold, and the sun was so hot that after only a few minutes with her head above water she could feel it beginning to dry off.

As they emerged from the water he held her from behind, his arms enfolding her, and she gasped as his fingers slipped down between her thighs, caressing her.

'Anyone could be spying on us!' she protested, not struggling very hard to resist because his fingers were rapidly firing her body into a wet, willing response.

'Don't be so worried,' he murmured, sweeping her hair to one side and bending to kiss her neck. 'This little spot is surprisingly difficult to find if you don't know precisely where to go. Trust me.'

'Trust you? Isn't that something of a tall order?' She twisted around to give him a sceptical, amused look from under her lashes, and he grinned back obligingly.

'I sense criticism in that remark.' They held hands and began walking back towards their clothes, which lay strewn at the scene of their lovemaking.

It hadn't been meant as criticism, or even to be taken seriously, but now that he had offered that observation she suddenly gave some consideration to what had just happened between them. For a minute, she had taken flight, but the earth was still under her feet and sooner or later she would have to land.

She thoughtfully slipped back on her sandy bikini and her even sandier shorts and then sat down, hugging her knees and waiting while he dressed and sat back down next to her.

'Actually,' she said slowly, turning to face him, 'I wasn't being critical.'

'But…? That expression on your face is telling me that there's a postscript attached to that little statement of yours…'

'This feels so unreal,' she started, with hesitation. She dropped one hand to the sand and began sifting through it, watching it filter through her fingers like castor sugar. 'Look…I feel you should know that I…' She sighed and mentally made an effort to work out where she was going with this one. 'I'm not the kind of girl who makes a habit of this sort of thing…' She gave an unsteady laugh and felt a rush of confusion at what she had just said. Not only was she *not* the sort of girl who did *this sort of thing*, she was not the sort of girl who had ever even contemplated it.

So how had it all happened so easily?

'I know.'

'Because your experience is with girls who would *easily* do that sort of thing?' She couldn't help it but she felt a stab of jealousy so deep that it was a physical pain in her chest.

'What do you want me to say to that?'

'The truth?' This conversation was not going where she had expected it to. Ten minutes previously, they had been swimming naked in the crystal waters, and she had felt as though she had no cares in the world. Now reality had come barging through and was refusing to budge until it had been dealt with.

Why did that fill her with such a sense of anger and regret? She had never had a problem facing up to reality, but now she wished that it would just go away and leave her alone.

'Okay, the truth is that I haven't had a string of women who particularly balk at the prospect of going to bed with a man. If you want to call them easy, then you can. So, as far as my trustworthiness goes, I guess it's never had to be put to the test.' He expelled a long breath and looked at her with utter seriousness. 'I work damn hard and I've never sought out the responsibility of a committed relationship. I never felt the need for it.'

'Well, at least you don't have a problem with honesty.' A breeze wafted and blew her hair into chaotic semi-dry tendrils around her face.

He hadn't told her anything that she hadn't already figured out for herself, but she still felt a little shocked at the brutality of his frankness.

'I try not to. Lying just ends up in a knotty situation.'

'So this weekend…'

'Can be whatever you want it to be.'

Jessica stared out to sea, curling a strand of hair around her finger. She knew what was on offer. A temporary liaison on an island that inspired magic.

She desperately wanted to ask him what happened once the weekend drew to a close, but she already knew the answer to that one. He neither wanted nor needed anything permanent in his life. In fact, she doubted he even wanted anything that remotely smelled of permanence. She wasn't his type, nor was he hers, but for a few days they could let the spell that had been cast run its course.

'What do *you* want?' she asked curiously, turning to look at him.

'You.'

'A holiday fling,' she said pensively. The way he looked at her filled her with a heady, drowning sensation. She looked away and distractedly flicked some sand with one finger, watching as it sprayed into the air.

'A time to remember.'

'Oh, very poetic.' Jessica laughed, not caring to look into the future beyond the weekend. He ran his fingers along her spine and she shivered. 'Perhaps we should be getting back.'

'I take it that's your answer?'

'I don't know *what* my answer is.'

And she truly didn't. But for the remainder of the day she felt his presence with such force that it left her breathless. This really was the stuff of memories. She didn't think that she would ever forget the way he made her feel, the way he sent her senses spinning into orbit.

She could feel his eyes on her, even when he was talking to everyone else, and it was like being touched. As dusk turned into inky blackness, and food was eaten and alcohol consumed, and the noise levels rose, the undercurrent running between them was like the silent buzz of electricity. Her eyes were drawn compulsively to him, as though her body had tuned into its own peculiar radio signal, but she only realised what she wanted to do when, as the last of the straggling crew drifted off to their bedroom, the worse for wear, she lingered behind, waiting and watching.

And even then, there were still the remnants of hesitation.

Was she cut out for this kind of thing? Was she fashioned for the one-off fling, no strings attached? She must surely be, she reasoned fiercely to herself, because she certainly wasn't fashioned for the whole marriage bit.

She didn't want commitment any more than he did, so why was she so scared at the prospect of this brief, intense fling, followed by nothing?

'Not heading off to bed?' She heard his voice from behind her, and jumped. He was switching off lights, checking the doors to make sure that everywhere was closed. In the darkness, he was a tall, shadowy figure, lounging indolently against the wall, his hands stuck in his pockets.

As she looked at him she could feel her breath quickening, and she raised her hand to her throat, forcing herself to be calm.

'Are you?' she asked in a ridiculously high voice.

'Actually…' he pushed himself away from the wall and walked slowly towards her, and with every step closer she could feel her heart rate accelerate '…I was thinking about a stroll on the beach. Care to join me?'

They both knew what he was asking, and after only a few seconds' hesitation she nodded.

'I've never strolled on a beach at midnight,' she confessed. He was now standing so close to her that she could feel her nipples hardening, pushing against her shirt, aroused simply at the thought of what he could do to her.

'It's quite an experience,' he murmured, and his voice was like a caress—a soft, velvety caress.

They silently left the house and walked down to the beach, then down to the water's edge so that the sea lapped against their bare feet. Everything around them was dark. The sea, the sky, the silhouettes of the trees like swaying black figures. They began walking away from the house, until they had left it behind. With every step, she could feel that thread of pulsating excitement growing stronger and stronger.

When he finally turned to her and cupped her face in his hands, she breathed a sigh of satisfaction, tilting her head upwards, parting her lips to meet his mouth as it descended and moved against hers in a soft, lingering, never-ending kiss.

Tomorrow was a point in time which no longer existed. For the first time in her life the only thing that mattered was the here and now, with no plans for the future, no looking ahead.

She wasn't wearing a bra, and a part of her wondered now whether she hadn't already made her mind up when she had changed clothes earlier in the evening.

His hands slid to her waist, circling it, his thumbs meeting and rubbing her navel, then climbing higher, under the baggy shirt, pushing it up until her breasts were exposed.

They sank slowly, entwined, onto their bed of sand, white and flawless in the burning daylight sun, dark with shadows now.

He buried his head between her breasts, then licked them gently, leaving no part of the full, swelling mounds untouched.

Somehow, this time, the embrace of darkness made things seem less frantic, less urgent. Their actions were unhurried, a slow, thorough exploration of each other's bodies.

He sucked on her nipples, taking his time, savouring their sweetness, and she, in turn, ran her tongue along the firm, hard lines of his torso, marvelling at the ridges of muscles she could feel under her fingers.

The build-up was exquisitely unhurried. It seemed as though everything could last for ever.

When he finally nuzzled the sensitised region between her thighs, she had to stop herself from crying out loud in ecstasy. Even then, there was no rush, no fast rhythm to propel her on to a shuddering, urgent climax. He licked and sucked, and she softly moaned as his tongue found the throbbing bud of her femininity and played with it, gently.

The minutes seemed to stretch on into eternity, with the lapping of the water blending with the lapping of his tongue in her moistness.

There was something shockingly tender about their love-making.

Even as he entered her, his movements were long and deep, and she felt as though her body had been created just for this: to receive him.

She arched back, and he bent forward so that with every thrust his tongue briefly found an engorged nipple and flicked erotically against it. There was no part of her body that wasn't on fire. If two bodies could fuse, then surely theirs must. They were slippery with heat, and she could feel him burning against her. Finally, when she could hold out no longer, his rhythm altered, speeding up, faster and faster until he tensed with the final pleasure just as she felt her body stiffen in response, and she gave a hoarse cry of fulfilment, rolling over so that she could continue the momentum, shuddering uncontrollably as ripple after ripple of pleasure ran through her.

Later, much later, when she rolled to her side and said to him, 'You're right. One weekend, but a weekend that will become the stuff of memories,' she almost felt as though she meant it. Here, in the middle of nowhere, nothing outside seemed to exist, and all her everyday problems appeared petty and meaningless. She could cope with all that, in time.

'And what if I want to see you when we get back?' he asked in a husky voice, and her body stilled.

No, she thought sadly. If only, but what they had here was unique and should remain what it was: a moment in time. She instinctively knew that to prolong their relationship, if that was what it could be called, would be a mistake.

'It wouldn't work,' she whispered softly, blowing into his ear and feeling him stir into life against her. 'You really don't want someone like me, and I'd rather...'

'Quit while you're ahead?'

'Enjoy what we have for what it is,' she amended. A wave of emotion rushed through her, making her feel giddy and faint, and she blinked it away.

'No commitment,' she said quietly. 'It's something neither of us needs.' Or did she? *Did she?* No. It had never been part of her master plan. A weekend she could control, but nothing beyond that.

## CHAPTER SEVEN

'YOU'VE been summoned.' Millie's face wore the same anxious, concerned look that it had held for the interminably fraught last couple of months, but at least, Jessica thought, she had stopped asking her repeatedly if everything was all right.

Everything was not all right. It never would be, and she knew that that was reflected in her every expression, in every move she made, but there seemed to be very little she could do to control that.

'I'm too busy, Mills,' Jessica said, sitting down suddenly and giving in to the overwhelming exhaustion that had been sapping her energy ever since she had returned from that fateful weekend abroad. She rested her head in her open palms and shut her eyes.

'I wish you'd tell me what's wrong,' Millie said worriedly, and Jessica sighed heavily by way of response.

'I'll be fine.'

Not long left to go at the company, then her problems would begin in earnest. She didn't know if she had the strength to face them, but there was no way out.

'Shall I tell Mr Carr that you won't be able to see him?' Millie asked gently, and Jessica's head shot up.

'Bruno Carr wants to see me?' Her voice was hoarse and shocked, and her secretary's face became pinched with consternation. 'Why?' she demanded. 'Why? Why would he want to see me all of a sudden? I've had no contact with the man for weeks and weeks and weeks! What did he say?'

'I don't know,' Millie stammered. 'I'm sorry, Jess...

perhaps he just wants to tell you goodbye personally...'

'How does he know that I'm leaving?' Every aching muscle in her body had sprung into life, filling her with a dreadful sense of apprehension.

How could he still do this to her?

When they had parted company all that time ago, she had cheerfully believed every word she had said to him. She had convinced herself that their very brief fling had been everything and nothing, and all that she had needed. Just what the doctor had ordered, she had told herself, every time his image crept into her head and wreaked havoc with her thoughts.

She barely knew the man, she had thought, and the fact that he seemed to have stuck in her brain was absolutely nothing to worry about. She was not accustomed to having a weekend lover. Of course, she would find it a little difficult to get out of her mind. She wasn't made of stone, after all.

It wasn't even that they were soul mates, she lectured repeatedly to herself, when the hours became days, and the days turned into weeks, and the thought of him still managed to evoke feelings of loss and misery. Time would cure her of her stupidity.

But time, she had discovered, had joined hands with fate and both were conspiring to turn her life on its head.

'He owns this company, Jess...' Millie's voice was confused and agitated, and Jessica knew just what she was thinking: The boss has finally lost it. She's been a mess for the past few weeks, and now she's finally waved goodbye to her sanity.

Jessica cleared her throat, looked up, and made an attempt to speak with at least a semblance of self-control.

'You're right. I'll see him right away.' She watched as

her secretary's expression of worry changed into one of relief. Of course, she had no intention of going to see Bruno Carr, but Millie wasn't to know that.

She stood up, smoothed her hair neatly behind her ears, and plastered a cheerful smile on her face.

'Where is he?' Polite look, a little quizzical, but definitely composed. Millie, she thought, must think I'm deranged.

'At his office. He said that he expects you within the hour.'

Fat chance.

'I'll go immediately.' She glanced at her desk, with the papers covering most of the available free space, and randomly selected a couple which she handed to her secretary. A couple of months ago, she would have been invigorated at the prospect of the work lying in front of her. Now, she couldn't care less. She had an insane urge to sweep her hand across the smooth, hard, wooden surface and watch all those little bits of paper swirl helplessly into the wastepaper basket on the ground. 'Reply to these for me, would you, Mills? And you'd better cancel my appointment to see James Parker this afternoon. I'm not sure what time I'll be back from seeing Mr Carr. If I get back at all.'

'Of course.'

There, there, there, Jessica wanted to say. Don't you feel better now, Mills? Now that I'm acting in character, even if it's all a charade?

She fetched her jacket from the back of her chair and stuck it on. The weather had finally broken after an endless winter and a spring that had seemed reluctant to part company with the cold. Now it had shed its indecision and was everywhere. New, little buds bursting out in the sunshine, daffodils sticking yellow heads through the grass, coats returned to wardrobes for their annual hibernation. Jessica barely noticed any of it. The sky could have been bright red for all she knew, and the sun could have been purple. She came to work in a daze, worked in a daze and returned home in a daze.

'I'll see you in the morning!' Millie called, and Jessica turned around to look at her.

'Oh, yes. See you in the morning.' Then she was gone. Out of the door and the office and walking briskly towards the underground. Several stops, then finally her own. She thought about Bruno, waiting in his office to see her, and shuddered with relief as her house drew closer.

She had yearned to see him. It was unbelievable how much she had yearned to see him. It was as though their one weekend together had opened her up to emotions she had spent a lifetime suppressing.

Now, she could envisage nothing worse.

She slipped her key into the lock, shut the door behind her, and did what she did every evening recently when she returned from work: kicked her shoes off and then collapsed onto the sofa and closed her eyes. There was a lot to do, but the mere thought of doing any of it made her feel faint. The ironing basket seemed to have taken on a life of its own, and was growing daily. If she didn't do something about it, she knew that she would be forced to contact an ironing service to come and take it all away. There were dishes in the sink, and a few of them had been sitting there for the past two days. She hadn't even bothered to soak them in water, and the grime would have hardened so that when she finally did get around to washing them they would stubbornly refuse to release their greasy layers.

None of it seemed to matter. In her head, the problems churned around and around, mutating and changing and shifting positions, but never going away.

How could they?

From her prone position on the sofa, she gave a little groan and rolled over onto her side, feeling utterly horrible in her work clothes. Her hair was coming undone, and she irritably released it from its tightly coiled bun, running her fingers through it and then draping it over one shoulder.

She could feel herself sliding into sleep when the doorbell sounded. It penetrated her fuggy brain like the sudden buzz of a wasp, and as she blinked her way to the surface became shrill and insistent until she could ignore it no longer.

Shoeless, hair everywhere, she stormed to the front door, yanked it open, and then felt her mouth turn to ash.

'I gave it half an hour,' Bruno said coldly, 'and then I phoned your secretary, to be told that you had left some time ago. To come and see me. At my office. As instructed.' He folded his arms and lounged against the doorframe.

'What have you come here for?' She could control her words, but not the tenor of her voice, and she heard the faint tremble in it with a mixture of disgust and panic.

He was everything and more than she remembered. Taller, leaner, more bronzed, and infinitely more disturbing. She felt suffocated by his presence, literally choking from the impact of seeing him here, on her doorstep. How on earth had she ever been able to tell him goodbye, to inform him that she was not open to his offer of casual mistress once they returned to England, to let him know that he had been no more than a wonderful but temporary liaison? How had she ever thought that she could return to her normal life and put him down to experience?

'To see you,' he informed her, his voice ice. 'I came here because it was obvious that you had left the office with no intention whatsoever of taking a taxi to the City.'

He reached inside his trouser pocket and pulled out a sheet of paper. 'Mind telling me what this is all about?'

It was her letter of resignation. She recognised the paper, and the glimpse of signature at the bottom of the typed page. In the absence of her direct boss, she had made sure to send it to the personnel department, never imagining that it would find its way to Bruno Carr. She should have known better. Hadn't he always made a point of saying how au fait he was with everything that happened in his various companies? Clearly it had been no idle boast.

'Come in.' She stepped aside to let him enter. It was strange seeing him like this after all this time. A wall had developed between them and it hurt to remember how easy they had been with one another. It seemed like a lifetime away. As he brushed past her she could feel her skin crawl, and her pulses began to race.

She didn't know what the hell she was going to tell him, but she knew that he wouldn't leave until she provided him with an answer. Any answer. Any answer but the truth.

'Would you like a cup of tea?' she asked politely. 'Some coffee?' With a change of clothes she could be a waitress, she thought, so impersonal was her voice, and by way of response he threw her a dark, brooding scowl, before walking towards the sitting room and making himself comfortable on one of the chairs.

'I'll pass on the drink,' he told her sarcastically. 'Sorry. I guess that means a little less time for you to try and fabricate an excuse.'

'I wasn't going to do any such thing.' She picked the end of the sofa furthest away from him and sat down. Even at this distance, she could feel him as strongly as if he were touching her.

'How did you get hold of my resignation?' she asked eventually. It was hard to maintain her composure and she found herself leaning forward, her elbows resting on her knees.

Oh, God. She had never envisaged laying eyes on him again. This was her worst nightmare.

'I keep tabs on everything that goes on in my company,' he informed her icily. 'It's my business.'

'Of course.'

'Correct me if I'm wrong,' he said, sitting back and tossing her letter of resignation dismissively on the table between them, 'but the last time I saw you, you were perfectly happy with your job.'

'Things change.' She shrugged and threw him an apologetic smile, which did nothing to alter his thunderous expression. The steady, polite smile on her face slipped a little. 'I decided that the job just wasn't challenging enough for me,' she told him, thinking on her feet, and steering far away from any possible excuse which might encourage him to smell a rat. 'I suppose it was the anticlimax of your court case. I realised that I no longer had anything to get my teeth into.' She could feel herself building up some very convenient momentum with this line of reasoning. It was beginning to sound more and more plausible.

She still couldn't quite meet his eyes though. So, instead, she addressed the space slightly to the left of his ear. Craven but necessary if her heart wasn't to start doing unmanageable things behind her ribcage. She could already feel most of her confident assertions, which she had made repeatedly to herself over the past few weeks—that he was insignificant in her life, a ship that had passed in the night—ebbing away at a furious rate.

'What a period of revelations for you,' he commented acidly.

'Yes. Yes, it was! And what's the problem here anyway?' she snapped, going onto the attack. 'I assume your employees aren't chained to your companies for life! I assume they're at liberty to move on! Tell me, do you subject each and every employee who has the temerity to try and resign to this kind of third degree?' Her heart was pounding and her face was bright red. She could feel it burning as though her whole body were on fire.

She desperately wanted to be angry with him. If need be, she would generate her own spurious argument, because the anger was her only point of protection. She knew that any other reaction would allow memories to seep through, and she couldn't allow that to happen.

'So you were suddenly disillusioned with your job. And I take it that you've already found something else? Or were you so disillusioned that you decided to throw it all in and to heck with the possibility of earning nothing? No,' he said slowly to himself, while she listened to his line of reasoning with helpless frustration. 'Surely not. You've always made such a point of being in control of your life, of needing to be in control of your life, that you'd hardly pack in a hefty pay cheque on wild impulse. Which leaves us with your new job. What is it? I'm all ears.'

He sat back and allowed himself the satisfied smile of the cat that had successfully cornered the mouse.

'I haven't found anything yet,' Jessica muttered under her breath.

'Dear, oh, dear. Now, that makes no sense at all. Does it?'

She said nothing, feeling trapped.

'Which is probably why I don't buy the *I'm suddenly disillusioned* excuse.' He stared at her coolly and with a degree of calculation that made her nervous system go into overdrive. Her mind raced ahead, attempting to pre-empt all possible arguments he could throw at her, but nothing in her head appeared to be working efficiently.

'I really don't care what you buy or don't buy.' Brave words, she thought miserably, if it weren't for the fact they were sabotaged by the shakiness of her voice.

'Sure about that?'

'What are you talking about?'

He folded his arms and surveyed her unhurriedly and dispassionately.

'I find it a bit coincidental that we shared a weekend together, and then suddenly you decide to quit.'

A chill was beginning to crawl up her spine.

'I've always enjoyed crosswords,' he mused pensively. 'I like the challenge posed to the intellect. The knowledge that, however convoluted the clue is, there's an answer and the answer is clear provided your brain's working in the right direction.'

That chill was now spreading outwards, numbing her. She felt as though she were being pulled along behind something very fast and quite unstoppable. She could barely breathe, never mind open her mouth and try to change the course of this remorseless reasoning.

'I looked at your letter of resignation and none of it made any sense,' he continued, relentless and implacable. 'Believe it or not, I did consider your original line of argument, that you had become turned off the nature of the work, but I dismissed that almost immediately for the reasons I gave you.' He smiled, but there was nothing remotely warm about it. Her hands, resting on her knees, felt clammy.

'Which made me wonder whether you had had a falling out with someone you work with, but I was certain that that wasn't the case... Of course, there was the slight chance that you found yourself unable to manage Robert's job, but that wasn't it, was it? I've been keeping tabs on you and I would have been the first to have heard. Which in turn led me to think that perhaps our weekend together meant more to you than you had said at the time.'

She felt her body still. Her brain had turned over that horrifying thought so often in the past few weeks that it had physically hurt, and still the answer to the question eluded her.

'Maybe you'd nurtured cosy little thoughts of togetherness... Maybe that was why you wouldn't contemplate seeing me on a casual basis once we got back...maybe you wanted more than that...much more...' He let the insinuation hang in the air between them, until mortification at the prolonged silence forced her into speech.

'Hardly. But of course you'd find that hard to believe because your ego wouldn't allow it.' She could feel herself on the brink of anger once again, but somehow she couldn't quite sustain the feeling. It slithered through her fingers like sand, until she was left clutching her fear and trepidation once more.

He shrugged, as though her observation was neither here nor there. Mere words.

His eyes were watchful now, though. She could sense him focusing every ounce of his attention on her, and it was debilitating.

'Perhaps, I thought, you'd been hit harder than you had anticipated, and you felt that your only move would be to get out of the company, to escape from my orbit. But that made no sense either. Because we could go for the next few years and not see one another, couldn't we? It's hardly as though we work under the same roof, in the same building.' He was leaning forward now, and his energy was so intense that she could feel it wrap itself around her like a vice.

'I don't know where this is taking us!' she said, springing to her feet. Panic had swept through her, turning her words into staccato bursts. 'Whatever my reasons for leaving, they're none of your business!'

'Sit back down,' he said with deadly quietness. 'Now!' His command cracked through the air like a whiplash, and she sank back into the chair, heart racing.

'I'm about to say something and if I'm wrong, then I'll walk out of that door and that will be the last you ever see of me again. But I've considered all the options, and I think the reason you've handed in your notice affects me quite a bit.'

Jessica swallowed painfully, aware that her mouth was dry.

'I have no idea what you're getting at,' she said bravely. 'And I think that it's time you left. I've quit and that's all there is to it. You can't force an explanation out of me, and you can't force me to go back to work for you.'

'You're pregnant, aren't you?'

It was a question, but posed as a statement, and the blood rushed to her head like a tidal wave, suddenly freed from all constraints. She found that she couldn't speak, couldn't think. The drumbeat in her ears was too loud, and even as she maintained her horrified silence she knew that it pronounced the truth of what he had just said.

She should have rushed in to defend herself, cried out in amused denial, anything but sit there in silence.

'Don't be ridiculous.' Her voice was barely above a whisper, and unsteady. Her hands, clasped on her lap, were shaking, and she quickly stuck them under her thighs, sitting on them.

'Why don't you save us forty minutes of pointless discussion on the subject, and just admit it? You're leaving because you're carrying my baby.' He raked his fingers through his hair and stood up, as though the words had generated a level of energy in him that had to be worked off.

He began pacing the room and she followed him with her eyes.

'And did you have any intention of telling me?' he asked grimly, walking over to her and leaning over her, his hands on either side of her arm rests, so that she was compelled to push herself into the chair.

'Please go.'

'I'm not leaving this house until you tell me the truth!' The words sliced through the air like a knife.

'It's true. I'm pregnant.' There was nothing to be gained by lying. She might get rid of him temporarily, but she knew that he would return, over and over, waiting to see her swelling stomach, waiting to see his accusations verified. And she could hardly move house in an attempt to escape him, could she?

'I thought…'

'That it was the perfect ploy to find yourself a husband?' he sneered, and she flung her head back, shocked and furious at where his thinking was carrying him.

'How dare you…?'

'How dare I what…Jessica? Push you into a corner?'

'Get out!'

'Or else what? You'll throw me out? Hardly.' He laughed coldly, and she struggled to match this ice-cold stranger in front of her with the sensuous, witty man who had made her laugh and made love to her, and changed the course of her life.

He was still looming over her, so close that his face was almost touching hers. 'Was that the plan? A carefully orchestrated weekend of lovemaking, with just enough protests about independence to stave off any worries I might have had about your becoming clingy, and a pregnancy at the end of it? Pregnancy and marriage? Was that the idea, Jessica?' His voice had grown steadily harsher, and as she looked at him in horror she could feel herself breathing quickly.

'You're mad,' she finally whispered. 'How could you imagine for a minute that I *planned* this pregnancy?' She gave a bitter, shallow laugh.

He couldn't have been further from the truth. She closed her eyes and relived that weak, collapsing feeling as she had stood in her bathroom and stared as two blue lines had appeared in their little windows on that tester. She couldn't begin to explain the emotion that had swept over her, but at no time had she felt the slightest inclination to tell him what had happened. From the start she had seen it as uniquely *her* problem.

'Are you denying it?'

'Does it matter one way or the other? You're going to believe what you want, anyway.'

'Answer me! Dammit!'

She almost expected him to get hold of her and shake her, but his hands remained gripping the sides of the chair, his white knuckles a testimony to what he was feeling. Fury, she guessed, suddenly weary with the whole thing. His mind was probably working overtime as well at the thought of how he could wriggle out of the situation. As far as she was concerned, he had nothing to worry about on that score.

'You're a sick man if you think that I would get myself pregnant for the sole purpose of trapping you into marriage. I made a mistake, it's as simple as that. I calculated that I wouldn't be in a fertile period, and my calculations were wrong, probably only by a couple of days, but a miss is as good as a mile in this instance, isn't it?' His breath fanned her face and she had to steel herself to meet his eyes. 'I know you think there's a huge female contingent out there, gasping for the privilege of trapping you into marriage, but I'm not one of them. Whether you believe me or not is up to you. I'm sorry you found out—'

'Because, fired as you are with moral ethics, you had no intention of telling me.' His mouth twisted angrily, and she flinched.

'This is *my* problem,' she said fiercely.

'And nothing whatsoever to do with me?'

'That's right!'

'An Immaculate Conception. The Pope would be interested.'

'You know what I mean.'

'Explain it to me, why don't you?'

'I don't understand you,' Jessica muttered. 'One minute you're raging at me because you think I'm a conniving gold-digger. The next minute, you're raging at me because you think I'm not.' Their eyes met and she held his narrowed stare, even though it was hard.

She was the first to look down, and it was a relief when he pushed himself away from the chair and went to sit on the sofa.

'You made it quite clear what sort of man you are,' she said, pausing in between her words to harness her thoughts into some semblance of order. 'Fast lane with work, fast lane with women. Wasn't one of your complaints that your last girlfriend was getting a little too cosy for your liking?' She stared mutinously at him, daring him to contradict her, but he remained silent. 'I respect that. The last thing I intended to do was push you into a corner, force you into premature responsibility with someone you barely know.'

'So your plan was…what? Exactly?'

'To cope on my own,' she told him. 'Isn't that obvious?'

'And coping on your own starts by your handing in your notice, thereby cutting off your income.'

'I had no choice,' Jessica said through gritted teeth.

'So now you have no job...what then?'

'I intend to find another job.'

'Doing what?'

'The same sort of thing I was doing before,' she snapped tensely.

'Oh, but correct me if I'm wrong. Permanent jobs are a bit thin on the ground for women who are pregnant, aren't they? Don't employers look askance at women who will only be available for work for a matter of a few months?'

'Temp work, then,' she said uncomfortably.

'Does that pay well?'

'I'm sure I could find something...' Her voice dwindled off and she stared down at her fingers, frowning.

'Filing? Typing? Temp workers get the dregs of the work and they're paid relatively little. A pittance when you consider that you intended to cover some substantial costs. Of course, you might have a large amount of savings stashed away somewhere, for just such a rainy day as this...'

'I could make do...'

'Without money and without family support...'

Jessica glared at him, wishing that she had never let slip confidences which were now being used against her.

'I can manage.'

'And your problems don't cease with the birth of the baby, do they?' he carried on relentlessly. She could feel tears gathering in the corners of her eyes and she blinked them away. 'You'll have to get your act together and find yourself a damn good job once the baby's born if you're to cover the costs of what...childcare? Nursery? And all that on your own.'

'Are you suggesting that I...terminate this pregnancy?'

She could barely form the words. The thought of doing any such thing disgusted her and if that was the route he was heading down, then he could walk right out of that door and carry on walking.

Not once had she contemplated an abortion. Her initial response had been one of confusion and fear, but she couldn't deny that from the start she had also felt a certain wild thrill at the thought of bringing a baby into the world. It hadn't been part of her plan, but she wanted this baby with an intensity she would never have thought possible. So much for the biological clock she had always assumed she didn't have.

'You insult me,' he told her with freezing disdain. 'I would no more think of suggesting such a thing than I would advise you to jump off a cliff.' He paused and appeared to turn his thoughts over in his head, like someone swilling a mouthful of fine wine, tasting, rolling it over on his tongue.

Eventually he said, 'So we've agreed that bringing up a baby on your own is as good as impossible.'

'We agree on no such thing! Thousands of women do it and cope quite satisfactorily.' She would never have admitted it, but he had managed to shake some of her self-confidence. She knew that she had deliberately adopted a rosy view of what lay ahead, more as a method of self-defence than anything else, but he had forced her to stare at all the pitfalls, and she hadn't liked what she had seen.

'In most cases because they have no choice.'

'And I do?'

'Oh, yes,' he said softly. 'You most certainly do.'

She didn't like the look in his eyes. It unsettled her.

'And what's my choice?' she heard herself ask, even though she knew that the answer to the question was not something she wanted to hear.

'You marry me.'

Jessica stared at him, open-mouthed. 'Marry?' she asked, on the verge of hysterical laughter. 'You?' She couldn't help it. She could feel the laughter rising out of her stomach. Her mouth began to twitch, and the more she acknowledged that that would be an unacceptable reaction, the less capable she felt of controlling the urge.

She began to giggle, and then a flood of emotion took over. All the confusion and stress and uncertainty seemed finally to find an outlet, and she heard herself laughing. Laughing until she thought she would never stop. Laughing until the tears came to her eyes, but somehow she knew that the tears were not of jollity, but stemmed from something else.

When he slammed his fist down on the table, the noise was so loud and so incongruous that she jumped back with a gasp.

'Stop it! Now!'

'I can't help it. I'm laughing at your ridiculous suggestion.'

'You're laughing because you know that if you don't you'll crack up,' he told her grimly.

Jessica looked at him dumbly. He was right. She could feel tears of anxiety and worry begin to collect in the corner of her eyes and she glared at him with savage resentment. She had managed to build a little cocoon for herself and along he had come and destroyed it in one fell swoop.

'You're going to marry me because you have no real choice in the matter.'

'How dare you...?'

'I have no intention of relinquishing my responsibility, nor do I intend to politely knock on your door once a week on a Saturday, so that I can see my child. I hadn't banked on fatherhood, you're damned right about that, but fatherhood has managed to come along and find me and I have every intention of doing my duty.'

'Doing your duty...? This is the twentieth century!'

'No child of mine is going to grow up a bastard,' he said quietly, and Jessica flushed.

'You ought to hear yourself, Bruno Carr! You sound positively medieval! Well, we're not in the Middle Ages now, and I'll be damned if I'm going to marry you just because you say so!'

'I could make life very difficult for you, Jessica...'

'How?'

'Jobs, for a start.' He stood up and began pacing the room, pausing every so often to inspect something, even though she knew that his mind was utterly focused on what he was saying. 'My connections are widespread,' he said casually, as though discussing how many pairs of socks he possessed. 'I know everyone. Word gets around...'

'You wouldn't dare! You would never jeopardise your own child's financial future by jeopardising my earning power. That makes no sense at all.' She was barely moved by this threat because she knew that it was empty. What frightened her was the motivation behind it. Bruno Carr did not relinquish what he felt belonged to him, and this child would belong to him.

He paused and turned to face her, his eyes narrowed. 'You can't win on this, Jessica.'

'I won't marry you for the wrong reasons! It would be unfair on us both, and on the child! Can't you see that?'

'All I see is a very selfish woman who would sacrifice her child's life for the sake of her own.'

'How can you say that? How can you imply that...?'

'You would rather scrimp and save and go without than marry me? And tell me, how do you think our child will feel about that when he's old enough to understand—?'

He had managed to hit her on a vulnerable spot, and one which she had never considered.

'Aside from closing the door on any possible future you might have, you'd merrily close the door on a child's future as well. For what? To hang on to your independence?'

'There's nothing wrong with that...' she protested, but her voice had weakened.

'Absolutely nothing...when you are the only one involved.'

'But you don't love me...' she said, horrified at the desperate tone that had crept into her voice.

'Who's talking about love? We're talking about an arrangement. A business arrangement, so to speak... You've said often enough that romance is not for you. Well, I'm offering the perfect solution.'

'I can't...'

'Oh, you can,' he said silkily, his eyes steel, 'and you will. Believe me, you will.'

# CHAPTER EIGHT

BRUNO CARR always got what he wanted. Hadn't he mentioned that to Jessica in passing somewhere along the line? She should have paid a bit more attention. She certainly should never have allowed a weekend's worth of charm to blind her to the man she had glimpsed at their very first meeting. A man who expected the world to dance to his tune.

Two days ago he had left her in a state of confusion and now, as she arranged herself in suitable clothes to meet him at a restaurant in Covent Garden, she stared glumly at her reflection in the mirror.

Her stomach was still flat, showing no indication of what lay ahead.

She still hadn't worked up the courage to telephone her mother and let her know of these latest, overwhelming developments in her life. Similarly, she had put her friends on hold, unable to face the barrage of questions that would greet her announcement. They had all cheerfully given up on her and the institution of marriage.

They would have to iron out the details of their little arrangement, he had informed her. As though her life, from now on, were nothing more than a piece of cloth, to be pulled and stretched and straightened into whatever shape he desired.

*I can't imagine why you're not enamoured of the idea,* he had told her coldly. Wasn't an arranged marriage the ultimate in control? She had heard his words, and watched his mouth as he formed them, and had felt anything but in control. Her life had never seemed so wildly disordered and unpredictable. .

She sighed and ran her fingers through her hair, sectioning it off into three, and absent-mindedly plaiting it in one long, thick braid down her back.

She knew, somewhere, that a part of her was being unreasonable.

After all, she had felt shock at the discovery of her pregnancy, but the shock had soon been replaced by a certain nervous elation. So why did something less significant fill her with such terror?

With absolutely no time to spare, she made it to the restaurant, to find him sitting on the far side with a drink in front of him.

'I wondered whether you'd chickened out of meeting me,' were his first words, though with no smile to accompany them.

'And if I had?'

She sat down, pulling the chair towards the table, and then relaxed back with her arms folded, in the classic pose of self-defence.

'Oh, I would have come and found you. And just in case the thought of running away ever crosses your mind, forget it. There would be no rock I would leave unturned to get you.'

'To get your baby, you mean,' she said bitterly.

'I stand corrected.' He gestured to the waiter for two menus, and she grabbed a few minutes' reprieve from looking at him by concentrating on the jumble of words in front of her. Salmon, steak, sauces and parcels of vegetables, whatever. She couldn't care less what she ate. A hearty appetite and the presence of Bruno Carr were two things that did not go together. Not now.

'You haven't put on much weight,' he said, settling back in his seat.

'Is that remark intended to put me at ease?'

'Is that what I'm supposed to do? Put you at ease?'

'No, of course it isn't,' Jessica said acidly. 'Marriages are best conducted in a state of cold war.'

She fiddled with the stem of her wineglass and missed the glimmer of a smile that tugged the corners of his mouth for a few seconds.

'So I take it that you've resigned yourself to the prospect...' He waited until a glass of wine had been placed in front of him and a glass of orange juice in front of her, and then leaned slightly forward. 'There's a lot to be sorted out.'

'You're a cold-hearted bastard, aren't you?' she answered.

'On the contrary,' he said smoothly. 'If I were a cold-hearted bastard, I would have allowed you to handle the entire thing on your own, as you had stupidly planned to do. The fact is, whether you like it or not, I have no intention of relinquishing my responsibility and I also have no intention of lurking on the sidelines, watching any child of mine grow up without my input. As I've told you before.'

'So you have.'

'Why aren't you looking pregnant?'

'What are you trying to say, Bruno? That you doubt me? That you think I've made the whole thing up?'

'Don't be ridiculous.' He flushed and looked away uncomfortably. 'I'm asking if you're all right. Physically, I mean. Things doing what they should be doing?' He looked at her briefly from under his lashes, and she was momentarily thrown by that glimmer of boyish charm that had captivated her.

'"Things doing what they should be doing?"' She raised

her eyebrows expressively. 'What a medically oriented question. Don't you know anything about pregnancy?'

'Well, having just been pregnant the one time...'

Jessica felt a sudden urge to smile and clicked her tongue with irritation instead. After all the defensive, hostile feelings he had recently aroused in her, she was stupefied that she could suddenly find anything he said remotely amusing. It wouldn't do, she told herself sternly. It wouldn't do at all. She couldn't let herself forget that, beneath any charm, this man would do whatever he wanted to get his own way. He would marry her for the sake of the baby and then what? Lifelong fidelity? Hardly. He didn't love her and it would simply be a matter of time before his sexual urges took him to newer hunting grounds. Because he occasionally had the knack of making her laugh meant nothing. It certainly didn't mean that a union between them wouldn't be a union on paper only.

'I doubt I'll show for another few weeks or so.' Her cheeks were burning and it was a relief when the food came and she had a chance to catch her breath.

'But you've been to the doctor...had checks...I mean, whatever checks you should have had...'

'Quite soon, but not just yet,' she informed him.

'Oh.' He appeared to digest this piece of information. 'Then how do you know...?'

'Bruno.' Jessica looked at him firmly. 'Pregnancy is a natural occurrence. I feel well enough, apart from the odd bout of morning sickness and that's on its way out. I'm sure everything is all right. There's absolutely nothing to worry about.'

'Who ever said anything about worrying?' He stabbed a piece of fish with his fork and treated her to a watered-down version of a glare.

Why did he have to be so damned *cute*? she thought

irritably. Why couldn't he be cold and detached all the time? *Cute* undermined her. His *mood swings* undermined her.

She felt a sudden gust of misery sweep over her. It was all such a parody of what should have been.

'You brought me here to discuss arrangements...' she reminded him unsteadily.

'Arrangements. Yes.' He seemed as relieved as she was to find their conversational footing back to where it should be. 'There's no need, first of all, for you to continue working out your notice.'

'You mean I can continue working until I'm ready to...have the baby?' Now that he knew the reasons for her resignation, there seemed no point in resigning after all. She knew that she would have to tell everyone at the office that she was getting married, having a baby, and that Bruno Carr was the man responsible, and she knew that there would be a buzz of gossip for a while after. But gossip died eventually. And she wasn't afraid of gossip. They were a good bunch of people, and after the initial shock and 'who'd have thought it?' remarks, they would accept it.

'I mean,' Bruno said patiently, 'you can leave immediately, *without* bothering to work out your notice at all.'

'And do what?' She looked at him questioningly, as though he had suddenly started talking a different language.

'Do nothing. Relax. Put your feet up. Plan a nursery. Whatever,' he finished irritably, watching her face.

'I intend to do no such thing,' Jessica informed him flatly. If there were one or two things to be ironed out, then they had hit the first major crease. 'I'm not going to *sit around doing nothing*. I'd go mad.'

'Lots of women do it,' he said impatiently. 'And there's no *financial* need for you to work. As my wife, you'll have whatever you need, and whenever you need it.'

Which, she thought, brought them swiftly to crease number two.

'Look, let's get one or two things straight here.' She abandoned her attempts to enjoy what remained of the food in front of her, and closed her knife and fork. 'I *am not* going to be giving up work from now and sitting around on my butt doing nothing, just because you think it might be a good idea. I am going to carry on where I am and when the time comes I shall have the baby and then go back out to work. I have no intention of becoming a financial burden to you.'

'Oh, for God's sake, woman—'

'And furthermore, while we're on the subject of money, I intend to keep my flat and rent it out.'

'As a bolt-hole?'

'As a source of income!'

'You *don't need* a source of income!'

'Nor do you, any longer!' she retorted. 'But that doesn't mean that you intend to pack in your job and sit around building shelves and doing the garden!'

They stared at one another and finally he expelled a long, frustrated sigh.

'It's a lousy idea. Pregnant women need to rest.'

'According to a man who freely admits he knows nothing whatsoever on the subject!'

'Lord, give me strength…' he muttered under his breath.

'If you're beginning to regret your little proposition,' she said hopefully, 'then now's the time to retract it.' If she was going to go along with this so-called business arrangement, then she intended to lay down a few ground rules before she found herself swept up into a world in which she had no say. There was no way on the face of the earth that she would follow in her mother's footsteps and become the silent partner in an unfair dictatorship.

She thrust out her chin belligerently, and he looked at her with a shadow of amusement.

'I wouldn't dream of doing any such thing.'

She noticed that he had similarly closed his knife and fork, and she wondered whether this blast of reality had affected his appetite as well. If it had, then all the better.

'Now, the wedding…' he began.

'*Business arrangement*, you mean?'

'Pick your choice of words. The sooner the better as far as I'm concerned.'

'Why?'

She felt a nervous flutter in her stomach at the prospect of fixing a date, but her expression remained unchanged.

'Wouldn't you like to become accustomed to *our* home before the baby comes along?'

No, she was tempted to say. She thought of sharing a home with him and was attacked by another queasy sense of anxiety.

'Oh, getting accustomed to some bricks and mortar doesn't take very long,' she said with conviction. If only, she thought, she didn't feel something for him. She wasn't too sure what she felt, but she could sense it there, deep inside, for ever stirring. A business arrangement involved two dispassionate strangers, but they weren't, were they?

'Stop being so damned obstructive. It won't work.'

'What won't work?'

'Trying to put off the inevitable.' He signalled for some coffee. 'And I don't want you getting cold feet at the last minute. We both know what the outcome is going to be and you might as well face the facts.' He sipped some of his coffee and regarded her calmly over the rim of the cup.

Those eyes. Those fingers curled around the handle of the cup. However much she tried to persuade herself that she found him unreasonable, lacking in the milk of human

tenderness and ruthless to the core, her body still responded
with eagerness at the mere sight of him. Why? *Why? Why?*

'So we've agreed that I continue working until the time
comes.'

'I can hardly drag you to my house and chain you to a
piece of furniture.'

'So you won't pass the word down that my employment
with your company is terminated.'

'Sir.'

'I beg your pardon?'

'You sound as though you should be adding *Sir* to the
end of that question. For God's sake, can't you relax a bit
about this whole thing?'

'How do you expect me to do that?' she almost shrieked.
'I feel as though I'm on a roller coaster all of a sudden.
How easy is it to relax on a roller coaster?' She looked at
her coffee with distaste.

'Life is going to change for the both of us,' he said
coolly. 'You're not the only one who's going to be feeling
the repercussions of this, are you?' He called for the bill,
but kept watching her, as though half expecting her to make
a sudden dash for the door.

'I can take the underground back to my place,' she said,
once he had paid.

'We're going back to my house.' He steered her towards
a taxi and she helplessly allowed herself to be ushered in.

'What for?'

'Because I say so.'

'You're not my lord and master,' she protested grimly
under her breath.

'If you want to be involved in joint decision making,
then you're going to have to act in a more mature manner.
Circumstance has put us both in a situation we hadn't

banked on, and now that we're here we might just as well make the best of it.'

'That's easier said than done!'

'Only if you don't wake up to reality.' He looked at her with steely-eyed hardness. 'You can either make things difficult for yourself, or else you can accept the situation we're both in and enjoy it.'

'"Enjoy it?"' she asked incredulously. 'Are you *enjoying* it? Are you looking forward to marrying someone you'd rather not marry? Does your heart thrill at the prospect of sharing a house with a woman who was meant to be a temporary blip?' Just uttering the words brought on an attack of self-pity, and she turned away and glared out of the window.

Her hormones were up the spout. Every word he had spoken was true and she knew that if a friend had come to her with a tale of pregnancy and marriage to a man whom most women would give their eye-teeth to have, her advice would have been to take it in her stride and enjoy it. She would have said that things could have been a whole lot worse. She would have counselled her friend to see the best in a man who was prepared to adopt the mantle of responsibility when he had no need to. Such men were few and far between.

It wasn't even as if she had nurtured romantic notions of white weddings with fairy-tale endings. This marriage of convenience was a logical step in a logical life, and as such she should have embraced it wholeheartedly.

So why couldn't she?

She wasn't going to make things easier for herself if she insisted on fighting him every step of the way.

The taxi drew up in front of his house and she looked at it curiously. She had pictured him as a man who lived in a penthouse suite at the top of an exclusive block of apartments somewhere very central. She couldn't have been further from the truth. His house was set back in gardens in a quiet street in the St John's Wood area, and as they entered it she was struck by a feeling of cosiness. It was no sprawling mansion, but neither was it a box. Warm, red brick, ivy clambering to touch the window-panes, and inside rich, deep colours and furniture that was old and comfortable.

'I thought all top businessmen who lived on their own inhabited apartments with lots of chrome and black,' she said eventually, gazing at the paintings on the walls and trying to place a couple of them.

'Yet another of your hare-brained notions.' He led the way to the sitting room, which was small and had, a rarity in London, a wonderful fireplace with the original tiles on it. On the wall above the fire was an exquisite mirror, and, flanking either side, two paintings that looked disturbingly familiar. Everything she had seen spoke of wealth, but wealth without any accompanying fanfare.

'The house has been in my family for generations,' he said, following her gaze and picking up on her surprise at her surroundings.

'It's…'

'A far cry from chrome and black?'

'Absolutely splendid.'

'Well, that's hurdle number one over,' he said dryly. 'Would you like something to drink? Tea? Coffee?'

'Tea would be fine, thank you. Milk, one sugar.' There were so many basic things he didn't know about her, and yet, every so often, she was struck by the strangest feeling that she had known this man for ever. She sat down in the sitting room, waiting for him to return, and thought that they should be writing down their CVs for each other to read. Filling in all the gaps which were normally filled in between two people during the period of courtship, when they got to know one another. They were doing things the wrong way around. The baby before the marriage and the marriage before the relationship. The scope for things going horrendously wrong was so enormous that she couldn't even dwell on it.

The most she knew she could hope for was the thing he saw as perfectly acceptable. That they would have the baby and would be able to communicate without friction. With no love to confuse the issue, their relationship would never soar to any great heights, but they might eventually become friends. Two friends sharing a house. She would turn a blind eye to his sexual adventures elsewhere, and presumably he would turn a blind eye to hers.

Not, she knew, that she would have any.

She had never considered marriage, but now that she was being forced to she might just as well face facts. She was no twentieth-century woman who carried the torch for sexual freedom, whether there was a ring on her finger or not.

For her, marriage was a commitment.

She stared blindly through the bay window at the glimpse of sky and garden outside.

It was all about love.

All about being in love.

Her mind began to travel back down the past few months, but this time all the connections were made. It was as though she was seeing her life, for the first time ever, with absolute clarity.

She had proudly thought that her background had hardened her, turned any thoughts of romance into cynicism. She had managed to convince herself for years that her career was all she wanted out of life. She had seen it as a positive sign, the fact that her relationships had been brief and pain-free. Men, she had thought, were objects of desire or at least temporary enjoyment.

She could see where her thoughts were taking her, and was powerless to drag them away from the route.

Outside, the sky was blue and flawless, undisturbed by clouds. It made the perfect canvas against which to view her life and to see how willingly she had succumbed to her illusions of independence and freedom from the rest of the human race.

The truth was that she had just never found love. Until Bruno Carr had arrived on the scene. All those intense, conflicting emotions she had felt in his presence had nothing to do with dislike. They had to do with opening her eyes for the first time in her life, and taking her first stretch, and finally coming alive. It was a shock in much the same way, she supposed, that a new-born baby feels the shock of taking its first breath.

She could feel her breath getting ragged, but she continued staring in an unfocused manner through the window, carried along with her thoughts like a stick floating randomly on an ocean tide.

When had she fallen? Impossible to tell, but fallen she had. Well and truly fallen in love with him. Little wonder that the pregnancy had caused her no real grief. Subconsciously, she had wanted his baby from the start. She closed her eyes to try and block out her thoughts, but they kept on rolling. She felt sick.

She didn't hear him enter the room. The first she knew of his presence was when he asked her if she felt all right.

'You're as white as a sheet.'

She opened her eyes and looked at him, and she felt as if she were seeing him for the first time. She accepted her cup of tea and blew gently on the surface, then watched in silence as he sat down opposite her and crossed his legs.

This terrible realisation would have to be her secret. She would be businesslike and calm because that was the only way to conduct herself without revealing what was inside her.

He was looking at her, waiting for some kind of response, and she took a deep breath.

'Just some passing nausea. My stomach hasn't been accustomed to rich food.' She hazarded a smile which met with a frown. 'How long have you lived here?' she asked politely, reaching for the first pointless remark she could think of, and his frown deepened.

'I've already told you. The house has been in—'

'Your family for generations. Of course. Forgot.'

'What's the matter with you?' He narrowed his eyes, searching to get inside her head, and she met his stare blandly.

'Amnesia and pregnancy. Well documented,' she told him. She sipped some tea and adopted a more relaxed pose.

'I don't think we should rush into the marriage thing,' she said. 'The baby's not due for another few months. I think we should take the time to at least get to know one another a bit.' She would need the time to let her emotions settle a little, or at least to learn to control them. The thought of sharing his house immediately filled her with horror.

'Actually, I think we know each other better than you imagine,' he remarked. 'But if you want to wait a couple of months as opposed to a couple of weeks, then that's fine by me. I take it you won't object to an engagement ring.'

'Do people still get engaged these days?' She knew that they did, but an engagement seemed almost a greater show of hypocrisy than the prospect of marriage. Engagements, she thought, were all about being wrapped up in dreams and hope and plans. Rings to be shown off as the glowing proof of love.

'I have no idea...' he shrugged '...and it's not something

that I care about one way or another. But my mother would find it very disturbing if the conventional rites of passage weren't adhered to. The gesture might mean nothing to either of us, but it would mean a great deal to her.'

His words stabbed into her with the precision of a sharp knife, but she forced herself to smile.

'In that case…' she shrugged as well '…it doesn't matter to me one way or the other, as you say, and if it would make your mother happier, then that's fine.' Things should have been different. They should have been planning a life of happiness, with a baby on the way. But maybe it was better like this. If there were no dreams, then there were no dreams to be shattered.

'Come on,' he said abruptly, standing up. 'You might as well have the guided tour of the place.'

'Why not?'

She followed him into all the downstairs rooms, and murmured favourably, and tried to close her eyes to thoughts of them happily growing old together, sitting on the sofa side by side, sharing laughter in the kitchen, entertaining friends in the dining room.

When they went upstairs, the beating of her heart quickened. Behind the closed doors lay bedrooms and the thought of bedrooms brought her out in a cold sweat.

The layout of the upstairs mirrored that of downstairs, with a large, central hall off which the rooms fell. Four huge bedrooms and a large sitting room which had been turned into a television area. Somehow, she couldn't imagine Bruno Carr finding the time to sit in front of a TV, but she refrained from saying that. Instead, she commented on the furnishings, peering at the paintings and delaying the onset of a further attack of nerves when confronted with the bedroom. His bedroom. Their bedroom. Their bed. God, would he want to touch her? Or would his eyes glaze over with disinterest?

His bedroom, as it turned out, was large enough to include a sitting area, in addition to a massive *en suite* bathroom.

'Big,' Jessica said weakly, not straying from the door.

'What the hell is wrong with you?' He swung around and stood in front of her, propping himself up with his hands on either side of the doorway.

'Nothing's wrong with me.' She licked her lips nervously.

'Does the thought of sharing a house with me frighten you?' he asked, reading her mind, and she shook her head vigorously.

'Shall we move on?'

'Not until you answer a few questions.' He pulled her inside the bedroom, towards the small, squashy sofa by the bay window, and she reluctantly sat down, averting her eyes from the king-size Victorian bed dominating the room.

How many women had he shared that bed with?

The question brought a surge of angry, jealous colour to her face.

'Ever since you walked through the front door, you've been acting like a zombie. Why?' It was less of a question and more of a demand for information. He was still standing over her, hands thrust into his pockets, but now he sat down next to her on the sofa, his thighs splayed against her own.

'It all seems unreal,' Jessica mumbled, inclining her body to look at him, and feeling the full force of his personality like a sledgehammer.

She knew every line on his face, the way his mouth curved when he smiled and became a thin line when he was angry. It amazed her that she had never sought to discover why it was that a man she had told herself meant nothing to her could still have become so familiar. How had she not added up all the signs before? How could love have overcome her so stealthily that she had been unaware of herself falling headlong into the ambush?

'What do you imagine life will be like once we're married? Once you've taken up residence here and there's no flat to run to?' His velvety voice seemed to reach her from a great distance and it was an effort to keep her eyes on his face with some semblance of normality.

'I don't know.' A shrug. 'Guess I'll have to wait and see. My mind will be on the pregnancy, anyway. And after that...well, babies require a lot of attention.'

'Which still hasn't answered my question.'

'What answer do you want?' she replied hotly. She resented his composure. She knew that he found all this much easier to deal with because the prospect of marriage didn't threaten him. He could quite happily cohabit with her because she meant nothing to him emotionally and so would never really disturb his lifestyle.

Quite honestly, she could have hurled something very big and very heavy at him.

'The goddamn truth!'

'No, you don't!' she snapped, close to tears now. 'The truth is the last thing you want! What you want is my total agreement with everything you say! You want me to nod my head all the time and tell you what a clever person you are!'

'You're talking absolute rubbish!'

She was leaning towards him, their faces almost touching, and through all her rage and misery she still felt a yearning to close her eyes and put her mouth against his. She still wanted his hands to slip beneath her shirt and caress her swollen breasts.

'No, I'm not, Bruno! Let's look at things dispassionately, shall we? I was good enough for a weekend, but that was all you were interested in...'

'If I recall, that was *your* point of view,' he grated.

'Okay, then! A weekend, a week, maybe a month but then I got pregnant and, now that you've found out, you've decided to launch yourself into fatherhood and wrap the whole business up with a phoney marriage, which means nothing to you...'

'And you want it to...?'

'I never said that!'

'Then what precisely *are* you saying?'

'I'm saying...' She miserably tried to work out an answer to his question. The only thing revolving in her brain was the hideous revelation that she loved this man and that her love wasn't reciprocated. What kind of answer could she give him? 'Oh, I don't know.' She buried her head in her hands, and was giving herself a strong lecture on self-control when she felt his hand against the nape of her neck, massaging it.

'Turn around,' he said roughly, and she obeyed, flexing her muscles, then allowing her head to drop. She didn't want to think and his hands on her neck were so soothing. His thumbs pressed against her bones, rotating along her shoulders, and she sighed with pleasure.

'Like it?' he murmured, and she nodded. His fingers found her shoulder blades, then her spine, pushing against the line of vertebrae, and she involuntarily gave a stifled moan of satisfaction.

His hands circled around to her ribcage, then back to her spine, then beneath her breasts and she gave a little gasp.

'You're bloody tense,' he said softly, his breath tickling her ear. 'I'm no masseur, and I can feel it. Just relax.' He unclasped her bra and spanned his hands across her back, gently pressing and kneading her flesh.

'I'm not tense.'

'And stop arguing. You argue too much.' He circled her waist with his hands, then rolled them up higher until his fingers lay provocatively beneath her breasts, fuller and heavier with the pregnancy.

With eyes still closed, Jessica leaned back against him, tilting her head over his shoulder, and shuddered as she felt him cup her breasts, then slowly he began to massage them. She sank deeper into him, and when he shifted slightly she lay fully back, her body still arched up to him, her head inclined over the arm of the sofa.

She felt as though the past few weeks had been spent in a state of constant need, a craving that she had refused to acknowledge.

He leant over her and his tongue flicked against her nipples. The moan that escaped her lips seemed to come from someone else. It was a moan of the deepest contentment. His mouth covered her nipple, then he was suckling on it and she squirmed and smiled and curled her fingers into his hair.

Between her legs grew damp and she spread them apart, knowing that his hand would find the hungry moistness beneath her lacy briefs. Her skirt had hitched up to her thighs and he began to stroke the inside of them, while he continued to lick and play with her breasts with his mouth.

'See. Don't be afraid. Marriage won't be nearly as bad as you anticipate.'

His words took a second to sink in, but as soon as they did her brain seemed to go into overdrive, analysing what he had said, dissecting every hidden nuance.

The thought of living with Bruno, married to him, having to conceal her love like a dirty secret, offered enough of a prospect of lifelong hurt. But to have him touch her, knowing that he didn't love her, knowing, in due course, that he probably touched other women as well, would be beyond endurance.

# CHAPTER NINE

THE shock of opening her eyes and seeing Bruno staring down at her, white-faced, was almost enough to make Jessica want to slip back into unconsciousness.

Then, hard on the heels of that, she remembered the sequence of events that had brought her to a hospital, and she struggled to sit up.

'The baby.' She knew that she was bleeding. She could feel it and a flood of sudden panic gripped her. She had lost the baby. She just knew it. She hadn't realised how desperately she had wanted this baby until now. 'How long have I been here?' Her voice was unsteady and she glanced around her with an expression of fear. White walls had never seemed more intimidating. She was in a gown. One of those hideous hospital gowns that automatically brought on an attack of malaise the second they were put on.

'Minutes. Do you remember what happened?' She hardly recognised his voice. Gone was the composure and authority. She looked more carefully at him and saw lines of anxiety and tension around his eyes.

'I ran into the road.' She shook her head and made no effort to stop the trickle of tears that ran down her face. Very gently, he wiped them with his handkerchief.

He was already treating her like an invalid. Confirmation enough that the pregnancy was no more.

'Don't talk about it if you feel you don't want to.'

'Was I hit?'

'The car braked just in time.' He managed a smile. 'You'd know if you'd been hit, I assure you. Speaking, you understand, as someone with a limited medical background.'

He was humouring her, and she smiled weakly back at him, appreciating his efforts to sustain her spirits.

'You came here by ambulance,' he continued. His voice was like a soothing balm. Just what she needed. She remembered his hands massaging her back. That had been just what she had needed as well. She squeezed her eyes shut for a few seconds to block out the image and then opened them and looked at him.

Now, of course, there would be no wedding. There would be no need to get married, and she felt a spreading void begin to wash over her. No wedding, no baby, no more Bruno Carr. She had been so terrified of marrying him and involving herself in a life of loving from the sidelines, but now the thought of never seeing him again filled her with a different type of terror. It was like staring into a black hole.

'Actually, you more or less came to on the way here. You've only been in the room for a short while.' He took one of her hands between his, and was it her imagination or could she feel the pity oozing out of him? 'The nurse will be back in a few minutes. You've already been examined by a doctor, and they'll be taking you to be scanned to see...' He didn't end the sentence, but there was no need for him to. She knew what he meant.

'What did the doctor say?'

'There's a heartbeat, but...'

'That might not last, might it? I might be heading for a miscarriage. Well, after all that...' She tried to laugh but couldn't and he didn't say anything.

It threatened to become a silence filled with dangerously raw feelings of self-pity and despair, when the nurse bustled in, looking starched and cheerful. Jessica looked glumly at her and wondered how hospital employees always managed to maintain such relentless good humour.

'Radiologist's all ready for you now, my love.' She was efficiently transferred from bed to wheelchair, which made her feel even more of an invalid, and she was immeasurably grateful when Bruno took her hand in his and held it.

This, she knew, was one of the many reasons why she loved him. He was a source of strength. However often she told herself that he was autocratic and over-forceful, she knew that those were just the desperate postulations of someone who recognised qualities she would rather not acknowledge.

The short spin passed in a blur. Fear had congealed itself like a ball in her head.

The room with the scanning machine was dark and she propped herself onto the narrow bed and lay down, watching as the radiologist swivelled the screen at an angle so that she could see what was happening on it. Or not, as the case might be.

Bruno was still clasping her hand, and now he squeezed it. The radiologist, a middle-aged woman with an expression of perpetual concentration, was talking in the background. Referring to the accident. Then she switched on the machine and began to roll the monitor across Jessica's well-greased stomach.

'There,' she said, finding what she was looking for. 'There's the foetus. And there, you see, is the heart. Beating away quite merrily.'

A blob. An indistinct grey blob with a merrily beating heart. The flood of relief was so intense that Jessica felt she might possibly pass out. She listened while Bruno began asking questions, and half absorbed what the radiologist was saying about measurements and stage of development.

A merrily beating heart. She stared, fixated, at the screen, just to make sure that she could still see the beating pinprick.

'Of course,' the radiologist said, switching off the monitor, 'you'll want to rest for a bit. Just until the bleeding settles, which should be quite soon. And then take it easy.'

'Oh, she'll be doing just that,' Jessica heard Bruno say. 'When I take her home.'

Home? Whose home?

'You can't stay in your flat on your own,' he repeated the following day as they were in the car and heading away from the hospital. 'Before you start launching into a debate on the subject. You're bloody lucky…' His voice stumbled a bit, but he carried on almost immediately in his usual tone of command. 'You heard what the woman said. You need to rest.'

'I can rest at my own place.' But it was a token protest. The fact was that she wanted to put her feet up, at least for a little while.

'Absolutely not. No way, no how, no debate,' he told her warningly, and she glanced across at him, trying to read his mind and unearth how he felt.

Relieved that everything was all right? Or disturbed that he had been given a glimpse of possible liberation from an unwanted marriage and was now forced back to square one? She daredn't ask him. The thought of what he might say by way of reply was enough to make her cringe inwardly.

'How are you feeling?' He glanced across at her. This was the third time he had asked that question.

'Still shaken, but all right. Why do you keep asking?'

'Why do you think?' He let the rhetorical question hang in the air and then evidently gave up on her saying anything. 'You could say that I was responsible for everything that happened, couldn't you?' he said conversationally. His face was impassive, but there were thoughts running through his head. She could tell from the tense set of his jaw.

'How do you work that one out?'

'Don't be obtuse, Jessica,' he ground out. He shot her a brief glance, then reverted his attention to the road. 'I touched you, and you obviously didn't want to be touched, so you fled. Without thinking.'

'Well, it's very good of you to take the blame, and I wish I could let you get away with it, but...'

'But...?'

'My reaction had nothing to do with you,' she told him bluntly. 'Yes, you touched me, but I allowed myself to be touched. I just felt, when it happened, that I needed to get away. To escape.'

'Which pretty much seems to sum up your feelings ever since we reached the decision to get married for the sake of the baby. Or maybe even before. You're terrified of commitment, even the sort of commitment that doesn't have the burden of love and romance to live up to. Am I right?'

'I suppose I am,' Jessica said carefully and he expelled a long, frustrated sigh.

'In which case, you're free.'

'What?'

'You heard me,' he said flatly, not looking at her. 'You're free. I'm not going to force you to live a life of terror and abhorrence simply because of my principles.'

'Are you being serious?' Her ears had taken in what he had just said, and her mind was slowly registering the fact that, far from feeling heady with a sense of release, she felt as though she were being sucked down a plug hole.

'I've never been more serious in my entire life,' he told

her grimly. 'I mistakenly imagined that we might have rubbed along harmoniously as a married couple for the sake of the baby, but what happened has proved that that's complete nonsense. Your aversion to me is so intense that it almost ending up endangering our child's life.'

So she had got what she had clamoured so loudly for after all. Didn't they say that you should be very careful what you wished for because wishes had a nasty habit of coming true?

'Naturally, we will have to have something drawn up by lawyers.'

'I really don't feel up to discussing this just at the moment, Bruno,' she said feebly. She rested her head against the window-pane and shut her eyes. Her ears were pounding and the trauma of her near miss was catching up on her. Or so it felt. She was very tired. All she wanted to do was get into a bed and drift off to sleep.

'You'll still be coming to stay with me for a while,' he continued, ignoring her lack of response. 'At least for a week. There's no way that your stubbornness is going to come before health.'

Jessica didn't answer. After a while, she was aware of the car slowing down, pulling up in front of the house, then she heard him open his door, and eventually she lugged herself out of the car and followed him inside.

'I'll need the key to your place,' he told her. 'I'll have to bring some of your clothes over.'

'I can always go and fetch them myself tomorrow,' she said.

'Still fighting for your independence up to the last, aren't you, Jessica?' She heard the cynicism in his voice and flinched. 'Still totally incapable of accepting even the smallest of favours just in case you might find a corner of your precious self-control eroded.'

'Please, Bruno. Not now. I'm feeling very fragile at the moment.'

She knew that he would respect that, but for how long? He was furious with her and she wondered whether that wasn't in part due to the fact that, just this once, he had found himself incapable of ordering events precisely how he wanted to.

He had wanted to marry her, had wanted to adopt the mantle of fatherhood, and now he must be seeing it slipping away from him.

How do you think *I* feel? she wanted to shout at him. She would be financially secure, she knew that, but the emptiness stretching out in front of her was almost beyond endurance.

Weekly visits. Just often enough to ensure that she never recovered from the havoc he had wreaked on her heart. And then watching from the sidelines as over time he found someone. In fact, probably not that much time before the inevitable happened. He was an intensely sexual man. Celibacy, she guessed, was not a word he was overly familiar with.

He walked her up the stairs, keeping pace with her, and then led her into one of the guest bedrooms.

'Your keys?' he reminded her, standing by the door and watching as she sank onto the bed.

'Yes, my keys.' She rustled around in her bag and unearthed them from underneath a half-empty packet of mints and an assortment of pens and stray items of make-up. Funny, with all her passion for control, she had never been able to control her bag. Was there a name for someone whose life resembled the state of their bag? 'I don't feel happy about you rummaging around in my flat—' she began.

'Tough. You've got zero choice in the matter.' He took

the keys from her and vanished. She waited a few minutes, then slowly changed into more comfortable clothes, drew the curtains and lay down on the bed.

She must have dozed off, because when she next opened her eyes evening had arrived, and Bruno was standing by the bed. On the chair by the bay window, she saw her suitcase, and she sat up, momentarily disoriented.

'How long have I been asleep?' she asked.

'Hours. I got back here and didn't want to disturb you, and I've been popping in every so often to check and make sure you were all right.'

The overhead light hadn't been switched on, so she couldn't properly make out the expression on his face, but at least his voice had no undertones of anger.

'Tea.' He nodded in the direction of the bedside table, and Jessica gratefully took the mug and drank. Warm but fortifying.

'How are you feeling?'

'Much better. Thank you.'

He pulled a chair across to the bed and sat down next to her, so that he was more on her level and she didn't have to crane her neck upwards to see him. She knew they would have to talk. They had worked out details of the marriage that wasn't to be, and now they would have to work out arrangements for her and the baby after it was born. And claiming exhaustion was an excuse that wouldn't hold water for ever.

How could she explain that marrying him and enduring the torment of her love in silence had seemed unbearable, but the alternative was even worse?

She couldn't. She had made her bed and she would now have to lie on it. Wasn't that what her mother had once said to her? That she had made her bed and would simply have to accept all that went with it? Ironic that her situation was reversed. Bitterly ironic.

'So,' he said casually, not looking at her, 'there's a baby inside you.'

'Could we turn the lights on? I can't see your face.'

'In a minute.' He relaxed back in the chair and stuck his legs out, crossing them at the ankle. 'I've never…had an experience…'

'I'm relieved to hear it,' Jessica said. 'It would be a bit off-putting to discover you'd fathered a herd of children before.'

'I doubt you'll be able to get back to work as rapidly as you had anticipated…'

She looked at his hard profile, and then found that the glance had turned into a stare.

'Possibly not,' Jessica admitted, taking advantage of his averted face to drink him in. There was an awkward pause, and she said, simply to break the silence, 'What did you pack? Perhaps I could have a shower…'

Without a word, he stood up, fetched the suitcase from the chair and deposited it on the bed next to her. His silence was beginning to rattle her. He had accepted that there would be no marriage, and now she wondered whether he had decided that he could cease to make all efforts with her. Why bother to build any kind of tenuous relationship when there was now no need? She had been reduced to being no more than the mother of his child. Once this week was over, she would return to her flat and he would visit occasionally, she guessed, to make sure that she hadn't flung herself in front of another passing car. But meanwhile he would carry on with his life and contact would only be resumed once the baby was born. By then, all legal arrangements would be in place. He would be super-efficient when it came to that.

'Are you going to be all right to manage yourself?'

'I'm not ill, Bruno. Had a slight shock, admittedly, but I'm fine.' She sat up and swung open the suitcase to find that he had packed several dresses, her entire underwear drawer, no pyjamas, one shirt and a pair of trousers which had clearly been the first pair his hands had happened to chance upon hanging in the wardrobe. Jade-green silk, appropriate only for evening wear.

Jessica tipped the suitcase upside down and stared at the contents.

'You envisage a series of cocktail parties for me over the next week, do you?'

'A series of cocktail parties?' He moved to turn on the light, which revealed the inappropriate selection in all their glory.

'Dresses?' She looked at him quizzically, momentarily forgetting her personal state of depression. 'I'm supposed to be relaxing for the next few days. Does this...' she held up a scarlet number which had not seen the light of day for years '...strike you as a relaxing outfit?'

'It's a very jolly colour,' he commented, flushing. 'Thought it might cheer you up.'

'Okay. So what was the reasoning behind the two little black affairs?'

'Those must have found their way in by mistake.' He cleared his throat and peered at the bundle on the bed. He picked one up and he held it up by one shoestring strap to the light. 'It's a very attractive number,' he said, observing it from several angles. 'It never ceases to amaze me the clothes that women somehow manage to squeeze their bodies into.' He dropped it back on the bed and folded his arms.

'That's as may be, but...' she looked at him with an inward sigh of despair '...it's not a useful lot of clothes. I shall have to go myself and fetch some more.' She prepared to swing her legs over the side of the bed.

'Not on your life! If you just tell me what to bring over, then I can do it myself.'

'But I wanted to have a shower now,' Jessica said a little plaintively.

'Fine. Stay right there. I'll be back in a second.'

He vanished, to return literally a minute later with a short-sleeved shirt in one hand.

'Here. You can put this on.'

'But it's yours.'

He looked at it as though seeing it for the first time. 'Oh, so it is. Well, it won't bite and it's been recently laundered. Have a shower and I'll be back up in half an hour with something for you to eat.' Before she could protest he was walking out of the door, and as soon as he had vacated the room she made her way to the bathroom, and had a shower.

The memory of the bleeding was already beginning to fade away, and her spirits began to lift a little.

She still couldn't seem to harness her thoughts, but at least she no longer felt on the verge of cracking up.

If she could manage to maintain her good humour, then it would give her time to build up her defences against him. It had worked for her in the past. She could remember, even as a child, learning to bring the shutters down over her eyes, to control her emotions when her father had been in one of his moods and jeering at her school efforts had become a form of fun. Tears had never worked then. They had only fuelled his cruelty. But gradually she had learned to blank out what he'd been saying and to look through him and past him. Out towards a happier future. Somewhere. And in time the self-imposed control had become second nature for her. She had carried it all the way through to her adult life when it had clothed and protected her like a second skin.

This was different, but wasn't the objective more or less the same?

She slowly dried herself, brushed her hair, leaving it hanging down her back, then she donned the oversized shirt which reached to mid-thigh and suitably disguised every scrap of her body.

This time she would not allow her emotions to ambush all her good intentions. She would smile on the surface and eventually the smiles would become a part of her expression whenever she was in his company.

She stared at the reflection in the mirror and practised a smile.

By the time he returned with a tray, she was back in bed and under the covers.

'You look better,' he said, glancing at her and looking away. 'Food.'

'You shouldn't have,' Jessica said politely as he placed the tray on her lap and, mysteriously, resumed his position on the chair next to the bed.

'You're absolutely right. I should have just let you fend for yourself.'

'Well, I've done it all my life,' she answered absentmindedly, tucking into a mound of scrambled egg and toast. Her hair slipped over a shoulder and she flicked it back, thinking that she should have tied the lot into a ponytail.

'Sounds exhausting,' he said eventually, and she stopped eating momentarily to look across at him.

'What does?'

'A lifetime of fending for yourself.'

Jessica flushed and resumed eating. This was normal conversation, she told herself. Getting uptight was only going to drag her back to square one, back to the place where every word he uttered had the ability to throw her off balance.

Step one in learning how to deal with her situation would be to answer his questions courteously and without flinching.

'Oh, it becomes a habit after a while,' she said airily. 'This tastes delicious, by the way. I've always admired a man who's not afraid of cooking.'

'Well, I personally wouldn't call two scrambled eggs the epitome of haute cuisine.'

'Small beginnings,' Jessica said, finishing the very last morsel and closing her knife and fork with some regret. Then she rested back against the pillows with her cup of tea and watched in silence as he removed the tray from bed to side table.

'There's no need for you to stay here, you know,' she said eventually, when he showed no signs of moving. 'I give you my word that I won't leave the room and hurtle outside in another fit of confusion.'

'Was that why you did it?' he asked softly. 'Because my touching you confused you?'

The sudden intimacy of the question wedged a splinter in her determined effort to keep up a smiling façade. She felt the smile begin to slip a little.

'I mean,' she said, disregarding his question, 'haven't you got some work to do? The odd fax to send somewhere?'

'Nothing that can't wait.' He paused and continued staring at her. 'You haven't answered my question.'

'There's nothing *to* answer.' She could feel her heart beating very quickly. Doing double time.

'What if I said that I would never lay another finger on you again?' A dark flush had spread across his face and he threw her a challenging look from under his lashes.

'I don't understand what you're saying.'

'We can simply live under the same roof.'

'It would drive me crazy!' Jessica blurted out. Tears were beginning to prick the backs of her eyes. How was she supposed to get all her defences in place, if he wasn't prepared to play the game according to her rules?

'I get the message.' He stood up abruptly and looked down at her with his hands in his pockets.

'You don't understand!' Imploring eyes met cold ice.

'I think I do. Forget I ever asked the question. You were right. I have work to do, so I'll leave you here to get on with your resting. Tonight, I'll give my mother a call and she can come up and lend a hand.'

'Your mother?'

'Good night, Jessica. Call me if you need anything. I'll be in the office downstairs.'

'Wait, Bruno.' He was already heading to the door. 'Why don't we talk about this?' She could feel herself on the verge of confessing everything to him and hang the consequences.

'There's nothing to talk about,' he said politely. 'Let's not go along the road of forcing something that's just not there. We're two people who happened to meet in passing, which, as you've been at great pains to point out, is precisely where it should have been left.'

With that he left the room, and Jessica crumpled back onto the bed. It was over. There had been a finality in his voice when he had spoken and beyond them now was nothing. He had made one last effort to accommodate her because of the baby, and she had spontaneously uttered the wrong words. Not that there would have been any right ones.

The past and the present tangled together in her head and she switched the overhead light off, waiting, dry-eyed, as the sky outside darkened. There were no noises in the house, and she wouldn't have been surprised to find that he had gone out. Gone to find himself a real woman, instead of a repressed, inhibited one who couldn't even say what was in her mind because heartfelt truths were something she had never felt the need to indulge in before.

When she next opened her eyes, it was to find light trying to get through the curtain, and there was a knocking on the bedroom door. She wasn't entirely sure which had awakened her. The light or the sound of knocking. Her watch, which she was still wearing, showed her that it was a little after eight.

The shirt—crumpled. The hair—a mess. The face—she daredn't look. If Bruno wasn't repelled by her enough already, then he was in for a treat.

She watched the door handle being turned, frantically tried to arrange her face into something loosely resembling a human being instead of a zombie recently roused from the local graveyard, and was already wearing a fixed, if jaw-aching, smile on her lips when a tall, dark-haired woman entered the room. She was dressed smartly in a tan-coloured cashmere twin set although, instead of the customary pearls, she wore three long strands of gold around her neck.

If this is the housekeeper, then I'm the Queen of England, Jessica thought, but she kept smiling until the woman approached the bed.

It then occurred to her that the constant smile might look a bit manic and she allowed her mouth to relax a little.

'You must be wondering who I am,' the woman said, and as soon as she had spoken Jessica knew precisely who the woman was. Right age, right look, right accent. Her heart sank.

'You must be Bruno's mother,' she said, feeling at a

disadvantage in her son's shirt, in bed. This sort of elegant, well-bred woman was best dealt with on fairly equal terms. The fact of the pregnancy was just another huge, added disadvantage. The woman had the same angular, strong face as her son although time had weathered it into something slightly less daunting.

'Victoria.' She stepped into the room, and, if she was horrified at the circumstances that had brought her to London from the sanity of her country mansion, then she showed no sign of it. 'And you're Jessica, of course.'

'I'm very pleased to meet you,' Jessica lied.

'Are you?' The bright, shrewd eyes examined her. 'I wish I could say the same but I'm very much afraid that it would be a complete lie.'

Okay, Jessica thought. Let's not beat about the bush here.

'I came up last night, actually, on Bruno's request. He's going to be out of the country for a few days and he thought that, in view of the situation, my presence here might be a help.'

Jessica nodded miserably, at a loss for words.

'You have no experience of children, as yet, but, speaking as a mother, I needn't tell you how disappointed I am with this situation.'

'Well,' Jessica said, firing on a few cylinders now that the immediate shock had worn off, 'and I would hate to appear rude, but, speaking as the person in the middle of the situation, I can assure you that it's not exactly a bed of roses for me either.'

For the first time, a glimmer of humour flitted across the woman's face, but she remained silent for a while, eventually moving to pull back the curtains, then to sit in still repose on the love chair by the bay window. Jessica followed her warily with her eyes.

'I had always expected, my dear, that Bruno would indulge his mother with a white wedding, with all the trimmings…' She smiled a little wistfully. 'No, perhaps not quite the full affair, but a wedding, at any rate.'

'I understand,' Jessica said uncomfortably. Had he told his mother that a wedding had been planned? Planned and then dismantled in the blink of an eye?

'He tells me that any such thing is out of the question.' She paused and looked carefully at Jessica. 'May I ask why?'

'Because weddings, marriage… I was a fool, Mrs Carr. A mistake and…' Her voice was beginning to go. She could feel her throat seizing up, but she forced herself to plough on. 'And here I am. Pregnant. I know that Bruno hadn't planned for his life to take this awkward course, and I certainly hadn't.'

'What *had* you planned, my dear?' The voice was soft but insistent, and Jessica sighed and lay back on the bed, with her eyes on the ceiling.

What *had* she planned? It was a good question.

'I'd planned a life of independence. A career. A life with no emotional involvement. I always thought that it would just be so much easier. I certainly hadn't planned on babies and on your son… No, all that had been the last thing on my mind…'

'All that?'

Jessica shifted her head so that she was looking at Bruno's mother. She shrugged. 'Involvement, I guess. I know there's a baby, but marriage…well, underneath it all, I guess I was more of a foolish romantic than I'd believed. I guess I'd thought all along that marriage and love needed to go together. Bruno and I won't be married because he doesn't love me, and I can't think of anything more unfair on him than shackling him to my side because of a mistake.'

'Unfair on you as well, if you don't love him either.'

Jessica caught the woman's eyes and opened her mouth to agree but found that she couldn't. No more lies.

'If only it was as easy as that,' she murmured, half to herself. 'If only.'

# CHAPTER TEN

IT WAS after midnight when banging on the front door dragged Jessica out of her sleep. For the first time since returning to her own place two days ago, she cursed the fact that she was no longer under Bruno Carr's roof, because if she had been there would have been no chance of hearing anyone knock or bang or possibly even break down his front door.

As it was, she yawned and staggered into her dressing gown and then headed to the door, which she opened by a couple of inches, making sure to keep the chain firmly in place. She lived in a relatively safe part of town, but it still didn't make sense to take chances, especially at this hour, notorious for drunken revellers heading home, only stopping off *en route* to cause a bit of random harassment.

The minute she saw who was standing outside her front door, all signs of sleep vanished.

'Open this door,' Bruno commanded, looking as though he might risk pushing it with his shoulder, despite the obstacle of the chain. He was dressed, mysteriously at this hour, in his work suit, although his tie was askew as though he had been tugging it down.

'What are you doing here at this hour? I thought you weren't going to be back in the country for another three days.'

'Plans changed.'

'In that case you can find your way back to your own house. Do you realise what time it is? I was asleep!' She didn't add that it had taken her long enough to get to sleep in the first place without having what little she had enjoyed ruined halfway through.

'I don't care if you were levitating six inches off the bed, Jessica. Open this door or else I'll break the thing down.'

'You're not strong enough,' she pointed out flatly.

'In which case, I'll yell so loudly that every neighbour in a sixty-mile radius will come running to see what's going on.'

She didn't doubt him either. She reluctantly unhooked the chain from the door and stood aside to let him enter. His absence over the past five days had been just what she'd needed to put him in perspective. Or so she reminded herself as she watched him divest himself of his jacket and stride purposefully towards her sitting room. The fact that it was after twelve o'clock was obviously something that hadn't registered with him, or maybe his body was still running on American time.

'So,' she said mutinously, following him into the sitting room, but then standing by the door with her arms folded defensively. 'What do you want?'

'I had a long chat with my mother when I got back from America this evening,' he said, perching on the window-ledge and staring at her, his eyes hooded and unrevealing.

'And? What does that have to do with me? I'm tired, and whatever you have to say to me can wait until another day.' Her sluggish brain began working furiously, trying to remember what she could possibly have said to his mother that might have been relayed back to him, but she had been very careful to keep her emotions to herself. Even when it had become patently clear that she and his mother got along really rather well, circumstances considering. Despite frequent references to maternal disapproval, there was something innately warm inside Victoria that Jessica had found herself responding to. So what could she have told her son that had made him find his way over here at this hour?

'I liked your mother!' she blurted out, confused. 'And I thought she liked me too!'

'And you're wondering how she might have betrayed one of your little confidences?' he said in a jeering voice.

'I didn't give her any!' Jessica retorted, whitening. Had she? She had been tempted, but she had held back, biting back the need to confess how she really felt about her son. She wrapped her dressing gown more tightly around her, but even so she still felt cold.

'Then why are you so frantic to try and remember what you said to her? No, don't bother to answer that. Not that you would. Denial is your instinctive response to any question you find even remotely troublesome.' He moved across to one of the chairs and sat down, rubbing his eyes.

'Why are you sitting down and making yourself at home at this hour of the morning?' Jessica asked coldly.

'I told you. We need to talk.'

'We've already talked. I don't remember it getting us anywhere.'

'My mother liked you. Have I mentioned that?'

'You've been drinking, haven't you?' Jessica asked, looking at him narrowly. He hadn't staggered into the house like a typical inebriate, and his words weren't slurring, but there was something aggressive and unpredictable about his behaviour.

'Don't try and change the bloody topic, Jessica. I'm sick to death of that ploy of yours. I'm sick of pussyfooting around all your little problems.'

'You? Pussyfooting? Don't make me laugh. I'm going to go and get you a cup of black coffee. You're going to drink it and then you're going to leave.' She didn't give him time to answer. Instead she swept out of the room, headed towards the kitchen, relieved to find that he hadn't followed her, and then slumped heavily against the fridge door while she waited for the kettle to boil.

Why had he come? She had never seen him under the influence of drink, but she was pretty certain he was there now, whatever he might say, and drunks were notoriously unreliable. They said what was in their mind, and she didn't think that she could stand an hour's worth of Bruno Carr raving on about all her inadequacies. But how could she get him out? He was bigger than her and stronger and if he decided to stay put until he had said whatever piece he had come to say, then he would stay put.

The kettle began to boil and she shakily poured the water into a mug and then stirred in two heaped teaspoons of strong coffee granules.

She half expected to find that he had passed out on the sofa in her absence, but when she got back to the sitting room it was to find him where she had left him, and if the drink was getting to him then he showed zero signs of it.

'Drink up.' She stood over him with her arms folded and watched as he took a mouthful and then recoiled, spluttering.

'What the hell have you put in this?'

'You've had too much to drink. The stronger the coffee, the better,' she told him calmly, and he muttered something unflattering under his breath. 'You need to get back to your house, get yourself into bed with a couple of paracetamol and go to sleep. In the morning, you might be coherent.' And you won't be here, she thought to herself. Whatever state he was in, she still didn't like what he could do to her. Just seeing him, looking down at that rumpled thatch of black hair, was enough to make her feel unsteady.

'Stop giving orders. I'm sick to death of you giving orders.'

'You're sick of a lot of things concerning me, aren't you? Is that why you came here? So that you could tell me just how sick you are of me and everything that I do and say? I wouldn't have thought that you would need drink as a prop to give you Dutch courage for that, though. You've always been just fine at telling me precisely what you think.'

'Oh, do me a favour. You're hardly the shrinking violet when it comes to saying what's on your mind.'

'Right, I'm off to bed.' She made a move to turn away and he grabbed her clumsily by the wrist.

'Oh, no, you don't. You're going to stay right here and listen to what I have to say.' He frowned, as though he had temporarily forgotten what he had to say, and Jessica watched him with an expression of long-suffering patience.

'Then hurry up and say it. I'm tired.'

'No, you're not. You're all wired up because I'm here.' He shot her a crafty look from under his lashes, which she did her best to ignore, but her heart had gone into overdrive.

'Don't flatter yourself.'

'I'm not.' He gave her a lopsided, knowing smile and she raised her eyebrows expressively.

'And that wolfish grin doesn't sit well on someone who's had too much to drink. You just look ridiculous.' The annoying thing was that he looked anything but ridiculous, even though he should have. 'And I don't recall saying anything funny,' she snapped, when he grinned delightedly at this remark.

'Did I tell you that my mother took to you?'

'Yes, as a matter of fact, you did.'

'Said you had a lot of fighting spirit.' He gave something that sounded like a snort. 'What could I do but agree with her?'

He was still loosely hanging on to her wrist as though

having forgotten that his hand was there, and she tried to jerk her hand away. Instantly, his grip tightened, though he was still staring thoughtfully into the distance.

'Would you mind letting me go?'

'Only if you promise not to hover over me like a school-teacher with your arms folded.'

She sighed loudly and nodded, then, when he continued looking at her, repeated woodenly, 'I promise not to hover over you like a schoolteacher with my arms folded.' At which he gave her a satisfied look, released her hand, and she gratefully went to the sofa and sat down, curling her legs underneath her.

'My mother never really cared for the women I've gone out with,' he said in a ruminating voice.

'Yes. I know.'

'You *know*?'

'She told me.' That, Jessica freely admitted to herself, had given her a buzz.

'And what *precisely* did she tell you?'

'She *precisely* told me that you always went for the same type of woman. Pretty, empty-headed, disposable.'

'My mother told you all that, did she?' His voice was blustering, but she could see that he was severely taken aback. 'So you two sat there, having cosy little confidential chit-chats at my expense over cups of tea.'

'Your name cropped up now and again.' Jessica shrugged. 'Bound to, I guess, under the circumstances.'

'And what other gems did she come up with?'

'She said that when you were three you rifled her lipstick drawer, smeared bright red lipstick all over your face and then fell down the stairs in her high-heeled shoes.' That had been such a gem of a confidence that she couldn't resist smiling now at the image, and Bruno scowled at her.

'God, the woman never lets me forget embarrassing incidents like that. I was three at the time!'

'That's probably because you've managed to put all embarrassing incidents behind you now.'

'Well, it would be extremely suspect if I was still prone to smearing lipstick on my face and tripping downstairs in high-heeled shoes, wouldn't it?'

'Anyway, we're getting off the topic of why you're here.' She felt she had to drag the conversation back into the boxing ring or else totally lose sight of the fact that Bruno Carr was to be kept at a safe distance.

'So we are.' He stretched his feet out and crossed them at the ankles, then he clasped his hands behind his head and sank into silence.

'Well?' Jessica prompted.

'My mother didn't expect to like you. When I first explained the situation to her on the telephone, she was horrified. 'Course, she blamed you for the whole mess.'

'Oh, of course,' Jessica said sarcastically. 'Because Archangel Bruno couldn't possibly have had a hand in it at all!'

'It seems she changed her mind after meeting you.'

'You mean...she thinks that you might be partly responsible for the situation? You amaze me!'

'I mean she expected to find that you followed the trend of my usual girlfriends.'

'Ah!' She was no clearer now as to the direction this conversation was going but she realised that she couldn't have halted it even if she wanted to. Which she didn't.

'Don't interrupt,' he ordered and she declined to point out that she hadn't. 'I came here fortified to say my speech and you'll sit there and listen to it. My mother...whom I love dearly and whose opinions I value greatly, seemed to think...' His voice petered out and he frowned accusingly at her, as though she were personally responsible for his failure to carry on.

'I haven't interrupted,' Jessica pointed out. 'You were saying…?'

'She seemed to think that you might possibly be the right woman for me.'

Jessica's mouth dropped open in sheer amazement. If his mother had told him that, then the woman was an actress of Oscar-winning standards because she had certainly said nothing to Jessica of the sort. In fact, she had pointedly steered clear of any matchmaking tendencies.

'She seems to think I might be better off with someone like you.'

'*Someone like me?* I'm not an act at a circus show! What do you mean *someone like me*? I can't think that your mother would have referred to me in those terms!' Her eyes started welling up and she blinked the tears back.

'No, she didn't. God!' He stood up and raked his fingers through his hair and began pacing the room as if he needed the physical activity to think better. 'You're not making this any easier for me,' he said, stopping in front of her. Looming so that she had to look up at him.

'She seemed to think that you and I are rather well suited, which happens to be my opinion as well.' Jessica opened her mouth and he held up one hand for her to be quiet, then he sat down heavily next to her on the sofa. 'And it has nothing to do with the baby. Well, obviously the baby comes into the equation. The fact is I happen to enjoy your company even if *you* spend half your time running away from my questions and the other half giving me a hard time for asking them in the first place.'

Jessica could feel her heart beating quicker and quicker, and she thought that she might well be holding her breath, so she exhaled very deeply and told herself not to get worked up over what he was saying because it probably wasn't leading where she would dearly have wanted it to lead.

'Well?' he prompted challengingly. 'Aren't you going to rush in here to defend yourself?'

'I'll wait until you reach the end of your speech. I wouldn't want to be accused of interrupting you.'

'There you go again! Throwing me off my stride!' He glared at her. 'You've done that from day one! I'm not accustomed to having to be alert one hundred per cent of the time when I'm with a woman, just in case some stray verbal arrow comes flying my way!'

'I *know* what you've been accustomed to, Bruno. Isn't that why marriage would never work between us? Because you're not accustomed to women like me? Because at the end of the day, whatever your mother says and however much your head agrees with her, your heart is firmly rooted in another type of girl?'

'So I've told myself for the past few weeks,' he muttered, and she strained across to hear what he was saying.

'What was that?'

'You heard me!' He looked at her, tilted his head slightly to one side and gave her a winningly boyish 'can't you see where I'm heading?' look, which she returned with a perplexed frown.

'It seems that I rather like the intelligent, bossy—'

'I am not bossy!'

'Answer-me-back at the drop of a hat style of woman.'

Jessica, listening intently to every word, found that she was having trouble swallowing. Her throat appeared to have become very dry.

'It seems that...' he began, and then, once more, left the sentence unfinished.

'I wish you'd get to the point, Bruno.'

'Because you can't wait to see the back of me?'

'No.'

'Are you telling me that you don't want me to go?' He gave her a sly, charming smile and she flushed. 'My mother informed me that she thinks you're not quite as hostile towards me as you like to make out...'

'Oh, she does, does she?' Traitor, Jessica thought.

'Yes. What do you say?'

'Oh, what does it matter?' she said on a sigh. 'It doesn't matter how many roads we go down, we always seem to end up right back at the place we started, which, in case you're wondering, is nowhere.'

'I disagree. Have I told you that I've been doing some thinking?'

'I think you might have.'

'I don't repulse you, do I, Jessica? Admit it. It's just the opposite, isn't it? I turn you on and that terrifies you. That's why you didn't want to continue what we had once we got back to England. That's why you've been fighting me every inch of the way. Because you're not indifferent to me at all. Okay, I'm going to lay all my cards on the table and tell you that I think you—'

'Don't you dare say it!' She felt the customary panic at the prospect of having her emotions laid bare for him to pick over, but hard on the heels of panic came a kind of weary lassitude. She was fed up playing games. What was the point of it all? It didn't change the way she felt.

'Why not? Because you might give yourself away?'

'Is that why you came over here, Bruno?' she asked quietly. 'So that you can gloat at yet another conquest?'

He looked at her startled, then confused, but she was too dispirited to react to the fact that he had just pulled off the greatest piece of bluffing he had probably ever done in his life.

'No, that's not why I came here.'

Jessica looked at him, mildly surprised at this admission.

'I came here to tell you that…it seems that…well, my mother put two and two together to be honest…nothing better to do with her time than try and analyse other people's motivations… I don't suppose you have a glass of whisky lying about, do you?' When she shook her head, he continued, flushing, 'If you really want to know, I think you've managed to pull the rug from under my feet…'

'Rug? What rug? What on earth are you on about?'

'You've made me fall in love with you.' He stared at her defiantly, and his admission was so overwhelming that for a few seconds she sat there and stared back at him with her lips parted. 'I couldn't stop thinking about you when I got back to England. I was pretty sure that you'd make contact, and when nothing happened I told myself that it didn't matter. In fact, that it was the best thing that could happen. I tried to launch myself back into my social life, I even dated a couple of other women, but it was a ridiculous farce. I compared all of them to you, and I missed you.'

'You *slept* with other women?'

'I don't think I could have even if I'd wanted to,' he replied with a dry, ironic laugh. 'How could I when my head was filled with you?'

Jessica could feel a foolish grin spread over her face.

'Good,' she told him comfortably. 'Carry on.'

'*Good?*' He shifted slightly. ''Course, I'm only admitting all this because I know you feel precisely the same way about me…don't you?' He paused. 'Don't you?'

'I…well, yes…I do happen to like you very much…' She smiled to herself.

'*Like?*'

'Perhaps a bit more.'

'You mean you're deeply, irretrievably, passionately in love with me?'

Jessica laughed and gazed at him tenderly. She inched her way towards him until she was curled against him, and could hear the beating of his heart through his shirt. He kissed her hair and stroked it, then kissed it again.

'I might well be,' she said softly. 'You might well have pulled the rug from under my feet as well.' She raised her face to his and her heart, which had been doing all sorts of odd things ever since he had appeared on the scene, seemed to settle in just the place it belonged. 'I thought I could do without men and I could. I just found that I couldn't do without you.'

'What do you mean by that?' he asked in mock hurt, kissing the tip of her nose while he stroked her neck very gently. 'I'm not an act at a circus show, you know.'

'I couldn't bear the thought of marrying you when you didn't love me and I couldn't bear the thought of leaving you, of only being tied to you through our child.'

He smiled and kissed her very thoroughly on the mouth and she moaned and guided his hand to her breast.

'So. Will you marry me?' he asked huskily.

'Do you know, Bruno Carr? I think I just might.'

# EPILOGUE

'MUMMY! Mummy! Mummy!'

Jessica looked at her daughter and against the flickering night shadows she could make out the glowing eyes and rosy-cheeked smile. Beyond her, she met Bruno's eyes and they smiled at one another. With Amy in his arms, her little face was at the same level as his, and even without the benefit of bright lights it was easy for her to see how closely they resembled each other.

'Strong genes,' he had told her with proud satisfaction two years ago when he had gazed down at that seven-pound three-ounce scrap of closed-fisted baby wrapped in blankets. 'Spit image of me. A little clone.'

'Poor child!' Jessica had teased, looking at the thatch of dark hair.

'Amy! Amy! Amy!' Jessica replied, reaching to stroke her daughter's face. It was after seven and they had wrapped her up warmly for this little expedition to the local village school.

'Isn't she a little nag?' Bruno murmured, nuzzling Amy's cheek with his nose and then planting a kiss on her neck. 'I knew she'd inherited certain important character traits from you!'

Jessica laughed, and wondered, not for the first time, how she could still be so thrilled with this extraordinary man. She still felt that magical tingle of awareness whenever he was near her and that warm feeling of security, as though the sweetest things in life had somehow found her and were there to stay.

'Me like de fireworks!'

'I can see that you do, darling.'

'She's so *advanced*,' Bruno said in wonderment, for the umpteenth time, and Jessica's arm around his waist circled him even closer.

'You're biased.'

'Not at all. How many children of her age do you know can hold a conversation?'

Jessica doubted whether her daughter's ability to string words together could actually be labelled 'holding a conversation' but she knew better than to argue the point. Bruno, the archetypal single man, had become the most devoted father.

'Absolutely none,' she agreed and she saw the glimmer of teeth as he smiled and looked upwards to where a shower of light was descending back to earth. The ground was packed to the rafters, but here, at the back, it was as though there were only the three of them in the entire universe. Amy's face, tilted upwards, was alight with childish amazement.

'Again!' she cried. 'Again! Again! Again!'

'Time to go, Amy,' Jessica said, laughing, as her daughter pushed out her mouth in stubborn disagreement.

'No!'

They walked past groups of milling people towards the car and, despite the childish protestations and tears, within five minutes Amy was sound asleep, her thumb half falling out of her mouth, her head curled to one side.

'Isn't she an angel when she's asleep?' Jessica said, resting her head back and half closing her eyes.

'Something else she's inherited from you,' Bruno said softly. She felt his hand cover hers and their fingers entwined into a solid bond. 'Now admit it, aren't you glad you persuaded me to marry you?'

She laughed and squeezed his fingers. 'Oh, yes, my lord and master!'

'And, of course, you can prove that when we get back,' he growled, and then he shook his head. 'But then again, maybe not. Not quite yet, anyway.'

'I know. Things *are* getting a trifle difficult on that front, aren't they, my love?' she said ruefully, glancing down at her stomach.

'And a more beautiful reason for that I can't imagine.' He smiled and glanced across to her, his eyes warm and loving. 'Just think, by Christmas, no more stomach.'

'I know,' she sighed contentedly. 'But lots of broken nights.'

'Could things be better?'

And they laughed in unison.

Award-winning author **Sandra Marton** wrote her first novel while still in school. Her doting parents told her she'd be a writer someday and Sandra believed them. In school and college, she wrote dark poetry nobody but her boyfriend understood. As a wife and mother, she devoted the little free time she had to writing murky short stories. Not even her boyfriend-turned-husband understood those. At last, Sandra decided she wanted to write about real people. That didn't actually happen because the heroes she created—and still creates—are larger than life but both she and her readers around the world love them exactly that way. When she isn't at her computer, Sandra loves to bird watch, walk in the woods and the desert, and travel. She can be as happy people-watching from a sidewalk café in Paris as she can be animal-watching in the forest behind her home in northeastern Connecticut. Her love for both worlds, the urban and the natural, is often reflected in her books. You can write to Sandra Marton at PO Box 295, Storrs, Connecticut, USA (please enclose a self-addressed envelope and postage for a reply) or visit her website at www.sandramarton.com

**Don't miss the next intense and engaging story
by Sandra Marton:
THE ONE-NIGHT WIFE
On sale June 2005, in Modern Romance™!**

# THE BEDROOM
# BUSINESS
*by*
**Sandra Marton**

# CHAPTER ONE

JAKE MCBRIDE was a man under siege.

A woman who'd spent the past couple of months on his arm and in his bed, couldn't accept the fact that their relationship was over.

"You don't love me," she'd wept, just last night.

Well, no. Jake didn't. He'd told her that days ago, reminded her that he'd never said he loved her, never even hinted that he might love her someday. He knew there were guys who said it in an attempt to score, but he wasn't one of them. Jake was always honest about his intentions. He made it clear that love, marriage, the "something old, something new, something blue" thing just wasn't on his agenda.

Besides, the immodest truth was that he didn't have to.

He was a healthy, heterosexual, thirty-year-old American male. He was six foot three with broad shoulders, a deep chest and a hard, flat belly, thanks to his passion for tough, sweaty workouts at his gym. His hair was dark, thick and wavy; his eyes were what one besotted female had called the color of the Atlantic in midsummer, which even now made him smile because he hardly ever noticed his eyes—what man would?—except when he happened to see them in the mirror while he shaved. He had a square jaw and a firm mouth set beneath a nose that bore a small bump, a souvenir of the year he'd spent working a jackhammer in a Pennsylvania coal mine.

He found it amusing that women seemed to like the faintly misshapen nose. The same babe who'd said his eyes were like the sea had told him it made him look dangerous.

"Whatever turns you on," Jake had said with a husky laugh, as he rolled her beneath him.

5

And he had money. Hell, why dance around the issue? He was rich, richer than he'd ever dreamed he could be, and he'd earned every dime himself, transforming a propensity for numbers, a talent for reading the market and a love for taking risks into a career in venture capitalism that was light-years away from the life he'd been born to.

Wasn't all that enough to make a woman happy? Yes. Yes, it was. He never had difficulty finding a woman.

The trouble was getting rid of them.

Jake winced.

It wasn't a nice way to think about it but it was the truth.

What he was going through with Brandi wasn't exactly new. It had happened to him before. A woman would agree, at the start of their affair, that she was no more interested in forever-after than he was. Then, for some unearthly reason, she'd change her mind a few weeks later and get that oh-how-happy-we-could-be gleam in her eye even though any fool could tell that marriage was not man's natural state.

The whole turnaround was beyond his comprehension but yeah, it happened. And it was happening again, despite his best efforts.

The only person who could save him from disaster was his personal assistant, Emily.

Emily, Jake thought gratefully. What would he do without her? She was smart, efficient, always on her toes. Emily not only kept his office running smoothly, but she protected him from the predations of women like Brandi. It didn't happen often, thankfully, but when necessary, Emily fielded unwanted calls, kept away unwanted visitors.

Jake wasn't unkind. That was the reason he'd told Emily to show Brandi into his private office yesterday, even though he knew it was a bad idea. He was right. It had been a miserable idea. All Brandi had wanted to do was tell him that she loved him but he didn't love her.

"You don't," she'd cried, "you don't, Jake!"

Why would he deny it? "No," he'd said, "I don't." He'd

handed her his handkerchief. ''But I like you,'' he'd added earnestly. ''A lot.''

Jake sighed, sat down at his desk, leaned his elbows on the gleaming oak surface and massaged his aching temples with his fingertips.

So much for being honest. Brandi had gone from weeping to sobbing while he stood there, feeling like an idiot for not having seen it coming but then, he really never did.

''Hell,'' he muttered, and shot to his feet again.

He really did like her. Why else would he have spent the last, what, two months seeing her? Exclusively, of course. He wasn't into sharing his women and besides, he was always faithful for as long as a relationship lasted. But he wasn't ready to spend the rest of his life with one woman. Not now, not in the foreseeable future, maybe not ever.

Life had only just begun to open for him in the past few years. Jake had grown up poor, lost his father in a mining accident when he was ten, lost his mother to a stepfather who believed that sparing the rod spoiled the child when he was twelve. At seventeen, he'd quit school and gone to work in the same mine that had taken his father's life. A year later, after almost dying under two tons of coal, Jake put down his hammer and scrubbed the black dust from his skin even though he'd known he'd never quite get it out of his blood. Then he'd headed east. It had taken a while but a quirky combination of luck, guts and a hard-won university degree had turned his life into a dream.

It was a life he liked, just the way it was.

He had an office in Rockefeller Center, an apartment on Park Avenue, a weekend house in Connecticut and a vintage Corvette.

He had Emily.

Yes, life was good…except for this current mess, with Brandi.

Jake groaned, kicked back his chair and put his feet up on his desk. How come he hadn't read the signs? Her career was all that mattered, she'd told him, but it wasn't true. First she gave him a key to her apartment. He hadn't asked for one, hadn't offered her the key to his, but she handed hers over, anyway, with a casual smile that would have made him look like an ass not to have accepted it. Then she bought him a tie at Bloomingdale's. Nobody bought Jake ties except Jake, but she said some hotshot actor had been wearing one just like it when she'd posed in an ad with him, and how could he possibly turn down such a simple gift?

And then, last week, the final touch. He'd taken her home, was in the process of saying good-night—he hadn't felt like spending the night with her which, in retrospect, he should have recognized as the beginning of the end—when she reached into her pocket, pulled out a pair of airline tickets and waggled them at him.

"Surprise," she'd said gaily, and explained that she was flying home to Minneapolis for the weekend and he was going with her.

"It's my parents' thirty-fifth anniversary, Jake. They're having the whole family to dinner and they're just dying to meet you!"

The tie around his neck—the very one she'd bought him, which he hated but had worn that evening because she'd asked him where it was—suddenly felt like a noose, growing tighter and tighter until he stabbed two fingers under the knot and yanked it away from his throat.

"I can't go," he'd said, and she'd said yes, yes, he could, and he'd said he couldn't and she, with her lip trembling, said he could if he wanted to and finally he'd said well, he *didn't* want to…

"Oh, Jake," she'd whispered, and the next thing he'd known, she was crying into his shirt.

What did women want, anyway? Well, not all women. Not the Emilies of this world but then, Emily wasn't a woman. Not a real one. She was his P.A.

Jake sighed, rose from the chair behind his desk, walked

to the window and looked out. Forty stories below, people crowded the street. He hoped Brandi wasn't one of those people. She'd been there this morning, waiting for him.

"Jake?" she'd said, and before he could decide what the heck to do, whether to pretend he didn't see her or hustle her into the lobby and up to his office before she started bawling, she'd thrown her arms around him and tried to kiss him.

"Hell," he whispered, and leaned his forehead against the cool glass.

Still, he had no desire to hurt her. He didn't want to say anything cruel or unkind…

"Mr. McBride?"

Because she was a nice woman. And even though it was time to move on, that didn't mean—

"Mr. McBride? Sir?"

Jake swung around. Emily stood in the doorway. For the first time in what felt like hours, he smiled. If only all women were as pragmatic, as sensible, as she.

"Yes, Emily?"

"Sir, I thought you'd like to know that I sent that e-mail memo to John Woods."

"Fine."

"His reply just came in. He says he likes your suggestions and hopes you're free to fly to San Diego to meet with him next week."

"Am I?"

"Yes, sir. You're free Monday and Tuesday. You have a meeting Tuesday afternoon but it can be easily postponed."

Jake nodded. "Make the arrangements, please. What else?"

"A fax from Atlanta. Nothing important, just a confirmation of your conference call."

"Good, good. Anything else?"

Emily looked down at the notepad in her hand. "You're

having a late lunch with Mr. Carstairs tomorrow at the Oak Room.''

''Ah. Thank you for reminding me.''

''Yes, sir. And you have a dinner appointment this evening. Eight o'clock, at The Palm. You asked me to remind you to mention that new oil field opportunity in Russia.''

Jake smiled and shook his head. ''What would I do without you?'' he said pleasantly. ''You're the epitome of efficiency.''

''Being efficient is my job, Mr. McBride.''

''Jake, please. I don't think we need to be so formal. You've been working for me for, what, a year?''

''Eleven months and twelve days.'' Emily smiled politely. ''I'm comfortable calling you Mr. McBride, sir. Unless *you* find it uncomfortable…?''

''No,'' Jake said quickly, ''no, that's fine. Whatever you prefer is okay with me.''

It sure as hell was. He'd never had an assistant like this one. When he looked ahead, he could see Emily Taylor by his side well into the distant future. Emily wouldn't find a man, get married and quit her job. Her career meant as much to her as his did to him.

He was fairly certain she never even dated.

He supposed he ought to feel guilty for being happy she didn't, but why should he? Emily was just one of those women who wasn't interested in men. There was a long and honorable list of them, going back through the centuries. Betty Friedan and the women's libbers. The Suffragettes. Joan of Arc. They'd all devoted their lives to Causes, not to men.

How could a man feel badly if a woman made a choice like that?

Emily wasn't even a distraction.

Some of the women he'd interviewed before hiring her had been stunners, but the word for Emily was ''average.''

Average height. Average weight. Average face. Average brown hair and average brown eyes.

"A little brown sparrow," Brandi had said after meeting her, with what Jake had recognized as a little purr of relief.

An accurate description, he thought. On his runs through Central Park, he saw lots of birds with flashier plumage but it was the little brown sparrows who were the most industrious.

Emily, Jake thought fondly. His very own little brown sparrow.

He smiled again, folded his arms and hitched a hip onto the edge of his desk. "Emily, how much am I paying you?"

"Sir?"

"Your salary. What is it?"

"Eight hundred a week, Mr. McBride."

"Well, give yourself a hundred bucks more."

Emily smiled politely. "Thank you, sir."

Jake smiled, too. He liked the no-nonsense way she'd accepted her raise. No little squeals of joy, no bouncing up and down, no "Oooh, Jake..." But, of course, she wouldn't call him "Jake" any more than she'd squeal. Squealing was for the women he dated, who greeted each bouquet of long-stemmed roses, each blue-boxed Tiffany trinket, with shrieks of delight.

"No." Jake strolled towards her. "No, thank *you*, Emily."

He clapped her lightly on the back. That was another thing he liked about his P.A. Her posture. She stood ramrod straight, not slouched or with her hips angled forward. So many women in New York stood that way, as if they were about to stalk down a runway at a fashion show.

Not his Emily.

Idly, he wondered what effect Emily's perfect stance had on her figure. Did it tilt her breasts forward? He couldn't tell; summer and winter, she always wore suits. Tweed, for the most part, like this one. Brown tweed, to match her brown hair, with the jacket closed so that her figure was pretty much a mystery. For all he knew, her breasts were the size of Ping-Pong balls. Or casaba melons. Who knew? Who cared? Not him. Yes, it was a definite pleasure to work with a woman who was both efficient and unattractive.

"I mean it," he said. "You're the best P.A. I've ever had."

Emily cleared her throat. "In that case, sir…"

"Yes?" Jake grinned. Evidently, the raise he'd just given her wasn't enough. That surprised him a little; Emily was never pushy but if she thought she deserved more money, she could have it. "Give yourself two hundred more a week. Is that better?"

A light blush suffused her cheeks. "One hundred is fine, Mr. McBride." She stepped back, her chin lifted, her eyes on his. "But I would much prefer to be called your E.A. instead of your P.A."

"Huh?"

"Your executive assistant, instead of your personal assistant. It's a more accurate description of my duties."

"My exec," Jake mused. "Well, sure. You want to be called my E.A., that's fine."

"Thank you again, sir."

"You're welcome." Jake smiled. "Just as long as you assure me you aren't changing your title to make your résumé look better."

"Sir?"

"You're not thinking of going job-hunting, are you?"

Emily looked horrified. "Certainly not, sir. I merely want an appropriate title."

Well, well, well. His little sparrow had an ego. Nothing wrong with that. Nothing at all.

"And you deserve it."

Oh, the sickly-sweet benevolence in his tone. Emily smiled, not an easy thing to do when what she felt like doing was throwing up on Jake McBride's shiny black shoes. The egotistical goon. If only she could tell him what she thought of him. But she couldn't. Jobs as good as this one were impossible to find. She had lots of responsibility; the pay was excellent; and, she supposed, as men went, McBride was easy enough to work for. She just wondered if he had any idea, any actual idea, of how invaluable she was to him. Of what a mess he'd be in, without her.

Why wonder? She knew that he didn't. He was as dense as every other man she'd ever known, as foolishly arrogant as the endless succession of idiots who'd trooped through the house when she was growing up, every last one of them thinking he knew what he was doing and why he was doing it when, in reality, her gorgeous sisters had been leading the jerks around by their...hormones.

Jake McBride was just like those silly stud puppies. He might be rich, he might be handsome—assuming you liked the type, which she certainly didn't—but he was as much a victim of his hormones as the tongue-tied idiots who'd filled her sisters' teenaged lives.

His problems with the latest twit was proof of that.

McBride had broken things off. No surprise there. Emily had sensed it coming, long before he had. And, she had to admit, he'd done it with his usual flair. Roses. A little bracelet from Tiffany's that she knew—after all, she'd placed the order—set him back six thousand dollars. But the brunette with the ditzy name wouldn't, couldn't, accept The End. She sent gifts. Notes. She phoned. She'd even taken to dropping by the office.

*I'm here to see Jake,* she'd whisper, in a voice Marilyn Monroe would have envied.

And Emily would pick up the phone, tell her boss that Miss Carole was here. And McBride would say, oh Lord, just get rid of her, please, Emily.

Emily almost felt sorry for the woman. She certainly didn't feel sorry for Jake. As if she had nothing better to do than clean up after his messes. Bad enough she'd cleaned up after messes that involved her sisters.

*Em, are you sure Billy hasn't called?* Or, *Em, I'm so un-happy. Jimmy's dating another girl.* And then, after they both got married, she'd been expected to soothe them through their other disasters. *Em, I think Billy's fooling around. Em, Jimmy just doesn't love me the way he used to...*

They hadn't learned anything, either, not even after mar-riages and divorces and affairs...

Ridiculous, the way women set out to snare men and ended up in the trap, themselves.

That had never been what she wanted out of life. A man? A lot of embarrassing slobbering to be endured and then, maybe, a wedding ring and promises of forever-after that wouldn't even last as long as it took a slice of good-luck wedding cake to go stale, and for what?

*For companionship, Emily. For those long winter nights when you think you'll die if you have to curl up with another book...*

Emily bit her lip.

Okay. So, maybe she wasn't getting any younger. Maybe it might be nice to know what it was like to go on an oc-casional date. To have some man send her flowers, the way McBride—correction. The way *she* sent flowers, to his women. It might even be nice to get to see all those elegant New York restaurants from the inside, instead of just tele-phoning to make reservations for her boss and his latest in-terest.

What would such an evening be like? To have a man smile across the table at you, have him pick up your hand and bring it to his lips? Even if she really wanted to find out, where would she find a date? Lately, she'd started reading through the Personals in the back of *GOTHAM* magazine. Just for laughs, of course. She couldn't imagine ever bringing herself to answer an ad. Or running one. What would she say?

*Average-looking mouse searching for gorgeous, sexy, ex-citing man but will settle for plain, nonsexy, unexciting, av-erage-looking rat...*

No. That wouldn't do at all. Then again, neither would the truth.

*Average-looking female interested in average-looking male. Object: to find out what a date is like because said female hasn't had one in forever. In fact, not since the night of her senior prom, when one of her beautiful sisters conned a would-be boyfriend into being said female's date and everybody knew it and laughed...*

"Emily?"

Okay. That was it. She *would* run an ad. After all, she wasn't eighteen anymore. She wasn't Serena and Angela Taylor's poor little sister, the one with all the brains and none of the looks. She wasn't one of Jake McBride's women, either, with the kind of face and figure men dreamed of, but she could still manage to find herself a date—

"Emily? Are you okay?"

A large, warm hand settled on her shoulder. Emily blinked, focused her eyes on her boss. He was standing a breath away from her, staring at her with a little furrow just between his eyes. And what eyes they were. Dark. Deep. So deep...

"Are you all right? For a minute there, you seemed to drift away."

"I'm fine," she said briskly. "Just, uh, just a cold coming on, perhaps."

His hand slid to her elbow. "Go home," he said gently, as he propelled her towards the door. "Take a nice hot bath. Make yourself some tea."

"Honestly, Mr. McBride..."

"Do it," he said, with a polite, teasing smile, "or I'll take you home and do it for you."

An image swam into her head. McBride, in her tiny apartment, so big and masculine against her chintz-covered furniture. McBride, smiling down at her, his hands warm and gentle as he unbuttoned her tweed jacket, unbuttoned her silk blouse. Or, perhaps, his hands not so gentle. Hard, in fact.

Rough, maybe, as he ripped the blouse from her and took her into his arms...

Color flooded her face as she stepped back.

"That won't be necessary, sir. I'm perfectly capable of taking care of myself."

"I know you are," he said. For one awful minute, she was afraid he was going to pat her on the head. "Now just run along home, Emily. Take that bath, have the tea, pop some vitamin C and get a good night's rest."

"But it's only four forty-five."

McBride gave her another of those I'm-So-Wonderful-and-You're-So-Lucky-To-Be-Working-For-Me smiles.

"I can do without you for a little while, I promise. Now, go home. I'll see you in the morning."

"Thank you, Mr. McBride."

"Good night, Emily."

"Good night, sir."

Jake shut the door and sat down at his desk. Damn, what dedication. He'd almost had to carry Emily out of the office. Well, that would have been simple enough. She was small. Slender. She'd be light, just like one of those little sparrows. He could carry Emily up the steps in his duplex, to his bedroom, set her down on her feet and find out just what, exactly, lay hidden under all those woolly layers of clothing...

He frowned, pulled a blank pad towards him. What crazy thoughts. Jake chuckled softly. Amazing, the things a man's brain could conjure up at the end of a long day. Better to spend the next couple of hours profitably, writing some memos to leave on Emily's desk for her to tackle first thing in the morning.

He worked for a while, went from the memos to sketching out an idea that had just come to him about that meeting in San Diego...

A knock sounded on the door.

Jake looked up, then checked his watch. It was after five. Emily was gone. Nobody else would...

Somebody would.

Brandi, he thought unhappily. She'd called earlier, when Emily was at lunch. He'd picked up the phone just as the answering machine did and he'd heard that little whisper that had once driven him crazy with lust and now just drove him crazy, begging him to see her tonight.

The knock came again. Maybe if he just sat it out, pretended he wasn't here...

"Jake?"

The door swung open. Jake, caught between deciding whether to duck for cover or tell Brandi to get lost, looked up and grinned in surprise.

"Pete?"

Pete Archer, a guy he'd worked with his first year in New York, opened the door wider and stepped inside.

"Jake, you old son of a gun. What's the matter? You afraid I'm a bill collector or something?"

Jake got to his feet. "Or something." He came forward and the men shook hands. They'd never been close friends but it was great to see someone from the past. "Why didn't you call me? If I'd known you were going to be in town, I'd have rolled out the red carpet."

"Didn't know it, until the last minute." Pete smiled. "You look like life's treating you well."

"You, too." Jake grinned, gave Pete a light jab to the biceps. "How long will you be in town?"

"Just overnight. I have to be back in Chicago tomorrow morning."

"Too bad. I have a business dinner lined up. Let me call the guy and—"

"No, no, I understand. How about drinks? You have time for that?"

"Great idea. Want to go out, or have something here?"

"Here would be cool. Got any ale?"

Jake laughed. "Some things never change, huh? Ale, it is."

He went to his built-in mini fridge, took out a couple of bottles and opened them. Pete waved away his offer of a glass. The two men sat across from each other, leaned close enough to clink bottles, took long, thirsty swallows, then smiled.

"So," Jake said, "how're things?"

"Couldn't be better. And you?"

"Terrific." Jake sighed. "Well, they would be, if…" He leaned forward, across the desk. "You know why I didn't answer when you knocked? I thought you were a woman."

Pete laughed. "Don't tell me you've decided you're giving up babes. I wouldn't believe it."

"Let me amend that," Jake said, smiling. "I thought you were a particular woman."

"Ah. A bowwow who's developed a thing for you, huh?"

"No, she's a definite ten." Jake grinned, but his grin faded. "But the thing ran its course, you know? She began to hear wedding bells."

"Oh, yeah. I know what that's like." Pete drank some ale. "So, you tried to end it?"

"I'm still trying. Trouble is, she's determined. She calls. She sends me notes. She shows up at my apartment, she shows up here…"

"Well, you have a secretary, don't you? Let her do the dirty work."

"I have an executive assistant," Jake said, smiling and lifting his eyebrows.

"What's that mean?"

"It means I'm lucky enough to employ a woman whose only goal in life is to make me happy."

"Jake, you dog, you! You stocked the front desk with a hot babe!"

"Sorry to burst the bubble, pal, but Emily's as far from being a hot babe as Arnold Schwarzenegger."

Pete sighed. "Too bad. I figured her for the fox I just saw at the elevator."

"Oh, hell," Jake said, and the color drained from his face. "Brunette?"

"Uh-huh."

"Big brown eyes?"

"Uh-huh."

"Great legs? A body meant to send a man straight over the edge?"

Pete shrugged, took a drink of his ale. "Definitely and probably."

"Probably?" Jake gave a forlorn laugh. "You'd have to be blind or dead not to notice Brandi's figure."

"Brandi?"

"Yeah. The lady who's decided I'm the love of her life. I half-figured she might show up here tonight."

"Well, she did. And the only reason I didn't notice her shape was because it was hidden under a layer of tweed."

"Yeah, well..." Jake stared at Pete. "Tweed? Brandi would sooner be caught during rush hour in a New York subway than in tweed."

"Either her tastes have changed, or the woman I saw wasn't... Who'd you say?"

"Brandi," Jake said automatically. He frowned. "Emily wears tweed."

"And Emily would be...?"

"I told you about her. She's my P.A. My E.A." Jake thought for a second, then shook his head. "Forget it. No way could it have been Emily. I mean, she's great. She's efficient. She's capable. She's the best assistant I've ever had." He smiled. "But a looker? No way."

Pete gave a dramatic sigh. "See, that's where we differ, Jake. I've learned to refine my tastes."

Jake grinned. "Sure."

"No, I'm serious. I look beyond the obvious." He leaned forward, gave a leering smirk. "Besides, you know what they say. Still waters run deep."

"Meaning?"

"Meaning," Pete said smugly, "if a babe doesn't think she's a looker, a guy can get into her pants a lot easier."

Jake shot to his feet. "Not into Emily's, he can't." His voice was cold; he could feel the sudden tension in his muscles.

"Hey." Pete stood up, too. "We don't even know it's Emily we're talking about."

"I'm just making a point, Archer. Forget about getting into Emily's pants."

"Yeah, but it's probably not even... Jake. I didn't..." Pete took a breath. "Listen man, no offence."

"None taken," Jake said, and even he could hear the lie in his words. Well, why wouldn't he be upset? Emily was a fantastic asset. He wasn't about to end up with a messed-up assistant on his hands. Anyway, it was all academic, he thought, and forced himself to smile. "Not that it matters. That couldn't have been Emily. She isn't a looker. You don't know my Emily but I can tell you, my Emily is average—"

"Your Emily isn't 'your Emily,' Mr. McBride!"

Both men swung around. Emily stood in the open doorway, her face pale except for two spots of crimson high on her cheeks.

"Oh, hell," Jake said softly. "Emily. Emily, listen, I didn't mean—"

"You *did* mean. And I don't mind being called 'average.' It's what I am." Her hands bunched into fists, fists she hid in the folds of her tweed skirt. "But I am not your property. You may assume I have no life away from this office, but that does not give you the right to—"

"Emily," Jake said unhappily, "please—"

"Emily." Pete's voice was soft. Smarmy, Jake thought. Gentle, Emily thought, and looked at him. "Emily," Pete said again, and smiled, "I'm sorry we have to meet under such difficult circumstances."

"You two were talking about me," she said stiffly.

Pete walked towards her. "We were, yes. I was telling Jake—Mr. McBride—that I'd just passed you in the hall."

Jake made a choked sound. "You mean, the woman you were talking about really was—"

"And that I wanted to meet you," Pete went on, as if Jake hadn't spoken. He held out his hand. "My name is Pete Archer."

Emily ignored his outstretched hand. "Why did you want to meet me?"

"Because I'd like to take you to dinner."

"Nonsense." Jake's voice was too loud, too sharp. He knew it but hell, this was his office and his exec. What right did Archer have to... "She can't go with you," he said, as he stalked towards the two of them. "She doesn't want to go with you. She—"

"I'd be delighted," Emily said firmly.

"Emily, don't be a fool. Pete's not really interested in..." Jake bit his lip. If looks could kill, the one she'd just given him would have left him stone-cold and on the way to the mortuary. "For heaven's sake, where's your common sense? You, and this man...?"

She shot him a look more vicious than the first, and then she swung towards Pete.

"Shall we go, Mr. Archer?"

"Archer," Jake roared, "you son of a—"

"The lady's made her decision, Jake."

"I have, indeed. You pay my salary, Mr. McBride, but you do not own me. I do as I wish after office hours. If I want to go out on a date, I will." Her eyes narrowed. "Unless you'd rather I tendered my resignation...?"

Emily waited. Pete did, too. And Jake, totally helpless for the first time in his adult life, could do nothing except stand in the center of his office and watch his former friend and his little brown sparrow flutter her wings as she headed for a night on the town.

## CHAPTER TWO

THE city awoke to snow the next morning.

Heavy wet flakes drifted down from the skies.

Fine, Jake thought. Let the sky turn to lead, for all he cared. He was in a mood almost as foul as the weather. Snow that would soon turn to gray slush was just about right this morning.

The doorman greeted him cheerfully. Jake muttered a response, waved off his offer of a taxi. Traffic in Manhattan always verged on gridlock; it would be even worse in weather like this. Besides, walking to work might be a good idea. He figured that the cold air, a brisk pace as he headed crosstown, would improve his mood.

It didn't.

Some bozo trying to get his truck through a blocked intersection sent a spray of wet, dirty snow flying onto the sidewalk and over Jake's shoes; a guy on Rollerblades—Rollerblades, on a day like this—damned near rode him down.

By the time he reached Rockefeller Center, Jake's mood had gone from glum to grim. He gave a cursory look around as he strode into the building but he knew Brandi would be a no-show on a day like this. Not even her sudden determination to keep their affair alive would stand up to the possibility that her hair or makeup might get damaged. It was an unkind thought but, dammit, he was in an unkind frame of mind.

That was what staying awake half the night did to a man. Left him ill-tempered and mean-natured, especially when there was no good reason for him to have spent more time pacing the floors than sleeping.

It had to be the caffeine, Jake thought, as he stepped from

the elevator onto the pale gray marble floor and walked to his office. The health food pundits made him edgy, with all their doomsaying. He liked coffee, and steak, and if he'd ever accidentally consumed a bite of tofu in his life, he didn't want to know it.

Still, what else could have kept him up until almost dawn, if it wasn't caffeine? Or maybe that Chinese takeout he'd picked up for supper had done him in. Not that he'd eaten much of it. Jake frowned as he reached his office. A hell of a night he'd put in, not eating, not sleeping...

The kid who delivered the mail came skidding around the corner.

"Morning, Mr. McBride," he said cheerfully. "Here's your mail."

Jake, in no mood for cheerful banter or a stack of mail, scowled at the kid.

"What's the matter?" he growled. "Don't you deliver it anymore?"

"I am delivering it. See?" The kid shoved an armload of stuff at Jake, who took it grudgingly.

"This goes to my P.A., not to me."

"Your what?"

"My P.A. My E.A...." Jake's scowl deepened. "My secretary," he said. "You're supposed to hand her the mail."

"Oh. Emily."

For reasons unknown, Jake felt his hackles rise. "Her name," he said coldly, "is Miss Taylor."

"Uh-huh. Emily, like I said." The kid grinned. "Nice lady. Pretty eyes."

What was this? Did every male who walked in the door have to make an appraisal of Emily? What about her eyes? She had two of them. So what? Most people did.

"I always hand the mail right to her. But the door's locked. It looks like nobody's home."

Jake's scowl turned to a look of disbelief. He shot back

the cuffs of his Burberry and his suit jacket, checked his watch and looked at the kid.

"Don't be ridiculous. Of course someone is home." He grabbed the doorknob. "It's after nine. Miss Taylor's always at her desk by—"

The knob didn't move. The kid was right. The door was locked.

Jake's mood, already in the cellar, began digging its way towards China. He shifted the armload of envelopes and magazines, dug out his keys and let himself into his office.

"If Emily is sick or something," the kid said, "when you talk to her, tell her that Tommy sends—"

Jake slammed the door, stalked across the office and dumped the mail on Emily's desk. It was, as always, neat as a pin. Even when she was seated behind it, not so much as a paper clip was ever out of place. Still, he could tell she wasn't there. Her computer monitor stared at him with a cold black eye. The office lights were off, too, and there was no wonderful aroma of fresh coffee in the air.

E.A. or not, Emily had no feminist compunction against making coffee every morning.

Jake turned on the lights, marched into his private office, peeled off his wet coat and dumped it on the back of his chair.

Sick? Emily?

"Ha," he said.

She hadn't been sick a day since she'd come to work for him. Yeah, she'd said she felt as if she were coming down with a cold yesterday afternoon but it couldn't have been much of a cold because not an hour later, she'd leaped at Archer's invitation to dinner like a trout going after a fly.

"Sick," Jake muttered.

Sleeping off her big night out, was more like it. Who knew where Archer had taken her for dinner, or what hour he'd gotten her home? Who knew how much wine she'd had to drink or how late she'd gone to bed or if she'd gone to bed at all...

Or if she'd been alone when she got into it.

Not that he cared. What she did, who she did it with, was her business. He'd tell her that, when—if—she deigned to show up this morning. The only question was, should he tell it to her before or after he told her she was fired?

From executive assistant to unemployed, in less than twenty-four hours.

The thought did wonders for his disposition. But why wait for Miss Taylor to put in an appearance? He could just as easily fire her right now.

Jake smiled coldly as he reached for the telephone but his smile changed, went back to being a frown. What was her number? For that matter, where did she live? In the city? In the suburbs? In one of the outlying boroughs? He had all that information. She'd filled out a form when she'd come to work for him. Actually, she'd filled out a zillion forms, thanks to all the tax information everybody required, but he'd be damned if he could remember anything about Emily's private life.

Why would he? Until Archer stirred things up, she'd been the perfect employee. He'd never had reason to think about her, once he was away from the office. And now he was wasting time, thinking about her instead of sitting down and doing all the things that needed doing today. Not that he was actually "thinking" about Emily. Where she'd gone with Archer. Whether she'd had fun. Whether Archer had come on to her. Whether she was late because, even now, she was lying in the bastard's arms...

"Son of a bitch," Jake said, under his breath.

He thumbed open his address book, ran his finger down the list of T's. There it was, Emily Taylor, the phone number written in Emily's own, careful hand. Her address was there, too. She lived in Manhattan. Good, he thought grimly as he punched the phone number into the keypad. Then, she could damned well get her tail in here, pronto, and never mind what she was in the middle of doing with Archer.

Let her trudge through the snow. Then, he'd fire her. In person, where he could watch her face become pale as he told her to get out of his life.

Jake waited, tapping his foot impatiently as the phone rang. And rang. And—

"Good morning, Mr. McBride."

"I'm happy you think so, Miss Taylor," he said coldly...and suddenly realized that Emily's voice wasn't coming from the phone in his hand, it was coming from behind him. Slowly, he put down the telephone and turned around.

She stood in the doorway. Snowflakes glittered in her hair—brown hair, he thought, but with a warm, golden glow that made a man think of dark maple syrup on a winter morning....

Jake's mouth turned down.

"You're late."

"I'm aware of that, sir. And I'm sorry."

She didn't sound sorry. Not the least bit. There was a chill to her voice that had nothing to do with the weather.

"And you're late because...?"

"The trains are running behind schedule."

"Really." Jake smiled thinly and folded his arms. "I wonder if that could be because it's snowing."

He was gratified to see a light flush color her cheeks. "I'm sure it is, Mr. McBride."

"In which case, Miss Taylor, you must also know that the trains always run late when it snows. Half the city runs late— or is that news to you?"

Emily looked down and brushed the snow from her coat. Her ankle-length, tweed coat, Jake thought irritably. Was tweed the only item in her wardrobe? Was he ever going to see her legs?

"I know what snow does to New York," she said calmly. She lifted her eyes to his. "I allowed for that contingency."

"Ah. You allowed for it." Jake glanced pointedly at his watch. "Interesting, since you're almost an hour late."

Damn, he sounded like an ass. Well, so what? He was the boss. He was entitled to sound like an ass, if he wanted.

"I'm twenty minutes late, sir." Emily still sounded calm but there was a bite to the "sir." "And I did allow for the weather. I left my apartment twenty minutes earlier than usual. If I hadn't, I'd be later than I already am."

"Does that mean you got out of bed twenty minutes earlier than usual?"

Emily's eyebrows brows rose. "I beg your pardon?"

"It's a simple question. I asked if you set your alarm back twenty minutes."

"I don't see what that has to do with anything."

Neither did Jake. What he really wanted to ask was if she'd had to set the alarm back or if something else had awakened her this morning. Somebody. Archer, for instance, moving above her, in her bed...

*Hell!*

Jake frowned, cleared his throat, went behind his desk and sat down. He reached for his appointment book and looked at the page. Letters and numbers danced before his eyes.

"Never mind," he said brusquely.

"Never mind, indeed." Her voice was frigid now; he could almost see the icicles forming on each word. "Perhaps we need to establish some boundaries, Mr. McBride. My private life—"

"So you said, last evening." Jake waved his hand in dismissal. "I left the mail on your desk. Go through it, see if anything needs my immediate attention and then come back and I'll dictate some notes."

She hesitated. He didn't look up but he didn't have to. He could all but feel her counting to ten, taking deep breaths, doing what she could to hang onto her composure. Well, wasn't he doing the same thing? The nerve of her, holding him up for a pay raise and a new title one day and coming in late the next.

"Of course, Mr. McBride."

The door snicked shut. Jake looked up, glowered at it, and closed his appointment book.

Of course, Mr. McBride, he thought furiously. As if nothing had changed, as if she hadn't shown up late, been insubordinate, done exactly the opposite of what he'd told her to do and gone off with a man who was only after one thing…

Jake closed his eyes. "Hell," he said, but with no heat whatsoever.

Emily was right. Her life, outside of the office, wasn't his business. Who she dated was up to her. What she did with who she dated was up to her, too. Why should he care, as long as she did her work?

Still, it was only human to wonder where she'd gone last night and whether she'd had a good time. He could just ask her. He'd known Emily for almost a year now. They were friends. Well, they were business associates. And he'd been the one who'd put Archer in her path.

Was it so strange he should be vaguely curious about how things had gone last night?

*Emily,* he could say, *I was just wondering, did you have a nice evening? Where'd Archer take you for dinner? Did he take you home? Did you invite him in? What time did he leave?*

*He did leave, didn't he?*

Jake rubbed his hands over his face.

Not only was her private life none of his business, but even thinking about it was none of his business.

The kid was right, though. She did have nice eyes.

A muscle knotted in Jake's jaw. He wondered if Archer had been right, too. About her legs. Were they great? He couldn't tell, not with that coat going straight down to her feet, and he'd certainly never noticed her legs in the past.

Why would he? Emily was his P.A. Check that. She was his E.A. She was a well-oiled, well-educated, well-paid employee. Her looks were none of his business.

She was a quiet little sparrow.

His little sparrow.

Jake shoved the appointment book halfway across his desk, swiveled his chair towards the window and gave the falling snow the benefit of his scowl. He knew it was foolish to bristle, but bristling was precisely what he felt like doing.

And it was all Emily's fault.

Emily took off her coat, shook it briskly and hung it in the closet. Then she sat, bent down and began tugging at her left boot while she told herself that bristling would get her nowhere.

Still, bristling was exactly what she felt like doing.

And it was all McBride's fault.

The great man was not in a good mood this morning. Too bad. Perhaps he'd had another run-in with the twit, desperate to tell him how wonderful he was.

''Idiot,'' Emily said, and gave the stubborn boot a whack.

Or was he still annoyed that she hadn't let him tell her what to do last night? Don't go, he'd said, as if he owned her, and the hell of it was she should have listened to him because her evening with his pal had been a disaster. A total, unmitigated disaster. Mr. Peter-Aren't-You-Fortunate-To-Be-With-Me Archer was so full of himself it was a wonder there'd been room for her at their all-too-cozy table for two in the restaurant he'd chosen.

Emily hung her head and groaned.

Oh, what an awful evening. The wine he'd ordered, even after she'd politely declined a drink. The way he'd leaned close and breathed moistly on her neck. The way he'd tried to feed her a bite of his meal from his fork. Yuck. As if she would want to take the fork into her mouth after it had been in his. And then all that smarmy, double entendre stuff which she'd been too dumb to recognize as smarmy and double entendre, until the waiter happened by just as Archer, the slimeball, said something that made the hapless waiter almost pour the coffee into her lap.

Emily attacked the boot again.

And this man, she reminded herself grimly, this—this human octopus, was Mr. Jake McBride's friend. His oldest, dearest, closest friend.

So much for thinking her boss was a nice guy even if he was dense. Nice guys didn't have lifelong buddies like Peter Archer.

Damn this boot! Why wouldn't it come off?

To think of McBride's gall, that *he* was angry with *her*. Whatever the cause of it, how dare he take it out on her? She'd been, what, fifteen minutes late? When she thought of all the times she'd come in early without McBride so much as saying, Why, Emily, how good of you to be here before nine.

But why would he? She was his personal property. He expected her to be there, at his beck and call.

"The Emperor McBride," she said, under her breath, and tugged harder. What was with these boots? They might as well be glued on.

"Uh," she said, and tugged again. "Uh…"

"Having a problem, Emily?"

She sat up so fast that her heel slammed against the carpeted floor. McBride was standing in the doorway, watching her. His arms were folded and one of his dark eyebrows was lifted in what looked like amusement.

"No problem, sir," she replied briskly.

Of course it was a problem. She'd been bent over, tugging at her boots, and her face was flushed with rosy color. Her hair—a few strands of it, anyway—had come loose of its clip at the nape of her neck and curled gently at her ears. Emily's hair was curly? He'd never noticed. She always wore it back, and straight.

Jake frowned.

"Here," he said, advancing towards her, "let me help you."

"It isn't necessary. I can—"

Too late. He was already squatting before her, lifting her foot into his lap and tugging.

"Really, Mr. McBride…"

Jake pulled off the boot. No wonder it had been hard to remove. Her boots were made of thin black leather and she was wearing heavy socks. Heavy wool socks, over feet that were attached to long, slender legs.

Oh, yeah. Archer, the bastard, had called it right. Her legs were good. Excellent, as a matter of fact.

"Thank you," Emily said.

Jake lifted his eyes to her face. "You're welcome." He cleared his throat, looked down at the foot, still in his hands, and tried to think of something intelligent to say. "You're wearing socks." Brilliant, he thought trying not to wince, just brilliant, McBride. "I mean—you're wearing—"

"Socks," she said stiffly. "Wool socks. Double knit. I guess that's the reason the boots are so hard to get off. I wore them because I thought I might have to walk at least part of the way home, if the snow keeps up, and these boots aren't really warm…"

Her voice trailed to silence. Why was she telling him all this? He was holding her foot in his hands, looking at it as if he'd never seen a foot before. And she was explaining why she was wearing wool socks, as if it mattered.

"Socks," he murmured, and looked up at her again. He had such a strange look on his face. That darkness in his eyes.

Maybe he thought she was going to walk around the office in heavy wool socks all day.

"Yes. But I'll take them off. I have panty hose underneath…"

Oh, good. Now she was telling him about her underwear. Emily colored and pulled her foot from Jake's hands.

"Thank you again," she said briskly. "I'll get to the mail immediately."

"Not without taking that other boot off."

"I can manage."

"I doubt it."

"Honestly, Mr. McBride—"

Jake knew he could get the boot off with one quick tug but considering the condition she'd put him in, with that comment about her underwear, he figured it was best to take his time.

"There," he said, when it was safe. He dropped the boot beside its mate and rose to his feet. "All done."

Emily nodded. "Thank you," she said again.

"You're welcome."

He looked as if he were going to say something more. A few words of apology, maybe, for the way he'd snapped at her before? No such luck. He gave her a quick nod, swung away and went back inside his office.

The door closed silently behind him.

Emily sat motionless. Her feet were tingling. Not the way they'd tingle if the circulation were coming back after they'd been freezing cold. She'd felt that, once, when she was a little girl and she'd missed the school bus and ended up walking home in the snow. No, they were tingling in a very strange way. As if they were still in McBride's lap. As if his big hands were still holding them. As if he were still looking up at her with his eyes all dark and hungry…

The room seemed to tilt.

Emily dragged air into her lungs. Then she took off her socks, slipped her feet into the shoes she'd brought with her, and got to work.

Hours later, she sighed, blinked owlishly at her computer screen and pushed back from her desk. It was almost one o'clock. Time for lunch, she thought, and rose from her chair. She gave a ladylike stretch, opened the drawer to get her purse…and saw the copy of *GOTHAM*, still opened to the personal ads.

She made a face, picked up the magazine and dumped it into the wastebasket.

"Goodbye and good riddance," she said, and dusted off her hands.

Last night had cured her of even thinking about going out for an evening with a man she didn't know anything about.

On the other hand, choosing a date from the Personals would be different.

She might not really "know" the man, but she wouldn't go into it blindfolded. At least, she'd have some information about her date beforehand. And she wouldn't have to waste an entire evening. She could suggest they meet for lunch, or coffee, or for nothing more complicated than a walk in the park. She could control the character of this kind of date and not end up finding out, as she had last night, that the only thing the man in question wanted was to get into her pants.

Emily plucked the discarded magazine from the wastebasket, opened it and laid it on her desk.

*Handsome, sexy, successful male, 40, D, Br & Br, ISO beautiful, sexy female, preferably br&br, too…*

*Handsome, successful, sexy, Romeo, 33, S, BL and bl, looking for his beautiful, sexy Juliet…*

*Sexy, handsome guy, 38, ND, blond and blue, very successful, ISO sexy, beautiful lady, preferably Br&B…*

It was like reading a code. ISO for "in search of." D for "divorced," S for "single," ND for "newly divorced." B's for hair and eye color. Unless you had red hair. Or gold. Or…

Oh, this was ridiculous. Advertisements by men for women. Reading them was a joke. They were so phony. If every guy who was dateless in New York was sexy, easy on the eyes and successful, why were they running these ads? She knew better than to fall for all those adjectives. In fact, if she had to come up with the name of a gorgeous, sexy, successful man, the only one she'd be able to muster was that of Jake Mc...

Emily's heartbeat stumbled. Quickly, she grabbed the telephone, punched in the Personals number, listened impatiently as a recorded female voice offered available options.

*To reply to a LoveNote,* the voice said nasally, *please enter the number of the LoveNote you've selected.*

Emily entered a number. She waited, heard a husky male voice say "hello," listened to what was, more or less, a repeat of the ad in the magazine, and waited for the ad to end and the tone to sound. At last, it did. It was time to leave a message for Mr. Handsome, Sexy and Successful, 40, D, brown and brown.

Her mouth was dry as sand. She thought, fleetingly, of the sad red geranium sitting at home on her kitchen table, which she kept forgetting to water...

*Beeeep!*

Emily swallowed, licked her lips and took a breath. Sound sexy, she told herself.

"Good afternoon." Great. Just great. She sounded about as sexy as a Girl Scout trying to sell cookies. "Hi," she said, trying for perky, if not sexy. "Uh, I'm calling to say—to say that I think I might be just the Brrr and Brrr—uh, the Brown and Brown you're looking for." She hesitated, checked the ad again. Sexy, it said. And beautiful. Emily chewed on her lip. "Well, maybe not. I mean, I have brown hair. And brown eyes. But I'm not exactly sexy. Or beautiful." Her voice cracked. "But, really, is that so awful? 'Beautiful' means having qualities that delight the senses. I know that because I had to look it up once, in the dictionary. I wanted the exact meaning because I was writing a term paper on Shelley. The poet, you know? Anyway, I'm just saying that beauty is in the eye of the beholder and handsome probably is, too. So even if you're not as handsome as you say you are, that's okay because I'm not..." She groaned, put her hand to her forehead. "As for sexy, well, what does 'sexy' mean, anyway? Different things in different cultures. For example, when I was studying anthro, I learned that sexual attractiveness varies enormously from tribe to tribe in the Amazon. Some view nudity as the norm. Others, perhaps after they've had some contact with the outside world, disdain nudity but see nothing wrong with indulging in coitus with a variety of partners. There's a particular pygmy tribe—"

A large male hand slammed down on the telephone cradle, breaking the connection. Emily jerked her head up. McBride was standing over her, looking down and glaring.

"Just what in the Sam Hill are you doing?"

Dear God, Emily thought, what *was* I doing? The telephone buzzed in her ear like an angry bee.

"Miss Taylor?"

"You've—you've always called me Emily."

"A mistake," Jake said coldly, "considering that I'm starting to realize I don't know the first thing about you."

He folded his arms over his chest. It was, she thought foolishly, a formidable chest. He'd taken off his suit jacket, loosened his tie, undone the top button of his white shirt and rolled back his sleeves. He did that often; he'd once said he felt choked in a suit and tie. Why was it she'd never before noticed that his arms were dusted with dark, silky-looking hair? That his chest was the width of The Great Wall of China?

"Well, Miss Taylor? What were you doing?"

Emily put the phone down, folded her hands in her lap and tried not to think about how long he might have been standing there.

"I was—I was making a call," she said carefully.

"To whom?"

"To…" She frowned as she looked up at him again. "It was a personal call, Mr. McBride."

"Yes." Jake shot her a predatory smile. "I imagined it was. Somehow or other, I didn't think you'd be discussing pygmy sex practices with any of my clients."

She could feel the heat flash into her face. "I was not discussing pygmy sex practices."

"What were you discussing, then?"

"Would you step back, please," she said coolly, "so I can stand up?"

"Answer the question, Miss Taylor."

"I don't have to." She could feel her courage rushing back, swirling through her blood in a wave of heat. "As I said, it was personal."

"Did you ask me if you could make personal calls?"

She blinked. "No. No, I didn't. But you never said—"

"You never asked."

Emily glowered up at Jake. "I'll pay for the call," she snapped.

"I don't want your money. I want to know why you were talking about pygmy sex practices, and with whom."

"Dammit!" She shoved her chair back and shot to her feet, her flushed, angry face lifted to Jake's. "I wasn't talking about pygmy sex practices. I told you that. I was leaving a message on an answering machine."

"An answering machine at the Museum of Natural History?"

God, that infuriating smirk on his face! How had she survived it, all this time?

"An answering machine at a man's apartment," she said tightly. Well, it wasn't a lie. It wasn't an apartment but Handsome, Sexy and Successful would probably phone in for his messages from his apartment.

"Well, well, well." Jake's dark green eyes narrowed.

"You're just full of surprises, Miss Taylor. No wonder ol' Pete was so eager to take you to dinner last night. He read you just right."

Emily flung her hands on her hips. "And what is that supposed to mean, Mr. McBride?"

"Never mind what it's supposed to mean. I'm waiting to hear who you were phoning."

"Oh, for goodness sake!" She swung away, grabbed the magazine and shoved it into Jake's flat belly. "You won't be satisfied until you wring the truth out of me, will you? Okay. Okay, here's the truth, McBride, and I hope you enjoy getting the last laugh."

She swung away from him, trembling with anger and humiliation. She could hear Jake reading the ads aloud in a soft, disbelieving voice. There was a long silence before he spoke again.

"You were answering an ad in the personals?"

"Yes."

"You were telling one of these men you'd go out with him?"

"Yes."

"You were going to meet a stranger, an asshole who identifies himself as sexy, successful and handsome with… What in hell is Brrr and Brrr? A description of the weather? A new liqueur?"

Emily spun around and faced Jake. Her eyes were huge, her face flushed, and he fought back the sudden, insane desire to take her in his arms and soothe her.

"It's brown hair and brown eyes," she snarled. "And for your information, lots of people meet through ads like this."

"To do what?" Jake said, his eyes getting that narrowed, intense look again.

"To—to go out. On a date. To have dinner together. Take in a movie. Just—just spend a little time with another person…"

Her voice broke. Jake looked bewildered. She thought, for a second, he was reaching towards her and she shook her head and stepped back.

"I don't expect you to understand. You're never home alone, unless you want to be. You never have to look at the calendar and say, look at that, it's the weekend and I don't have a thing to do except clean my apartment and wash my hair."

Holy hell, Jake thought.

"That's what this is all about?" he said slowly. "That you don't date?"

"That's what I just said."

"You don't have any, uh, any men in your life?"

Emily's chin lifted to a dangerous angle. "Are we going to have to go through this, line by line?"

"So, that's why you accepted Archer's invitation last night? Because you're lonely?"

"I'm not lonely," she said defiantly. "I have friends. Hobbies. I have a canary."

"You're lonely," he said. "That's why you went out with that snake."

"Are you deaf, Mr. McBride? I am not..." Emily frowned. "You think he's a snake?"

"Of course."

"That's what you've always thought?"

"Yes." Well, it was true if you figured "always" referred to yesterday evening, when Archer had sneaked up on Emily. "I tried to tell you that, but you wouldn't listen."

"You didn't try to tell me anything, except how to run my life." She cocked her head. "Pete Archer said you and he are best friends."

"Ha."

"He said you've known each other forever."

"Only if forever means a year working for the same brokerage firm, a long time back."

Emily puffed out a breath. "He lied to me." She looked at Jake. "You're right, by the way. He *is* a snake."

Jake's face darkened. "Did he—"

"Oh, I can handle men like Pete Archer." A smile ghosted across her lips. "When I was sixteen, one of my sisters dated a guy who was into karate. He taught me some great moves. I still remember them."

"Ah." Jake moistened his lips. "Let me get this straight. You, uh, you'd like to date. To meet some nice guys and go out. Is that it?"

What was the sense in trying to pretend otherwise? Jake McBride knew virtually everything about her now, from her shoe size to her sexless sex life.

"Yes."

"Well." He ran his hand through his hair again, turned away from her, paced back and forth, back and forth. "I've got it," he said, and swung towards her. "I know a lot of people. Some of them are nice guys, too. I'll introduce you."

"Oh, no. I couldn't ask you to—"

"You haven't asked, I've volunteered. Look, it's no big deal."

Emily collapsed into her chair. "What are you going to do," she said, with a nervous laugh, "go to a meeting and say, 'oh, by the way, my personal assistant would like to have a date this weekend'?"

Jake grinned at her. "My executive assistant," he said. "And I'll be subtle, I promise. For instance...well, I go to lots of cocktail parties. Business stuff. From now on, you'll go with me."

"Mr. McBride, really—"

"I'll introduce you as my good right hand, you'll circulate, network... Emily, don't look at me that way. It'll work, I know it will."

"It won't. I'm—I'm not good at this male-female thing, Mr. McBride."

"Jake."

"Jake," she said, because it was silly, really, to go on with such formality now. "Look, I appreciate your offer but it's pointless. I'll feel ridiculous."

"More ridiculous than you'd have felt if you'd left your number on that answering machine?"

Emily bit her lip. "Even if something came of it... For one thing, I don't know how to make small talk. "

"There's nothing to it. I'll teach you."

"Yes, but..." She waved a hand. "It's more than that. I don't dress right. My sisters used to tell me I had no idea of style."

Jake took a step back, looked her over slowly from head to toe. "We can take care of that with ease."

"I don't even know how to—" she blushed "—how to handle the, uh, the end of the evening thing."

"The...?" He colored. "Oh."

"Exactly. I mean, it was simple enough, last night. When your friend—"

"Archer's no friend of mine," Jake said grimly.

"The point is, when he, uh, when he tried to, you know, kiss me, I just put my hands up, the way you do in karate—"

Jake began to laugh. "I'd have given anything to have seen that."

"But—but if a man tried to kiss me and I wanted him to, I'd just mess it up. I'd—"

He felt his body tighten. "You mean you've never..." He cleared his throat, did a mental ten-count, reminded himself that Emily was a sparrow, not a thrush, and his lifelong preference was for songbirds. "Well," he said briskly, "never mind. I'll teach you everything you need to know. How to talk with a man. How to dress for him. How to make him want you, and only you."

"I don't know. It all seems to—so—"

"I'll teach you all you need to know, Emily." Jake's voice

roughened. ''Including how to conduct yourself at the end of the evening.''

Color swept into her face. ''I can't believe I told you that,'' she whispered. ''I feel so foolish!''

''I'll teach you,'' Jake said gently. He reached down, clasped her shoulders and lifted her to her feet. ''You'll see. I'm an excellent teacher.''

So saying, he bent his head, took Emily's face in his hands, and covered her mouth with his.

# CHAPTER THREE

HIS mouth fit hers, perfectly.

His lips were warm, and dry, and pleasant. No tongue, Emily thought dazedly. None of that disgusting swapping spit stuff that the insufferable Pete Archer had tried last night.

Still, why was McBride kissing her? And why was she letting him? That was a better question.

Because he'd caught her by surprise. Why else? she told herself, and she put her hands against his chest and pulled back from his kiss.

"Mr. McBride," she said, a little breathlessly, "I really don't think—"

"Call me Jake," he said hoarsely but before she could call him anything, he put his arms around her, drew her against him and kissed her again.

The kiss wasn't the same.

She might have known it wouldn't be. His lips nudged hers, tugged at hers, moved against hers. And, when she tried to protest, to tell him there was no reason for them to kiss and certainly no reason to kiss like this, he used the moment against her and parted her lips with his.

Emily's hands came up, flattened against Jake's chest again.

No, she thought, no, please. No tongue, no spit, no awful wet kiss...

He didn't take the hint. He went right on with what he was doing, changing the rules, changing the kiss. What he was doing now—angling his mouth differently so that she had to tilt her head back as he slipped the tip of his tongue between her lips—what he was doing was—it was—

Oh, it was wonderful.

The feel of his arms around her. The hardness of his body against hers. The taste of his mouth. His hot mouth. His tongue. The glorious, mind-bending, mind-blowing heat and, yes, the wetness of his kiss...

Emily moaned. She curled her fingers into Jake's shirt, rose on her toes and pressed herself against him.

Was this what a kiss, a real kiss, was like? Was a man supposed to be able to turn a woman into a mindless, breathless, boneless creature with a kiss? Or did Jake know something other men didn't?

Not that Emily cared about any of the answers. She only knew that she wanted this feeling to go on forever.

Jake did, too.

It was crazy, to get so turned on by a kiss. But turned on, turned up, turned inside out was what he was, all right, and he was aching for more.

Emily wasn't just kissing him back, she was making the soft little noises a woman made when she wanted more. Her sweet body was pressing against his—grinding against his. Yes, indeed; there were curves under that boxy tweed jacket and bulky skirt, curves and warm, eager flesh.

And then she moved, and moaned, and Jake gave up thinking. He slid one hand down her spine, cupped her bottom, lifted her into the hardness of his arousal, knotted his hand in her skirt, pushed it up, stroked his hand along her thigh, her hot, silken thigh...

*Told you,* Archer's voice whispered smugly, way, way in the back of Jake's mind. *Didn't I say still waters run deep?*

Jake shoved Emily's skirt down, clasped her arms, tore his mouth from hers and stepped back. She swayed unsteadily, her eyes still shut, her lips rosy and parted.

Desire burned hot in his blood.

She wanted him, desired him, as much as he wanted her. And he wanted to assuage that desire. He wanted to reach out for her again, drag her back into his arms, carry her into his office, kick the door shut and rip away the tweed that hid her from his mouth and from his eyes...

But sanity prevailed. The last thing he wanted was an affair with his P.A. Uh, with his E.A. Hell, the last thing, absolutely the last thing, he wanted was an affair with a little brown sparrow who'd undoubtedly confuse sex with love.

Jake tried to speak, cleared his throat and tried again.

"You see?"

Emily blinked and opened her eyes. They were dark with passion and he felt himself teeter on the brink of that upside-down, inside-out feeling all over again.

He took another step back, shoved his hands into his trouser pockets and knotted them so he wouldn't be an idiot and reach for her.

"See what?" she croaked.

Jake tried for a nonchalant shrug. "I was just showing you that you don't have anything to worry about. I can teach you everything you need to know. It's not a problem."

Emily touched her fingers to her mouth. The simple action almost brought him to his knees.

"Not a problem at all," he said, and before she could respond, he went back into his office, fixed his tie and shirt, put on his jacket and coat, strode past her and headed out into the snowstorm for his lunch at the Oak Room...

And tried not to think about the kiss, or the fact that she'd been busy at her desk, fingers flying industriously over the keyboard as if the whole thing had never happened, as he went out the door.

Emily paused in her typing when Jake got back.

She looked up, greeted him politely and told him he'd find some faxes on his desk.

"Thank you," he said, and went straight into his office.

The door swung shut, and she almost collapsed with relief.

He wasn't going to mention what had happened. Thank God for that.

She'd worried that the kiss would affect their relationship. Foolish her. She should have known that it wouldn't. The kiss had meant nothing. Jake had, as he'd explained, been establishing his credentials, that was all.

Evidently, that was the way he always kissed a woman.

No wonder the twit wanted to keep him.

Any woman would. Well, not any woman. She wouldn't. Jake McBride wasn't her type at all, no more than she was his, and a kiss wouldn't change that. Not that he'd kissed her for that reason. To change her mind. To get her interested in him. No, it wasn't like that and a good thing, too, because she wasn't interested.

Emily looked at her computer screen. Her fingers had been busy but she'd been typing gibberish.

She took a breath, put her hands in her lap and folded them.

Okay. That was it. Enough. This was ridiculous, every bit of it, starting with Jake's nonsensical idea of introducing her to eligible men. Eligible for what? Was he going to run a Date My Assistant bureau?

All she'd wanted was to know what it was like to look forward to an occasional date but using your employer as a dating service was totally unacceptable. In the seven years since she'd come to New York, she'd heard of some strange employer-employee arrangements. She knew a secretary who baby-sat for her boss's golden retrievers on weekends, another who read all the books on the New York Times list, then wrote up one paragraph synopses for the man she worked for so he could sound as if he were well-read. She'd once met a P.A. whose boss baked him cookies. Awful cookies, but the poor guy had never worked up the courage to tell her so.

But a boss who got you dates?

No way.

That was what she'd tell Jake, if he brought up the subject

again. There wasn't a way in the world she was going to let her boss play matchmaker for…

"Emily?"

She looked up. Definitely, the kiss had meant nothing. Jake stood in the doorway between his office and hers. He looked the way he always did. Intense. Focused. Just a little bit forbidding.

The wings of hope fluttered in Emily's breast. Maybe she wouldn't have to tell him she was declining his offer. With luck, he might say it first.

"Yes, Mr. McBride?"

"Emily, I've given this some thought."

"Yes?"

"And I've decided you should leave."

The wings of hope faltered, folded and were still. "Leave?"

"That's what I said. I want you to go, right now."

"But…" He was firing her, because of that kiss? She pushed back her chair and stood up. "But it wasn't my idea."

Jake lifted his brows. "Obviously not."

"Then why…" *Why should I lose my job over your mistake?* "Why should I leave?"

"Look, I'm not going to debate this. I want you out of here, pronto."

Emily folded her arms. "I don't see any reason for this."

"No." Jake smiled tightly. "I didn't think you would."

"It's not fair. You've said, yourself, I'm good at my job."

"Of course you are. But whatever you're doing can wait until tomorrow."

"Now, just one minute, mister…" Emily frowned. "Tomorrow?"

"Nothing's so important that it can't be put off for a day."

"I don't…" She stared at him. "Are you telling me to leave early?"

Jake nodded. "I know you can't see the street from here—"

"No," she said, fumbling desperately for words, "uh, no, I can't. I don't have a window..."

"Exactly." Jake gave her a quick smile. "The snow's stopped and the streets are clear, but it's freezing out there and you know what happens to the subways when the temperature drops to zero."

"What?" she said stupidly. "I mean, yes. Yes, I know..."

"What's wrong?"

"Nothing," she said quickly. "I mean...well, I thought— only for a minute, you understand—I thought..."

She couldn't say it. What an idiot she was, thinking he'd fire her because of a silly kiss. He was a man who kissed women all the time, kissed them until they were clinging to him as if he were a lifeline and they were drowning in his arms.

"...I thought the temperature was supposed to stay in the mid-thirties," she said briskly. "Thanks for the warning."

Oh, yes. Most definitely, the sooner she was out of here, the better. This had been the weirdest day of her life. Thankfully, she'd come to her senses. McBride had, too. He hadn't even mentioned the Introduce Emily Around campaign. Better still, she had the feeling he'd never mention it again.

Life was still good, she thought, and smiled brightly in Jake's direction.

"Thank you again, sir. I appreciate your concern." She shut off her computer, cleared off her desk, got her things from the closet and sat down to put on her socks and boots.

"Emily."

She looked up. He was leaning against the wall, eyes hooded, arms folded, watching her.

"Do you need me?"

"Do I... do I need you?"

"All you have to do is tell me you want me, Emily. You know that."

"I don't." She spoke quickly, too quickly, she knew, but

what kind of question was that to ask? Here she'd thought the kiss wouldn't stand in the way of their continuing to have a good working relationship, and then he'd asked if she—

"Of course, if you're sure you can get those boots on by yourself…"

The boots. Oh the stupid boots. Emily wanted to laugh but she didn't dare. Instead, she gave him another bright smile.

"I'll be fine, thank you, Mr. McBride."

"You're sure."

"I'm positive."

Jake nodded. "In that case, I'll see you in the morning."

"Certainly, Mr. McBride."

"Jake. I thought we agreed on that."

"Jake," she said, and beamed at him again. "I'll try and remember that, sir."

"'Sir' and 'Jake' don't go together, Emily."

He smiled. She smiled. She was tired of smiling. Her lips felt as if they'd been stretched on a rack.

Jake strolled into his office, stopped, and swung towards her. "Oh, Emily?"

"Mr. Mc…? I mean, Yes, Jake?"

"While you're remembering things, remember not to wear tweed tomorrow."

Her face creased in puzzlement. "I beg your pardon?"

"Tweed," he said patiently, jerking his chin towards her. "That's what that stuff you're wearing is called, isn't it?"

Emily glanced down at herself. "Well, no," she said slowly, "actually, it's not. Tweed is nubby and coarse. This is just a heavy wool worsted—"

"How about silk?" Jake said, before she could treat him to a dissertation on fabrics.

"How about it?" she said, looking at him with caution.

Jake sighed. He was starting to regret the deal they'd made. First, for reasons he couldn't figure out, he'd teased her about helping her with the boots and he'd seen that she'd taken him seriously. Now she was staring at him as if he'd asked her if she had anything in her closet made of chain mail.

"Silk," he said. "You know, that soft stuff made by silk moths?"

"Silk worms, sir. Yes. Yes, I do."

"A dress?"

"A suit. But—"

Jake sighed again. "A suit. Well, that figures. Okay. Wear it tomorrow."

Emily furrowed her brow. "Why?"

"Because," he said, through his teeth, "tweed—"

"Wool worsted."

"Whatever. It won't go over, tomorrow night."

"Tomorrow…?"

"Internet Resources is giving a cocktail party. You penciled it into my appointment book."

"I remember, sir. Jake. But what does that have to do with me?"

"Emily, Emily, what a short memory you have. Our plan? For you to meet men? You'll go with me." He smiled. "Actually, there's an even better thing tonight but…" His voice trailed off. But, you're not dressed for it, he'd almost said, but why hurt her feelings? "But, considering the weather, I wouldn't want to see you having to ride the subway all the way to… Where is it you live again? Brooklyn?"

"Tribeca," Emily said stiffly. "Mr. McBride—"

"Tribeca," he repeated, as if she'd said she lived in Outer Mongolia. "Too bad. Tonight's affair—"

"What affair?"

"The one I've been talking about. Cocktails and dinner, for United Broadcasting. I thought they might call it off, because of the weather, but I spoke with one of the V.P's a while ago and he said—"

"No!"

"Yes. I just told you, the Veep said—"

"No, I am not going with you tomorrow night."

"Of course you are. That's the plan, remember? You'll network, I'll introduce you around—"

"Absolutely not."

"What do you mean, absolutely not?" Jake straightened up and walked towards her. "We agreed this was a good plan."

"Well, it isn't." Emily tucked her socks into a desk drawer and quickly pulled on her boots. No socks; she wasn't going to leave herself open to that problem again. She stood up, put on her coat and buttoned it. "I've thought about your idea, Mr....Jake. And I just don't see myself meeting men that way."

"Ah," Jake said, and folded his arms. "Of course. You'd rather meet them through ads in magazines."

She could feel color rising into her cheeks. "Whatever I choose to do, it isn't your concern."

"Meaning, I should mind my own business."

"Meaning, I'm an adult. I can take care of myself."

"Listen, Emily—"

"Why should it matter to you, who I go out with?"

Why, indeed? "Because I'm your employer. I'm your friend."

"We have never been friends, sir," Emily said politely. "That's as it should be. You're my employer, as you said. I am your employee. That has always been the extent of our relationship."

She was right. She was his P.A. His E.A. She wasn't his friend. But, dammit, that didn't mean he wasn't concerned about her welfare.

"That doesn't mean I'm not concerned about your welfare," Jake said with self-righteous indignation. "I'd much rather know the men you date than worry about you meeting up with the Boston Strangler."

"Oh, for goodness sakes... Look, Mr. McBride. Jake." Emily put her hands on her hips and tried her best not to glare. "You're blowing this out of all proportion. I don't go out with men."

"You went out with Archer."

"Only because I was angry at you."

"Well, that's certainly reassuring," Jake said, his words ripe with sarcasm. "You don't go out with men but you went out with this one because you were mad at me. That's a heck of a way to pick a date, isn't it?"

"I just told you, I don't have dates!"

"Then, what were you doing with *GOTHAM* magazine?"

"Reading it," she said sharply. "You do understand the concept, don't you?"

Jake's eyes narrowed. "Don't try and play smart with me, Miss Taylor. You know damn well what I'm talking about." He reached past her, snatched the magazine from the wastebasket and waved it in front of her. "You were in the process of leaving your name and phone number at the local loony bin when I stopped you!"

"The local..." Emily laughed. "You're being ridiculous," she said and started past him, but Jake snagged her by the elbow.

"Ridiculous? When hardly a day goes by there isn't something in the paper about a woman getting robbed, raped and murdered? When this city's full of perverts?"

"Let go of me."

"You want to be a statistic? You want the cops to call me and ask me to come identify the body?"

"You're not just being ridiculous, Mr. McBride. You're stark-raving mad."

Hell. Maybe he was. She wanted to go out with the reincarnation of Vlad the Impaler, was it his business? No, it was not.

"Okay, then." Jake took his hand from her arm with deliberate exaggeration. "Answer the Personals. Pick up guys on street corners, for all I care."

"Thank you. It's good to know I have your permission."

"Go out with guys you just met because you're pissed off at me."

"An excellent idea," Emily said, eyes flashing as she tried to step past him.

"Date any Tom, Dick or Harry who comes up to you on the subway and says 'Hi, honey, how about a movie?'"

"I would never," she said icily, "accept a date from a man I didn't know."

"Except for last night," Jake snarled.

"Except for last night…but then, why would I assume that my boss would introduce me to an octopus?"

"Is that what he was?" Jake's eyes glittered. He took hold of Emily's shoulders and propelled her backwards. "What did that son of a bitch do to you? Tell me. I'll hunt him down and beat the crap out of him."

"I told you, he didn't do anything. And I don't need a protector!"

"You're right." He slapped his hands on either side of her, palms flat against the wall. "What you need is a keeper."

He was only inches from her, so close that he could see a tiny muscle just beside her mouth. It was moving in time with her heartbeat, fast and furious, and he wondered what would happen if he put his lips against it, if he'd somehow absorb the race of her blood into his.

"Jake," she said, in a low voice.

His eyes went to hers. She was looking at him as if she'd never seen him before and maybe she hadn't. He felt like a stranger in his own body, a man wanting to do things he knew were crazy.

This was his assistant. This was Emily Taylor, she of the efficient brain and unremarkable body. Except, he knew that body wasn't unremarkable at all. He wanted to prove that to her, to put his hands into her hair, pull it free of the clip and let it spill like dark silk through his fingers. He wanted to unbutton her coat, lift her skirt, seek out her heat.

Most of all, more than any of that, he wanted to kiss her again.

"Emily," he said huskily, and his gaze dropped to her mouth. "Emily…"

She moved fast, ducked under his arm and reached for the doorknob. But Jake was quicker. He grabbed her arm and swung her around.

"Look," he said, in what he hoped was a tone of reason, "try and see this from my angle, okay? I, ah, I feel some responsibility for you, Emily. You work for me. You don't have any family in the city."

"How do you know that?"

Because he'd pulled out her job application again and read it thoroughly, that was why. All of a sudden, he'd wanted to know her age, her marital status, as much as he could find out about her. It was perfectly logical, too. A man had to research his subject before he could play matchmaker.

"You told me so, when you applied here. You said you were from Rochester. Right?"

"Right," she said, a little grudgingly. "But that doesn't mean—"

"Look, I feel guilty about last night. If I hadn't introduced you to Archer, if I hadn't made you so angry at me…"

"It isn't your fault." She sighed, looked up, managed a quick smile. "What I told you was the truth. I'm an adult, and I take full responsibility for my actions. Accepting Archer's dinner invitation was foolish. I'm to blame, not you. As for the personal ads… You're right. They're not for me."

Jake smiled. The tendrils of hair he'd noticed this morning were still clinging to her temples. He reached out, touched one, watched as it curled around his finger.

"Good. I'd hate to end up paying a visit to each of those guys in that listing."

Emily's eyes widened. "Why would you do that?"

He shrugged, caught the curl between his thumb and index fingers, let it slide against his skin.

"To warn them that they'd have to answer to me, if they tried any funny stuff."

She laughed. Her whole face lit up, when she laughed. How come he'd never noticed that before?

"Just what I need," she said. "A bodyguard."

"Yeah," Jake said. His gaze dropped to her mouth, then returned to her eyes. "That's what you need, all right."

"Well, you can stop worrying. I promise, I won't go out with anybody who describes himself as H, S, and S."

"H, S, and S?"

"Handsome, sexy and successful. I figure it's only a matter of time before those ads are all initials and numbers. You know, H, S and S, B and B, ISO for B, S and S… Jake? What are you doing?"

Slipping the clip from her hair, that's what he was doing. He felt her shudder as he moved his fingers lightly against her scalp.

"Is this natural?"

"Is what natural?" she whispered. Her mouth was too dry for anything but a whisper.

"This." He took a handful of her hair, let it sift though his hand. "The color. What do you call it?"

"What do you call the color of my hair?" Emily laughed nervously. "Brown. As in, 'mouse.'"

"Brown, as in 'sparrow,'" Jake murmured, and smiled. "I like it." He leaned forward, took a sniff. "I like the smell, too. What is it?"

Emily could feel her heart, pounding in her throat. "It's— it's just shampoo. Whatever was on sale last week."

"Nice. Smells like sunshine and flowers."

"Mr. McBride. Jake. I really have to leave, if I want to miss the worst of the subway rush—"

"What about the others?"

"The other what?" It was hard to talk. She wanted to shut her eyes, lean into his stroking hand, draw his scent of cold air and hot male deep into her lungs. "What others? The shampoos? I don't know. I only buy whatever is—"

"The other guys you'll date." Jake shifted his weight. His body brushed hers. She felt soft. So soft. So wonderfully, marvelously soft. "What about them?"

"What *about* them?" she said, because the only way to respond to a question that made no sense was with an answer that made no sense. How could it, when she was feeling so strange? So warm. So liquid. So...

"The guys you'll go out with. Those you'll meet that I don't know. How am I going to know they're harmless?"

Emily stiffened. Jake McBride was leaning over her, smelling her hair, stroking her cheek, breathing in the same air she was breathing, and he was asking her about the men she intended to date?

How on earth had she let him maneuver her into such a situation?

Emily scowled, put a hand in the center of Jake's chest and shoved him away.

"That's easy," she said crisply. "You won't have to worry about a thing because I won't be dating anybody."

He blinked. "What?"

"You heard me." She dug into her coat pocket, took out a sensible wool scarf and wrapped it around her neck. Then she dug into the other pocket, took out a pair of sensible woolen gloves and pulled them on. "I've rethought things, Mr. McBride."

"Jake," he said automatically, while he stared at her and tried to figure out how he'd ended up playing with Emily Taylor's very proper hair.

"Mr. McBride," Emily corrected politely. "I really do think it's advisable to maintain decorum in the office, don't you?"

"No. I mean, yes. Calling me by my first name doesn't change office decorum. Actually, I don't think I know another secretary who calls her boss 'Mr.'"

"I am not your secretary, Mr. McBride."

"I know that. I only meant… You're in a very contrary frame of mind lately, Emily."

"I don't think so."

"Well, I do. And, as you've just pointed out, I'm your boss and you're my employee. If I say you're contrary, you're contrary."

She smiled politely. "Whatever you say, sir."

"Dammit, this is ridiculous. Calling me 'sir,' and 'Mr.' I've got a good mind to—"

The door squeaked open. "Jake?"

Jake froze. He looked up, past Emily, and groaned.

"Brandi," he said tonelessly, and took a couple of steps back.

Brandi slipped into the office and put her arms around his neck. "Jake," she whispered, "have you been trying to avoid me?"

Did flies avoid flypaper?

Jake reached up, grasped her wrists and drew them to her sides. "What are you doing here, Brandi?"

"I came to see you. To ask why you've been ignoring my calls."

She smiled up at him, or pouted. One or the other. It was hard for him to tell. She had what she called bee-stung lips. Collagen stung, was more like it. Whatever, Jake wanted no part of her lips or her.

"Brandi," he said kindly, "I've already explained that what you and I had is—"

"Don't say it! It isn't. It can't be."

"Brandi…"

"I reserved a corner table at Alfredo's. We can have a nice quiet dinner and talk things over."

"No," Jake said firmly. "I'm sorry, Brandi, but there's no point in that."

"Of course there is."

"There isn't."

"There is."

"Well," Emily said brightly, "it's getting late, Mr. McBride. And you know what you said about the cold. So, if you don't mind—"

"You're right," Jake said quickly. "It is getting late."

"Exactly. Which is why I'm just going to—"

"Wait right there, Emily. Don't move a muscle."

Jake hurried into his office. The women's eyes met. Emily's lips turned up in a faint smile. Brandi's turned down, or would have, if she'd been able to move them. Enough, Emily thought, and reached for the door...

"I'm ready," Jake said.

She turned and looked at Jake. He'd put on his jacket, his coat and gloves. Smiling, he reached for her hand. She pulled it back. He trapped it with his leather-gloved fingers, wound them through hers.

"What are you doing?" she hissed.

"We have to leave now or we'll be late." He smiled, but his eyes flashed a warning. "You know how Donovan is about people being late."

"Who?"

"Donovan. The chairman."

"What chairman? Jake, what—"

He bent his head, silenced Emily by brushing his mouth gently over hers. Then he looked at Brandi, who was staring at him with a stricken expression on her perfectly made-up face. Two perfect tears rose in her eyes and trickled artistically down her cheeks.

"You and this—this creature? You don't mean it."

"Ah," Jake said, and smiled at Emily. "But I do."

Emily would have protested but how could she? Jake had already drawn her into his arms so he could kiss her, just the way he had the last time, until she felt her toes curl inside the too-tight boots.

# CHAPTER FOUR

WHO would show up at a party in snowy Manhattan on a frigid January night?

Everybody who'd been invited, or so it seemed.

Emily had expected to see ten or twenty lost souls with nothing better to do than attend the UBS celebration. But when the elevator doors slid open to the Sunset Room on the fortieth floor of the Ascot Towers, she could see that even the corridor was alive with people.

Famous people. People whose faces lit up TV and movie screens from coast to coast...

People dressed for the occasion.

Emily touched an uneasy hand to her dampness-frizzed hair, glanced down at her sensible coat and equally sensible boots, and blanched.

"Uh-oh," she whispered.

Jake, who figured the "uh oh" was an exclamation of delight, put his hand lightly in the small of her back and moved her forward.

"See?" he said softly. "Aren't you glad you let me talk you into coming?"

No, she wasn't. She was as out of place here as she'd been at that long-ago high school prom, where she'd showed up in a full-skirted, pale blue satin gown with puffy sleeves and a bow when every other girl in the room had been wearing clingy, slinky black silk.

As for "talk..." The man didn't know the meaning of the word. He'd hustled her out of the office, into a cab and towards Fifth Avenue so fast that it had made her head spin. All the "talk" had been hers. She'd demanded he let her out of the taxi so she could go home but Jake had ignored her protests. He hadn't "talked" her into coming here, he'd shanghaied her.

Still, Emily had to admit, if reluctantly, that being here might have its uses, now that Jake had promoted her. There were more business contacts just in the corridor than she'd ever imagined a person could find in one place, and from the "hello's" and "how are you's" Jake was exchanging as they moved slowly towards the Sunset Room, her boss knew every last one of—

"Jake. Great to see you."

"You, too, Thad." Jake smiled and looked at Emily. "Thad, I'd like you to meet Emily Taylor, my executive assistant. Emily, this is Thaddeus Jennett."

"Miss Taylor."

Emily blinked. "Thad" was none other than the handsome, debonair anchor on UBS's top-rated evening news show.

"Nice to meet you," she said, and took the hand Thad extended to her.

"We'll catch up to you later," Jake said, taking Emily's elbow, "just as soon as we find the checkroom and get rid of these coats."

Get rid of these coats? Emily clutched her collar in a death grip. She felt out of place enough as it was. The last thing she was going to do was peel off her coat and stand around like a plain gray goose in a sea of sexy swans.

"I don't want to find the checkroom," she hissed.

But Jake didn't hear her. He was stopping again, introducing her again, to the star in the newest UBS romantic comedy, then to the guy's publicist. Emily said hello, did her best to make small talk and tried not to wonder what people must be thinking.

"Not so bad, is it?" Jake whispered as he drew her forward.

"Why didn't you tell me this would be so—so dressed up?"

Jake lifted an eyebrow. "Let's see. One, you didn't ask. Two, bringing you with me was a last-minute decision."

"That's an interesting way to put it," Emily said coolly.

"Three," he said, ignoring the interruption, "you didn't want to come, anyway. Four…four, would it have mattered? Do you own anything that would have worked tonight?"

Emily's mouth turned down. "That's none of your business."

"I didn't say it was. You were the one who raised the issue. Besides—"

"Jake!"

The shriek was loud enough to shatter glass. A tall, exquisite blonde hurled herself into Jake's arms.

"Jake, lover, is it true you and Brandi are…" The blonde drew back, made a face and slid her hand across her throat.

Jake grinned. "Hello, Crystal, news travels quickly in this town."

"Good news, you mean," the blonde replied, and looped her arm through his. "Come get me a drink and tell me how I can help you recover from the loss."

"A little later, maybe. Let me get rid of my coat, first…" He paused, frowned, and looked at Emily. "Sorry," he muttered.

"No problem," Emily said sweetly, and held out her hand. "I'm Emily Taylor, Mr. McBride's executive assistant. How do you do, Miss…?"

"How nice," the blonde said, in a tone that made it clear it wasn't, and turned her attention back to Jake. "Darling, I'm so glad to see you! Honestly, it's been so long…"

The sexy voice droned on. Emily felt her face turning hot. She'd been dismissed, totally and completely, as only one woman can dismiss another. Well, so what? She was here as Jake's business associate, not as his date. Exchanging names with someone like this—this person wasn't important. It wouldn't do a thing for her career, or for McBride Investments…

Oh, who was she kidding?

Never mind careers. What about egos? She had one, even though she hardly ever let it show its face to the world, and it was her ego that was warning her what the rest of the evening would be like.

She was here as a stand-in for Brandi, but that was a joke. The blonde, draped over Jake's arm with the determination of a boa constrictor on its prey, was determined to be Brandi's successor. She was also a harbinger of what lay ahead.

Women would swarm around Jake like bees around honeysuckle. They'd all be beautiful. They'd have perfect hair, perfect smiles, perfect makeup, perfect bodies. Her prom, all over again. She'd be the plain-but-brainy wallflower on the sidelines, whose date had wandered off, smiling until her face hurt, pretending it didn't matter that she was alone, that no boy had come near her...

No. It would be worse than her prom. This was real life, not high school. And Jake, gorgeous, sexy Jake, would laud her as his executive assistant—his sexless executive assistant—and then flirt with every woman in the place except her.

She didn't care, though. He could do what he wanted, with whatever woman he wanted. She really didn't...

Emily turned on her heel, pushed her way through the still-crowded corridor, made her way to the elevators and stabbed the call button.

She didn't have to be here. She didn't have to spend the evening with her boss. Her day began at nine and ended at five, thank you very much, unless you counted the endless overtime she put in and never, ever bothered mentioning to Jake.

Well, he was in for a surprise.

Emily pushed the button again. Where was that miserable elevator? You'd think, in a hotel like this, one would come when you wanted it.

Jake would have to learn that she had a life of her own. That she couldn't trot along behind him like a well-trained puppy. That when she said no, no was what she meant. No more letting him dictate commands, or bait her into dizzy arguments she couldn't win. She wouldn't permit it. She wouldn't let Jake get under her skin...

Or touch it. Stroke it, with his hand. With his lips...

"Dammit!" Emily growled, and slammed the call button again.

As if in response, the doors slid open and disgorged a carful of laughing, chattering party guests. Emily tapped her foot impatiently, waited until the car emptied, slipped inside...

"What do you think you're doing?"

Jake suddenly loomed in the space between the slowly closing doors. She could see only his face, dark with annoyance, and his hand as he jammed it between the doors, forced them open and stepped into the car with her.

The doors swished shut. Suddenly, the car felt small. Very small, and very, very airless but there wasn't a way in the world she'd let him know that.

"I'm going home," she said briskly, and pressed the lobby button.

"Going home, or running away?"

"You're wasting your time if you think you'll bait me into going back, Mr. McBride. You want to think I'm running away? Fine. Think it."

"Don't be silly." Jake spoke calmly. So calmly that she wanted to slug him. "We just got here."

"So?"

"So, I'm not ready to leave."

"I'm not asking you to." Emily slapped the button again. Why was the damned elevator moving so slowly? "In fact, I don't want you to leave. Not when you're obviously having such a good time."

Jake's dark brows lifted. "Interesting. Who'd have suspected the formidably efficient Ms. Taylor has normal female instincts?''

''I've no idea what you're talking about.''

''Could it be,'' he said, with just a hint of smug satisfaction, ''that you're jealous of Crystal?''

''Is that her name?'' Emily folded her arms and stared straight ahead at the blinking lights on the control panel. ''You sure it isn't Brandi the Second?'' The elevator came to a stop. The doors slid open but no one got on. After a minute, the doors shut and the downward journey resumed. ''Your companions are difficult to tell apart, considering that they're always tall, leggy, and brain-dead.''

Jake laughed. ''You *are* jealous.''

''Jealous? Of your women?''

''I don't have 'women.' Anyway, I've known Crystal for years.''

''You can know her for centuries, for all I care. Dammit, what is with this elevator? Why doesn't it move?''

''It is moving,'' Jake said. ''If anything, it's moving too fast.''

And, just like that, he reached out and hit the Stop button. The car lurched to a halt. Emily staggered and landed against Jake's chest. His arms went around her but she jerked away.

''What do you think you're doing?'' she demanded.

Jake leaned back against the wood-paneled wall and folded his arms. ''We came here so you could network.''

''You came here to network.'' Emily glowered at the closed doors. ''I came here so you could save yourself from a fate worse than death.''

''Yeah.'' He gave a sigh of apology. ''Listen, about that. I'm really sorry but—''

''But,'' Emily said coldly, ''that's okay. It turns out I *did* network. I met three people. Four, if I expand the list to include life-size mannequins with improbable names.''

She reached towards the Stop button but Jake's hand shot out and clamped around her wrist.

"There are lots more people to meet, if you're going to be my exec."

"I thought you brought me here to meet eligible men."

"Yeah, that was part of the plan." Jake's jaw tightened. "But you changed your mind... Didn't you?"

"I've changed it again," she said coldly. "Yes, I want to meet men. The more the better."

"In that case, let's go back to the party."

"No."

"Emily, don't be an idiot. That party's loaded with candidates."

"Oh, I'm sure it is. Crystal-clones are probably everywhere!"

"I'm not talking about Crystal, I'm talking about..." Jake scowled and let go of Emily's hand. What *was* he talking about? If she wanted to meet men, that was her business. But if she was serious about being his exec, that was his business. She had to start spending some time with him at functions like this one. That was reasonable, wasn't it? "Look, we won't stay long."

"I stayed too long, already."

"Will you stop being so foolish?"

"I am not being foolish. I am being sensible."

"The hell you are. You want to meet men? Well, there they are, a dozen floors above us. Men. Young, old, in between. Fat ones, thin ones, lawyers, bankers and corporate types, all arrayed for your pleasure like hors d'oeuvres on a buffet table."

"I'm not interested," Emily said sharply. "Can't you get that through your thick head? I want to meet men, not have you play go-between."

"You sure as hell need somebody as a go-between! When you search for dates on your own—"

"I do not search for dates!"

"—when you run your own campaign, the guys you come up with are creeps."

"All right," Emily said furiously, "this has gone far enough."

Jake grabbed her and swung her towards him as she reached for the Stop button. His eyes had turned a dark, forbidding green. "Okay. We'll forget whether or not you're in the mood to start behaving like a real woman. Let's stick to business. I promoted you yesterday. You want to be my exec? Start acting like one."

"I will. I *have,* for months now. I do your research. I soothe your clients. I see to it that your office runs without a hiccup. But I *don't* have to subject myself to—to standing around on the sidelines in a room filled with overdressed, overmade up females who think life begins and ends with you."

"Listen to me, Emily. We're going upstairs. You're going to that party, by my side."

"What for? You don't need me there. I'm not Jacob McBride, Super-Macho Investment Broker. And before you tell yourself that's a compliment, it isn't."

"P.A's go home at five. E.A's network. That's why you're going to smile, shake some hands, let me introduce you around." Jake smiled through his teeth. "Or I can take you downstairs, put you in a taxi, and you can go back to being my secretary and my personal assistant. Your choice."

Emily stared at him. "Why are you doing this?" she finally asked. "I mean, it's just a party. You really think I should go to these things, okay. I will. But I don't see what's so important about tonight."

Actually, he didn't, either. Yeah, it would help if she met some of the UBS people but it wasn't vital. Keeping her at his side tonight was going to cramp his style; he'd be so busy making sure she didn't make a run for the elevators or bolt for the fire stairs that he'd probably spend more time concentrating on her than on the people he'd come to see.

And she was right, about not being dressed for the occasion. She'd look out of place. Well, so what? Crystal was a sight every man in the room would enjoy but she wasn't bright, the way Emily was. She didn't have Emily's sense of fun. And she'd never drive him crazy, making him want to throttle her one minute and kiss her the next...

Jake frowned, took an involuntary step back.

"I told you the reason," he said brusquely. "Now, do you want the promotion or don't you?"

The cool, insolent look on Jake's handsome face was infuriating. Emily debated the wisdom of telling the mighty McBride what he could do with both the job and the promotion, thought better of it, and lifted her chin.

"I really don't like you, Mr. McBride," she said coldly. "But I do like my job." She undid the belt at the waistline of her coat, snatched the wool scarf from her throat, the wool gloves from her hands, tucked them into her pockets and took the coat off. "Very well. I'm ready."

She said it as if she'd just agreed to an evening of root canal, Jake thought. And she looked about as eager.

He sighed, took her coat and let it fall to the floor.

Emily's eyes widened. "Hey," she said, "what do you think you're—"

Jake reached out and tugged the clip from her hair. The damp, snowy weather had turned it to a mass of curls; freed of constraint, they tumbled around her face and to her shoulders like a frothy mass of coffee-colored silk.

"Are you crazy? Give me that clip!"

Jake dropped the clip in his pocket, then ran his fingers through her hair.

"You *are* crazy!" Emily slapped at his hands. "Stop that!"

"You have beautiful hair," he said. "Why don't you make the most of it?"

"What do you know about it? Curls aren't professional."

"Dressing like your grandmother is?"

"You don't know anything about my grandmother, either. Jake. Jake! What are you doing?"

"Getting rid of this horse-blanket," Jake said grimly, as he tugged her suit jacket from her shoulders and dumped it on top of the coat that lay at her feet.

"Dammit, Jake..."

"It's a cocktail party," he said, as he undid the first button of her blouse, "not a wake. You're the one who pointed out that you weren't dressed right." Emily grabbed at his hand as he started working on the second button but he shrugged her off. "We'll do what little we can. Let your hair down, get rid of that jacket, open a few buttons..."

"Hey," a voice called, from somewhere outside the elevator, "anybody stuck in there?"

People, Emily thought desperately, people near enough to save her. But save her from what? It was hard to concentrate, when she was so furious at Jake...

...when Jake's fingers were at the next tiny button on her blouse.

Emily grabbed his wrist. "Stop it!"

He didn't stop. He kept going, opening buttons, muttering that it was time she stepped into the twenty-first century and let herself look like a woman, until she glanced down at herself and saw the first hint of...

"Lace?"

Jake's voice cracked. He looked up. Emily did, too. Their eyes met, and she could see that his were no longer cold and dark but a deep, hot emerald. Her heart did a strange two-step before lodging in her throat.

"Lace," he said again, very softly, "under all those layers of wool."

"I happen to like..." Emily licked her lips. Jake followed the movement of her tongue with an almost unholy fascination. She took a step back but there was nowhere to go; her shoulders hit the wall of the car. "I happen to like lace," she said, in a voice that sounded as if she were a marathon runner approaching the finish line. "Besides, what I wear under the wool is none of your—"

"Shut up, Emily," Jake said, and kissed her.

It was a gentle kiss, hardly a kiss at all. Only their mouths met, his moving over hers in soft, exploratory touches.

And then he groaned, or maybe she did. The only thing Emily knew for sure was that, suddenly, she was in his arms.

His kiss changed, then, became the kiss of a conqueror, hungry and rapacious, demanding surrender. And even as she told herself not to give in, she curled her arms around his neck, opened her mouth to his and kissed him back.

Jake gathered her tightly against him. She swept her hands into his hair, tugged his head down and lifted herself to him. He pressed her back against the wall. She moaned. He was so hard. So strong. So aroused and so completely, magnificently male.

He wanted her.

Wanted her, as much as she wanted him.

His arms offered no escape and she desired none. This, this was what she yearned for. Jake's lips, plundering hers. His tongue, in her mouth. His erection, against her belly.

Emily whimpered, twisted in his arms, wanting something more now, wanting it with sweet desperation. Jake pulled her blouse out from the waistband of her skirt, swept his hands beneath it and up to her breasts. He groaned her name, moved his thumbs against her lace-covered nipples and she sobbed with the ecstasy of it.

This, yes. This was what she ached for. Jake's touch. The pads of his thumbs moving, like that. Just like that, stroking her there. The curling ribbon of fire that lanced from her breasts to her belly. The answering tug of liquid heat between her thighs.

"Emily," Jake said thickly.

He drew back. She moaned, refused to let him go until she realized he only wanted enough room to undo the rest of her buttons.

"Let me," he said, "Emily, let me..."

"Yes," she whispered, against his mouth, "Jake, yes..."

Off in the distance, an alarm bell began to ring. Emily didn't hear it. The beat of her heart, the sexy-sweet rasp of Jake's whispers, drowned out everything else as he eased her blouse open.

"Beautiful." His eyes, so hot and dark, locked onto hers as he ran the roughened tip of his index finger along the soft, warm curve of flesh that rose above the lace of her camisole. "Such a beautiful little sparrow."

He bent his head, let the tip of his tongue follow the same path as his finger and she cried out, arched towards him...

Emily's shoulder hit the Stop switch. The car lurched into motion. After a few seconds, so did her brain.

She was in an elevator in the Ascot Towers. It was heading up, towards a floor filled with people. And she was half-undressed, making love with her boss.

"Jake!" She shoved against his shoulders, tugged at his hair. "Jake! The elevator. The car's going up!"

Right, Jake thought dazedly, and slipped his hand under her chemise. Everything was going up. And the ground was shifting under his feet.

"Stop it," Emily hissed, into his ear. "Do you hear me? Stop!"

Stop? How was he supposed to...

"Jake!"

Emily pounded her fists against his back. He blinked, looked up, and realized that it wasn't the ground shifting, it was the elevator. It was rising, and fast. Thirty, said the panel indicator lights. Thirty-one. Thirty-two...

"Hell!"

Jake grabbed Emily's jacket from the floor, draped it around her shoulders, draped her coat over that. He ran his hands through her hair, through his hair, tugged at his tie, his shirt...

The elevator stopped. The doors slid open and a small sea of faces peered at them.

"Hey, McBride," a male voice said, "you guys okay? This thing must have been stuck for twenty minutes."

Jake peeled his lips back from his teeth. "We're fine."

"Fine," Emily croaked.

Fine? Jake smothered a groan. She was as pale as a ghost; he could feel her trembling in the curve of his arm.

"Miss Taylor," he said, "my, ah, my assistant. She, uh, she has a touch of claustrophobia…"

"Claustrophobia," Emily said, and smiled brightly.

Jake tightened his hold, led her through the little crowd, down the hall and towards the party. Halfway there, she dug in her heels and balked.

"I can't go in there looking like this," she hissed.

He nodded. Of course she couldn't. Neither could he. What they could do was turn around, get back into the elevator, stop at the reservation desk in the lobby and take a room for the night…

Oh, hell.

He cleared his throat, looked around, saw the discreet signs for the lounges, and pointed her towards the ladies' room.

Emily disappeared through the door. Jake stumbled into the men's room. It was empty, but he wasn't taking any chances. He went into a stall, locked the door, took off his coat and hung it up. He straightened his shirt, his tie, his suit jacket, checked out his fly. Then he sagged against the wall and tried to figure out what had just happened.

Actually, what hadn't happened, no thanks to him. If the elevator hadn't started moving, he'd have made love to Emily right then and there. Made love to a sparrow, when there was a nest full of brightly plumed chicks just aching to be plucked only seconds away.

He groaned and rubbed his hands over his face.

Never mind that, he thought grimly, forget the bird analogy. The bottom line was that no man with even half a brain in his head got involved with his secretary. Okay, so Emily was his executive assistant, not his secretary. Whatever she was, he had to be out of his mind, even sniffing the air in her direction.

He hissed with frustration.

An intelligent man did not get involved with a woman who worked for him, even if she looked like a goddess, which Emily most certainly did not. Just imagining the repercussions of such a relationship were staggering. The sexual harassment charges. And even if there weren't any, the emotional complications…

He was a civilized man. He ended relationships in ways that were bloodless. Jake thought of Brandi and winced. Okay. Relatively bloodless. And that would never be possible if he had an affair with Emily. It was bad enough to have a woman stalking him like the ghost of Hamlet's father but if that woman worked for him, there'd be no avoiding her at all. She'd be there, all day, every day, sniveling into a hanky and giving him damp-eyed, woeful looks.

No way. No, no, no. A smart man didn't ever mix business with pleasure, and Jake had always been smart, when it came to both.

He put his coat over his arm, unlocked the stall door, walked to the sink and turned on the cold water.

Emily was an excellent secretary. An excellent associate. He had no intention of losing her and he would, if he let his gonads get in the way.

He draped his coat over a chair, splashed cold water over his face.

Okay. So he'd done something stupid but the damage wasn't irreversible. He knew the reason things had gotten out of hand, in the elevator.

It was the shock of seeing that white lace.

"Hey," he said softly, to his reflection in the mirror over the sink, "who expects to see Mary Poppins wearing white lace?"

Not him. Definitely, not him.

He took a towel from the stack neatly piled on the marble countertop, dried his hands and face, then tossed it aside.

That was all of it. The unexpected glimpse of lace. And, yeah, that cloud of silken curls. And all right, the surprising roundness, the feel of her breasts. The smell of her skin. The taste of her mouth. The way she'd responded to him, all that heat and fire...

"Dammit, McBride!"

Was he crazy? He was supposed to be reminding himself of how foolish it would be to take things even a step further; instead, he was turning himself on.

Okay. That was it. What had happened tonight was the start and finish of his relationship with Emily.

She'd be disappointed.

He knew she would be, Jake thought, and sighed. After what had happened just now, Emily had to figure this night would end with him in her bed. He'd have to reason with her, make her see that even though he'd like that, too, it was out of the question. It would only make for trouble. She'd just have to understand.

There was no sense letting her think that things could progress between them.

Jake nodded at his reflection. "She'll have to understand," he murmured.

She would. Emily was an intelligent woman. She'd listen to reason, put this behind her and get on with business.

Jake let out a breath he hadn't realized he'd been holding. Then he slung his coat over his arm and went outside, into the corridor. Emily wasn't there. He frowned, glanced at his watch, tapped his foot.

The door to the ladies room swung open.

"Emily," he said briskly...

It wasn't Emily. It was Crystal. When she saw Jake, she smiled.

"Hi, handsome. Waiting for me?"

"Uh, not exactly. Did you happen to see Emily Taylor in there?"

"Who? Oh, you mean that dowdy little... Your secretary?" Crystal batted her lashes. "Nope." She moved closer, her head tilted, her smile brilliant. Too brilliant, everything about her. The sprayed-to-stay hair, the bright red mouth, the endless eyelashes. "Is it really important? To find her, I mean?"

"Yes," Jake said, "it is."

Crystal's face fell but he didn't notice. Of course it was important, he thought, as he made his way through the crowded corridor. He had to find Emily so he could tell her that what had happened—what had almost happened—was a mistake.

On the other hand, he didn't have to tell her tonight. It might be best to let her down easy. Yeah, that was it. Take her home, see her in, maybe just kiss her again a few times, so she wouldn't be as upset when he said—

"Jake?"

Jake cocked his head. "Emily?"

"Jake. I'm over here."

Over where? There. Inside the jammed main room, he could just make out a hand waving in his direction.

"Excuse me," Jake said, and started towards that hand.

Emily, in the thick of the party? It amazed him, that she'd worked up enough courage to move ahead on her own. Well, that was an improvement. Getting her out among people had been a good idea. If only he could convince her to let him put his plan into motion. Introduce her to guys. Get her to go out on dates. It would be the right thing for her, especially if she harbored any silly ideas about him, now that they'd had that insane business in the elevator...

"Jake? Jake, here I am."

Jake almost skidded to a stop. "Emily?"

It was Emily, all right, but an Emily he'd never seen before. Her coat and jacket were gone. She'd taken all those

loose curls and piled them high on her head, though several
fell sexily around her face. Her blouse was closed but only
as far down as the button that had started all the trouble
because he could see that hint of white lace emphasizing the
sweet curve of flesh rising above it.

Jake stared.

What had happened to her skirt? What had she done to it?
A little while ago, it had hung somewhere between her calves
and ankles. Now it hung just above her knees. It wasn't
shapeless anymore, either; she'd cinched something around
her waist. A belt. The belt from her coat? Yes, that had to
be it. The belt, hugging her waist, holding up the skirt…

"Jake," she said pleasantly.

He blinked. She was smiling, smiling and hanging on to
Thad Jennett's Armani-clad arm. And Thad was beaming
down at her.

"We've been looking for you."

"Really," Jake said, when he could find his voice.

"Yes." She smiled at him, then at Thad, and just for a
minute, Jake wanted to pound his fist into Jennett's slickly
handsome face—but that would have been stupid because
this was exactly what he'd hoped for, that Emily would meet
some man to date.

"…waiting for you, when Thad came along, and…"

But not Jennett. Not without knowing more about him.
Was he okay? Pete Archer was supposed to have been okay
but look what had happened. The bastard had come on to
Emily like an octopus.

"…that I had to wait until you…"

So, okay. Tomorrow, he'd do this the right way. He'd sit
down, draw up a list of names. Guys he knew well enough
to let Emily date them. It might take a while. He'd have to
check their backgrounds, talk to people who knew them, talk
to the guys themselves…

"…leave now, Jake, if you have no objection."

"No," Jake said. He smiled politely and reached for her

arm. "No, on the contrary. I was just thinking the same thing. Let's just get your coat and—''

"Oh, I didn't mean I was leaving with you," Emily said, with a brilliant smile. She looked up at Jennett, who smiled back at her. "Thad's asked me to supper."

"Supper?" Jake repeated, as if the concept was alien to him. "You, and Jennett?"

Jennett leaned forward, man to man. "Food's not up to par tonight, Jake, not up to par at all. Looks as if UBS had to cut corners, to make up for that extra two mill a year they've agreed to pay me on my new contract."

Jennett laughed. Emily smiled. Jake knotted his hands and jammed them into his trouser pockets.

"Thad? Would you get my coat, please?" Emily shifted closer to Jake as Jennett hurried off. "Jake, I want to be sure you understand that—that what happened in the elevator..." She licked her lips. "It was a mistake."

"Says who?" Jake snarled, as all his good intentions flew out the door.

"Oh, come on. You know it was."

"What I know is that going to supper with Jennett is a damn-fool idea!"

"It's an excellent idea." Emily touched his arm. "It was good of you to do what you'd said. Introduce me to a nice man, I mean."

"Jennett? That's your idea of a nice man?"

"Uh-huh. He's charming."

Jake's mouth thinned. "What he is," he said coldly, "is a one-man publicity machine. That smile's as phony as a three-dollar bill. I'll bet every tooth in his mouth is capped." He clasped her elbow and pulled her towards him. "And I don't know enough about Jennett to agree to a date."

Emily pulled free of Jake's hand. "Then it's a good thing he asked me out instead of you," she said sweetly.

"Dammit, Emily! You can't go out with anybody unless I say you—"

"Ready?"

Thad Jennett smiled at them both as he draped Emily's jacket over her shoulders.

"Completely ready," she said, with a cold look at Jake.

Jake thought about answering. He thought about punching out Jennett's lights. He even thought about slinging Emily over his shoulder and heading straight back to the elevator...

But he was a civilized man. And anyway, what did he care who his exec dated? Her life, and the men in it, were her business.

He got himself a drink, then scoured the room until he spotted Crystal.

"Crystal," he called, and when she turned and smiled, he held out his arms in welcome.

# CHAPTER FIVE

JAKE stood at the window in his office, sipping a cup of what was supposed to be coffee.

It smelled right. It even looked right. But if coffee tasted like this, the world's tea-leaf growers would be billionaires.

He took another mouthful, shuddered and swallowed. This was what you got for relying on someone. It was Emily's job to make the coffee. Every morning, promptly at nine, she brought him a cup.

But she'd come to work too late to do it yesterday. Jake shot a scowling look at his watch. And she was going to be late today, too. There was no excuse this time. No snow. No tangled traffic. No subway trains running late. He'd had to make his own coffee and dammit, Emily obviously knew something about the coffeemaker he didn't because the stuff she made never tasted like this.

"Never," Jake growled, as he strode into his private bathroom and dumped the sludge down the sink.

The day was definitely not off to a good start.

Jake stomped back to his desk and sat down in his chair.

How could the day begin well, without a proper cup of coffee? Without the presence of his executive assistant? Without having a memory of an evening that should have been, to say the least, memorable?

"Damned right, it should have been," he mumbled.

Crystal was beautiful. Beautiful? She was spectacular. Yards of blond hair. Silky skin. A lush-looking mouth, a body that should have graced a centerfold. Oh, yes. Spectacular was the word. On a scale of one to ten, she was a twelve.

And what had he done? He'd taken her to supper, then home. He'd taken her to *her* home, and left her at her door with a chaste kiss on the cheek and a sort of promise he'd phone sometime soon.

Jake groaned, propped his elbows on his desk and buried his face in his hands.

In other words, the evening had been a disaster, and who was to blame for that? Not Crystal. Not him.

"Emily," Jake said, lifting his head and glaring at the door. Emily, that was who.

She'd ruined his evening, ruined his night, because he'd ended up so ticked off that he'd spent most of it tossing and turning instead of sleeping. She'd put him into a foul mood, and for what reason? All he'd tried to do was look after her. He'd taken her to a party, offered some helpful advice and had she appreciated it?

"No," he said, answering his own question.

In a city like this, most women would surely give anything for a man's concern. But his testy executive assistant hadn't just disregarded his advice, she'd tossed it in his face. She'd gone out on the town with a man who was wrong for her and now it was the next morning, and she was late.

Jake looked at the open door between the inner and outer office, then at his watch again.

Did she think he'd tolerate lateness, now that he'd promoted her and given her a raise? Maybe she thought that fooling around in the elevator had really meant something. It hadn't. She'd simply caught him by surprise with the lace thing. So what? Some men got turned on by high heels, some by silk. He just happened to like lace.

Not that he'd ever known it, until last night. Lace was, well, it was lace. Sexy, sure, but no more so than, well, than silk. Or satin. It was only that the lace had been so unexpected. Cotton, was what he'd have figured, if he'd figured anything at all…although even cotton would have done it, against Emily's soft, sweetly-scented skin. Against that smoothly curved breast that he'd barely tasted…

The outer door swung open. Emily stepped into the office,

covered from head to ankle in her usual layers of shapeless wool. But she wasn't shapeless. She was delicately curved, lushly female. He knew that, now.

Did Thad Jennett, that smarmy excuse for a human being, know it, too? Had Jennett kissed that sweet mouth, that delicate flesh? Had he stripped away Emily's coat, her jacket, her blouse...

"You're late," Jake snarled, and shot to his feet.

Emily shut the door, looked calmly at the clock on her desk, then at him. "And a cheerful good morning to you, too, Mr. McBride."

"There's nothing good about it." He folded his arms. "Well?"

"Well, what?"

"Well, aren't you going to explain why you're late?"

Emily went to her desk, put down her purse, pulled off her gloves and scarf, unbuttoned her coat. Carefully, she tucked her scarf and gloves into the pockets of the coat, hung the coat in the closet, then sat down and pulled off her boots. No heavy socks, Jake noticed. Just a quick, tantalizing flash of nylon-covered leg.

"I am not late. In fact," she said, with a nod at the clock, "I'm early." She smoothed down her skirt, pulled out her chair and sat. "Perhaps you've forgotten that I'm not due in until nine."

Jake's scowl deepened. The skirt was nubby wool, at least a hundred sizes too big, and hadn't he asked her to wear something else for tonight's cocktail party?

"I have forgotten nothing," he said coolly. "And I'd suggest *you* not forget that you have an obligation here."

"I beg your pardon?"

She didn't beg anything. He could tell, from the way she spoke, from the way she was looking at him. What had happened to business demeanor? Was this what came of a meaningless few fumbles in an elevator, or was it what happened after a meal with Thad Jennett?

"I asked you to wear something appropriate for this evening."

"This evening?"

"Yes. The party at Internet Resources. A business commitment which I see you've already forgotten."

"I didn't forget. I just..." Emily swallowed. "I can't go with you."

"Why not?"

"I—I just don't think it's a good idea."

"Perhaps I should remind you that you have an obligation—"

"You already did. And I'll continue to fulfill that obligation, each and every day."

Jake's eyes narrowed. "If that's a polite way of telling me that your nights are your own, I'd suggest you keep in mind that your days belong to me. You can carouse—"

"Carouse?"

"Exactly. You can carouse from dusk to dawn. You can light up the night, if that's your preference." He strode towards her, his expression chill, his hands on his hips. "Just don't expect to waltz into this office late."

"I told you, I am not late."

"My coffee is usually on my desk by nine."

"Only because I usually come in early."

"Well, then."

"Well, then, what?"

Well, then, Jake thought grimly, he was making a colossal ass of himself again. So what if she'd gone out with Jennett? So what if she didn't want to go out with him tonight? Go out? No. He'd intended to have her accompany him to a business function, that was all, and maybe she was right. Maybe it wasn't a good idea...

He clamped his lips together, marched into his office, shut his door and buried his nose in his work.

Ten minutes later, he shoved aside what he was doing,

pushed back his chair, went to the door and flung it open. Emily was typing away at her computer.

"You're right," he said.

She looked up. "Excuse me?"

"Your life is your own, to do with as you see fit."

"Am I supposed to say thank you?"

Jake's eyes glittered. "I'm trying to apologize, dammit."

Emily sighed. "I know. It's just... I'm not in the best of moods this morning."

"Yeah." He nodded, ran his hand through his hair. "Well, that makes two of us." He hesitated. Her life was her own, but there was nothing wrong in asking. After all, he was the one who'd introduced her to Jennett. "So, how'd things go?"

"Things?" she said brightly.

Too brightly, Jake thought, and cocked his head.

"Your date with Jennett. It, uh, it went well?"

She looked at him for a long moment. "Fine," she said, and smiled, but she wasn't fooling him. The smile was as phony as the perky voice.

"Emily?"

She shook her head, swiveled her chair so that her back was to him. "I have a lot to do, Jake. Those memos you left me yesterday..."

"Emily," he said again, and went to her. He put his hands on the back of the chair, turned it towards him. She dropped her head so he couldn't see her face and he squatted down beside her, gently cupped her chin in his hand and brought her eyes level with his. "Emily, what is it?"

Her shoulders lifted and fell. "Nothing. I told you, I'm just not in the best of moods this morning."

Jake sighed. "My fault. I'm sorry. I shouldn't have chewed your head off. Of course you weren't late. You never are."

"Yesterday," she said, and sniffed. "I was late yesterday."

"Yeah, well, so was half the city."

Was that a hint of dampness in her eyes?

"That cold I mentioned," she said, as if she'd read his thoughts. Jake nodded, dug in his trouser pocket, took out a folded white handkerchief and gave it to her.

"Blow," he said. He waited while she did, then cleared his throat. "It's just, well, when you didn't show up early, the way you usually do, I began to worry."

"About me?"

"Sure. I mean, I sort of feel like I'm responsible for introducing you to Jennett." He waited for her to say something. When she didn't, he cleared his throat again. "How'd it go? I mean, no octopus last night?"

Emily smiled. "Thad was a perfect gentleman."

Jake let out his breath. "Good. That's, ah, that's a relief to hear."

"But the date was a disaster."

"A disaster?" Jake frowned and rose to his feet. "How come?"

"It just was," she said, in a small voice.

"You didn't have a good time?"

"I was too nervous to have a good time."

"Nervous? About what?"

Emily sighed. "About everything. What to say. What to do. What to order, from the menu…"

"Where'd he take you for supper?"

"A little place on Third. It had a French name but Thad kept calling it a perfect bwaht, whatever that means."

Jake nodded. *"Chez Louis?"*

"That's it. But I've no idea what a 'bwaht' is."

"It's French, Em," he said gently. Oh, she was so innocent. Her mouth was trembling, and he thought about kissing it. Just to soothe it, of course, not for any other reason. "A *boite* is a box. Jennett meant the restaurant is like a little jewel box. A special sort of place." Indeed, it was. Jake knew it well. *Chez Louis* was one of midtown's most romantic,

most seductive restaurants. His jaw tightened. "He was trying to impress you."

"Oh, it was impressive, all right. Soft lights. Not a word
of English from the waiters or on the menu..." She looked
up at him. "I was never very good at languages. I took a lot
of science courses. I wanted to be an anthropologist. I
thought I did, anyway, until I decided I'd like to try my hand
at business..." Her words trailed away.

"Well," he said briskly, "dinner must have been nice."

Emily shrugged. Her eyes glittered again and she lifted his
handkerchief to her nose and blew.

"It wasn't?"

"I guess. But Thad ordered snails." She shuddered and
folded her hands in her lap, the handkerchief bunched in her
fist.

"Yeah." Jake smiled. "Well, some people love 'em. Me,
I've never been able to get past the idea that they leave a
trail of slime behind them when they... What?"

"He ordered them for me."

Jake's eyes narrowed. She'd let Jennett order her meal,
when she wouldn't even let *him* give her advice?

"I see," he said coldly.

"No. No, you don't. 'Why not let me order for both of
us?' Thad said, and I said, fine, because the menu was in
French and the only language I ever took was beginning
Spanish and..." She paused, took a deep breath. "He said
they were es cargo."

"*Escargots,*" Jake said helpfully.

"Yes. Well, I'd heard the word. I mean, of course, I knew
it was some kind of French dish..."

"Of course." Was it possible his little sparrow regretted
her first flight? Jake squatted down beside her again and took
her hand. "But you didn't know exactly what."

"Not until the waiter put the plate in front of me." A
shudder ripped through her again. "Oh, when I saw those

slimy shells…'' She sighed. "I couldn't eat them. And I felt so silly. I mean, I should have known he'd asked for snails.''

"Lots of people wouldn't.''

"I'm twenty-six years old,'' Emily said sternly. "I live in New York City. I'm going to meet lots of sophisticated people, now that I'm your exec. Don't you think it's time I could make my way through a restaurant menu, even if it's written in French?''

"It's probably a good idea, but it's not—''

"I made a fool of myself, is what I did, Jake!'' Emily snatched back her hand, plucked some papers from her desk and got to her feet. Jake stood, too, and followed her slowly into his office. "I turned green at the sight of the snails, I nearly gagged over the drink he'd ordered for me…''

"What was it?''

"I don't know. Thad said it was an apéritif but it tasted more like cough medicine.''

So much for Jennett's Let-Me-Thrill-You-With-My-Sophistication suaveness, Jake thought with satisfaction. That had obviously been the plan, but it had fallen flat on its cosmetically enhanced face.

"So,'' he said, trying to sound sympathetic, "it wasn't a memorable meal, huh?''

"I guess it depends on your definition of memorable.'' Emily blushed. "I felt like an idiot by the time it ended. You know, the poor little country mouse? That was me.''

"Don't be silly. There's nothing wrong with not being familiar with menus deliberately written so you can't understand them, or with a drink that tastes like you ought to have somebody clamp your nose shut with one hand and pour it down your throat with the other.''

He'd hoped for a smile. Instead, Emily dumped the papers on his desk and swung towards him, her expression taut.

"Don't patronize me, Jake. You said I'm going to have to attend business functions with you. Well, you won't think it's so amusing if I end up making an ass of myself when we're together.''

Jake sighed, eased a hip onto the edge of his desk and folded his arms.

"When I came to New York," he said, "I thought the height of fine dining consisted of a hot dog served with chili.''

Emily's lips twitched. "No, you didn't.''

"Yeah, I did. Back home, you ate a frank in a bun with mustard and, if you were lucky, sauerkraut. Then I came to the big city and discovered those pushcarts where you can order a hot dog smothered in mustard, ketchup, onions, relish, and chili.'' He grinned. "I can still remember standing on the corner, eating a frank with everything and thinking that was *haute cuisine*. Well, I'd have thought it if I'd known the phrase. As it was, I just figured I'd died and gone to heaven.''

Emily laughed. Damn, Jake thought, watching her, she had a wonderful laugh.

"Chili dogs are gourmet dining, huh?''

"Hey, this is New York.''

She laughed again. Had her laugh always been like this, so open and easy and infectious? Or had he just never noticed it before?

"Thank you, Jake. For making me feel better, I mean. All through supper, I just kept wanting the evening to end.''

"Ah.'' He cleared his throat. "Speaking of endings, how did it? End, I mean. What time did Jennett get you home?''

"I'm not sure. It wasn't late.''

"No?''

"No.'' Emily's smile faded. She took some papers from the desk and began leafing through them. "You left me a memo about that trip to San Diego. I have it here, somewhere…''

"Emily? What's the matter?''

"Nothing.''

"Come on, don't hand me that. Something's wrong."

Emily bit her lip, spun around and started towards th
door. "I don't want to discuss it."

Jake could feel his muscles knot. "Well, I do," he said
He moved past her, shut the door, leaned back against it an
folded his arms. His face was blank. "I thought you said h
wasn't an octopus."

"He wasn't."

"So?"

"So…" Color suffused her face. "I don't think this is a
appropriate topic of conversation for an employer and an em
ployee."

Jake thought about taking Emily in his arms, kissing he
until she clung to him, reminding her with his hands an
mouth that what had gone on between them last night wasn
what either of them would have called "appropriate" just
few days ago, but that would only have taken things back t
where they'd been in the elevator, and he wasn't going to le
that happen.

He'd already reached that decision.

There wasn't a way in the world he was going to get in
volved with Emily…but he did have an obligation here.

"Remember what I said after your date with Archer
About feeling responsible?" He spoke calmly. Why wouldn
he? Just because her color was deepening and his imaginatio
was running wild, why wouldn't he speak calmly? "I intro
duced you to him, too, and look what happened. Come or
Em. Tell me about last night."

Emily sighed. She put her hands behind her, placed ther
against the edge of Jake's desk and leaned back. The simpl
action thrust her breasts forward. Not that he could see them
she had on another of those big, bulky suit jackets. But h
could imagine the way they were lifting, rising towards him
Towards his hands. His mouth…

Jake frowned and stood up straight.

"What did he do?" he demanded. "If that bastard got out of line—"

"We kissed," she blurted.

Jennett had kissed her. Jake curled his hands into fists until he could feel his fingernails biting into his palms. Well, so what? A kiss wasn't anything. And she had the right to kiss any man she liked. She had the right to sigh in a man's arms, open her lips to his, take his tongue into her mouth...

Jake cursed, grabbed his suit jacket from the back of his chair and made for the door. Emily flung herself in front of it.

"Jake? Where are you going?"

"To kill Jennett," he growled. "I don't know why you tried to protect him, why you said he wasn't all over you if he was, but—"

"He wasn't. He didn't. It was me. I...I kissed him!"

Jake felt everything inside him become numb. "You kissed him? But you just said—"

"I know what I said." Emily blushed. "This is so embarrassing!"

"Just tell me what happened, dammit." Jake tossed aside his jacket and dug his hands into her shoulders. "You kissed Jennett?"

"He kissed me first. At the door. On my cheek. And I— I thought, well, of course he's only going to want to kiss my cheek, after that dumb performance in the restaurant..."

"You wanted him to kiss your mouth," Jake said slowly. "You actually wanted that—that—" he drew a harsh breath "—that man to kiss your mouth?"

"You have to understand," Emily said, the words a breathless rush, but how could she make him understand when she still didn't? She'd told herself she'd wanted Thad to kiss her because he was handsome, and sexy; because he was only the second man who'd asked her out in years...

But the truth was far more complicated. It had to do with wanting, with hoping, that Jake's kisses hadn't turned her inside out because they'd been from Jake. That her response to him had been no different than it would be to any man, that it wasn't just his particular kisses that could make her feel as if time were standing still.

"Well?"

Emily looked up into Jake's face. He was waiting for her answer but she knew better than to tell him the things she'd been thinking. She might have been naïve about French menus and good-night kisses, but she knew better than to tell a man like Jake that his kisses robbed her of coherent thought and all but liquefied her bones.

"After the restaurant thing...I just—I felt like a ninny. I wanted to be cool and sophisticated. So, when I realized he was aiming for my cheek, I turned my head at the last second and—and he ended up kissing my mouth, instead." She swallowed hard. "And—and..."

"And?"

"And..." Her voice fell to a whisper. "Nothing."

"Nothing," Jake said. He knew he sounded like an idiot trapped in an echo chamber but what was a man supposed to say to a woman when she told him what it was like to kiss another man? "What do you mean, nothing?"

"No bells. No lights. No flutter in my... No flutter," she said, her face flaming. "It was pretty much like kissing a friend. I just didn't feel anything."

Jake wanted to shout hosannas. "Really," he said calmly.

"Really. And Thad knew it. He had to. I pulled back and I stuck out my hand and thanked him for supper and..." She gave a long, deep sigh. "And, that was it. There I was, kissing a man women dream about, and I bungled it."

"You didn't bungle it when I kissed you," Jake said softly.

"I know. And I don't understand it." Her eyes sought his. "A kiss is just a kiss, after all."

Jake smiled a little. "That's what an old song says, yeah."

Gently, he framed her face with his hands. His gaze fell to her lips, then rose again. "But it's not true."

"No?"

"No." His voice was calm. That, in itself, was remarkable because her embarrassed whispers were turning him on as much as if she were touching him. "Every man has a different technique."

"You think?"

"I know. Show me how you kissed him," Jake said, in a voice he barely recognized as his own.

"How I kissed Thad?" A warning bell sounded softly in Emily's ears. Don't, she told herself, oh, don't do this. But Jake's thumbs were moving over her skin; his eyes were blazing into hers. "Well…" Her heart began to race. "I told you. He bent down to kiss my cheek."

"Like this?" Jake said, tilting his face towards hers.

"Exactly. But at the last second, I sort of turned my head…"

"Turn it," he said, and his voice grew even deeper. "The way you did last night. Fine. Now, do the rest."

"Kiss you?"

"Yes. Kiss…"

She did. She tilted her face to his, brought her lips to his in a kiss so innocent, so gentle, that he felt his heart turn over.

"And Jennett didn't intensify the kiss?" he said, or thought he said. The blood was pounding in his ears; he was having trouble hearing anything but its heavy beat.

"He tried," Emily whispered.

"How? Did he put his arms around you, like this?"

Jake slipped his arms around her and drew her to him. Emily bit back a moan.

"No. I didn't give him the chance."

"Well, just in case he does, the next time, let's work on this a little, okay? Look up at me. That's it. Now, tilt your head, just a bit…" God. Oh, God, what was he doing? Why didn't he let go of her? Why didn't he write her a check for six months' salary, for a year's salary, give her a glowing letter of commendation and send her packing? "Now, part your lips, Em. Excellent. Stay like that. That's fine. Fine."

He bent his head and lightly, very lightly, feathered his mouth over hers. It was barely a kiss; it was a whisper of a kiss but the feel of her lips, the sweetness of them, instantly drove all the blood from his head straight into his groin.

"Like that?" she said shakily.

*Yes. Like that. Exactly like that...*

"No," Jake said. "Not quite. You have to open your mouth just a little bit more. Good girl. Now, relax. Lean into me..."

He groaned. He couldn't help it. The taste of her. Oh, the taste.

"How's that?" he said, his voice low, his body hard, his brain on the brink of combustion. "Better?"

"Better," Emily said, and sighed. "Much better."

Jake dipped his head again, settled his mouth over hers, slid the tip of his tongue between her lips and she made a sound, the sound a woman makes as she surrenders herself to a man, and he knew that if this went any further, if he didn't stop it now, he was going to take her. Strip away her clothes, all that foolish wool, carry her to the couch and take her...

"Jake?" she whispered, and she arched against him, kissed him, bit delicately into his bottom lip...and shattered his control, completely.

He sank down into the chair behind his desk with Emily in his lap. The clip fell from her hair as he tunneled his fingers into it; he felt her shudder and then her arms were tight around his neck, his hands were under her skirt, on her legs, her thighs; she was moaning into his ear and he was lost, he was lost, he was...

The phone rang.

"Jake," Emily gasped, but he shook his head, cupped her face, took her mouth in deep, hot kisses...

The phone rang, and rang, and finally Jake snarled, reached for it and jammed it against his ear.

"Hello," he said, "and this better be..."

The look on his face changed. He sat up straight, so suddenly that Emily almost fell off his lap. One glance at Jake's face and she scrambled to her feet.

"Glad to hear it," he said, after a minute. His voice was frigid, his eyes icy as he hit the mute button and held out the telephone. "It's for you."

"For...?"

"It's your boyfriend. Jennett." Jake's teeth glittered in a predatory smile. "You forgot to tell me why you can't make that party. You have another date with him this evening."

Emily's heart tumbled. "I didn't forget. Anyway, you didn't ask."

"No. No, I sure as hell didn't." He shot her another terrible smile. "Why would I? It's your life, Emily. Who you see is none of my business. Besides, I'm flattered."

"Flattered?"

"Sure. It's not every day I'm used as a stand-in for the real performance."

Emily turned pale. "You can't believe that!"

"Can't I?" Jake grabbed his jacket from the back of the chair. "Have fun tonight, babe. Just remember to give credit where credit is due, when you start turning ol' Thad on."

"It's Thad who'll deserve the credit," she hissed, "not you!" Angry tears blurred her vision. She turned her back on Jake as she put the phone to her ear. "Hi," she said brightly. "No, no problem. Uh-huh. Yes, I'd love to. I had fun, too. *The Gondola,* at six? Great, Thad. I'll see you then."

She heard the click as Thad hung up. Then she slammed the phone into its cradle and swung around, ready to do battle, but she was alone in the office.

Jake was gone.

# CHAPTER SIX

EMILY looked up from her computer monitor and checked the clock.

It was almost five, time to stop work and get ready for her date with Thad.

She finished what she'd been typing, saved it to a disk, exited the program and shut off her computer.

Jake still hadn't returned to the office. She'd spoken to him once, in midafternoon, when he'd phoned to issue some crisp commands. The call had been brief and to the point, with no time wasted on pleasantries. He'd simply ticked off a list of things he wanted done, she'd said "Yes, Mr. McBride," or "No, Mr. McBride," and that was it.

Well, that was fine. It was the way it should be, the way it would be, from now on.

She'd had lots of time to think, after Jake had stormed off, and she'd reached a decision. Not the obvious one, she thought as she put away a file folder, not the first one that had popped into her head, because what was the point of quitting a perfectly good job when there was a far simpler solution?

All she had to do was turn back the clock.

Everything had been great until that fateful moment Jake had smiled and told her to stop calling him Mr. McBride. Such a simple thing, that easy descent into informality, but it had turned life upside down. Well, it was time to set things straight again.

When she saw Jake—when she saw Mr. McBride—tomorrow morning, she would tell him that they were going back to the old rules. She'd call him by his proper name, and he'd stay out of her personal life.

It went without saying that he'd never kiss her, or touch her, again.

Emily rose from her chair, took her purse and made her way to the ladies room. She switched on the light, went to the sink and briskly washed her hands and face.

She was glad she'd decided against leaving her job. It would be foolish to give up an excellent position with excellent pay for what were, basically, simple lapses in judgment. And Mr. McBride wouldn't fire her. He might be an easy mark for the Crystals and Brandies of this world but when it came to business, he was a tough, take-no-prisoners warrior. She did her job well, and he knew it. Hadn't he promoted her and given her a fat raise just a few days ago?

Emily turned off the water, reached for a towel and dried her hands and face.

Yes, he'd stormed out of the office in a rage but by now, he'd have calmed down enough to realize that the best thing he could do, the best thing they could both do, would be to go back to where they'd been. She'd be Emily, he'd be Mr. McBride, and the closest they'd ever come to anything of a personal nature would be on Friday evenings, when he'd smile politely and wish her a pleasant weekend.

Now to get ready for her date with Thad Jennett.

She leaned closer to the mirror and looked at herself critically. She saw wide-set chocolate-brown eyes, a nose that was okay set over a mouth that was nothing special. Average, she thought, just plain, average Emily.

She poked at her hair, neatly confined at the nape of her neck. It looked all right, she supposed; not sexy or glamorous the way the hairdos on all those women last night had looked, but at least the strands weren't curling this time. She hated those curls; they looked wild and uncontrolled and that wasn't her, that wasn't her, at all.

A touch of dark brown mascara might have been a good idea, if she'd known Thad had really meant it when he'd said he'd call. So would a better-looking outfit. Not that she had one. The only nonpractical things in her closet were the silk suit she'd mentioned to Jake—to Mr. McBride—and a bridesmaid's gown. She'd bought the suit for Serena's wedding and the gown for Angela's.

The gown was out of the question. It was long. It was frilly. Mostly, it was puce. The suit wouldn't have worked, either. It was an okay shade of pale apricot but she'd have frozen wearing it in weather like this, although none of those women last night had seemed terribly concerned about freezing in their excuses for dresses. That Crystal creature, especially, hadn't been concerned about frostbite but then, she'd probably figured some man would warm her.

Not some man.

Jake.

Had he? Had he taken Crystal out, after the party? Had he taken her home, put heat and color into her skin with his hands and mouth...

Emily glared at her reflection.

"Stop it," she said sharply.

What Jake did with women was none of her concern. She worked for him, that was all. Besides, she had Thad to think about now. There wasn't a woman alive who wouldn't sigh at her good fortune. Thad was handsome. He was interesting. He was famous enough so that women shot her envious little glances when they'd had supper last night...

But he wasn't Jake.

Emily frowned.

No. He wasn't Jake, and a good thing, too. Thad was a gentleman. He'd never hold her prisoner in a public elevator, kiss her until she was breathless, press her back against the wall and touch her until she was mindless with need...

Just thinking about it made her head swim.

Maybe some women liked that approach but she wasn't one of them. She'd never fantasized about being conquered. Why would she? An intelligent woman wanted time to think, to make informed, clearly planned choices. Thad was a man who'd give her that time. No sudden moves, with Thad. No hot, demanding kisses. Just reason, and a careful telegraphing of his intentions, the way it had been last night.

Thad wouldn't overwhelm her senses, as Jake did. He wouldn't drive all rational thought from her head.

Emily lifted her chin and eyed herself in the mirror again. She was really looking forward to tonight. Too bad she hadn't told Thad she needed time to change. Well, it wasn't too late to do a little touch-up. She pulled off the hair clip, fluffed her hair. Then she opened her jacket, undid a couple of blouse buttons. She hiked up her skirt, too.

It had worked last night. She'd proven she could get attention from men. But she didn't want attention from men, she wanted it from Jake...

Emily blinked. She pulled her hair back into its clip, buttoned her blouse, closed the jacket and rolled down the waistband of her skirt.

"Take it or leave it, Thad Jennett," she said, "this is the real me."

*La Gondola* was *Chez Louis* by another name, or at least in another language.

It was small, intimate and dimly lit. And if the captain's greeting was anything to go by, she wasn't going to understand the menu here, either.

Still, only a coward would turn tail and run. So what if her comprehension of menu-Italian began with Chianti and ended with lasagna? So what if she was wearing more yards of fabric than all the other female diners were wearing, combined, or if each of them must have spent the whole afternoon on hair and makeup?

Looks, as her mother had often told her, weren't everything. She was bright, she was well-educated. She could carry on a conversation, get by with ordering Chianti and lasagna. As for the rest...wearing a designer dress and having a perfect face and an even more perfect mane of hair wasn't everything.

On the other hand, maybe it was.

And maybe turning tail and running was the better part of valor, but it was too late for that. Thad had already risen to his feet to greet her as the captain bowed her into the booth.

"EmilyDarling," he said, touching his cheek to hers as he clasped her hands, "you're here, at last."

Yes, she thought, she was here. And now that she was, she wished she weren't. Not because she was dressed wrong, or because she knew she'd never be able to read the menu, but because she was here with the wrong man.

Her name wasn't EmilyDarling, and she hated air-kisses, and Thad was wearing half a bottle too much of cologne. Jake never wore cologne; his scent was simply of soap and man, and she had the feeling that sharing chili dogs on a sidewalk with him really would be the best kind of fine dining...

She blinked.

"Yes," she said gaily, "I'm here, at last."

Thad drew her down beside him. "Did you have a long day, EmilyDarling?" He smiled. "You probably did. That boss of yours doesn't give you time to think. I'll bet he keeps you chained to the desk."

"He doesn't. I mean, that's not why I'm late. The crosstown bus—" She stopped, took a breath, and started again. "Sorry. You were joking, of course."

Thad smiled. "Your innocence is so charming. Well, I know just the way to relax you. Let's have a drink."

"Chianti," Emily said quickly.

Thad laughed. "Chianti," he said, and laughed again. "Don't be silly, EmilyDarling. *La Gondola* is known for its wine list."

A hovering waiter handed him what looked like the Manhattan telephone directory. Thad opened it, glanced through it, and ordered something unpronounceable. Moments later, a bottle was brought to the table and opened. Thad sniffed the cork, swished some wine in his mouth, and nodded.

"Excellent," he said briskly and the waiter poured the wine. Emily lifted her glass when Thad lifted his and took a sip of what surely had to be paint thinner. "Isn't that delightful, EmilyDarling?"

"Lovely," Emily replied, and tried not to cough.

"Well," Thad said briskly, "did you hear what happened at the Bishikoffs' the other night?"

Emily didn't know who the Bishikoffs were, much less what had happened. It seemed to involve a dining-room table, a frantic rodent, and a rather athletic Persian cat. She tried to make sense of the story, got as far as feeling sorry for the poor mouse, then gave up listening and just smiled and nodded and said "oh, really," whenever it seemed appropriate.

"Wonderful story," Thad said, chuckling at his own humor, "don't you think?"

"Wonderful," she agreed.

What am I doing here? she thought. And where was Jake, right now? Was he out with some woman? Was he looking across a table like this one, smiling into her eyes? Would he go home at the evening's end or would he spend the long night locked in another woman's embrace...

"Emily?" Thad said. "What would you like?"

Emily jerked her head up. There was a menu lying in front of her. It made the wine list look like a short story.

"Sorry," she said quickly, and opened the menu. If lasagna was listed in elegant gold script anywhere on those parchment pages, she didn't see it. Determinedly, she snapped the menu closed. "I'll have pasta."

"Excellent choice, EmilyDarling. How about trying the house special? You'll love it."

"I'm sure I will." Well, she would. She liked lasagna better but pasta had just popped into her head. How wrong could you go with spaghetti?

Thad started talking again, about the cat and mouse chase at the Bishikoffs'.

"Of course," he said, "we all had to pretend we hadn't noticed…"

Oh, of course not, Emily thought, with growing irritation. Jake wouldn't pretend, if something like that were taking place right under his nose. He'd laugh out loud, if it were funny. Or he'd have gone to the rescue of the hapless mouse, which somebody should have done, if she was getting parts of the story right.

"That poor mouse," she blurted.

Thad's eyebrows lifted. "Mice are just mice," he said gently. "Besides, what could anyone possibly do? It was the most undignified situation imaginable."

As if dignity mattered, at such a moment. Jake wouldn't think so. He wouldn't be trapped by convention…

And he would not eat what was being placed in front of her right now. Creamy tendrils of pasta, laced with a strange, midnight-black liquid. Emily shrank back in her seat.

"That's not mine," she said quickly. "I ordered—"

*"Pasta alla Gondola,"* Thad said, leaning over her plate and inhaling. "Wonderful!" He looked up at the waiter. "I can never remember, Paolo. Is that ink from squid or octopus?"

Emily looked at her plate. "It must be octopus," she said faintly, staring at the tiny, eight-tentacled creatures she'd just noticed delicately peeking out from under the pasta, "unless those are made of rubber…"

Her stomach lurched. The fork dropped from her fingers and fell to the floor. "I can't—I just can't…"

Thad put a sympathetic hand on her knee. "Can't what, EmilyDarling?"

"Can't eat seafood," a familiar male voice said. "She's allergic to it. Isn't that right, Emily?"

Thad snatched his hand from Emily's leg. She jerked her head around…and saw Jake.

"Surprised to see me?"

Stunned, she thought. Stunned and delighted. God, he was so handsome. So big and gorgeous. And so smart! He'd saved her from her fate with one quick sentence.

"A little," she said carefully, and wondered if he could see the race of her pulse in her throat.

Jake sat down beside her in the booth. Thad shifted closer to the wall.

"It's a good thing I came along," Jake said, looking over Emily's head at Thad. "She's got this rare allergy to cephalopod mollusks"

Cephalopod what? Emily thought. "Oh, I certainly do!"

The booth was small; Jake was big and solid. Wonderfully solid, like an anchor in a storm, she thought as his thigh pressed against hers.

"Strange she didn't mention it, when I ordered dinner," Thad said coldly.

"Well, she was only recently diagnosed. Right, Em?"

"Oh, yes." The lie sailed from her lips with ease.

"It's terribly rare. Not many things contain cephalopod mollusks." Jake reached under the table and took her hand. Her fingers lifted, wove tightly into his. "Well," he said briskly, as he pushed her plate aside, "let's order you something you can eat. *'Pasta Amatriciana,'*" he told the waiter, who'd come hurrying to the table. "For the lady, and for me." He smiled at Emily. "No allergy problems with that, I promise."

Emily smiled back. Her heart was still bumping against her ribs. It was so wonderful to see Jake, to have him with her. Only because he'd dug her out of a hole, of course. Why else would she be this happy to see him?

"McBride?"

Thad's voice was icy. Jake smiled politely and looked at him. "Yes?"

"What are you doing here?"

"What are *you* doing here, Jennett?"

"Having dinner, but—"

"What a coincidence." Jake laid his hand, still joined with Emily's, on her thigh. "So am I. At least, I was about to when I noticed you guys. You don't mind if I join you, do you?"

"No," Emily said. She blushed. "I mean, if it's all right with you, Thad..."

Thad offered a taut smile. "Of course."

"Great," Jake said, and waved the waiter over again to order some wine.

The wine was delicious. So was the pasta. Emily dug into it with pleasure. Jake squeezed her hand and leaned closer.

"Good?"

"Yes." She smiled at him. "Thank you."

"No need to thank me," he said quietly. "I like my ink to stay in ballpoint pens, and things with too many arms belong in nightmares."

She laughed. Jake did, too.

"Did I miss something?" Thad asked stiffly.

"No," Emily said, with a guilty smile. It was too bad. Thad was a nice man. He just wasn't—he wasn't—

"So," Jake said, "did you hear what happened at the Bishikoffs' the other night?"

He told the story but it wasn't the same. He'd actually been there; he made the incident seem funny, even for the mouse.

"...grabbed the first thing I could find, which just happened to be the salad bowl, trapped the little guy in it, and took him away. The cat wasn't very happy. Neither was the lady seated to my right because the salad ended up in her lap, but..."

She was laughing by the time he finished. Thad wasn't. He sat beside her stiffly, his eyes fixed on his plate. Gradually, her laughter died. This was terrible. She'd agreed to dinner with one man but she was really spending the evening with another. Thad might be a pompous ass, but he deserved better than this.

"Thad?" she said softly.

"Yes?"

"I'm sorry."

Thad put down his fork. "I doubt it."

"But I am. I didn't expect Jake to—"

Thad swung towards her, eyes glittering. "I don't like playing stand-in for another man, Emily."

"Jake isn't anything to me!"

"I don't believe you."

"What would you like me to do? Sign an affidavit? Jake's just my employer. He isn't—"

"Sweetheart?"

*Sweetheart?* Emily looked at Jake. "What did you call me?"

"Ah." Jake gave her a crooked grin and lifted their entwined hands to the top of the table. "Sorry. I know how you are about keeping things private."

"Private?" Dammit, what was she doing, repeating his insane comments this way? She twisted her hand, tugged it free of his. "Really, Jake…"

"Really, Em." Jake's tone was soft, his smile pleasant but his eyes were dark, and narrowly focused on her face. "I think it's time I took you home."

"Are you crazy? You're not—"

"Now," Jake said coldly. "Right now." He looked past her, at Thad. "Unless you have a problem with that, Jennett?"

Thad didn't answer. His skin had taken on a pallor that showed through his out-of-season tan. Even the waiter, who'd been approaching with dessert menus, seemed frozen in place.

Emily flushed, dropped her napkin alongside her plate and rose to her feet. "It's been a lovely evening but Mr. McBride is right. I have to get home."

Jake rose, too, his actions as slow and deliberate as those of a panther. "The party's on me," he said. He pulled out his wallet and tossed a handful of bills on the table. Then he looped his hand under Emily's hair, around the nape of her neck. There was nothing casual in it; it was the touch of a possessive male, and a look at Thad, staring up at them, assured Emily that she wasn't the only one reading it that way.

"Em?" Jake said.

She thought of all the responses she could make, everything from calling Jake McBride a fool to slugging him, but making a scene would only make matters worse than they already were.

"Jake," she said calmly, and she let him drape her coat over her shoulders, put his hand in the small of her back and guide her away from the table, through the restaurant and out the door.

"Taxi," Jake snapped at the doorman.

"Not for me," Emily said. She wrenched free of his hand and swung towards him. "Just who do you think you are?" she demanded, her voice quivering with rage.

"Did you expect me to sit there and let Jennett paw you?"

"He was not 'pawing' me!"

"Come off it, Emily. Or maybe you didn't think I could see what was happening right under my nose."

"Nothing was happening, except maybe poor Thad was trying to figure out what you were doing, elbowing in on our date."

"Oh, give me a break! You were damned glad to see me."

"Only because you were better looking than that stuff on my plate!"

Jake glared at her. "You were glad to see me because I'm me, and you know it."

"My God, you're impossible! Six feet of outlandish ego."

"Six feet plus," Jake growled, and pulled her into his arms.

His mouth took hers with heat and hunger; his arms closed tightly around her. Emily made a little sound of indignation…and then she groaned, rose on her toes, flung her arms around Jake's neck and kissed him back.

"Sir? Uh, sir, your cab…"

Jake stepped back, kept one hand on Emily and dug in his pocket for a bill with the other. Then he marched Emily to the curb but she'd recovered her equilibrium by then.

"I'm not getting into a cab with you!"

Jake muttered something, opened the door and none too gently pushed her inside, got in after her and gave the driver her address. The taxi shot off down the street.

"Damn you, Jake!"

"You ought to thank me," Jake said coldly, "instead of cursing me."

"Thank you?" Her voice rose shrilly. "For what, huh? For letting Thad think that you and I—that I…"

"You don't give a damn what he thinks. Not unless you've lost all your common sense."

"Don't you get it? You made it look as if you—you had the right to—to—"

"I do have the right." Jake shot her a quick look. "We agreed on that, remember? I'm going to find men for you to date, vet them, see if they're a good match for you."

"We didn't agree. And even if we had, I don't want you involved in my private life. Not anymore."

"Forget the octopus on your plate," Jake growled. "If I hadn't turned up, you'd be dealing with a human octopus in another half hour."

"You are beyond belief, do you know that?" Emily folded her arms and glared at him. "If Thad wanted to give me a bad time, he'd have done it last night."

"I saw the way he was looking at you, as if his brand were stamped on your forehead."

"And how do you think you were looking at me? When you announced I was leaving with you, when you—when you touched me that way. When you—when you kissed me just now…'' Emily looked away from him and stared out the window. ''This whole thing has gone wrong. You're my boss, not my keeper.''

''Yeah, well, maybe you need a keeper.''

''You had no right to turn up at that restaurant.''

''Coincidence,'' he said airily.

''Coincidence, my foot! I was on a date. A date, Jake! Do you understand the meaning of the word?''

Jake's mouth thinned. She was right. She'd been on a date and, no, he hadn't turned up by coincidence but what else could he have done? Emily had made him angry as hell earlier today, but that didn't change the facts. One, Jennett had a reputation. Two, Emily was naïve. And three—the biggest piece of the equation—three, it was his fault she was out with the guy.

He'd offered to introduce her to men but not men like Jennett. There were other guys out there, guys he'd be glad to introduce her to, and if he couldn't think of one of them, well, that was only because he hadn't had time to work on the problem.

Plus, Emily needed some pointers. She needed to know how to dress, how to look, how to handle herself in fast company, which was the kind she'd been with tonight. And he'd need time to teach her all that, every last bit of it…

The taxi jolted to a stop. Jake looked up. They were outside Emily's brownstone, and she was half out the door.

''Wait for me,'' he said to the cabby, and scrambled out after her.

''I do not wish you to see me in,'' she said coldly, as she marched up the steps.

''I don't care what you wish. I always see my…''

Jake frowned. Emily looked at him. ''I'm not your anything, Jake, except your assistant.''

His assistant. Yeah, she was. And that was fine; it was all he wanted her to be. Still, he'd made a deal and if there was one thing Jake McBride always did, it was keep his end of a bargain.

"You're right," he said.

Emily's brows lifted. "Well, well, well. Two apologies, in one day? Will miracles never cease?"

"I probably shouldn't have shown up at *La Gondola*."

"Probably? Try 'definitely.'"

Jake ran his hand through his hair. "It's just that I felt responsible."

"I don't need anybody feeling responsible for me. I'm a grown woman."

"Yeah. But I said I'd introduce you to guys, and—"

"Are we back to that?" Emily swung away, took her keys from her purse and jabbed one into the lock. "You are hereby absolved from all responsibility for introducing me to men. Okay?"

"Not okay." Jake caught her shoulders and turned her to face him. "It was a lousy idea," he said roughly. "Me saying I'd introduce you to guys. You're not ready for it. You were completely out of your league tonight."

"Thank you for that generous assessment."

"If Jennett sat any closer to you, you'd have been in his lap."

"Only because you crowded your way in."

"It's a good thing I did. He had a hand on your leg, when I got there."

"It wasn't on my leg. It was my knee, and it was only for a second. And it was a friendly gesture. He saw that I was upset when the waiter put that plate in front of me…"

"And why did that happen?"

"Because I couldn't read the menu," Emily said coldly, "and I was too proud to admit it. Any other questions?"

"Did it ever occur to you that Jennett should have told you what that dish was when you ordered it?"

"He just assumed—"

"He assumed you were as innocent as Little Red Riding

Hood, and that turned him on. Dammit, you don't need to learn about menus, you need to learn about men." Jake moved closer to her. "I looked at you tonight—hell, I looked at you last night—and I felt..." *What? What had he felt, watching her laugh at another man's jokes? Smile into another man's eyes?* "I felt as if I'd tossed a sparrow into a room filled with hawks." His voice roughened. "There are things you need to learn, Emily."

Emily shuddered. The wind had shifted; it was blowing in over the East River, chill and forbidding. Surely, that was the reason she was shivering. It couldn't have had anything to do with Jake, with his proximity, with the sudden crazy desire she had to fling herself into his arms again.

"Is that the reason you kissed me?" she said quietly.

"Yes. No. Dammit, Em—" Jake drew a ragged breath. "Look, I can help you. I can teach you about men. What they want from women. What they look for, what they expect. The male-female thing, the thing you don't seem to understand at all."

Emily stared at Jake. He was right. He could teach her. He already had.

"Is that what you want to do?" she said huskily. "Teach me about the male-female thing?"

It seemed a long time before Jake answered. When he did, his voice sounded low and far away, even to his own ears.

"Yes. Yes, I do. And I promise you, Em, I'll teach you all you need to know."

Everything came to a stop. The whispers of the city night, the moan of the wind, even the thump of Emily's heart as she lifted her eyes to Jake's face.

"Jake," she whispered. "Jake, I don't think—"

No, he told himself wildly. No, she wasn't thinking. Neither was he. He felt as if he were standing in a dark tunnel, trying to find his way out only by feel.

He took a step back, jammed his hands into his coat pockets, knotted them into fists. "It's too late to think," he said gruffly. "It's been a long day for both of us. We'll talk to-morrow morning. Ten o'clock."

"Ten..." Emily cleared her throat. "Ten o'clock?"

"Right."

He took another step, backed carefully down the stairs. Did she have to look at him like that? With her eyes so wide and dark, her lips parted? He could kiss her now. Hell, he could have her now. Take her in his arms, lead her upstairs, let it all happen, everything they'd both been fighting the past days or maybe the past year; he was beyond trying to figure it out.

But he wouldn't do it. What he'd do would be to teach her the things she needed to know about men. How to talk to them. How to see a pass and head it off. Nothing else, because Emily wasn't his kind of woman, or maybe he wasn't her kind of man. She was innocent and sweet; she had no idea how the game was played. She'd open her heart to a man, offer him everything and expect everything in return. Not little blue boxes from Tiffany's or long-stemmed hothouse roses but an intimacy that had nothing to do with what two people did together, in bed.

And that wasn't his thing.

He wanted her, yeah, but if he had her, what then? It would be over for him but not for her, and it wasn't his ego talking now, it was reality. Emily was a forever kind of woman but he wasn't a forever kind of guy. She'd look at him with those big eyes, she'd probably cry, and he'd feel like the worst kind of SOB as he walked away.

It was better to walk away now.

Jake took a deep breath.

It wouldn't kill him. Years from now, it might even make him feel pure and righteous to look back and remember that he'd done it. He'd walk away from temptation. Hell, he'd do more than that. He'd see to it Emily really did meet a man, not just one to date but one who cared about her. A guy she could be happy with.

It was the right thing to do.

"Ten o'clock," Jake said gruffly.

Then he did the hardest thing he'd ever done in his life. He turned his back on Emily, got into the waiting taxi, and rode off into the night.

# CHAPTER SEVEN

AT NINE the next morning, the clock radio beside Emily's bed shattered the silence with an earsplitting blast of guitar-twanging, drum-thumping, cymbal-crashing acid rock.

She shot up against the pillows, threw out her hand, knocked over a book, an empty cocoa mug and a box of tissues as she groped for the Off button.

The music stopped. Her heart pounded on. She waited until it slowed. Then she swung her feet to the floor and blinked at the radio.

She kept it set to a classical music station. Promptly at six each morning, Monday through Friday, the radio awakened her to the soothing strains of Debussy or Bach. Once in a very great while, she opened her eyes to something as modern and daring as Stravinsky.

But not rock. Never rock. It was too loud, too boisterous, too obvious, too everything. She'd always thought so. So, why would the radio be playing rock music this morning? For that matter, why would it go off at all, on a Saturday? And if it did, why would it go off at...

Nine?

"Nine," Emily gasped, and hurtled from the bed.

She remembered, now. Remembered it all. How she'd paced the floor last night, instead of sleeping. How she'd tossed and turned, once she'd finally fallen into bed. How she'd felt herself tumbling into the kind of exhausted sleep she feared would leave her feeling groggy, and how she'd reached out, fumbling in the dark, to reset the clock from six to seven so she'd have one more hour of sleep but would still awaken early enough to phone Jake and tell him there

109

wasn't a way in the world she'd see him at ten or any hour on a Saturday, in this lifetime.

Emily groaned.

There were two morals to that sad little tale. The first was never to try and set a clock radio in the dark. The second was never, ever, to let Jake McBride get the last word.

Nine o'clock! Hurriedly, she grabbed the phone and dialed his number.

"Come on," she whispered, "pick up, pick up, pick…"

"Hi," Jake said cheerfully.

Thank God!

"Jake?" Emily cleared her throat. "Jake," she said briskly, "I'm glad I—"

"This is Jake McBride. Sorry, but I can't take your call right now. Just leave your name, a brief message, and—"

Emily slammed the phone down. She scrubbed her hands over her face, ran them through her hair. She could feel curls springing up all over her head. What to do, what to do?

Calm down, an inner voice said.

But how could she calm down, when it was nine-fifteen and Jake was due here at ten? Okay. Okay, forget about calming down. She'd just concentrate on getting ready. Showering. Dressing. Doing something with her horrible hair, which seemed to know that there was snow forecast for later today. Then she'd put up coffee, straighten the house…

She sagged against the nightstand.

Forget about straightening the house. Forget about coffee. Just shower and get dressed, because the last thing she wanted was for Jake to ring her doorbell while she was standing here in her flannel pajamas.

No. He wouldn't be able to ring the doorbell. He'd have to press the downstairs buzzer. Then she'd have to press the Talk button. She'd say, "Who is it?" And he'd say, "Jake. Buzz me in," and she'd say, "Sorry, but I've changed my mind, Jake. I'll see you Monday morning, at the office…"

*Buzzzz.*

Emily spun around and stared into the living room. That was either the downstairs buzzer or an angry hornet had gotten into the house. It couldn't be a hornet, not in the winter. And it couldn't be the buzzer. Jake was coming at ten, and it wasn't even half past...

*Buzzzz.*

Then again, it didn't have to be Jake. It could be someone else. The super, calling to tell her when the painters would be coming. Or old Mrs. Levy, from apartment 3G, who forgot her keys half the time she went out and then just pressed buzzers at random until somebody buzzed back and let her in...

*Buzzzz, buzzzz, buzzzz.*

Whoever it was, was getting impatient. Her canary, its cage still covered for the night, gave a wistful chirp from the kitchen in response. Emily hurried to the intercom in the wall beside the front door.

"Yes?"

"It's Jake."

She groaned, closed her eyes, leaned her forehead against the wall. Actually, she felt like banging it against the wall but Jake might think she was trying to tap out a message.

"Emily?"

"Yes, Jake. I heard you. What are you doing here? It's not ten yet."

"Yeah, well, I got an early start."

"I'm not..." She looked down at her old pajamas, at her bare feet. "I'm not ready."

"No problem. I brought the paper. I'll just read it and wait."

"Fine. I mean, not fine. I mean, I've changed my..." Emily sputtered to a halt. Okay. Jake was here. In that case, she'd do the right thing. Get dressed, go downstairs, tell him her decision in person. "Look, just sit on the stoop and read the paper. I'll be down in twenty—"

"Are you nuts? It's zero degrees out here, Emily."

"Five minutes, then. That's all it'll take me to get ready."

"What's that, dear?"

"And don't 'dear' me!"

"I was talking with a charming lady name of… What's your name, sweetheart? Ah. Her name is Mrs. Levy. She says she forgot her keys and she's getting awfully cold, standing out here while you refuse to buzz her in."

Emily narrowed her eyes. "I hate you, Jake McBride," she said dispassionately, and pressed the buzzer. She thought about combing her hair, putting on her slippers, washing her face…

Instead, she flung open the door, folded her arms, and waited.

Jake bounded up the stairs a moment later. Her heart bounded, too. She'd never seen him dressed in anything but a suit. Today he wore scuffed leather boots, faded jeans and a scarred black leather jacket. Not that it mattered. He was an unwelcome sight…

But a magnificent one. Her heart leaped like a jackhammer when he smiled.

"Good morning, Emily."

"There's nothing good about it."

Jake went from a smile to a grin. "That's what I love," he said, "being greeted by someone who's cheerful, first thing in the morning."

What he hadn't expected to be greeted by was a barefoot, sleep-tousled Emily in a pair of flannel pajamas. He was a man who'd seen more than his fair share of slinky black nightgowns, negligees and spike-heeled sandals. How could a pair of bare feet and oversized flannel pj's be a turn-on? Not too oversized, though. He could see the rounded outline of Emily's breasts beneath the softly faded fabric, even see the thrust of her nipples…

Jake frowned. "We had an appointment," he said gruffly. "You look as if you just got out of bed."

"Our appointment was for ten o'clock. Besides, I changed my mind."

"Yeah, I figured you would."

Emily spun around as he brushed past her. "Where are you going?"

"I'm looking for the kitchen. You do have one, don't you?"

"Yes, but—"

Jake dumped the *Times* and a white paper sack on the kitchen table. "Two containers of coffee, two bagels with cream cheese, and two jelly doughnuts. My penance, for showing up early." He folded his arms. "I figured I'd better, or you'd chicken out."

"I am not, as you so elegantly put it, 'chickening out.' And I'm not interested in starting my day with a carbohydrate high."

"No problem. I'll eat the doughnuts by myself." Jake looked around the room. He'd have looked anywhere, if it meant not looking at Emily. Her hair was a mass of silky curls; her mouth was pink. What would she taste like, without even a touch of lipstick? What would she feel like, in his arms? Desperate for diversion, he jerked his chin in the direction of Horace's cage. "Is this the bird you told me about?"

"Yes. That's Horace. And he doesn't like strangers."

"Horace, huh?" He whisked the cover off the cage. "Named for the Roman poet?"

"Why—why yes. How did you—"

"Hello, Horace." Jake raised an eyebrow. "Does the lady underestimate you as often as she underestimates me?"

Horace sent up a trilling song. Emily glared at him, then at Jake, and gave up.

"Enjoy your breakfast," she said coldly, and started from the room. Jake snagged her wrist.

"I brought breakfast for two."

"And I told you, I don't like—"

"I heard you. Well, at least have the coffee, while it's hot. Oh, come on. It's not as if I've never seen the early-morning you."

Damn the man. He was making her blush. "You've seen me in the office," she said stiffly.

He smiled. Slowly, as if he had all the time in the world, he looked her over from the top of her head to the tips of her toes, then back up again.

"Right," he said softly. "In the office. And I have to tell you, this is a big improvement."

Emily's blush deepened. "I hardly think so."

"Well, that's where we differ. I find flannel and a wild mane of hair a lot sexier than a clip at the nape of your neck and an oversized tweed suit."

"I do not dress to look sexy, Mr. McBride."

"No." Jake's smile tilted as his eyes locked on hers. "You most certainly don't, Miss Taylor. But you should. That's going to be at the top of today's agenda. Lesson one—How To Dress For A Man."

"There is no agenda, today or any day. No lessons. I phoned to tell you that, but you'd already left your... What are you doing?"

It was a dumb question. What he was doing was curling his hand around the back of her neck, threading his fingers into her hair, moving closer to her, so close that she could smell the cold and the promise of snow on his skin.

"Jake." Emily cleared her throat. "Didn't you hear me? I've decided against your—your proposal. If I meet men, I'll do it on my own, and my own way. I don't want you to—"

Jake bent his head, brushed his lips gently over hers. Emily caught her breath. The touch of his mouth was light, so light she might have imagined it, but oh, she hadn't. She'd felt the kiss, the electricity, straight down to her toes.

"Jake." Her voice was shaky. "Please..."

"Please, what?"

His arms went around her. One hand slid under her pajama top and pressed gently against her naked back.

"Stop," she said, or tried to say, but Jake was tugging her closer, smoothing his hand up and down her spine.

"I'm just demonstrating," he whispered, his mouth soft against her ear. "Think of it as lesson one. How To Say Good Morning."

"You said…" Emily bit back a moan. "You said lesson one would be—would be How To Dress For A…"

Oh. Oh, he had to stop doing that. He had to let her go. Or maybe she had to let him go because somehow, her hands had stolen up his chest; her fingers had danced into his hair; she was drawing his head down to hers, his mouth to hers…

Jake clasped her shoulders and stepped back.

"Coffee," he said hoarsely. "I'll have coffee while you get some clothes on."

Emily swayed unsteadily. "Yes. Good. You have coffee while I…"

She turned, fled for the safety of the bedroom. Jake watched her go, told himself not to be an ass, not to go after her…

The door swung shut. He swallowed hard, felt for a chair, and sank into it.

So much for all his good intentions. He'd spent the night telling himself he'd done the right thing, when he'd walked away from Emily. That he was wrong for her. That she was wrong for him. He'd even gone through his address book, searching for the names of guys she might like. He had the list right here, in his jacket pocket.

And then he'd seen Emily standing in the doorway wearing an outfit that not even Marilyn Monroe in her heyday could have turned into something sexy, with her hair uncombed and her eyes a little puffy from sleep, and he'd had to work at not sweeping her into his arms and carrying her to bed.

Jake popped the lid off one of the cardboard containers,

dumped in half a dozen packets of sugar, stirred the resultant mess and gulped a mouthful. Caffeine, a sugar high and whatever the cardboard residue might add to the mix was just what he needed. Either that, or a cold shower.

He groaned, downed the rest of his coffee, grabbed one of the bagels and bit into it. He'd bought plain bagels, not the garlic ones that were his favorites. Big mistake. All those old movies on late night TV about werewolves and vampires... Wasn't it garlic that was supposed to keep them away?

Maybe it did the same thing when it came to keeping a man away from a woman he knew he shouldn't want.

Jake gave a soft, unhappy laugh. Where was a garlic necklace, when you need one? And how in hell was he going to make it through the day?

He paced, paced some more. He could hear the shower running. Not a cold one. A warm one. And Emily was in that shower. She was naked, waiting for him...

Jake grabbed the paper, buried his face in it and went through the motions of reading, but he'd given up the pretence by the time Emily entered the kitchen again. He was standing at the window, his back to her, and her breath caught at the sight of him.

He'd taken off his leather jacket; he was wearing a blue chambray shirt with the sleeves rolled midway up his muscled forearms. His hands were tucked into the back pockets of his jeans. His shoulders were broad, his waist and hips narrow, his legs long and slightly spread. It was the posture of a man who was self-assured and just a little dangerous.

Emily's throat tightened. She'd thought about Jake, while she was showering. There was no lock on her bedroom door, or on the adjoining bathroom. And she'd shut her eyes, while the water beat down, and imagined the shower door opening and Jake, a naked Jake, stepping into the shower with her. She'd imagined the strength of his arms, the feel of his mouth...

She must have made a sound because suddenly Jake turned towards her.

"Ready?"

She didn't trust herself to speak, not right away. To kill time, she went to the hall closet and got her jacket.

"Yes," she said, when it was safe to face him again. "I'm ready. What's on the agenda? New clothes? New hairdo? I made up my mind, Jake. I'm yours to command."

Jake felt his jaw knot so tightly it hurt. She wasn't. She was his for today, and only so he could ready her for another man.

What the hell kind of idiocy was that?

A sane idiocy, he told himself, without even wincing at the contradiction. He reached for his jacket, shrugged it on, and followed Emily out the door.

Snow did funny things to Manhattan.

On weekdays it snarled traffic, slowed buses and subway trains, piled up along the curbs and turned rapidly into slush.

It could do all those same things on a weekend...but nobody seemed to notice. The lacy white flakes touched the city with magic. People had even been known to smile at each other as they hurried along the streets.

Not Jake.

He didn't feel a bit like smiling.

He was seated in a leather and chrome chair built for contortionists in the waiting area of a place called *THE BEAUTY SPOT*. Mirrors surrounded him; music assaulted his ears. It came from every possible direction, some stuff he couldn't imagine anybody could possibly enjoy especially if their mood, like his, kept alternating between mean and downright nasty.

This was their third, and last, stop of the day.

He'd sat through a session in Saks, while a gushing saleswoman brought out suits and dresses, pants and blouses and sweaters, shoes and handbags and who knew what else, for Emily to try on...

Try on, for his approval.

At first, he'd liked the idea.

He had a pretty solid notion of how Emily ought to look. He knew she should wear soft colors and earth tones, that she had legs that deserved showcasing, that she had a body that deserved gently clinging cashmeres and silks. So, for a while, it had been a kick to sit in a velvet chair that was half a size too small for comfort, arms folded, head cocked, and say "No," "Yes," "Great," each time Emily stepped out of the fitting room.

"Your lady is so lovely," the saleswoman kept saying, and all at once, maybe the sixth time she said it, Jake had stopped grinning like an idiot and saying yes, yes, she was, because it had suddenly hit him that Emily wasn't his lady. She was his executive assistant and now she was his development project, and what he was "developing" her for was another man.

How come he'd forgotten that, somewhere between leaving her apartment and sitting through a fashion show?

Things had gone downhill from there.

He must have looked it, too. The saleswoman had stopped gushing, Emily had started giving him quick little glances, and when they'd finally left Saks with her wearing a cashmere dress in softest rose, a pair of high-heeled black leather boots and a belted black coat that looked soft as velvet, she'd said that if he wanted to call it a day, that was fine.

What he'd wanted was to call her beautiful, as she stood there with her face turned up to his—a face now heightened with artful applications of soft black mascara and lip gloss that matched the rose dress, after a stop at the cosmetics counter.

Instead, he'd taken an armful of elegant boxes from her, scowled and said that he'd made a deal and he was going through with it.

Which was how come he was sitting here, in *THE BEAUTY SPOT,* surrounded by glassy images of himself, images that pretty much showed a man coping with a growing frustration that made absolutely no sense at all. What was there to be frustrated about? This had been his idea, this makeover. And it was going well. Emily looked beautiful and, until he'd turned into a snarling beast at Saks, she'd been happy.

Well, that was her problem. She wanted to be happy because he was grooming her for another guy, let her. He didn't have to do anything except sit here with his arms folded, his back straight, his feet crossed at the ankles.

Jake glowered at himself. Half a dozen Jakes glowered back, all of them looking like police bulletins for the criminally insane. It didn't help that he hadn't bothered shaving this morning and he had a dark stubble on his cheeks and jaw. All in all, he might as well have been wearing a sign that said Keep Away. And people were. The place was crowded but the chairs on either side of him stayed empty and a good thing, too, because the last thing he wanted was to end up with some damned fool trying to engage him in polite conversation.

He was having a rotten time, and he didn't much care who knew it.

Emily, on the other hand, was back to enjoying herself.

Jake's eyes narrowed.

Eric, who was cutting her hair, was having a blast, too. Jake could see him from here, standing over Emily, smiling and laughing as he wielded a pair of scissors and a comb. She was laughing, too.

Jake's mouth turned down.

What the hell was there to laugh about?

The SOB better not be taking off too much of all that sexy hair. "Just trim it," Jake had warned, when he'd handed Emily over.

"Trust me, Jake," Eric had said.

Well, yeah. That was the reason he'd brought Emily here, wasn't it? He and Eric worked out at the same gym. They'd had some beers together. And Eric owned one of the trendiest styling salons in the city.

He was also straight, Jake thought grimly. And it was just possible some women might be turned on by his Viking good looks.

How come he hadn't considered those things before he'd brought Emily here and put her in Eric's hands? How come it hadn't occurred to him that Eric wouldn't just cut her hair, he'd also see how beautiful she was, how much fun; he'd see that she wasn't anything like the other women who crowded *THE BEAUTY SPOT,* that she was...

"Hi."

Jake lifted his glowering face. Emily stood before him. Eric was there, too, but at first all Jake could see was Emily. Emily, with her hair loose, with her curls set free, shiny and dark as coffee as they tumbled around her face.

"Well?" She smiled nervously. "What do you think?"

What did he think? Jake rose from the chair. What he thought was that he wanted to reach out and touch one of those curls, feel the silken whisper of it as he brought it to his lips....

"Not bad," he said calmly.

Emily's smile drooped. Good, Jake thought savagely. Had she really imagined he'd tell her she looked—she looked—

"That's typical," Eric said. He grinned, looped an arm lightly around Emily's shoulders and gave her a quick hug. "Last time I beat him at racquetball, he said the same thing."

Jake looked at Eric. "You got it wrong, buddy," he said quietly. "I beat you. And since when do stylists get so cozy with their clients?"

Emily flushed. Eric raised his eyebrows. Jake felt like an idiot.

"Oh, hell," he muttered, "man, I'm sorry. That was a stupid thing to say. I just—"

Eric let go of Emily and smiled. "No harm done, Jake. I'd probably have the ol' green-eyed monster on my back, too, if this were my lady."

"But I'm not," Emily said quickly. "I'm not—"

"See you," Jake said. He clasped Emily's arm and hustled her out of the salon.

"You shouldn't have done that," she hissed. "Now he thinks you and I—he thinks we're—"

"Did he ask for your phone number?"

"No!" Emily wrenched free of Jake's hand and glared at him. "But what if he had?"

What, indeed? Jake dug his hands deep into the pockets of his jacket. "Don't worry about it," he said coldly. "I'll set him straight when I see him next time. Once he's sure you and I aren't involved, he'll ask you out."

"I don't want him to ask me out! That's not what this is about."

"Sure it is. What else am I doing this for, if not to make guys interested in you?"

"I don't like your attitude!"

"You don't have to like it," Jake snarled. "Just do as you're told so we can get through the day."

"You know what?" Emily blew a curl off her forehead. "I've changed my mind. I don't want to get through the day. I don't want you in my face. In fact, I'm going home."

She swung away. Jake reached out, caught her arm and spun her towards him.

"You'll go home when I say you can go home."

"I know this may come as a shock, Mr. McBride, but I don't have to take orders from you."

"Yeah, you do. You're my exec, remember?"

"Five days a week. Even Scrooge gave Bob Cratchit weekends off."

"So, you're telling me you won't work overtime?"

Emily blinked. "What kind of question is that?"

"What do you think today is, if not overtime?"

"Huh?"

Huh, was right. Think fast, Jake told himself, go on, find a way to dig yourself out of the mess you're in.

"I have to drive to Connecticut, to, ah, to check on some property." Well, he thought, it could have been the truth. He had been planning to head north; he just hadn't thought about doing it today.

Emily frowned. "So?"

"So, I need you to come with me."

"To Connecticut?"

"Isn't that what I just said? Yes. To Connecticut."

"I don't understand. What does property in Connecticut have to do with me?"

"I want to see if you have a feel for this sort of thing."

"*What* sort of thing?" Emily shook her head. "I'm not following you at all."

Jake took her arm again. He led her up the street, around the corner, to where he'd parked his Corvette, unlocked the door and closed it after her. It took a couple of minutes, just the time he needed for it all to come together.

"There are times I invest in land," he said briskly, as he dumped the packages in the car and got behind the wheel. "You know that."

"Actually, I didn't. I know you have a weekend place in Connecticut, but—"

"Exactly." He checked for traffic, then pulled away from the curb. "The two acres next to mine just came on the market. I have to decide whether or not to buy them."

True again, he thought. Yes, it made more and more sense that she spend the rest of the day with him.

"And?" Emily said, sounding even more puzzled.

"And, I want your opinion. As my executive assistant."

He glanced over at her. She was looking at him as if he'd lost his mind and maybe he had. But his mouth was already working, even though his brain seemed to be shutting down.

"I have the data. Prices in the area. Tax info. Resale, all

of that.'' Jake cleared his throat. ''Of course,'' he said politely, ''if you think you'd be in over your head—''

''I'm perfectly capable of understanding the data,'' Emily said coolly. ''I just don't understand why you didn't mention this before.''

''I didn't think of it.''

That was true enough, too. Suddenly, he knew how crazy he had to sound. And this *was* crazy. Why would he want to take Emily to Connecticut? He'd said he'd spend the day getting her new clothes, a new hairdo, new makeup. Well, he'd done it. She wanted to go home and it was time to let her do just that, then head to his place, check his address book, figure out who he felt like seeing tonight...except he didn't feel like seeing anybody, except Emily.

*McBride, what are you doing?*

''Listen,'' he said quickly, ''if you don't want to do this... If you'd rather I took you home...''

He fell silent. The seconds ticked away and then Emily cleared her throat. ''No,'' she said softly, ''no, don't take me home. Take me with you, to—to Connecticut.''

Suddenly, Jake felt as if the car were filled with electricity. He looked at Emily. She was sitting very still, her hands folded in her lap.

''Okay,'' he said gruffly, and he took the 'Vette onto the highway that led out of the city, then onto the Hutchinson River Parkway, headed towards northwestern Connecticut. He was silent. Emily was, too. He glanced at her once in a while, as they left the city behind and entered the wooded hills of southern New England. She sat as she'd been sitting, hands folded, staring straight ahead.

What was she thinking?

The roads were fairly empty. The snow, falling more and more heavily, was keeping people home. Hell, home was where he ought to be. There was no sense to this. He'd get Emily to his house and then what? Show her the stuff about taxes and prices in Litchfield County? What for? The truth was that he didn't need her opinion. He'd already decided to buy the land, not as an investment but because he loved the house, loved the hill it stood on, the forest that surrounded it.

Jake cursed, swung the wheel hard to the right and pulled onto the shoulder of the highway. He stared straight ahead while he gripped the steering wheel hard. His knuckles turned white.

"This is crazy," he said gruffly. "I'll take you back."

"Jake?"

"Yes?"

"Jake, look at me."

He did. For the first time in hours, he looked straight at her. His heart turned over. She was so beautiful. So beautiful...

"Is this really about property that's for sale?" she said softly.

Her eyes lifted to his, and what he saw in their chocolate depths stole his breath away.

"Hell, no," he whispered. Quickly, he undid his seat belt, undid hers, and reached for her. She came into his arms with a little sob, turned her face up to his and met his hard, hungry kiss with an eagerness that almost undid him.

"Emily," he whispered, "come with me. Let me teach you the things that really matter."

She put her hands in his hair and dragged his mouth down to hers.

"Yes," she said, against his lips, "oh, Jake, yes."

# CHAPTER EIGHT

THE country road wound through the trees like a black ribbon, glittering wetly in the headlights of Jake's Corvette.

The windshield wipers beat a steady, swift pattern as they tried to keep up with the falling snow.

Emily was surprised the road was passable at all. She'd said as much, to Jake.

"It'll be clear," he'd said tersely. "The plows are always out early, especially in a storm like this."

The brief exchange had taken place almost an hour ago. Jake hadn't spoken a word since then.

Emily couldn't blame him. Ever since he'd pulled away after kissing her, she'd sat stiffly in her seat, her fingers almost painfully knotted together in her lap. Jake had to be thinking exactly what she was thinking, that the two of them had made an awful mistake.

Lights glinted ahead.

"Litchfield," Jake said.

The sound of his voice startled her. She looked over at him, nodded, searched desperately for something to say in reply as they drove through the town, which lay quiet under its heavy white mantle of snow.

"It's—it's beautiful."

"Yeah."

"It looks familiar. I know that's impossible. I mean, I've never been to this part of Connecticut before, but…"

"You've probably seen pictures of it on postcards. Typical New England scene, etcetera, etcetera."

It was a short, almost abrupt answer, delivered in a gruff tone. So much for conversation, Emily thought, and looked straight ahead again.

125

There was no question about it. Jake was definitely sorry he'd asked her to come with him. She could hear it in his silence, see it in his stern profile, in the way his hands gripped the steering wheel. He was as tense as an overwound spring.

Well, so was she. Jake's regrets couldn't be any greater than hers.

Emily clenched her hands together in her lap.

What insanity had made her say yes to his proposal? Why had she said she wanted him to teach her all those things she didn't know? It wasn't as if she'd misunderstood him. He was talking about things that happened in bed.

And she'd agreed. She hadn't even been subtle about it. She'd made it clear sleeping with him was precisely what she wanted but she shouldn't have. She wasn't cut out for a quick tumble in a man's bed.

In Jake's bed.

Yes, she wanted to know what sex was like. There was something pathetic about reaching this age and knowing only what you'd been taught in Sex Ed, back in high school, or what you'd picked up, over the years, from other women's comments. Her sisters, especially, made lots of references to sex. Barbed references, that suggested the whole thing wasn't half as terrific as it was cracked up to be.

Emily wanted to know for herself. She'd thought she did, anyway.

Now, with all this time to consider what came next, she wasn't so sure.

Was she really supposed to have sex with Jake tonight, go home tomorrow, then show up at work on Monday as if nothing had happened? She had no foolish illusions; this wasn't an affair she was entering into with him. He'd made that clear. This was part of her transformation from wallflower to woman.

Next week, maybe even sooner, she'd be ordering flowers for his latest conquest, making his dinner reservations, behaving politely when some new candidate for McBride's Playmate of the Month telephoned.

"May I speak to Jake, please?" they always said, in breathy voices that made her think of satin sheets and chilled champagne.

Or they'd show up at the office and she'd be expected to smile politely when he slid his arm around a slender waist and left for the weekend with some oversexed, overdressed, overeverythinged female...

*Oh, God!*

Emily swung towards Jake. "Stop the car!"

He responded instantly and stood on the brakes. The Corvette gave a sickening lurch. Emily gave a thin scream as Jake fought for control of the car as it slid crazily across the slick blacktop and spun in a drunken circle.

When the car finally came to a stop, it was pointed towards the forest, its headlights burrowing a cavern of light into the darkness. The engine coughed and died. In the sudden silence, Emily could hear the roar of the wind, the rasp of Jake's breath and the thump-thump of her own heart.

"Holy hell!" Jake reached for her hand and squeezed it hard enough so she felt the imprint of his fingers. "Em? Are you all right?"

"Yes," she said, past the lump of terror high in her throat. She looked at him. His face was white, his eyes deep, dark pools. "Are you?"

"Yeah, I'm fine." He flashed a reassuring smile, squeezed her hand again before putting it into her lap. "Let me just see if the car's okay. The last thing we need is to have somebody come around that curve and straight into us." Jake turned the key, held his breath until the engine caught and purred. "Damn," he said roughly, as he swung the car back into the lane and edged forward, "we almost bought it, that time."

Emily nodded. "I know. I'm sorry, Jake. I—I guess I wasn't thinking. It was stupid to yell like that."

"No need to apologize." He shot her a quick smile. "Nobody wants to kill Bambi."

"Bambi?"

"Uh-huh." Jake leaned forward, peered intently out the windshield. The wipers were working as hard as they could but the snow was too heavy for any real visibility. The turnoff that led to his driveway was just a little further up the road. He could only hope the guy he paid to keep it plowed had already been there. "You'd think the deer would have finally figured it out by now, wouldn't you? That running across the road in front of a car isn't a good idea?"

"Oh." Emily bit her lip. "I didn't see a deer." Her voice was soft and small. "I just—I just..." She took a breath. "I thought about what we were doing. And I decided it was a mistake."

Jake took his eyes off the road long enough to stare at her.

"Excuse me?"

"I said—"

"I heard what you said. I just don't believe it. You're telling me you almost got us killed because you suddenly decided you wanted to go home?"

"It wasn't sudden. I've been thinking about it for a while. And how was I supposed to know you'd react by almost crashing the car into a tree?"

"Oh, forgive me." His words were thick with sarcasm. "The next time I'm driving blind through a storm and the person seated next to me yells 'Stop,' I'll just keep going and hope for the best."

Emily lifted her chin. "I said I was sorry, didn't I?"

"You'd be sorrier if we were lying dead back there."

"Look, what I did was stupid. But I meant what I said, Jake. I want to go back to New York."

Jake gave a short, sharp laugh. "Yeah? Well, trust me, lady. So do I."

Emily's heart felt as if somebody were crushing it, which was even stupider than yelling "Stop." She'd already known

Jake had regrets. Why should it upset her, to hear him confirm it?

"Fine," she said coolly. "That makes the decision unanimous."

"It damned well does. Unfortunately, neither your vote nor mine counts. This blizzard owns the ballot box."

"This isn't a blizzard." Her voice wobbled a little and she cleared her throat. "I'll bet you never saw a blizzard in your life. Back home, in Rochester—"

"Trust me. We had blizzards in Pennsylvania, too."

Pennsylvania? Not New York? Was that where he was from? It was impossible to picture Jake living anywhere but in the elegant canyons of the city. She wanted to ask him where he'd grown up, and how, and what he'd been like as a boy...

But she wouldn't.

What was the matter with her tonight? You didn't ask questions like that of a man who'd just told you he was sorry he'd asked you to sleep with him.

"The wind has to blow at least thirty-five miles an hour for a snowstorm to be a blizzard," she said, blanking her mind to everything but the night and the storm. "And the visibility—"

Blah, blah, blah, Jake thought grimly. There she went, the Emily he knew, who could quote you chapter and verse on everything and anything—except how to be a woman.

He gritted his teeth, tuned her out, and concentrated on the road. There it was, just ahead. The turnoff. And yes, the guy had cleared it. He signaled for a right turn, not that there was anybody in back of him. Who'd be fool enough to be out on a night like this?

Only a man who'd been letting his gonads lead him around for the past week.

Well, no more.

He'd had lots of time to think, the past few hours, and what he'd thought was how dumb this whole escapade was.

He'd set out on a mission of mercy, been snared by his own hormones, and now he was taking a woman to the last place he'd ever thought he'd take a woman.

Not just a woman. Emily. Emily, for God's sake, who probably thought sex was another word for romance and love and lace-trimmed Valentine's Day cards. He'd backed himself into a corner he was going to have trouble getting out of, and for what? For a couple of hours in bed?

Jake almost laughed.

He could have taken the prim and proper Miss Taylor to bed one hundred and sixty miles ago. Back in the city, at his place. Or at hers. Or at some damned hotel, in a suite overlooking Central Park, if that was her preference. He could have had her anyplace but here, in a house that was his own personal hideaway from the real world.

He didn't want her here. He didn't want any woman here but, thanks to a momentary lapse in judgment, he sure as hell had one. And, as if that weren't bad enough, it looked as if they might end up stuck here for at least part of tomorrow.

What would they talk about? What would they do when the sex was over? It wasn't as if he'd never spent a whole weekend with a woman but it had always been in a place where there were things to do so you didn't have to sit around, looking at each other. Besides, those women knew how to play the game.

Emily didn't. She'd expect... What? Earnest conversation? An exchange of life stories?

Jake bit back a groan.

And come Monday morning, what would his life be like? Could he still walk into the office and greet her as if they were nothing more than two people who happened to work together?

No. Dammit, no. Women weren't like that. They put on a good act, said they were the same as men, said sex was sex and that it didn't have to be confused with love. And, he supposed, some of them even meant it.

Not Emily. Certainly, not Emily.

She was naïve to a fault. She'd probably only been with a couple of men. Every instinct warned him that she'd turn this one night into more than it was, more than he'd ever meant it to be. If he'd had himself under control, he'd have figured that out a lot sooner.

And that was another thing. He didn't like the feeling he had when he was around her, as if he weren't quite in charge of his own destiny, because he was.

Of course he was.

If only the roads were clear. If only the snow weren't coming down. If only he'd thought of all this before he'd asked her to come with him, before he'd started dreaming about her and yeah, okay, he dreamed about her, and wasn't that a laugh? What kind of man had dreams like that, when he knew that there were a dozen beautiful women just waiting to do in reality what Emily only did in those dreams?

Jake glared out the windshield. The house was just ahead. Normally, he felt good just at the sight of it, but not tonight. One huge master suite with an oversized tub and shower, a den, a living room, a half bath the Realtor had insisted on calling a powder room, and a country kitchen.

It was plenty big enough for him, but for him and a woman? For him and Emily?

It was too late for turning back but not too late for regrets.

Jake reached to the dashboard, depressed the button for the automatic garage door opener. The doors rolled up; he drove the Corvette inside and shut off the engine. Okay. Time to make the best of a bad situation.

"Well," he said, trying for pleasant and not quite making it, "here we are."

Emily wrenched open her door. "Thank you for telling me," she said coldly. "I'd never have figured it out if you hadn't."

Jake sighed. Oh, yeah. It was going to be a memorable

night. It was just a good thing the sofa in the den was comfortable.

He walked ahead of her, unlocked the door that led from the garage into the kitchen. The house was dark and cold. He was half tempted to leave it that way. It suited his mood. But he did the right thing, turned up the thermostat, then went from room to room, switching on lights before returning to the kitchen.

Emily was still standing where he'd left her, her back to him. Jake thawed, just a little. She looked lost, small and lonely...

No, she didn't. She turned around and she looked as if she'd been carved from the icicles that dangled from the eaves.

Okay, fine. That was the way she wanted it, that was the way it would be.

"I'll bring in your things," he snapped.

"What things? You mean, the stuff you bought today?"

"Yes."

"Don't bother. None of that's mine. You picked it, you paid for it. You can return it."

Jake peeled off his gloves, stuck them in the pockets of his leather jacket. "We've been all through this, remember? In Saks."

"How could I forget? You made such a scene..."

"I simply said you were to consider the clothes a gift."

"And I," Emily said sharply, "told you that I wouldn't."

"Dammit, I am not going through this again. Buying all that stuff was my—"

Emily unbuttoned her coat and shrugged it off. Jake swallowed dryly. He'd almost forgotten how she looked in that rose-colored dress and those high-heeled leather boots.

"It was my idea," he continued. "And it's a ridiculous thing to quarrel over. You'd never have done all that shopping if I—if I hadn't—"

"What's the matter?"

"Nothing." Nothing, unless he kept wondering what she had on under the dress. How come he hadn't thought of that before? How come he hadn't seen any underwear going in and out of that fitting room?

"Well, I'm not keeping the clothes."

"Yes, you are."

"No, I'm not."

"You are, and that's the end of it." Jake ripped off his jacket and tossed it on a chair. What did it matter, what she was wearing under the dress? He didn't care. For all he gave a damn, she could be wearing red flannel long johns. "I'm going to start a fire. How about you check out the kitchen and see if you can rustle up something to eat?"

"Oh, I see. You're the man, so you get to build the fire. I'm the woman, so I get to open a can of soup."

Jake threw out his arms. "You want to start the fire? Great. Be my guest. I'll be more than happy to switch jobs."

Emily lifted her chin. "I'd just as soon do the cooking, thank you. Why risk ptomaine poisoning, at your hands?"

She turned on her heel. Jake glared at her. "Women," he muttered, and then he marched into the living room, squatted down before the fireplace, and set to work.

Half an hour later, Jake sat on the carpet, cross-legged, before a roaring fire.

He was feeling a little better. A good fire always did that for him. And there were interesting smells coming from the direction of the kitchen.

He sighed, thought about the endless hours that lay ahead and figured it probably made sense to make the best of them. So he added another log to the blaze, got to his feet, headed for the wooden wine rack at the far end of the room, and frowned.

Red or white? He had no idea what Emily was cooking and he didn't much feel like invading her territory to ask. It was peaceful right now; why spoil things with a question about wine?

Red, he decided. Red seemed to suit a cold, snowy night.

Jake opened a bottle of Merlot, sniffed the cork and decided he'd made a good choice. Mmm. What was she making in there? Whatever it was, it smelled wonderful. His stomach gave an anticipatory growl. Damn, he was hungry. Starved was a better word, but then all he'd had for breakfast was that bagel. Now that he thought about it, they'd managed to blow right past lunch.

Well, that figured. Why would he have thought of lunch, when his sparrow had been turning into a songbird, right before his eyes?

Jake plucked a pair of wineglasses from the shelf.

The truth was, she'd always been a songbird. She'd just managed to keep it hidden from the world. You didn't see the real Emily until you took a long look. A long, wonderful look. Then you realized that she was beautiful.

Jake poured the wine.

More beautiful than any woman he knew, and maybe part of the reason was that she didn't think so.

But she was. That soft mouth. Those dark, drown-in-me eyes. That elegant little nose, the incredible hair, the lovely, curvy body... And her smile. Her laugh, so open and easy. Her honesty, her intelligence, her lack of pretension...

The amazing thing was that Pete Archer had seen the real Emily right away, despite the fact that Archer was an ass. So had Thad Jennett. And now Eric had been added to her list of admirers. Eric, who probably had his hands in the hair of more gorgeous women in a day than most men did in a year...

Was he the only guy who'd been so blind?

Jake picked up the glasses of wine and headed for the kitchen.

Emily was at the stove. She'd put on the denim apron he'd bought for himself but never quite found the courage to use, even though it said Chef on the front in bright red letters. The apron was enormous on her; the sides overlapped in the middle of her back. She was stirring something in a big pot. That was what he'd smelled and now he sniffed the air again, smiling appreciatively at the mingled aromas of garlic, tomatoes and—

"Sausage?"

Emily spun around. Heat from the stove had flushed her cheeks; steam from the pot had turned her hair into a riotous mane of curls and she had a smear of something red on her chin.

Jake felt something twist around his heart.

Beautiful, he thought, Emily, you're so beautiful...

He stiffened. Okay, so she was beautiful. So were a million other women. And there wasn't a reason in the world to get into an affair with her when he knew it would end badly.

Jake fixed a smile to his lips and strolled towards her.

"Vino for the cook," he said briskly, "but only if you tell me that really is sausage I smell."

She hesitated. He could almost see her weighing the benefits and drawbacks of a temporary thaw. After a few seconds, she gave him a little smile and accepted the glass he offered her. A truce had been declared, at least for the moment.

"It is," she said. "You said to poke around the kitchen. Well, I did—and I found some sausage in the freezer."

"You could have found a mastodon, and it wouldn't surprise me. I bought the freezer when I bought the house, filled it—and never opened it again." He held out his glass. "Salud."

They touched glasses. Emily took a sip of wine.

"Mmm. That's lovely."

"I'm glad you like it. I wasn't sure what your preferences are."

"Except when it comes to cephalopod mollusks."

Jake grinned. "Dangerous things, those mollusks."

"Mmm." She drank some of her wine. "Actually, I don't know much about wines. I just know what I like."

"Yes. So do I."

Their eyes met and held. Emily's color deepened and she turned away. "Anyway," she said, "I found the sausage. There were some canned tomatoes in one of the cupboards, along with a box of spaghetti. And you had garlic and cheese in the fridge, so I figured I'd make a sauce. It won't be anywhere near as good as that stuff at *La Gondola,* but—"

"How could it be?" Jake leaned back against a granite-topped counter and crossed his feet at the ankles. "I mean, heck, without some tentacles and a blob of ink, who'd want to eat spaghetti?"

Emily laughed. "Who, indeed?"

"Is the sauce going to take a while to simmer? We had a neighbor when I was a kid, lady named of Mrs. Rossini. She used to make this terrific sauce—it would make the whole street smell great. I remember it took forever to cook."

"Oh, this won't take that long. Just another half hour or so."

"Good. 'Cause I'm as hungry as a bear."

Emily picked up a wooden spoon and stirred the sauce. "So, where was this, where Mrs. Rossini used to make her sauce? Pennsylvania?"

"Uh-huh. How'd you know that?"

She shrugged. "You mentioned Pennsylvania before, when we were in the car."

"Ah. Yeah, Pennsylvania. That's where I grew up."

"I've never been there."

"Not much to see in my part of it," Jake said, and smiled. "Trees, trees, more trees…and coal mines."

"Coal mines, huh? That sounds interesting."

"It isn't," Jake said flatly. He stepped away from the counter. "Looks as if we have just enough time to sit by the fire and enjoy our wine."

"All right," she said, after a second's hesitation. "That would be nice."

Yes, he thought, yes, it would be. Sitting beside the fire, his arm around her shoulders, her head on his chest...

Jake put down his glass. "The thing is," he said gruffly, "I'm not a guy who believes in forever after."

He spoke before he could stop himself, because the words needed saying, but if he'd taken Emily by surprise, she didn't show it.

"I know that, Jake."

"Do you? I want you, Emily. Hell, I want you so badly it makes me ache." He took a slow step towards her. "But I don't want to hurt you. And I'm not sure what you expect out of tonight."

Emily didn't have to think about her answer. She'd come to grips with reality while she'd been making the sauce. She was an adult and so was he. Oh, she'd tried to pretty things up by telling herself she wasn't a woman meant for a one-night stand but the truth was, just as the sauce was made up of a bit of this and a bit of that, so was life.

Tonight was about sex, not romance. That was fine. She didn't believe in romance, anyway. This—being with Jake, learning what other women knew—was part of life. And here, at long last, was her chance to live it.

"Just tonight," she said softly, her chin level, her eyes steady on his. "That's all I expect, Jake. I just want—I want what you said you'd give me. What you said you'd teach me."

She sounded calm, almost cool. She wasn't, though. Jake could see the glass trembling in her hand. She was afraid, and excited, and the knowledge that she was both sent a lightning bolt of anticipation through his blood.

He took her wineglass from her hand and set it aside.

"Come here," he said softly, and drew her to him. "Em." He ran his hands down her back, then up again. "Em, you're so lovely."

"You don't have to lie to me. I know I'm not—"

Her voice was shaking. Well, why wouldn't it? She was terrified. Where was she supposed to put her hands? What was she supposed to do and say?

Her breath caught. Jake had nuzzled her hair aside. His mouth was hot against her neck.

"It's true, though," he whispered. "You're beautiful, and sweet, and perfect."

"Jake." Emily shut her eyes. "I don't—I don't know what you want me to do."

He took her hands, looped them behind his neck. "Just do whatever you want to do, sweetheart."

"Yes, but I—I—"

He kissed her gently, the brush of his lips against hers like a feather against her skin. Emily caught her breath.

"Jake? I don't think…"

"Good." He put his hand under her chin, tipped her face up to his. "Don't think, Em. That's it. Don't think. Just feel."

His eyes were deep and dark; she knew she could tumble into them, get lost in them forever. "Jake? Maybe we were right the first time. That coming here was a mis—"

He kissed her again. His lips pressed hers more firmly this time but his mouth was soft. Soft, and cool, and wonderful.

Her heart began to race. And there was a strange tingling sensation low in her belly.

"Jake. Jake, listen. I said that maybe coming here was—"

He silenced her by fitting his mouth carefully over hers, stroking the tip of his tongue against the seam of her lips.

"Emily," he said gruffly, "just turn off that brain of yours and kiss me back."

She did. She wrapped her arms around his neck, kissed him, and knew, at long last, that being here, with Jake, being in his arms, was what she'd waited for, all her life.

Jake groaned as she opened her mouth to him. He cupped her face in his hands, accepted her invitation, delved into the heat and sweetness of her mouth. Emily moaned, lifted herself to him, against him, pressed her soft, soft body against the hardness of his.

"Emily," he said, and he lifted her into his arms, carried her into the living room, to the fireplace, before he lowered her to her feet.

She'd knotted the apron; he'd always been good at knots, he thought incongruously, hell, he'd almost been a Boy Scout when he was a kid. He'd have sewn a hundred merit badges on his shirt if his mother ever had enough money for the cost of the uniform. But his hands were shaking now; it took forever to undo the knot and get the apron off.

Ah, he was right. She was beautiful. The rose-colored dress matched the color in her face. Her eyes were dark pools, wide with expectation and wonder. Her breasts were high, the nipples hard and visible beneath the soft wool.

"Em," he whispered.

He watched her face as he lifted his hand, brushed his thumb over the distended bit of wool. She cried out; her head fell back and Jake caught her, gathered her close, eased the dress off one creamy shoulder and pressed his mouth to her flesh, to the pulse racing in the hollow of her throat. She smelled of roses and sweet cream; she tasted of honey and heaven, and he told himself to go slow, go slow…

How could he?

The blood was pounding in his veins. And Emily… Emily was whispering his name as he cupped her breast, teased it to life.

"Please," she said, "Jake, please…"

He could feel the room spinning around him. She was crooning to him, begging him, arching against him. She tugged his shirt out of his jeans, ran her hands up his back.

Go slow, he told himself fiercely, dammit, go slow…

"Jake?" she said, and touched him. Touched his erection as it strained against his jeans, and he was lost. Lost, to everything but needing her, wanting her, having her.

"Take me," she said. "Please, Jake. Come inside me now."

Jake growled. He pulled her down to the carpet before the fire, thrust his hands under her skirt, felt the whisper of silk on her thighs, the slickness of silk between them.

She was wet and hot. Wet and hot, for him.

The world, and all his reason, disappeared.

"Now," he said, and he ripped away the wet silk, opened his fly, freed himself and thrust deep, thrust hard...

And felt the barrier, the one he'd never, in his entire life encountered. Stunned, he held still. Tried to think. To pull back. Emily wouldn't let him. She dug her hands into his shoulders, dragged him down to her, lifted herself to him.

"Em," he said, "Em, wait..."

Too late. She thrust her hips forward and impaled herself on his hard flesh.

A moment of shimmering pain, and then Jake was inside her, deep inside her, and she knew, she knew why she'd let this happen, why she'd wanted it to happen.

"Jake," Emily whispered, " oh, Jake, I..."

Jake groaned, thrust one last time, and the world came apart in a shattering explosion of light.

# CHAPTER NINE

JAKE buried his face in Emily's throat, kissed her damp skin, then rolled onto his side and curved her tightly against him.

"Em." He looked deep into her eyes. "Are you all right?"

All right? She was wonderful. Her body tingled; her skin felt flushed and hot. Was she supposed to tell him that?

"Baby," he said, drawing her closer and running his hand gently up and down her spine, "sweetheart, I'm sorry."

"For what? I wanted... I wanted you to make love to me, Jake."

"Yeah." A teasing smile angled across his lips. "Oh, yeah, Em. I know that." Jake threaded his fingers into her hair, brought her mouth to his for a long, tender kiss.

What did he mean, he knew she'd wanted him to make love to her? Yes, of course he knew. She'd told him. But there was something in that little smile...

"Really," she said quickly, "it was—it was fine, just the way you did it."

"Fine, huh?" He laughed softly. "Is that the best you can do?"

His tone was gentle. He was teasing her, she knew, just as she knew she should make some equally teasing response. She couldn't. Her heart was still racing but her mind was blank. There had to be a protocol for this but for the life of her, she had no idea what it was. Did you say thank you to the man who'd just shown you ecstasy? Or did you just lie here and wonder where this magic had been, all your adult life?

Nothing she'd read, nothing she'd imagined, had prepared her for the reality of what had just happened. The feeling of Jake, deep within her. His hot skin. His clever mouth. His

141

slow hands. She didn't want to ruin it now, by saying the wrong thing. As it was, she'd come close to doing just that. She'd almost said…almost said…

She'd almost said, Jake, I love you. And she didn't. Of course, she didn't. She'd just been so overwhelmed by sensation…

"Em, talk to me." Jake eased her onto her back and leaned over her, his weight on his elbows as he looked into her face. "Did I hurt you? I know I went too fast. I'm sorry. I couldn't…" He took a breath, laid his forehead against hers. "You should have told me," he said softly.

"Told you…"

Heat flooded her face. That she was a virgin. That was what he meant. And he was right. She probably should have. Jake was accustomed to being with women who knew about sex. He'd signed on to teach her about passion, not to spend a night with a trembling novice.

"I'm sorry," she whispered, and closed her eyes. "I guess I should have, but—"

"I'd have slowed down, if I'd known." He gave a little laugh. "At least, I'd have tried." He took her face in his hands, brushed his lips over hers. "To be honest, I don't know if I could have. I wanted you so badly, Em. And when you let me know you felt the same way…"

"I did?"

"Uh-huh." Jake kissed her again, and she felt his lips turn up in a smile against hers. "'Take me,' you said. 'Come inside me,' you said. What man could think straight, after that?"

Take me? Come inside me? Had she…could she possibly have…Emily felt a stab of anguish. Yes. Yes, she had. That was what he'd meant when he gave her that smug little smile. She'd said all that. She'd begged him.

And now, she wanted to die of embarrassment.

She'd done everything wrong. She'd pleaded for him to take her, made him come too quickly, been a virgin when a virgin was the last thing a man like Jake would expect. And she'd come within an inch of saying she loved him when, of course, she didn't.

Perfect, she thought. An absolutely perfect debut, Emily. Too bad there was nothing left for an encore.

"Jake."

"Mmm?"

He was kissing her throat, lightly nipping her skin. And she, dammit, she was getting aroused again. She could feel it happening: the liquid rush deep inside, the tingle in her breasts...

"Jake, let me up, please."

"In a minute."

He moved lazily, settled himself lower on her body, kissed the rise of her breast. "You have too much clothing on," he said huskily. "Does this dress have a zipper?"

Her dress. Oh, it was worse and worse. She still had her dress on, even her boots. Jake was fully clothed, too. She hadn't even given him the chance to—

"Jake. I want to get up!"

There was a note of panic in her voice. She heard it; she knew Jake did, too, from the way he reacted.

"I *did* hurt you." He drew back. "Em, baby, I'm sorry. I—"

"Dammit, will you stop saying that?" Her face flamed. "Look, I don't want to talk about it. I just—I want you to get off me." He did, and she shot to her feet. "Where's the bathroom?"

"Down the hall, but I can make things better, if you'd just—"

She didn't let him finish. Instead, she tugged the bodice of her dress up and the hem of it down. She could feel Jake's eyes boring into her as she made her way down the hall. Maybe it was just as well she was still dressed. Walking away naked, with him watching, would have been the final humiliation.

Why had she come here? Why had she done this? She'd never be able to look at Jake again, without thinking—

Emily slammed the bathroom door behind her and locked it.

"Oh my God," she said, in a choked whisper.

After a few seconds, she turned on the light, took a steadying breath and faced herself in the mirror. It was worse than she'd expected. Her hair was a tangle of wild curls, her lip gloss was gone, her mascara was smudged. She looked like a woman who'd been doing exactly what she'd been doing...except she hadn't been doing it very well.

A sound burst from her throat. Turning on the water muffled it; she cupped her hands under the stream. It was icy-cold; she gasped as she splashed it on her face.

Now what?

If only this were New York, she thought, as she dried her hands and face. *Thank you for everything, Jake,* she'd say. *No, no, don't get up. I'll see myself out.* Two minutes later, she'd be in the street, hailing a taxi or finding the nearest bus stop or subway station. Forget the snowstorm. Snowstorms didn't stop anybody, in the city.

But she wasn't in the city. No buses, no taxis, no subways. She might as well have been on the moon.

"Em?"

Emily spun around and stared at the door.

The knob rattled. "Baby, are you okay?"

Baby. What kind of name was that for a man to call a woman?

"Yes," she said brightly, "I'm fine."

"You don't sound fine. Are you crying?"

"Don't be silly." Emily swiped at her streaming eyes with the back of her hand. She *was* crying. And wasn't that dumb? Okay, so she'd made a fool of herself but still, why would she cry? "Why would I cry, Jake?"

"I don't know, but I'd like to find out. Open the door, Emily."

"No."

"Emily." Jake's voice hardened. "Open this door!"

"I don't have to. This is a bathroom. People are entitled to privacy, in a bathroom."

Jake leaned his forehead against the door. Dammit, now what? Of course she was crying. He'd dealt with enough teary females to know what a woman sounded like when she was crying. It usually sent him running in the opposite direction but where could he run to? This was his house, the wind and the snow were howling outside...and besides, it was doing funny things to him, hearing his sparrow weep.

Why would she cry? Okay, things hadn't been perfect. He hadn't made love to her the way he'd intended, so that it would last, so that he could seek out all her most sensitive places, hold her in his arms and watch her lovely face as she found the fulfillment he, and only he, could bring her...

He, and only he?

Jake frowned. What in hell was that supposed to mean? He was teaching Emily about passion. That was what he'd promised, what she'd accepted.

Easy. He needed a minute to get things in perspective. What had happened had thrown him. He'd expected Emily to be inexperienced, but a virgin?

No way.

That had come as a shock. No wonder he'd—he'd—

Who was he kidding? He'd lost control. That had never happened to him before, not since he was a kid. He loved sex: the musky scents; the hot, whispered sounds; the swift rocket-ride to the stars, but a little piece of him always stayed outside, kind of like an observer. What had happened to that observer this time? How come, at the end, nothing had mattered but being deep inside Emily?

The answer was simple. All that prim propriety, hiding all that heat. What man wouldn't lose control? What man wouldn't find the experience exceptional?

In fact, he wanted her again. Right now. The truth was, he

hadn't stopped wanting her, even after they'd both come. Did she know how rare that was, that a man and a woman found release at the same instant? No. She wouldn't know. She was so innocent. So…

Jake rubbed his hands over his face. His body was hardening, his pulse starting to do the samba, because he wanted to make love to Emily again. And what did Emily want?

She wanted to lock herself inside the powder room and cry.

Had he failed her that badly?

"Emily," he said, trying to sound stern, "I want you out of there this second."

Silence greeted his demand. He frowned, eyed the door narrowly.

"Em? Come out. I'll bust the door down, if I have to."

Emily gave a ladylike snort. "Oh, that's the ticket, Jake. You don't get what you want, just start barking!"

"Dammit, Emily…" A nerve ticked in Jake's temple. He laid his palms flat against the door, touched his forehead to the wood. "Let's not turn this into a battle. Just open the lock, okay?"

"No."

"You have to, sooner or later."

"I don't."

"Of course you do. You'll get hungry, or tired or thirsty…"

"I'm not hungry. There's plenty of water and I can always curl up on the floor."

Jake looked at the door, considered beating his head against it, and decided Emily would simply stand by and let him do it.

"Em?"

"Yes?"

He hesitated. "Are you sure I didn't hurt you?"

"Positive." She spoke softly, so softly that he could hardly hear her. "You didn't hurt me at all."

Jake cleared his throat. "Yeah, but I disappointed you."

"You didn't disappoint me, either."

"Sure, I did. I was—I was way too fast. I didn't mean it to be like that but when you said—"

"Don't repeat it!" Emily closed her eyes in misery. "I know what I said. If I could take it back—"

"Take back that you wanted me inside you?"

"Please," she whispered, "don't talk about it. I'm so embarrassed…"

"Embarrassed? That you let me know you wanted me? Em, don't you know what that did to me? Hearing you say those things?"

Emily slid down to the floor and leaned her head against the door. "You don't have to be polite, Jake."

Jake gave a choked laugh as he slid to the floor on the opposite side of the door. "Hell, Sparrow, good manners have nothing to do with this. I'm just sorry I made it all so quick. I wanted it to be perfect."

"It *was* perfect. It's just that I… What did you call me?"

"Sparrow. My sweet, hot little sparrow."

Emily cringed. "'Hot' isn't a word a lady appreciates, Jake."

"A woman's not supposed to be a lady when a man makes love to her, Em."

"No?"

"No. Is that what this is all about? That you weren't a lady?"

Another long silence. "Maybe."

"Baby, listen to me. A lady's the last thing a man wants in his bed."

He waited. She didn't reply.

"Emily? Sweetheart, please open the door. I promise, next time will be better."

"There won't be a next time." She paused. "And—and even if there were, how could it be better?" She thought back to that hot explosion of light. "How could it?" she said again, but very softly.

Jake rose slowly to his feet. "Open the door," he said huskily, "and I'll show you."

He waited. After a few seconds, he heard a sound, a soft rustle of clothing. The door opened a crack. Emily peered out.

"I think it would be best if I went home now."

Jake's smile tilted. "How're you going to manage that, Sparrow? Do you have a toboggan parked outside?"

She opened the door wider and stepped into the hall. Jake's heart did that funny upside down thing in his chest again. Her new hairdo was a mess, her lip gloss was all kissed off and the artfully applied mascara had dried into raccoonlike smudges under her teary eyes.

She was beautiful.

"Just look at you," he said gruffly. He took a step forward, gently dried her tears with his thumbs. "You've ruined all that goo that woman spent hours putting on your face."

"It wasn't goo," she said, sniffling a little but managing to sound defiant anyway, "and she spent two minutes."

Jake took her hand. "Come sit by the fire with me."

"I'd really like to go home."

"Yeah, well, you can't."

He led her into the living room. What he really wanted was to pull her into his arms, kiss her until she trembled and begged him to make love to her again, but he wouldn't do it. This was the time for seduction. Yeah, he'd seduce her. Slowly. Tenderly. Until she was on fire for him, the way he was on fire for her.

He sat down on the sofa, tried to pull her into his lap, but she wouldn't let him.

"I'd rather sit in the chair."

"How am I going to kiss you if I'm sitting here and you're sitting in the chair?"

''Jake. You said you'd teach me…things. And you have. You already—''

He tugged harder. She tumbled into his lap and he silenced her with a kiss. His mouth was warm; the tip of his tongue teased her lips. She swayed towards him, moaned, then pulled back.

''No,'' she said, a little breathlessly, ''once was enough. Honestly, Jake—''

''Honestly, Sparrow,'' he whispered, as his hands spanned her waist, ''once is never enough.''

''It is. It was. And then there's our supper. The sauce, and the pasta…''

''To hell with supper,'' Jake said in a husky whisper that made her breath quicken. ''Kiss me, Em.''

When she didn't, he kissed her, instead, and slipped his tongue into her mouth. The heat of it, the taste of him, made her dizzy.

''Jake.'' She leaned her forehead against his. ''Jake, stop. You make me feel—you make me feel—''

''What? Tell me. I want to know.'' His hands cupped her face, tilted it to his. ''I want to know what you like. What things you want me to do.''

Everything, she thought, oh, Jake, everything.

''This?'' he said, and kissed her again. ''And this?'' he whispered, and cupped her breasts in his hands. ''This, too,'' he murmured, and ran his thumbs over her nipples. ''Ah, Sparrow, Sparrow, I want you so badly…''

Emily moaned, put her arms around Jake's neck and kissed him. She wanted him, too. Wanted his mouth, his hands, his body. Wanted his soul, and his heart…

Suddenly, she tore her mouth from his. ''No,'' she gasped, and scrambled to her feet, but Jake went after her, put his arms around her, drew her back against his chest.

''Yes,'' he whispered, and buried his face in the soft, sweet place where her neck and shoulder joined.

She fell back against him, lifted her arm and lay her hand

against his cheek. Her fingers skimmed across his lips. He
caught them, sucked them into the heat of his mouth as he
undid the zipper that ran down the back of her dress. He
wrapped a handful of her hair around his fist, dragged it aside
and kissed the nape of her neck.

Her skin was like silk. He wanted to tear the dress away,
feast on her with all his senses. Instead, he eased the dress
to her waist and covered her breasts with his hands, teased
the crests with his thumbs, felt her tremble, shudder, felt his
body turning into steel.

"Do you like that?" he whispered.

Emily's breath caught. "Yes. Oh, yes. I—I—"

He turned her in his arms, took her mouth with his, nipped
at her bottom lip until her mouth opened and he could slip
his tongue inside. She trembled, pressed herself against him,
and he shuddered with almost savage exaltation.

She was his. His, and no other man's. She had never belonged to anyone else and she never...

His mind whirled, teetered on the brink of a dangerous
chasm. But Emily was holding him, kissing him, whispering
his name and he couldn't think, couldn't do anything but feel.

He kissed her, hard, tilted her head back as he took possession of her mouth. The dress tore under his hands as he
slid down her body. It pooled at her feet and he saw Emily,
his Emily, for the very first time.

She was every dream he'd ever had, and every hope. Her
body was slender, her curves feminine, her skin flushed with
desire. She was wearing lace. White lace. Bra, tiny panties,
stockings that ended at her thighs. White, all of it, as soft
and pure as the snow.

But her boots were black. Black as midnight, black as sin,
tight, sleek and high on her legs.

Jake shuddered again, knotted his hands, swore to himself
that he would make this second time perfect.

He bent to her and put his mouth against hers, holding her
captive only with his kiss. Then he knelt and eased the boots

from her feet, one at a time, pausing to kiss her ankle, her arch. He heard her make a whispered sound, felt the brush of her hand against his hair as he rose and he paused at the juncture of her thighs, told himself again to go slow, go slow, not to frighten her...

"Em," he whispered, and his hands closed around the backs of her thighs as he pressed his face against the white lace panties.

Her cry of pleasure was almost his undoing. He could feel the heat, the dampness of her through the lace; the woman-scent of her arousal was perfume to his soul. His sparrow was trembling with desire and it was all for him.

For him, he thought, and he stood straight and gathered her into his arms.

"You're beautiful," he said softly, "so beautiful that you make my heart stop."

She looked at him through those wide, dark eyes. "You are, too. I never knew a man could be beautiful, Jake."

"Do you want to see more of me, Sparrow?"

The tip of her tongue snaked across her bottom lip. "Yes," she said. "Yes, please."

Eyes locked to hers, Jake unbuttoned his shirt. It fell open and Emily's breath hitched. It was true. He *was* beautiful. All that taut muscle. The tanned skin. The whorls of black, silky hair...

She reached out a hand, hesitated, started to pull it back but Jake clasped her wrist, put her palm flat against his chest. He caught his breath; she gave a little hum of pleasure. His skin felt hot, his body hard. Without thinking, she leaned forward and pressed her lips to the strong column of his throat.

Jake trembled. "Oh Lord, Em," he whispered, and for the first time in her life, she knew what it meant to have a man want her. No. Not just a man. Jake. Jake, who she...

She jerked back, would have spun away, but he caught her shoulders, pulled her close and kissed her. There was nothing gentle about the kiss. His mouth was rough and demanding, the stroke of his tongue possessive, and Emily let it happen, the feeling that her bones were melting, that Jake was taking her, claiming her, that he was marking her as his own...

That she loved him.

She loved Jake McBride. She loved everything about him. His beautiful face. His powerful body. His intelligence, his humor, his hot temper and now, his heart-stopping passion.

No. No! She didn't want to love Jake. She didn't want to love any man, especially not one who was everything she'd sworn to avoid, everything her sisters had foolishly thought fascinating. Jake was too handsome, too macho, too reckless, too restless...

Emily caught her breath.

It was too late for thought or for regrets. Jake was touching her. Opening her bra. Claiming her breasts as they tumbled into his waiting hands. Sucking her nipples. Licking them while he eased her panties down her hips, down her legs.

She cried out, clasped Jake's shoulders for support. He said her name, tore off his clothes, swept her into his arms and took her down with him, in front of the fire.

"Jake," she said, her voice trembling with emotion, her hands clasping his face.

"Don't be afraid, Em," he whispered.

She wasn't afraid. Not of Jake. She was afraid of what she felt, what she wanted, what she could never have.

"Please," she said, "Jake, please."

Emily opened her arms. Jake groaned, parted her thighs and sank deep, deep, deep into softness. The sweet softness that belonged only to him.

The softness of Emily.

# CHAPTER TEN

THE snow continued all through the night.

Jake and Emily fell asleep before the fire, awoke and made love again.

Afterwards, he carried her to his bed.

"Mmm," she sighed, as he gathered her close against him under the soft down comforter.

Jake kissed her, tucked her head against his shoulder, and they tumbled back into sleep. When he awoke next, it was morning and the sky, visible through the bedroom window, was a peaceful cerulean blue.

The storm was over, which meant the main roads leading back to New York were probably clear.

Jake looked at Emily, still sleeping in his arms.

But he hadn't heard the sound of a snowplow.

The highways could be as smooth as glass. It didn't matter. Until the guy who plowed his driveway and road showed up, he and his sparrow were snowbound. He knew, from past experience, that his house was last on the list.

What a pity, he thought, smiling again as he drew Emily closer.

She sighed. Her fingers spread just over his heart but she didn't wake. Good. He didn't want to disturb her. She was new to all this and she had to ache, just a little. Her muscles had to be sore.

But he knew how simple it would be, to wake her as he'd done during the night. He had only to kiss her, taste her mouth, savor its sweetness. Even asleep, her lips would part in response to his. Mmm, she'd say, Jake…and he'd say yes, Em, yes, baby, and her arms would tighten around him, her warm, naked body would move against his…

153

Oh, hell.

Jake bit back a groan, relaxed his hold on Emily and tried to put some distance between them, but she wouldn't let it happen. She made a soft sound of distress, burrowed against him, threw her leg across his.

"Emily." His voice was hoarse, and he cleared his throat. "Baby?"

"Mmm."

No. He couldn't. He wouldn't...

She shifted her leg higher. Jake caught his breath.

"Sparrow, just move away a little. Just..."

Emily opened her eyes. Jake watched as the blur of sleep gave way to awareness. A delicate blush rose in her cheeks.

"Jake," she whispered.

"Yes." He kissed her. Her mouth was warm and soft under his. "I didn't mean to wake you."

"Is it morning?"

"Uh-huh." He kissed her throat, inhaling the sweet woman-scent of her skin. "The storm's over."

"Then, we can head back to—" her voice broke as his mouth found her breast "—to New York."

"Not yet," he said softly, and drew her nipple gently between his teeth. "We're still snowed in." He lifted his head and looked at her. Desire had turned her eyes dark. Slowly, he moved over her, kissed and licked his way down her body.

"Jake," she whispered, "Jake, what—"

"I just want to kiss you. Here. Right..."

She cried out, put her hands in his hair, arched towards him. Jake groaned, slid his hands under her bottom, touched his mouth to her again, and she tumbled with him into a whirlpool of dazzling sensation.

It was late morning before Emily stirred again.

She knew it was late. Sunlight filled the room; she could hear the steady *pit-pat* of the icicles melting from the eaves.

She was alone in the rumpled bed. The bedroom door was open…and she could hear a male voice singing downstairs.

Emily smiled, rolled onto her belly and took Jake's pillow in her arms.

She didn't know much about rock and roll but either the radio stations in this part of the northeast featured really bad artists or Jake was singing his heart out. And, if he was, there wasn't a singer in the world who had anything to worry about.

Jake was no threat to them… He was only a threat to her.

Emily's smile faded. She sat up, her knees tenting the blankets, and ran her fingers through her tangled curls. The reality of morning sent the dreams of the night skittering into the shadows.

Sleeping with Jake hadn't been on the agenda. Neither had falling in love with him. But both had happened, and now…

And now, what? What was a woman supposed to do, the morning after she'd slept with a man?

"Oh, Lord," Emily whispered, and laid her head against her knees.

What had she done? Falling for Jake wasn't just foolish, it was disaster waiting to happen. He didn't love her. He didn't even want an affair with her. He'd been perfectly clear about that. He'd wanted to show her what sex was all about….

And he had.

The weekend would end, and so would everything else. Monday morning, she'd show up at the office. So would Jake. And…

And?

And, nothing would be the same. Jake would look at her but not the way he always had. He'd look at her the way he'd looked at Brandi. With sadness, or maybe with embarrassment…

Emily fell back against the pillows.

A woman who slept with her boss was a liability, but a

woman who fell in love with him was a calamity. How many times had she heard the same story? Secretaries, assistants, falling for the men they worked for. It happened with pathetic frequency, and always ended the same way, with the woman not just nursing a broken heart but doing it while she stood on the unemployment line.

Who was she kidding? The job was the least of it. It was Jake's inevitable rejection that would be what would kill her. She'd laughed at the way Brandi had pursued him but it wasn't quite so easy to laugh, now that she'd been with Jake, now that she'd fallen in love with him.

Okay. Emily drew a resolute breath. The thing to do was to end this, quickly. The snow had stopped. Even here, in the middle of nowhere, the roads would be clear. She'd dress, phone for a taxi, thank Jake politely for—for all his efforts...

"There you are, woman."

Emily sat up. Jake was standing in the doorway, a rakish smile on his lips. He wore jeans and a black T-shirt; his feet were bare, his hair hung over his forehead and the stubble on his jaw was dark and sexy-looking.

Just seeing him made her feel dizzy.

"I figured you were going to sleep the day away."

She drew the blanket to her chin and looked at the bedside clock. "I didn't—I didn't realize it was so late."

"Yeah." His voice softened, his smile tilted. "Well, you were tired."

Her eyes flashed to his. He was coming towards her, and the way he was looking at her made her blush.

"Jake," she said quickly, "I'm getting up."

"Yes, you are." He sat down next to her, on the bed. "You're absolutely getting up, considering that I've spent the past thousand hours making pancakes, bacon, sausages and toast."

"Bacon *and* sausages?" she said, smiling before she could stop herself.

"I didn't know which you preferred."

"Actually…" Emily sat straighter as she remembered her plan. "Actually, I think I'll skip breakfast."

"No way." Jake reached out, brushed a curl from her forehead. "Didn't you pay attention to your teachers, when you were a kid? It's the most important meal of the day."

"Yes, but—"

"Besides, you'll hurt my feelings."

"Jake, honestly—"

"Honestly, I'll think you're trying to get out of eating what I've cooked."

He looked crestfallen, and about as serious as a puppy caught with a sock in its teeth. Emily fought back the desire to laugh.

"It's very nice that you've cooked breakfast, but—"

"But, you have to get back to the city."

"No. I mean, yes. The roads must be clear by now."

Jake looped a finger under the edge of the blanket and tugged it off her shoulder.

"They are," he said softly. "Clear enough so we can go out for dinner. I made reservations at The Hilltop Inn. You'll love it."

"I can't stay. Really." Emily caught her breath. His mouth was on her throat, his teeth and beard rasping sexily against her skin. "Jake," she said weakly, "I have things to do."

He pushed the blanket to her waist. "Uh-huh. So do I."

"Horace needs…" Her breath hitched. "He needs fresh seed."

"Call Mrs. Levy," Jake whispered, as he stroked his hand over her naked hip. "She has a set of keys to your apartment."

"Mrs. Levy? How do you know…"

"She told me, while we were freezing on that stoop, waiting for you to ring the buzzer." Jake licked her belly, blew lightly on her damp skin. "She told me lots of things, Em. That you were sweet, and generous. That you were sexy and beautiful."

Emily's hands rose. She stroked Jake's hair, cupped his strong jaw.

"She didn't," she said, and laughed softly.

"Not the sexy and beautiful part, no." Jake parted her thighs, watched her face as he touched her, felt his heart leap as she moaned. "I found that out, all by myself."

"Oh. Oh, Jake, please..."

"Please, what?" he said in a husky whisper.

"Please make love to me," she sighed, and went into Jake's arms.

Nobody had ever asked Jake to describe himself but if someone had, he'd have said he was a normal, healthy, heterosexual male of the twenty-first century.

In other words, he thought as he sat across from Emily in a candlelit booth at an inn a few miles west of Litchfield, in other words, he'd been with his fair share of women. What the heck. Maybe more than his fair share. He'd taken them to dinner, to the theater, to concerts, to parties. And to bed.

"...and," Emily was saying, her eyes filled with laughter, "Angela said she wanted to be blonder, no matter what our mother said. So she locked herself in the bathroom. A little while later, we heard this awful screech..."

Oh, yes. An impressive number of women, to bed.

"...green. I mean, bright green, Jake! And Serena and I tried not to laugh, but..."

Except, it had never been an entire weekend in bed, now that he thought about it. Saturday night, maybe Sunday morning, and that was it. By noon, he was always feeling restless. By two, he was out the door.

"I could set my clock by you, Jake," Brandi had said, with a sad little laugh.

Well, it was true. Saturday night, Sunday morning—that was a weekend. Anything that stretched beyond that, the lady might get ideas that would complicate things.

Plus, there was the boredom factor.

What did you do, when the sex was over? What did you talk about?

Everything, as it turned out. Everything, if Emily was the lady.

They'd finally gotten around to breakfast, even though it was so cold they'd had to start all over, from scratch.

Don't throw all that food out, Emily had said. It's wasteful.

So he'd cut up the pancakes for the birds, the bacon and sausages for the raccoons, while she'd made eggs—over easy, as it turned out, exactly the way he liked them—and bacon, and biscuits from a box of mix he'd bought and buried in the depths of a kitchen cupboard.

Then they'd bundled up, gone outside, left breakfast for the birds and the raccoons in the back of the yard, near the tree line. And yes, he'd shown her the lot next door, had a serious discussion about its value until Emily had sighed and said well, its real value was in its beauty, at which point he'd hauled her into his arms and kissed her so that they'd stumbled back into the house, made love again, slept awhile, awakened, listened to CD's because, as it turned out, she didn't really hate all rock and roll and he didn't really hate all classical stuff...

And they'd talked.

He loved listening to her. She'd told him about her first few jobs, about her sisters—her incredibly beautiful sisters, she called them. About her first apartment, and about Horace. How she'd spotted him languishing in a dingy pet-shop window, his feathers all dirty and mussed. How she hadn't intended to buy a pet at all, but how she couldn't possibly have left him there...

"What were you like, as a little girl?"

Emily blinked. Jake had interrupted her in the middle of a sentence and it was as much a surprise to him as it was to her. But, all of a sudden, he wanted to know about the Emily who'd existed before she came to New York. He wanted to be able to see her, in his mind's eye, although he thought he already could. She'd have been delicate and shy, with a mane of untamed hair and a stack of books always in her arms.

"Well…" She hesitated. "Well, there was nothing special about me, Jake. Compared to my sisters, I—"

Jake reached for her hand. "You're the one I want to hear about."

"I was, um, I was small."

"Delicate," he said, and smiled.

"I was quiet."

"Shy," he said, and lifted her hand to his mouth.

"And I always had my nose in a book."

Jake grinned and laced his fingers through hers. "Tell me more."

"No, it's your turn. Tell me about you."

"There's nothing much to tell."

"Ah. You mean, Jacob McBride was born in a well-furnished office, wearing a custom-made suit?"

Jake thought of the tiny house he'd been raised in, of the patched clothes he'd worn until the fabrics were too worn to fix, and he laughed.

"Not by a long shot."

"Well, what then? Was your father a banker, or… What's so funny?"

"Nothing," Jake said. "Hell, it's not funny at all. It's just the thought of my old man as a banker in a custom-made suit. I never saw him wear anything but overalls and a flannel shirt except on Sundays." His smile tilted. "His day of rest, you know? And he'd spend it trying to figure out how to pay the bills…"

"Jake." Emily's fingers tightened over his. "I'm sorry."

"No, that's okay. He was a good man. I just don't usually…" He shrugged. "I don't talk about him much."

Emily nodded. Jake didn't talk about himself much, either, even though she'd tried to get him to do it. She yearned to know more about him.

"Was your dad a farmer, then?"

Jake shook his head.

"I just thought... You said you're from Pennsylvania. And you said he wore overalls..."

"He was a miner," Jake said tonelessly. "At least, he was until he got buried under a few tons of coal."

"Oh, Jake. I'm so sorry."

"No need to be. It was a long time ago."

"It must have been awful for you to lose him."

"Yeah."

Emily heard the world of meaning behind the single word. Her fingers pressed Jake's.

"Losing your father...it must have turned your life upside down."

"Yeah," he said again. Carefully, he withdrew his hand from Emily's, curved it around his coffee cup and lifted the cup to his mouth. "Well, I was just a little kid, you know? But my mother had never thought of herself as anything but a wife. She married the first guy that showed any interest. My stepfather and I...let's just say, he'd signed on for a wife, and the rest was baggage."

"Ah."

"Ah, is right. As soon as I was old enough, I took off."

"For New York?"

"For the army, for Wall Street, for a little of this and that."

"You make it sound easy."

"Life is life, Em. You deal with whatever comes out of the box, that's all."

"Uh-huh." Emily looked at him. "And now you're light-years from the coal mines."

"Light-years, is right." Jake flashed a brittle smile. "Okay."

"Okay, what?"

"Okay, that's my life story. Now, can we get back to talking about other things? The kitchen here turns out an apple pie that—"

"I just wanted to know more about you, that's all."

"Why?"

"What do you mean, why? Because I—because I…"

Emily bit her lip. Whatever she said next would be a mistake. Because I love you? Because I like you? Even that would be disastrous.

She felt her heart break.

She was having an intimate little dinner with her lover, except Jake wasn't her lover. He was her—her instructor. And when had an instructor ever wanted to share his life story with a pupil?

She sat back.

"You're right," she said quietly. "There's no reason for either of us to share the stories of our lives."

Jake's eyebrows rose. "I didn't say that."

"I'm saying it." Emily put her napkin on the table. "It's late. And I really do have to get home."

"Tonight?"

"Tonight."

"But I thought—"

"I know what you thought," she said, with a momentary flash of anger. She could feel her hands shaking and she pushed her plate aside and folded them neatly on the table. There was no reason to be angry. She was the one who'd made all the mistakes. "I know," she said carefully. "You thought we'd spend the night at your house. That we'd make… That we'd sleep together again."

"And you're about to tell me I thought wrong."

There was a cool edge to his words. Oh, Jake, Emily thought, Jake, get out of your chair. Come and pull me into your arms. Tell me you don't just want to sleep with me, that you love me…

"Yes," she said, "as a matter of fact, I am."

There was a long silence. When Jake spoke again, the coolness in his voice had turned to ice.

"In other words, the weekend's over."

''Well, it is. Saturday, Sunday...'' Emily forced a smile to her lips. ''Tomorrow's Monday, Jake. There's no way to turn back the clock.''

Jake's lips tightened. How could she sit there and look at him that way? With eyes as cold as stones on a winter morning, with a polite little smile on her mouth.

He could change that smile, that stony look. All he had to do was take her in his arms and kiss her until she melted with desire, until she begged him to take her, to bury himself within her. Because that was all he was, to her. A damned walking, talking version of the Kama Sutra.

All right. It was what he'd signed on for. And that was fine. It was a relief that she understood that some good sex— okay, some incredible sex—was all that it was.

He wasn't a forever kind of man.

''I'm not interested in turning back the clock,'' he said. ''I just figured we could have a little more fun before the weekend's over.''

Fun, Emily thought, and felt the swift, stupid press of tears behind her eyes. Don't you cry, she told herself, don't you dare cry!

''Ah. Well, that would be nice, Jake, but really, I have a lot of work waiting at the office. And you have that trip to San Diego scheduled for tomorrow.''

Jake frowned. What was wrong with her? How could she talk about work, how could she look so calm, when he wanted to—when he was going to...

Wait a second. Maybe she figured it was up to her to end things. Maybe she was doing what she figured was the proper thing, after a weekend spent in a man's bed.

''Emily.'' He reached across the table and caught both of her hands in his. ''Listen to me.'' He gave her the kind of smile he knew always worked on women. ''I know this was supposed to be a temporary arrangement but we didn't put a deadline on it. So let's not worry about tomorrow. We'll stay the night, drive back early. As for that trip... I have a great idea. You're my exec, aren't you? Come to California with me.''

Emily felt her heart shatter. And wasn't that stupid? She'd known how this would go. Hadn't she begun the day by telling herself as much? And really, what Jake was suggesting was better than she'd expected. He didn't want to end things immediately. He just wanted to keep a good thing going until he wearied of it.

The bastard.

Emily's chin rose.

Just looking at him made her angry. The sexy smile, the was-it-as-good-for-you-as-it-was-for-me glint in his eyes? And to think she'd been on the verge of tears.

''Sparrow?'' He lifted her hand to his mouth and kissed the palm. ''Let's not spoil it, hmm?''

''Spoil it?'' Emily tugged her hand from his and shoved back her chair. ''Spoil such an interesting weekend? I'd never do that.''

Jake's smile slipped. ''Is that the best you can do? Call this 'an interesting weekend'?''

''I meant it as a compliment. You said you'd teach me to be a woman and you did. I'll always be grateful.''

His smile disappeared completely. ''What the hell is this?''

''It's my way of saying thank you. For the hair. The clothes. For everything.''

She could see him trying to figure out what was happening. No way would he believe she was kissing him off but it was better to be the kisser than the kissee. Something like that, anyway. Her anger was giving way to despair; her heart felt heavy and she knew, oh, she knew, that she'd been too quick to tell herself she wasn't going to cry, too quick to tell herself she hated Jake McBride...

''For everything,'' she said again, in a bright, cheerful tone. ''It was—it was great.''

''Great,'' Jake repeated, his voice low, his features taut, his fingers almost crushing hers.

Why did he have to look at her that way? As if she were hurting him when, dammit, she was the one who was in pain.

"We're finished?" he said. "That's it?"

"Yes. I mean, I really appreciate all you did, Jake—"

"Stop making it sound like an act of charity, goddamn it! I didn't make love to you because it was the right thing to do."

All at once, Emily felt revolted by the part she'd been playing. She was weary, and sick to the depths of her soul. Sick of Jake, of herself, of what had happened.

"Actually," she said shakily, as she pulled her hand free of his, "you didn't make love to me at all."

"Dammit, Emily!"

"Dammit, Jake! Isn't that what you wanted to hear? That what we did this weekend, what you want to keep doing until it gets boring, has nothing to do with making love?"

He glared at her. She was right but hell, there was no reason to lay it out like that. To make things sound so cold-blooded.

Emily shot to her feet. "Don't look so wounded. I know you think every woman over the age of consent is out to put a wedding ring through your nose. Well, I resent you thinking I'm one of them."

Jake stood up, took out his wallet and dropped a handful of bills on the table. Emily had already grabbed her coat and tossed it on; now, she was striding through the place with the other diners in the restaurant doing their best to pretend they weren't watching.

Well, so what? He'd take his time. He'd never run after a woman in his life, especially a crazy one, and he sure wasn't going to start now but, dammit, she was already going to the reservation desk near the door, motioning to the man behind it…

"Emily," Jake shouted, and ran after her. He caught her arm, swung her towards him. "What do you think you're doing?"

"I'm getting a taxi," she said calmly. "This gentleman is—"

"The lady doesn't need a taxi," Jake snarled.

"Don't listen to him." Emily looked at the manager, who was doing his best to become invisible. "I need a ride back to New York."

"Where do you think you are, Em? The Bronx? You can't get a taxi to Manhattan from here."

"I'm afraid the gentleman is right," the manager said nervously. "You can't—"

"You want to go home?" Jake closed his hand around her wrist. "I'll take you home."

"There's no need. I'm perfectly capable of handling this on my own."

"I brought you here. I'll take you back."

He was right. He'd brought her here; he could take her back. Emily nodded stiffly.

"Very well."

Jake marched her out the door, into the parking lot and to his car. She got inside, winced when he slammed the door, and stared straight ahead. The engine roared, the tires slewed sideways on a patch of ice, then squealed as they gained purchase and the car shot out of the parking lot onto the dark road.

Emily looked at the road, then at Jake.

"I don't want to go back to your house. I thought you understood that."

"Neither do I," he said coldly. "But your stuff is there."

"There's nothing of mine at your house."

"Listen," Jake said, his voice humming with tightly repressed fury, "you want to be stupid about us? Okay. Okay, be stupid. But what am I supposed to do with all that clothing, huh? Give it away?"

"There is no 'us.' As for the clothes…save them, for the next woman who walks into your life."

Jake banged his fist on the steering wheel.

"I don't believe this! We spent a weekend together. One weekend, and now you're jealous of somebody who doesn't even exist!"

"But she will!" Emily swung towards him. "She'll exist, and there'll be another one after her and one after that and another and another and another. And you know what? I don't care." Her voice broke, and she took a deep, deep breath. "If you'd only asked me, if you'd said, 'Emily, how do you feel about forever after?' I'd have told you I think it's all hogwash. I'd have said, any woman who thinks love lasts longer than a roller-coaster ride ought to have her head examined. What happens in bed isn't love. People tell themselves it is, well, women do, because they need to make sex sound like—like Mozart."

Jake shot her a look. "What in hell does Mozart have to do with this?"

"That's just my point. He has nothing to do with this. This is all about hormones, and—and random combinations of—of basic animal instincts and—and emotions and—" Emily began to weep.

Thank God, Jake thought frantically. Now, it all made sense. Hormones, instincts, emotions...

He reached across the console and squeezed her knee.

"Baby," he said gently, "you should have told me. Look, if you're approaching that time of the month...if your hormones are going up and down..."

She hit him. Not hard, because she wasn't a complete fool. The night was black, the road slick, and yesterday's near accident had made an impression. But she hit him, nevertheless, a good, solid shot to the arm, delivered with enough power to make him say "oof."

After that there was nothing but merciful silence, all the way through Connecticut, into the city, and to the sidewalk outside her apartment building.

Moments later, Emily was sitting on the floor before Horace's cage, weeping while Horace sang. Ten blocks away,

Jake got pulled over by a policeman who asked, warily, if Jake would like to explain how come he'd gone through the last three red lights in a row.

Jake explained.

"Unbelievable," the cop said when he'd finished, and Jake drove away without a ticket but with the officer's warning that there wasn't a woman in the world worth getting himself killed for...and the assurance that even if there were, no mortal man could possibly hope to understand her.

# CHAPTER ELEVEN

JAKE put his car into the garage, rode the elevator to his apartment and stormed inside.

He yanked off his jacket, tossed it in the general vicinity of a chair, headed for the kitchen and switched on the lights.

The room was big, bright, and handsomely done in stark black and white. It was the complete opposite of the kitchen in his Connecticut place, where the walls were old brick and the floor was made of wide-planked wood, although what in hell that had to do with anything was beyond him.

It was just that Emily had made a fuss about the Connecticut kitchen.

"I love this room," she'd said, smiling as she'd fried their eggs this morning, and he'd said yes, it was a terrific room, and then he'd taken her in his arms and kissed her, and found himself wondering what it would be like to spend all the Sundays of his life that way, with coffee on the counter, eggs and bacon on the stove, and Emily in his arms...

Which only went to prove how easily a woman could turn a perfectly intelligent man into a sad, confused ghost of his former self.

Jake opened the refrigerator, took out a bottle of ale and slammed the door shut.

How did women manage these things? How did they put such crazy ideas into a man's head without his even knowing they were doing it? And Emily, of all females...

Unbelievable!

She was the one woman he'd have thought incapable of such witchcraft, but he'd been wrong. The idea hadn't lasted—how could it? But the fact that she'd managed it was terrifying, and never mind her little speech about not wanting forever any more than he did.

"Ha," Jake said as he twisted the cap off the bottle and tossed it into the sink.

They all wanted forever. Nature had hard-wired them that way. Women were nest-builders, plain and simple, but men were meant to fly free—and, dammit, if he came up with one more stupid bird analogy, he was going to explode.

Jake tilted the bottle to his lips and took a long drink.

Women were all the same. Sooner or later, every last one of them brought things down to basics. Man, woman, sex, marriage, and never mind Emily's fancy denials.

Okay, so she'd ended things between them. So she'd made the speech that was usually his, smiled that little smile, said this was it, thank you and goodbye. No more sex. No more laughter. No more walks in the snow or soft little touches, no more sleeping in his arms as if she belonged there after making love.

No. After sex. Because she was right, it was sex, not anything else.

Jake glowered and brought the bottle to his mouth again.

On the other hand, maybe it was a trick. She might have been saying one thing and hoping for another. Why not? No man could ever figure out the twists and turns that the female brain could manage. For all he knew, Emily was sitting by the phone right this minute, waiting for him to call and say, Em, baby, I didn't really want this to end after one weekend or a thousand weekends, I want—I want—

Jake took a swig of ale.

Maybe a monk's cell. Or a padded one. Sanity. Peace and quiet. That was what he wanted. Maybe there was a place out beyond Jupiter where a man could enjoy being with a woman without all these ridiculous complications.

His life was fine, just as it was. Better than fine. He was free. He was doing things he'd never even dreamed of, when he was growing up. In other words, he was happy. Why did women think a man couldn't be happy, unless the poor sap put a ring on her finger and she put a matching one through his nose? Even those who pretended otherwise, thought it. The ones who said they didn't were just lying to themselves...

But Emily hadn't sounded as if she were lying.

*Any woman who thinks love lasts longer than a roller-coaster ride ought to have her head examined because what happens in bed isn't love.*

Jake took another drink.

That was what she'd said. And it was true. He had always known it. But if Emily believed it, really, honestly believed, as he did, that love was an illusion, why had she gotten so ticked off? When you came down to it, she'd simply told him what he'd already told her, that forever wasn't a viable plan.

Unless—unless it was him she didn't want any part of, not just a relationship that might go on for a while. Hell, he hadn't considered that, the possibility she hadn't liked being with him.

No. Forget that possibility. She had. He knew she had. Those sweet sighs, when they made love. The way she laughed at his jokes, hung onto his every word. The touch of her hand on his, when they were talking...

There'd be no more of that, now. And he'd miss it. All of it, although how he could miss things he'd barely had were beyond him.

So, what was the bottom line here? Why would a woman walk away from an affair when it was still at the hot, electric start?

And "hot" was the word.

Lord, what a weekend. They were perfect together. Better than perfect. Emily was an incredible combination of innocent and sexy.

"Let me," she'd whispered this afternoon, after he'd brought her to release with his mouth. And she'd knelt between his legs, touched him with her tongue, tasted him, pleasured him, and oh, the joy of it, the unbelievable pleasure because sex was different with his sparrow, everything was different, it was—

"Dammit-to-hell!" Jake snarled, and slammed the empty bottle on the counter.

He was wrong. Nothing was different with Emily except, maybe, the way she played the game. Yeah, that was it. She'd lured him on. The shapeless suits. The pulled-back hair. The polite, impersonal way she spoke. "Yes, Mr. McBride." "No, Mr. McBride." Even those horrible personal ads she'd said she was going to answer. It was all part of the game, designed to—

To what?

She'd worked for him for almost a year. And in all that time, she'd never looked at him as if he were a man any more than he'd looked at her as if she was a woman. She hadn't been playing a game. If anyone had been playing games, it was him.

Oh, he'd explained, told her he was going to help her change into a woman men would desire but, in the end, he was the man who'd desired her.

Now, she could go out and practice what he'd taught her with someone else.

Jake felt as if a hand had torn open his chest and ripped out his heart.

His Emily, with another man?

No. No, he couldn't let that happen. He wanted—he wanted…

He didn't know what he wanted, and it was all Emily's fault. She'd taken a perfectly simple thing, a weekend in bed, and turned it into an equation as complex as quantum mechanics.

Jake's jaw tightened. He switched off the kitchen light, strode into his bedroom, and got undressed.

He would tell her that, tomorrow morning. He had that

California meeting but no way was he going to fly west until this was settled.

"Emily," he'd say, "you overreacted. But because you're new to all this, I'm going to give you another chance. We'll forget all about that nasty little scene Sunday night. We can pretend it never happened..."

And if she laughed in his face, then what?

Jake got into bed, folded his hands beneath his head and stared into the darkness.

He could fire her. That was what.

He switched off the light, rolled on his belly and pummeled his pillow into shape.

Half an hour later, he switched the light on, folded his hands under his head again and glared at the ceiling.

He wouldn't fire her. How could he, when that was probably exactly what she expected so she could call him a vindictive bastard on top of everything else?

Anyway, it wouldn't come to that. She wouldn't laugh when he offered her the chance to turn back the clock. She'd go into his arms, kiss him, and just that easily, they'd agree to keep the office business in the office and the bedroom business where it belonged.

Jake smiled.

He knew, in his heart, that was what Emily really wanted. It was just that women were such emotional creatures. Not that he'd say so. Hell, that comment he'd made, about hormones and the time of the month...

"You were just asking for trouble, pal," he muttered.

Still, it was true. Female feelings gyrated like the stock market on a really bad day. Victims of emotion, all of them, even Emily. Really, what would women do without men to ensure that the world remained a logical place?

Okay. He had it all sorted out. Go to San Diego tomorrow, come back on Tuesday, don't phone her or do anything until he saw her at the office on Wednesday. Give her lots of time to think about the mistake she'd made. Keep her worrying, even turn panicky when she realized how much she missed him...

Yes, indeed.

When he turned out the light, Jake McBride fell into a deep, dreamless sleep.

The snow that had blanketed Connecticut had left the city of Rochester untouched, which was a rare event because, growing up, Emily had thought of her hometown as the Snow Capital of the Universe.

She thought of that now, as she began preparing dinner for her sisters in the house the two of them shared, and wasn't it great that it wasn't snowing?

Coming back to the place you thought you'd escaped, having to ask your sisters if you might stay with them for a while, was difficult enough. Doing it while the city was trapped under an inverted white bowl would have made it seem twice as dreary.

Not that she didn't like Rochester. Her roots were here, and her family. Of course, her parents didn't know she was back. Not yet. She'd wait, give herself time to find a job, an apartment and, most of all, a logical excuse for coming home.

She didn't want her mother looking at her father with her eyebrows raised, the way Serena had looked at Angela when she'd arrived on their doorstep with a bird, a birdcage, and three big suitcases Monday evening.

"Hi," she'd said brightly. "Can I move in with you guys for a while?"

"Of course," her sisters had said, and then they'd looked at each other, and she'd read all the questions in their faces but they were her sisters, and it was okay to look right back and tell them there wasn't a way in the world she was going to answer any questions.

Emily sighed.

She'd never imagined coming back for anything but a visit.

She'd had such big plans when she left for New York all those years ago. An exciting career, in an exciting city...

Emily blew a curl off her forehead, opened the oven door and checked on the meat loaf baking inside.

And she'd had that, until she'd ruined it all.

The sad thing was that she'd never thought about having a man in her life, except in the most casual way, until she'd gone to work for Jake. And then, as the months passed, she'd begun to wonder if she wasn't missing something...something like her tall, dark and handsome boss, who often visited her in her dreams.

Strange, how she'd never admitted that to herself until Sunday night, when she'd done nothing but dream of Jake. Of course, those dreams had been different. She'd buried him alive in a snowbank, in one dream. And she'd chained him to his bed and fed him cephalopod mollusks until he begged for mercy in another.

Emily slammed the oven door, went to the pantry and took out an onion and some potatoes.

So much for dreams, and so much for Jake. She was home and happy to be here. Rochester was a big place. She'd find a good job, a great apartment, and she'd never waste another second of her life, thinking about Jacob McBride.

She'd already wasted a lot of tears on him, and for what? The thing they'd done, the bedroom business, had been nothing but an aberration. It had taken her all of Monday to realize it, but that was all it was.

Her heart, thank goodness, was intact.

Serena and Angela didn't think so.

"It's a man," they'd kept saying. "It has to be, Emily. You fell in love and he broke your heart. That's why you ran away."

And finally Emily had admitted that yes, there'd been a man, but she hadn't fallen in love and she hadn't run away.

"I just got tired of New York, that's all. Nobody broke my heart."

Certainly not, she thought as she peeled the onion and diced it. Just because she'd packed her things, sold her furniture to the superintendent, arranged to have her books, her CDs and some other stuff packed and shipped, and put herself and Horace on a train all in one day, didn't mean she'd run away.

A tear ran down her cheek. "Damned onions," she muttered, and wiped the dampness away with her apron.

She had not run. Why would she? She had ended her relationship with Jake, if you could call a night a relationship. Then, after she'd thought it over, she'd decided a preemptive strike made sense. So she'd quit, before he could have the satisfaction of firing her, quit without notice or warning and left him in the lurch.

It was a great feeling.

Emily smiled tightly as she peeled the potatoes and cut them in quarters.

Oh, if only she could see the look on his handsome face when he came into the office Wednesday and found her gone. No Emily to make his appointments. Type his letters. Keep his files. No Emily to make his coffee, take his dictation, organize his notes...

Lie in his arms.

She frowned, took out a pot, dumped the potatoes in and filled it with water.

Where had that silly thought come from? Jake would hardly notice. He'd have some other woman in his arms before the week ended. Yes, maybe she'd dented his ego a little because he was the one who was supposed to end things.

After all, he was the Great Jake McBride.

"Great Egotistical Jerk, is more like it," she muttered, as she put the pot on the stove and turned on the burner.

Did he think every woman he bedded really wanted to spend the rest of her life with him?

"Ha," Emily said.

She didn't want to spend her life with any male, except

for Horace. As for that nonsense she'd spun in her head, that she'd fallen in love with Jake...

"Ha," she said again, and Horace chirped and fluttered his wings as if he found the idea as preposterous as she did. She didn't love Jake. It was just sex that had made her think so. All those shooting stars going off...

Yes, the sex had been terrific. But love?

"No way," she muttered, but the conviction in her head didn't connect with the anguish in her heart and, dammit, there she was, crying again. It was ridiculous. She'd been weeping, on and off, since Sunday night, which was why Serena and Angela kept exchanging those looks...

"Who is he?" Serena had asked, just this morning.

"Probably some fast-talking used-car salesman like the one I divorced," Angela had said, answering the question when Emily wouldn't.

"No," Serena had replied, "he's probably a duplicate of the skirt-chasing SOB I got rid of." Then she'd put her arm around Emily and hugged her. "Sweetie, what can we tell you? Men are all the same. Even the ones who look like pet mice are only rats in disguise."

"Jake doesn't look like a pet anything," Emily had said, her voice wobbling, "but you're right, he's a grade A, 100% rat."

And he was.

Emily yanked a paper towel from the roll, wiped her eyes and blew her nose.

This was ridiculous. She had not, repeat, not, loved Jake. Why would she? He was gorgeous and sexy and fun to be with but he wasn't the lovable kind.

If she cried, it was over her own foolishness in falling for him. In *thinking* she'd fallen for him, because she hadn't. She hadn't. She—

"Emily? I'm ho-ome."

Emily blew her nose again and tried, unsuccessfully, to tuck her hair behind her ears.

Angela was here. That meant Serena would be coming in, too, in just a few minutes. And she wasn't going to have either of them sneak little looks at her, or at each other, anymore. The very last thing she needed right now was to have her two beautiful sisters feeling sorry for her. She'd had enough of that in high school to last a lifetime.

"There you are, Emily." Angela, looking elegant as always, her blond hair shiny and smooth, her blue eyes sparkling, slipped an arm around Emily's waist and hugged her. "Mmm. Something smells good."

"Meat loaf," Emily said, and felt two gigantic tears trickle down her cheeks.

"Oh, Em." Angela sighed and put her hands on Emily's shoulders. "Sweetie, don't! Whoever he is, he's not worth it."

Emily nodded and wiped her eyes. "You're right," she said briskly. "And—and I'm not crying. I was—I was chopping onions."

"Onions?" Serena said, as she entered the kitchen. "Great. I don't have a date tonight, so..." She bit her lip, shot a guilty look at Emily. "I mean, I adore onions. And what's that luscious smell?"

"Meat loaf," Angela said, and shot a warning look at her sister.

Serena raised her eyebrows. "What? I like meat loaf. I wouldn't say anything bad about meat..." She looked at Emily. "Oh, Emily. Sweetie, you're crying."

"I am not crying. What's with you two? Don't you know onion tears when you see them?"

Serena turned her crystalline blue gaze on Emily, put an arm around her and hugged her. Strands of perfectly groomed, dark gold hair brushed Emily's cheek.

"You have to believe us," she said firmly. "Whoever he is, he's not worth it."

"For heaven's sake, I am not crying about a man. Can't you two get that straight?"

"You've been crying since you got here," Angela said sternly. "And just look at what it's done to you. Serena, have you ever seen a redder nose? And those swollen eyes, all red-ringed. Honestly, Emily…"

"Honestly, Angela," Emily said, with a little laugh, "I hoped you'd appreciate the fact that I'm color-coordinated. Red nose, red eyes…" She waited for her sisters to smile, but they didn't. "Oh, come on, guys. Lighten up. After all, it's just like old times, right? You're portraits of perfection. And I'm a mess."

Angela and Serena, each three swanlike inches taller than Emily, exchanged looks over her head.

"You don't have to be," Serena said gently. "You could use my cucumber pads on your eyes. And I have a cream that would do wonders for your nose."

"Yes," Angela said, just as gently. "Emily, you know, looking better would make you feel better."

Emily sighed. "I don't think so."

"Oh, it would. I mean, just look at what you're wearing. Baggy old jeans. A ratty sweatshirt. And your hair…"

"Would you believe I had it cut and styled on Saturday, by a guy who styles the hair of half the models in New York?"

"No," her sisters said, with one voice.

Emily put on a pair of mitts, opened the oven and peered at the meat loaf.

"Well, I did. And his hair was blonder and longer than yours."

"Now, Emily…"

"Look, both of you." Emily took a deep breath. "I know you mean well. But I have to work this out for myself."

Angela and Serena exchanged looks again. "Ah-ha."

Emily yanked off the oven mitts. "Okay. So I ran away. Well, you would have, too. I made the mistake of getting involved with a no-good rat. A fast-talking, lying, cheating, miserable rat who—who—"

"They're all liars, and fast-talking rats," said Angela.

"Yes," Serena said. "And they cheat, too."

Tears rose in Emily's eyes again. "He didn't cheat," she said miserably. "He didn't lie, either. That's the problem. He told me, straight out, that he wasn't the forever kind. That he just wanted me for—for sex."

"I never, ever said that, Sparrow," a man's voice said.

Emily, Angela and Serena all spun around. Emily's eyes widened with shock. Angela's and Serena's eyes widened too, but not with shock.

"Jake?" Emily whispered.

"You're damned right, it's Jake," Jake said coldly. "And you're lucky it is. What's the matter with you women? You think you can just leave doors open and only the good fairy will take you up on the invitation?"

Angela looked at Serena, who blushed. "I forgot. I wore boots, because it was supposed to snow, and I took them off outside…"

"Jake?" Emily said again. Her heart felt as if it were trying to leap out of her chest. She put her hand over it, as if that might slow its race. "Jake, what are you doing here?"

Jake stared at Emily. What *was* he doing here? He'd had a speech all planned, about how she'd scared the hell out of him by running off like that, about how he was totally and completely ticked off, that a really good executive assistant would never do such a thing…but now that he was here, he was tongue-tied.

Well, no wonder. What time zone was this, anyway? What day? What year? Yesterday, he'd been in California, sitting through a meeting with all the attentiveness of a chimpanzee at a ballet. People were spouting facts and numbers like hyperactive geysers but the only thing he could think of was what would happen to him if he lost Emily.

Eventually, he'd excused himself to the bewildered CEO, gone into the hall, pulled out his cell phone and called her. He'd tried to, anyway. But she didn't answer the phone in the office and when he called her at home, he got a recorded voice that said the number had been disconnected.

The panic he'd felt had made his blood run cold.

He'd gone back to the meeting, made some halfhearted excuse, headed for the airport and paced the first class lounge and dialed Emily's apartment and his office until the battery on his cell phone died.

While he paced, he came up with half a dozen scenarios to explain her absence, each one worse than the last.

The only thing he knew for certain was that his Emily, his sweet little sparrow, his impossible, pigheaded sparrow, had disappeared from his life.

How would he find her? Detectives? Private investigators? The police?

At last, he'd boarded a plane. And halfway over the country, the solution had come to him. He had Mrs. Levy's name. He had her address. He had an inflight phone...

"Jake? I asked you a question. How did you find me?"

"Mrs. Levy told me."

Emily felt behind her for a chair. Her legs were wobbly. Jake looked so angry. So enraged.

So handsome.

Oh, so handsome. And so disheveled. He'd tossed his overcoat on a chair, undone his jacket, loosened his tie. He kept running his hands through his hair so that it lay in heavy waves against his forehead. He hadn't shaved, either; his jaw was stubbled and with what she knew was painfully bad timing, she remembered how it had felt that first time he'd made love to her, when his stubbled jaw had rubbed against her skin. Against her breasts...

Color shot into her face.

Angela noticed. "Oh, my," she whispered. "Serena?"

"Yes." Serena licked her lips. "Emily? Is this the man?"

"No," Emily said. She took a deep breath and lifted her chin. "He's not *the* man. He's just a man."

"Oh, but he's gorgeous," Serena said softly. "Isn't he Ange?"

Jake narrowed his eyes. "Who are these women, Emily?"

"My—my sisters." Her beautiful sisters, who were all bu drooling. Well, Jake would drool, too, once he took a good long look at them. "This is Serena. And Angela."

"Hi," Angela cooed, and smiled.

"Hello," Serena hummed, and smiled.

Jake looked at each of them. "Hello," he said, and scowled. "Now would the two of you please get the hell ou of here and give us some privacy?"

Emily blinked. Serena and Angela did, too, but then they laughed, kissed Emily, one on each cheek, and did exactly as Jake had commanded.

Emily stared at him.

"You—you just told my sisters to go away."

"Damned right, I did."

"But—but they're beautiful."

"Are they?" Jake shrugged his shoulders and started to wards her. "I didn't notice."

"What do you mean, you didn't notice? You have to no tice. Serena and Angela are—they are… Jake. Jake, what are you doing?"

"Kissing you," Jake said, as he threaded his hands into Emily's hair and tilted her face to his.

And he did. Oh, he did. Not gently. Not politely. Hi mouth covered hers and he kissed her with all the hunger that he'd kept locked within his lonely, hungry soul.

Emily told herself not to respond. There was no reason to because this was only sex. It was only sex…

It was sex, and it was love, for her, anyway, because the man holding her in his arms was all she had ever wanted.

After a long time, Jake drew back.

"Dammit," he said huskily, "I am furious at you, Spar row." He proved it by kissing her again. "I ought to turn you over my knee and spank you."

"Kiss me instead," Emily whispered, and he did. Eventually, she pushed gently against his chest. "Jake," she said softly, "you came after me."

"Of course I came after you! Did you think I was the kind of man you could walk out on? The kind who'd let you go without a fight?" He drew a deep breath. "I won't let you leave me."

Emily hesitated, but not for long. She rose on her toes, clasped Jake's face and kissed him. It was, she knew, what a real woman would do, what she'd have the courage to do, if she loved a man.

And she loved Jake. She'd always love him, and she was woman enough, too, to accept whatever he offered, for as long as he offered it. Besides, miracles could happen. Jake might change. He might fall in love with her.

The risk was terrifying, but risk was what made life worth living. She knew that, now.

Emily smiled. "I won't leave you. I thought I had to, but I was wrong."

Jake kissed her again, over and over. He couldn't get enough of her taste, her sweetness, of the way she fit so perfectly into his arms, and into his heart.

"Sparrow." He pulled back, just a little. "Sparrow, you were wrong."

"I know. I just said so. I shouldn't have—"

"I *am* a forever kind of guy. And you're a forever kind of woman. We just needed to find the right person to be forever with." Jake gave a soft laugh. "I'm making a mess of this. I was going to do it perfectly, say it poetically…"

"Say what?" Emily said carefully, because it was too much to hope for.

Jake took a deep breath. "I love you, Em. I love you with all my heart, and you'd damn well better tell me you love me, too, and that you really do believe in forever because if you don't…" He stopped and looked deep into her eyes. "If you don't," he said softly, "I'll be lost and lonely, for the rest of my life.'' He lifted her face to his. ''Em? Tell me you love me, too.''

Emily wanted to laugh. She wanted to cry. Instead, she kissed Jake's mouth.

''Of course I love you. And I believe in forever, so long as it's with you.''

Jake grinned. ''The only things I don't believe in,'' he said, ''are long engagements.''

Emily laughed. Jake did, too, and he drew her close and kissed her. She kissed him back. Horace, observing all this, burst into song.

Beyond the kitchen, in the living room, Serena and Angela sighed, smiled tearily at each other, slipped into their coats and tiptoed out the door.

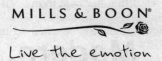

0305/62/MB123

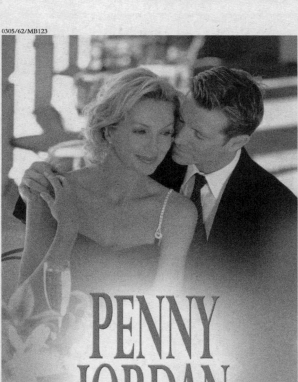

# PENNY JORDAN

*Sweet Seduction*

*From lust…to love*

## On sale 1st April 2005

*Available at most branches of WHSmith, Tesco, ASDA, Martins,
Borders, Eason, Sainsbury's and all good paperback bookshops.*

**Published 18th March 2005**

*New York Times* Bestselling Author

# Jennifer Crusie

# Charlie All Night

"Crusie has a gift for concocting nutty scenarios and witty one-liners…" —*People* magazine

MIRA®

M404

# A Regency Invitation

## to the House Party of the Season

*Nicola Cornick, Joanna Maitland,*
*Elizabeth Rolls*

**On sale 3rd December 2004**

*Available at most branches of WHSmith, Tesco, ASDA, Martins,*
*Borders, Eason, Sainsbury's and all good paperback bookshops.*

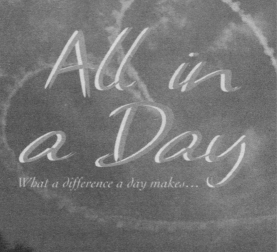

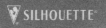

## SILHOUETTE®

Love Is In The Air...

# Stuck On You

Cait London
Carolyn Zane
Wendy Rosnau

## *Available from 21st January 2005*

*Available at most branches of WHSmith, Tesco, ASDA, Martins, Borders,
Eason, Sainsbury's and most good paperback bookshops.*

# WIN a romantic weekend in PARiS

*To celebrate Valentine's
Day we are offering you
the chance to WIN
one of 3 romantic
weekend breaks to Paris.*

Imagine you're in Paris; strolling down the Champs Elysées, pottering through the Latin Quarter or taking an evening cruise down the Seine. Whatever your mood, Paris has something to offer everyone.

For your chance to make this dream a reality simply enter this prize draw by filling in the entry form below:

Name _____

Address _____

_____ Tel no: _____

**Closing date for entries is 30th June 2005**

Please send your entry to:

## Valentine's Day Prize Draw
## PO Box 676, Richmond, Surrey, TW9 1WU